THE PRINCESS BRIDE

Rebecca Winters   Jennie Adams   Melissa McClone

MILLS & BOON®

THE BRIDE OF MONTEFALCO
© 2006 by Rebecca Winters
Australian Copyright 2006
New Zealand Copyright 2006

First Published 2006
Second Australian Paperback Edition 2015
ISBN 9781488766831

INVITATION TO THE PRINCE'S PALACE
© 2012 by Jennie Adams
Australian Copyright 2012
New Zealand Copyright 2012

First Published 2012
Second Australian Paperback Edition 2015
ISBN 9781488766831

NOT-SO-PERFECT PRINCESS
© 2011 by Melissa Martinez McClone
Australian Copyright 2011
New Zealand Copyright 2011

First Published 2011
Second Australian Paperback Edition 2015
ISBN 9781488766831

Except for use in any review, the reproduction or utilisation of this work in whole or in part in any form by any electronic, mechanical or other means, now known or hereafter invented, including xerography, photocopying and recording, or in any information storage or retrieval system, is forbidden without the permission of the publisher.

This book is sold subject to the condition that it shall not, by way of trade or otherwise, be lent, resold, hired out or otherwise circulated without the prior consent of the publisher in any form of binding or cover other than that in which it is published and without a similar condition including this condition being imposed on the subsequent purchaser.

All rights reserved including the right of reproduction in whole or in part in any form. This edition is published in arrangement with Harlequin Books S.A.
Cover art used by arrangement with Harlequin Books S.A. All rights reserved.

This is a work of fiction. Names, characters, places, and incidents are either the product of the author's imagination or are used fictitiously, and any resemblance to actual persons, living or dead, business establishments, events, or locales is entirely coincidental.

MIX
Paper from responsible sources
FSC
www.fsc.org   FSC® C009448

Published by
Mills & Boon
An imprint of Harlequin Enterprises (Australia) Pty Ltd
Level 13
201 Elizabeth St
Sydney NSW 2000
AUSTRALIA

® and ™ are trademarks owned by Harlequin Enterprises Limited or its corporate affiliates and used by others under licence. Trademarks marked with an ® are registered in Australia and in other countries. Contact admin_legal@Harlequin.ca for details.

Printed and bound in Australia by Griffin Press

CONTENTS

THE BRIDE OF MONTEFALCO 5
Rebecca Winters

INVITATION TO THE PRINCE'S PALACE 199
Jennie Adams

NOT-SO-PERFECT PRINCESS 359
Melissa McClone

Rebecca Winters, whose family of four children has now swelled to include three beautiful grandchildren, lives in Salt Lake City, Utah, in the land of the Rocky Mountains. With canyons and high Alpine meadows full of wildflowers, she never runs out of places to explore, and they—along with her favorite vacation spots in Europe—often end up as backgrounds for her Harlequin Romance® novels. Writing is her passion, along with her family and church. Rebecca loves to hear from her readers. If you wish to e-mail her, please visit her Web site at www.rebeccawinters-author.com

The Bride Of Montefalco

Rebecca Winters

CHAPTER ONE

"LIEUTENANT DAVIS?"

The Portland police detective looked up from his computer. "I'm glad you got here so fast, Mrs. Parker."

"Your message indicated it was urgent."

"It is," he said in a solemn tone. "Come in and sit down."

Ally took a chair opposite his desk.

"I take it there's been a new development in the case."

"Major." He nodded. "The woman who died in the car accident with your husband four months ago has finally been identified through dental records and a DNA match-up."

Though Ally had buried her husband two months ago, she'd needed this day to come if she were ever to find closure. Yet at the same time she'd been dreading it because it meant getting painful facts instead of wallowing in useless conjecture.

"Who was she?"

"A thirty-four-year-old married female from Italy named Donata Di Montefalco."

Finally the woman had a name and a background.

"The Italian authorities have informed me she was the wife

of the Duc Di Montefalco, a very wealthy, prominent aristocrat from a town of the same name near Rome. According to the police investigating the case, her husband has had his own people searching for her all these months."

"Naturally," Ally whispered. Had he been in love with his wife? Or had his marriage been unraveling like Ally's?

Though the detective had never said the words, she knew he suspected her husband of having been unfaithful. So had Ally who'd known her marriage was breaking down but hadn't wanted to believe it.

Jim had changed so much from the seemingly devoted family man she'd first married, she'd slowly fallen out of love with him though she wasn't able to pinpoint the exact moment it happened.

During the latter part of their two and half year marriage she'd seen signs that something was wrong. The long absenses from home because of his work, the lack of passion in his lovemaking when he did come home, his disinterest in her life when he made brief, unsatisfactory phone calls home, his desire to put off starting a family until he was making more money.

Despite the fact that there was still no definitive proof of an affair, this news gave added credence to her suspicions.

A fresh stab of pain assailed her. She needed to get out of his office to grieve in private.

Though she'd already had two months to absorb the fact that he hadn't died alone, a part of her had hoped the other woman would have been middle-aged. Possibly an older woman he'd given a lift to because of the storm. But this latest information put that myth to rest. It increased her turmoil that she hadn't loved him as much as she should have, otherwise why hadn't she confronted him before it was too late?

"Thank you for calling me in, Lieutenant." Any second now and she was going to lose control. Living in denial was the worst thing she could have done. Her guilt worsened to recognize she hadn't fought harder to recapture the love that had brought them together in the first place.

"I appreciate what you've done to help me."

She got up to leave. He walked her to the door of his office.

"I'm sorry I had to call you in and remind you of your loss all over again. But I promised to let you know when I had any more information.

"Here's hoping that in the months to come, you'll be able to put this behind you and move on."

Move on? a voice inside her cried hysterically. How did you do that when your husband had died at the lowest ebb in your marriage?

How did you function when your dreams for a happy life with him were permanently shattered?

The detective eyed her with compassion. "Would you like me to walk you out to your car?"

"No thank you," she murmured. "I'll be all right."

She hurried out of his office and down the hall to the front door of the police station.

Dear God—how was it possible things had ended like this? *Nothing* was resolved. If anything, she was riddled with new questions.

Her thoughts darted to the woman's husband. He would have only just learned his wife's body had been found and identified. Besides months of suffering since her disappearance and now this loss, he had to be wondering about Jim's importance in Donata's life.

Wherever the Duc Di Montefalco was at this moment, Ally knew he was in hell.

She could relate…

* * *

"Uncle Gino? How come we're going to stay at your farm for a while?

Rudolfo Giannino Fioretto Di Montefalco, known only to his family and a few close friends as Gino, eyed his eleven-year-old niece through the rearview mirror. The girl sat next to Marcello, Gino's elder brother.

"Because it's summer. I thought you and your father would enjoy getting out in nature instead of being cooped up in the palazzo."

"But what if Mama comes back and we're not there?"

Gino braced himself. The dreaded moment had come.

He pulled up to the side of the farmhouse. In the dying rays of the sun, the cypress trees formed spokes across the yellowed exterior.

He turned in his seat to make certain Sofia was holding her father's hand. Since Marcello had been stricken with Alzheimer's and could no longer talk, it was one of the ways she could express her love and hope to feel his in return.

"I have something to tell you, sweetheart."

A full minute passed. In that amount of time the color had drained from his niece's face. "What is it?" she asked in a tremulous voice. The strain of going months without knowing anything about her mother had robbed Sofia of any joie de vivre.

"Sofia, I have some bad news. Your mama, she was in a car accident, and...she died."

Four months ago in fact, but Gino had only been informed of her death last night. Today he'd been making preparations for Sofia's move to the country with Marcello.

The details surrounding the tragedy were something neither she nor the trusted staff both at the palazzo and the farmhouse needed to know about.

His gaze took in Sofia's pain-filled expression. When his news computed, he heard the sobs of an already heartbroken girl who buried her dark brown head against her father's shoulder.

Marcello looked down at her, not comprehending, not able to comfort his daughter.

Gino felt her sobs from the front seat. Tears welled in his throat. Now that Donata's body had been found and identified, the nightmare of her disappearance was over. But another one had just begun...

His motherless, already introverted niece was going to need more love and understanding than ever.

As for Gino, once he'd arranged with the priest for a private memorial service away from prying eyes so Sofia could say goodbye to her mother in private, he needed to increase security to protect his family from the press.

Carlo Santi, the region's top police inspector and one of their family's best friends was doing his best to stop information from the police department leaking to the various newspapers and media in Rome and elsewhere. But there were those rabid, insatiable vultures from the tabloids who invaded without mercy, always lurking to find something juicy on Gino and his family. It was the price they paid for their title and wealth.

If it weren't for Carlo running interference for him all these months, the situation could have gotten uglier much sooner.

With the sudden debilitating onset of Marcello's disease two years ago, Donata's selfish streak had created havoc in his brother's marriage, and had damaged their daughter irreparably. In Gino's opinion, Donata had to have been one of the world's most insensitive, neglectful wives and mothers on record.

He'd fought hard to protect his brother and niece from the worst of her flaws.

As a result he'd been forced to guard the family secrets with a certain ruthlessness that Donata enjoyed publicizing to anyone who would listen. Her indiscriminate venting had made its way to the press, casting a pall over all their lives, Gino's in particular. Through innuendo she'd made him out to be the grasping, jealous brother-in-law who wanted her and the title for himself.

The only thing Donata hadn't ever considered was her own death.

Once the media got wind of the accident that took her life, everything Gino had done to keep family matters private was about to become a public scandal. The fact that an American man close to Donata's age had been driving the car when they'd been killed provided the kind of fodder to cause a paparazzi frenzy. This kind of story would sell millions of papers with far reaching consequences for Sofia. His niece could be destroyed by the facts, let alone the malicious rumors surrounding them.

Aside from physically removing the two in the back seat to a protected place away from media invasion, there didn't seem to be a thing in hell he could do about unscrupulous journalists digging up old lies on him in order to sell more newspapers. Since his teens, battling the press had been the story of his life. Now it was about to be the story of Sofia's, but not if he could help it!

The orchestra conductor put down his baton. "Take a ten minute break. Then we'll pick up the Brahms at bar 20."

Thankful for the respite, Ally placed her violin on the seat and filed out of the music hall behind the other members of the string section.

She walked down the corridor where she could be alone and reached in her purse for her cell phone.

She was expecting a call back from her doctor. After the meeting with the detective yesterday, she'd developed a migraine that still hadn't gone away. To her dismay there was no message from the doctor. Maybe he'd tried her house phone and had left one.

Sure enough when she retrieved her messages, she learned his nurse had called in a prescription for the pain. If she could just get some relief...

Right now nothing seemed real. The hurt of her failed marriage and the circumstances surrounding Jim's death had gone too deep.

There was one more message, but she'd wait until she got home because the throbbing at the base of her skull refused to let up.

"Ally?" Carol called to her. "Are you all right?"

"I-it's a migraine giving me grief. Do me a favor and tell the maestro I had to go home, but I'll be here in the morning for rehearsal."

The Portland Philharmonic Orchestra's end of May concert was the day after tomorrow.

"I will. Don't worry about your violin. I'll take it home with me and bring it back tomorrow."

"You're an angel."

After getting a drink from the fountain, Ally found the strength to leave the building and head for her car.

Once she'd stopped at the pharmacy where she'd taken one of her pills on the spot, she drove straight home and went to bed with an ice bag across her forehead.

An hour passed before she started to feel a little better. But there was no pill to stop the questions that wouldn't leave her alone.

For one thing, she wanted to see the place where Jim had died. Her mother hadn't thought it a good idea because visiting the scene of the accident would be too painful.

But Ally couldn't be in any more pain than she was right now. She needed to look at the bridge where Jim's car had skidded on ice into the river. It had happened during a blizzard outside St. Moritz, Switzerland.

She also felt a compulsion to see Donata's family home, maybe even commiserate with the Duc on the phone after she arrived in Montefalco. He wouldn't be human if he didn't have questions, too. Maybe talking together would help both of them cope a little better with the tragedy.

Filled with a sense of purpose she hadn't felt in months, she reached for her cell to phone the airlines. Using her credit card she booked a flight out of Portland for the next day. She would fly to Switzerland, then Italy.

By midafternoon she felt well enough to drive to the bank for traveler's checks. The decision to do something concrete about her situation was probably more therapeutic than taking pills because she found the energy to get packed and arrange for her neighbor to bring in her mail while she was gone.

Once she'd showered, she took another pill and went to bed. When she awakened the next morning she felt considerably better.

With her car safely parked in the garage, all she had left to do was phone for a taxi. While she waited for it to come, Ally listened to the message that had been on her home phone since yesterday morning.

"Hey, Jim! This is Troy at the Golden Arm Gym. Since

new management is taking over, we've been cleaning out the lockers. I found something pretty valuable of yours. I don't have a phone number or address on you, so I've been calling all the J., Jim or James Parkers in the city trying to find you. Call me back either way so I can cross you off the list. If you're that Jim, drop by within twenty-four hours or it'll be gone."

Ally had buried her husband two months ago. Just hearing someone ask to speak to him today of all days sent a chill through her body. This call was like a ghost from the past.

Since Jim had never joined a gym, she phoned the number to let them know.

"Golden Arm Gym."

"Is Troy there?"

"Speaking."

"You're the person who called my house yesterday morning. I'm Mrs. James Parker, but I'm afraid you have the wrong Jim Parker."

"Okay. The Jim I'm looking for works in Europe a lot, and he doesn't have a wife. Thanks for letting me know."

He clicked off, but Ally's fingers tightened around the receiver. Much as she wanted to dismiss his words, she couldn't. Too often in her marriage she'd ignored little signs because she hadn't wanted to believe anything could be wrong.

But those days were over. She was no longer the naïve idealist he'd married.

Once the taxi arrived, she instructed the driver to stop by the gym. It was on the other side of Portland near the freeway leading to the airport. There was no time to lose.

The driver waited while she hurried inside the gym.

When she entered, there were several people already working out. The trainer at the counter flashed her a look of male interest.

"Hi!"

"Hello. Are you Troy?

"That's right."

"I'm Mrs. Parker, the woman you spoke to this morning."

He squinted at her. "I thought you told me I had the wrong person."

"Something you said forced me to reconsider. Did this Jim tell you what kind of work he did in Europe?"

"Yeah. He sells ski wear. In fact we worked out a deal. I gave him free workouts in exchange for his top of the line ski equipment."

She took a fortifying breath. "Then that was my husband."

He blinked. "What do you mean 'was'?"

"Jim died four months ago."

"You're kidding. So that's why I haven't seen him around. What happened?"

"He died in a car accident."

Had there been other women before Donata, and she'd happened to be the unlucky one who'd gone off the bridge with him?

"I'm sorry, Mrs. Parker. Maybe I misunderstood about him not being married."

She shook her head. "No. I'm quite sure you didn't. When did he join this club?"

"About a year ago."

A whole year?

Struggling to remain composed, she pulled the wallet from her purse. Inside was a little photo holder. She showed him the one of Jim.

The other man stared at it, then nodded. "Just a sec and I'll get what he left here."

Half a minute later he came out of his office with an unfamiliar looking silver laptop. The power cord had been taped to it.

He tore the attached slip in half. "Sign here."

Ally complied, trying her best not to tremble.

"Thank you for the call, Troy. I'm anxious to keep anything that belonged to my husband."

"Of course. I'm glad you came when you did, otherwise we'd have sold it. I really am sorry about your husband."

"So am I," she muttered in a dull voice.

She'd known nothing about the purchase of this laptop. Jim's company had supplied him with the one he'd always used to do business.

The only reason for this computer to exist meant he'd had something to hide.

She would have to take it to Europe with her. She didn't have time to go back home. After she returned to the States, she'd look inside. If she discovered painful secrets, hopefully by then she'd be better able to handle them.

After going out to the cab, she packed the laptop in her suitcase then told the driver to step on it.

As she sat back in the seat, she shuddered to realize that her husband had been working out in a gym for eight months, and she'd had no knowledge of his activities. He must have stopped by either coming or going to Switzerland on business.

It was one thing to recognize that the two of them had drifted apart, but quite another to realize he'd been living a separate and secret life. How humiliating to be confronted by the truth in front of Troy, a total stranger to her.

Oh, Jim. What happened to the man I married? Did I ever really know you?

Ally was beginning to wonder…

* * *

With the aid of the staff, Gino helped his grieving Sofia and her father into the limo outside the local parish church. They'd just buried Donata in the adjacent cemetery. It had all been carried out in secret while word of her death had finally been announced by the media.

One day when the furor had died down, he would have her remains removed and buried on the grounds of the Montefalco estate in the family plot.

"I'll join you at the farm in a few minutes, sweetheart."

Sofia's face was ravaged by fresh tears. "Don't take too long."

"I promise. I just want to say goodbye to a few people and thank the priest."

She nodded before the farmhouse caretaker Paolo drove the car away.

Vastly relieved this part was over, he turned swiftly to Carlo whom he'd asked to wait until they could talk in private.

"The onslaught has started in earnest, Carlo."

"What's going on?"

"One of the security guards at the palazzo just left a message that a woman claiming to be Mrs. James Parker tried to get in to see Marcello a few minutes ago. It's another ploy on the part of the paparazzi to ruin my family."

The other man pursed his lips. "I must say I'm surprised they'd be audacious enough to impersonate the wife of the deceased."

Gino grimaced. "Nothing surprises me anymore. She came in a taxi. As a precaution, the guard wrote down the license plate number."

Carlo's brows lifted. "Want me to track her down and have her vetted?"

Gino was way ahead of him.

"If you could locate her, I'd like to do the interrogating for a change."

"What's your plan?"

"How long could she be held at the jail?"

"Only twelve hours. If you can't make the charges stick, then we'd have to release her."

Gino's eyes glittered. "Don't worry about that. She's going to wish she'd never ventured into my territory."

Carlo pulled out his pocket notepad. "Give me the plate number. I'll alert the desk sergeant at the jail to cooperate with you."

"As usual, I'm indebted to you."

"Our families have been close for years. I'm not about to see you and Sofia destroyed."

Those words meant more to Gino than his friend would ever know.

"*Grazie*, Carlo."

There was a jarring knock on the bedroom door.

"Signora Parker?"

Ally had only been in bed an hour and groaned in disbelief. Her long connecting flights from Oregon to Switzerland, then Rome, had been bad enough. But it was the horrendous day she'd spent on a hot, overcrowded train to reach the hilltop town of Montefalco that had done her in.

To compound her troubles, every hotel in the town had been booked months in advance for some festival. If her taxi driver hadn't taken pity on her and brought her to his sister's house to sleep, she would have been forced to return to Rome for the night. Perish the thought!

The rapping grew louder.

"Signora!"

Ally couldn't work out what was happening.

"Just a moment!"

She sat up, unconsciously running a hand through her short, blond curls. They made her look younger than her twenty-eight years.

Grabbing her robe lying across the end of the bed, she slipped it on, then hurried over to the door and opened it.

The elderly woman looked tired. Ally thought she sounded out of breath.

"Quickly! You must get dressed! A car from the Palazzo Di Montefalco has come for you."

Ally's green eyes widened. "But that's impossible!"

Earlier in the day she'd been turned away from the palace gates by armed guards. No one knew where she'd gone after she'd gotten back in the taxi.

"You have to be a very important person for the Duc Di Montefalco himself to send for you. Hurry! You must not keep the driver waiting."

"I'll be out as soon as I can. Thank you."

Unless one of the guards had followed the taxi here, Ally was mystified as to how he'd known where to find her.

But that didn't matter now. In a few minutes she was finally going to meet with the man she'd flown thousands of miles to see. After her futile attempts to reach him by phone from Rome before boarding the train, and then the fiasco that took place earlier in front of the palace, she'd almost given up hope.

She shut the door and reached for her suitcase. In a few minutes she'd donned fresh jeans and a green print blouse.

At one-thirty in the morning she didn't feel like dressing in the suit she'd brought.

Once she'd put on her sneakers, she finished the little packing she had to do. Before leaving the room, she found her purse and left two hundred dollars on the dresser.

One more look around to make sure she hadn't left anything behind and she joined the older woman who stood in the foyer waiting.

Ally rushed up to her. "I'm so sorry you had to be wakened at this late hour because of me. Especially after you were kind enough to take me in. I've left money on the dresser for you and your brother. Thank you again for everything, including the delicious meal and the chance to shower. Please tell your brother thank you, too. I don't know what I would have done without your help."

The other woman nodded impatiently. "I'll tell him. Now you must go!"

She opened the door onto an ancient narrow alley. The woman's house was one of several built at street level. Yet all Ally could see was a gleaming black sedan parked right outside the door.

The light from the foyer illuminated the gold falcon insignia of the Montefalco crest emblazoned on the hood.

As Ally ventured over the threshold, a man dressed in black like the palace security guards stepped away from the stone wall connecting the houses.

Since Ally was only five foot five, she was immediately aware of a tall, solidly built male with hair black as night. Something about his imposing demeanor and the almost hawkish features that distinguished him from so many other Italian male faces she'd seen today sent a little shiver of alarm through her body.

With breathtaking economy of movement he relieved her of her purse and suitcase.

"Give that back!" she cried. Ally tried to wrest the suitcase from his hand, but it was no use. She was no match for him. Besides, he'd already stashed everything in the trunk.

She felt his glance mock her before he opened the rear door.

The interior light revealed a broad shouldered man of unquestionable strength. The sun had darkened his natural olive toned skin. He was more than conventionally handsome. The words splendid and fierce came to Ally's mind before she climbed in the back seat.

Following that thought she wondered if she wasn't crazy to let a total stranger whisk her away from her only place of refuge in this foreign country. She didn't know a soul here except the taxi driver and his sister.

Worse, she'd somehow lost her cell phone during the train ride, so she couldn't call for help. Someone had probably pilfered it.

The premonition that she might need a phone to the outside world was growing stronger as he climbed in behind the wheel and set the locks.

After he turned on the engine, they shot down the empty alley to the main road. Three blocks later and Ally sensed she was in trouble.

Instead of climbing to the top of the hill, the driver drove them through the lower streets of the town. He appeared to have a destination in mind that wasn't anywhere near the ochre-colored ducal palace clinging to the side of the cliff.

Rather than leave the old woman's protection at such an unorthodox hour, Ally should have obeyed her instincts and stayed in her room until morning.

She leaned forward in the leather seat. "This isn't the way to the palace." She'd said it in as steady a voice as she could muster.

"Please take me back to that woman's house."

The enigmatic guard ignored her demand and kept driving until they entered another alley behind some municipal buildings.

"Where are you taking me?"

"All in good time, *signora*." The first words out of his mouth were spoken in impeccable English with only a slight trace of accent.

He pulled in front of a steel door with a single light shining overhead. In the next instant he'd come around to her side of the car and opened the door for her.

"After you, *signora*."

She lifted her proud chin, refusing to budge. "Where have you brought me?"

His heavily lashed eyes looked like smoldering black fires.

"The Montefalco police station."

Police? "I don't understand."

"Earlier this evening you asked to speak to the Duc Di Montefalco, did you not?"

"Yes. Are you telling me I didn't have the right?"

"Let's just say he doesn't grant interviews."

"I didn't want an interview. I've flown a long way to talk to him in private."

He shifted his weight, drawing her attention to the play of raw muscle power in his arms and chest.

"Anyone who wants to make contact with him has to go through me."

That explained why she could never get anywhere on the phone or in front of the security guards.

Ally couldn't prevent her gaze from traveling over his distinctive masculine features. Those piercing eyes were framed by startlingly black brows. Never had she looked into such an arresting face.

"Are you a police officer who doubles as one of his bodyguards or something?"

A dangerous smile curled the corners of his mocking mouth. "That's one way of describing me."

CHAPTER TWO

A STRANGE CHILL rippled across Ally's skin. "How did you know where to find me?"

"The guards took down the license plate of your taxi. A simple phone call to the driver told me what I needed to know."

As easy as that.

"I told the palace guards who I was. They didn't even try to help me."

His lips twisted unpleasantly. "Any woman could claim to be Mrs. James Parker."

"But that's who I am! I have my passport to prove it."

"Passports are a dime a dozen. I believe that's the American expression."

She shook her head in exasperation. "Why are you being so hateful to me? I came to Italy expressly to meet with Mr. Montefalco for very personal reasons. You act like I've committed some crime."

"Trespassing *is* a crime," he muttered just loud enough to heighten her anxiety.

"This is impossible! I demand you call the American Embassy and let me talk to someone in charge."

His mouth formed a contemptuous line.

"No one there will be available before morning."

"In America you're innocent until proven guilty!" she flung at him, starting to feel desperate.

"Then you should have stayed there, or wherever you really came from, *signora*," he retorted in a voice of ice.

Trapped and painfully tired, Ally made the decision not to fight him. He was too formidable an adversary. This was all a terrible mistake, the kind you were supposed to be able to laugh about after you'd returned home from being abroad.

Once this man went through her belongings and found out the truth of her identity, she didn't expect an apology. However she could hope for a quick release and the chance to talk to Mr. Montefalco before too much more time passed.

Wrapping her dignity around her like a cloak, she got out of the car and waited for him to open the door.

He pressed a button on the wall of the building. In a minute the door swung open electronically.

She'd never been inside a jail of any kind. In the small reception area there were two armed police officers, one of them seated at a desk.

They nodded to her captor.

After an exchange in Italian she couldn't possibly understand, he left her in their charge and disappeared out the door.

"Wait—" she called out to no avail.

At that point she was photographed, fingerprinted and escorted down a passageway to a tiny room with a cot and a chair.

The door closed behind her, leaving her to her own devices.

The whole situation was so surreal, she wondered if she was hallucinating on the painkiller she'd taken before going to bed. It had been a preventive measure to ward off another sick headache.

Suddenly she heard the click of the electronic lock and the door opened. She swung around in time to see the driver who'd abducted her step inside. The door shut behind him, enclosing her in this tiny closet of a holding cell with a man who could overpower her before she took her next breath. He'd brought her purse with him.

"During your interrogation you have your choice of the chair or the bed, *signora*."

She was feeling pretty hysterical about now.

"I'd rather stand."

"So be it."

He opened her purse. After examining the contents including her wallet and bottle of medication, he pulled out her passport.

She watched him study the picture that had been taken three years earlier. At that point in time she'd been a radiant fiancée with long blond hair and sparkling green eyes, anticipating a skiing honeymoon in the French Alps with Jim.

Ally could no longer relate to that person.

The stranger's enigmatic gaze flicked to her face and hair. He scrutinized her as if trying and failing to find the woman in the photo.

He put the passport in his pocket, then tossed her purse with its contents on the cot next to the pathetic looking lump that was supposed to be a pillow.

Only now did she realize her suitcase was still in his car.

"I'd like my luggage. There are things I need," she explained. "I have to have it, you know? Like clean clothes?"

"First things first, *signora*. Until I get the answers I'm looking for, we'll be at this all night. Since you already appear unsteady on your feet—no doubt from fear that you've been caught in the act—I suggest you sit down before you pass out."

"In the act of what?" Ally questioned, totally shocked by his assumption she'd done something wrong.

"We both know you're one of the unscrupulous paparazzi, willing to do anything for an exclusive. But I'm warning you now. After trying to impersonate someone else, you're facing a prison sentence unless you start talking."

"I *am* Mrs. James Parker."

"Just tell me the name of the tabloid that sent you on this story."

Heat swept through her body into her face. "You're crazy!" she blurted in exasperation. "My name is Allyson Cummings Parker. I'm an American citizen from Portland, Oregon. I only arrived in Rome from Switzerland this afternoon, or—or yesterday afternoon. I'm all mixed up now about the time. But I'm the widow of James Parker. He was a ski clothes salesman who worked for an American manufacturing company called Slippery Slopes of Portland. He died in a car accident outside St. Moritz, Switzerland, with Mr. Montefalco's wife four months ago!"

"Of course you are," he said in a sarcastic aside that made her hackles rise.

Her breathing grew shallow.

"Since you tracked me down through the taxi driver, he'll tell you he picked me up at the train station, and had to do all the translating while I tried to find a room because I don't speak Italian."

Her captor nodded. "He admitted you put on a convincing performance. That is…until you gave yourself away by asking him to drive you to the palazzo. That was your fatal mistake."

Her hands curled into fists. "How else was I supposed to talk to Mr. Montefalco? He doesn't list his phone number. When I reached Rome, I was on the phone with an Italian operator for half an hour trying to get a number for him."

"He doesn't talk to strangers. If you were an innocent tourist who didn't have a place to spend the night, you would have been much more concerned about that than brazenly attempting to ramrod your way into the ducal palace that has always been off limits to the public."

"But I didn't know that!"

"You're a good liar, I'll grant you that, but it was a dangerous act of idiocy on your part no matter how greedy you are for money. It's the one credential you sleazy members of the media carry every time you trespass on sacred ground for a story. You have no decency or thought for the precariousness of the situation. None of your kind has a conscience."

He folded his arms, eyeing her with chilling menace.

"As you're going to find out, I don't have one, either. So you can start talking now, or look forward to being incarcerated here indefinitely."

Her mouth had gone dry. "You're going to be sorry you're treating me like this," she warned him with a mutinous expression. "When Mr. Montefalco finds out I'm here anxious to talk to him, you'll be lucky if it's only your job you lose."

His black eyes felt like lasers, scanning beneath the surface for any abnormalities.

"Who sent you to do their dirty work?" he rapped out as if she hadn't spoken. "Tell me now and I'll use my influence with the judge to get you off with a light sentence."

A pulse throbbed at the corner of his hard jaw. He was

in deadly earnest. That made the situation so much worse for Ally.

She spread her hands. "Look—there's been a huge misunderstanding here. If you think my passport and driver's license are doctored, then look at my airline tickets again. It proves I just flew here from Portland, with a stopover in Switzerland to see where my husband's accident happened."

His gaze searched hers relentlessly. "You call that proof when you could have flown from Italy to Oregon on your tabloid's money to begin your impersonation? You're wasting my time."

He pressed a button above the door, no doubt sending a signal that he was ready to leave. This was a nightmare!

"No—don't go yet—" she begged as the door swung outward.

He paused in the aperture, almost filling it with his tall, powerful body.

"Please—" she beseeched him. "There's someone you could call who will vouch for me. His name is L—"

She broke off talking because she suddenly realized she didn't want him to talk to Lieutenant Davis. She would be too embarrassed for the detective to know she'd flown here to satisfy her curiosity about Donata. It was a private matter she'd rather no one else knew about. Until she talked to Mr. Montefalco, it was absolutely crucial her activities and whereabouts remain a secret to everyone including her mother. Ally's mom thought she was spending the weekend with friends from the orchestra. If she knew the truth, there would have been a battle Ally couldn't have handled.

"Yes?" her adversary mocked again. "You were saying?"

He stood still as a tree trunk. By now she was so beside herself she felt light-headed. Her ears started to buzz.

Out of self-preservation she sank down on the end of the cot and lowered her head so she wouldn't faint.

"Anything you'd like to confess before lights out, *signora*?" he asked without an ounce of concern or compassion.

His voice sounded far away. Ally had to wait until the worst of her weakness had passed before she could talk.

By then, he'd gone...

Vaguely disturbed by the woman's insistence that she really was the wife of Donata's last lover, Gino sped faster than was prudent through the dark streets toward his family home at the top of the mount. He wanted total privacy before searching the woman's suitcase. En route he phoned Carlo.

"Thank you for helping me carry out my plan. The suspect is in her cell, but I realize we won't be able to hold her for long. I asked the desk sergeant to run her passport through the scanner for verification, then report to you. Do me a favor and let me know what he finds out. When we've learned it's counterfeit, I'll expose her in my own way so she never gets another job. I'm sick of the media."

Once they'd hung up, he used his remote to enter the estate.

After slipping in a private side entrance to the palazzo with his prisoner's luggage, he entered Marcello's study and set it on one of the damask couches.

Upon opening it, he was surprised to see how lightly she traveled. The interior was redolent of her flowery scent. There were only a few changes of outfits and feminine underclothing, all modest and for the most part American brands.

Frowning because he couldn't find a camera or film, in fact nothing that sent up a red flag, his hands dug deeper.

"What's this?"

He felt something solid, wrapped in a towel.

"I knew it!" he whispered fiercely as he pulled out a silver laptop.

No wonder she'd wanted to hold on to her luggage.

He carried it over to the desk and plugged it into the wall adaptor.

"You and your paper are about to be exposed. Believe me, *signora*, you're going to pay—"

He turned it on, then sat down in the leather chair and waited to see what flashed on the screen.

He was ready to seize on anything that linked her to one of the tabloids.

Her home page popped up. He immediately clicked on her favorite pictures icon. Before long he came face-to-face with photos of Donata.

Gino let out a curse. He counted thirty pictures showing his sister-in-law in various stages of dress and undress. The outdoor pictures had been taken in Prague. He recognized the landmarks.

How in the hell had that impossibly green-eyed imposter gotten hold of these?

Donata, Donata.

He gritted his teeth. If these were to make it onto the streets… If Sofia were ever to see them…

He felt his gut twist in reaction.

There was only one reason why the champagne-blonde with the voluptuous curves locked up in the cell hadn't gone public with them yet. Perhaps she'd decided to approach Marcello first to extort more money from him than her paper would pay out.

Sick to the depth of his being because he knew these photos were only the tip of the iceberg, he packed up the laptop, closed her suitcase and carried both out to the truck he kept on the estate.

Leaving by a hidden road that came out on a side street, he headed for the jail.

Later at the farmhouse when he had the luxury of time, he'd delve into the e-mails and other secrets of the computer's hard drive. Until then, Gino would break her down until she was grist.

He wanted the name of the tabloid she worked for, how many more photos existed and the length of time she'd been on Donata's trail in order to obtain those particular photos.

Ally heard the door open. When she saw a tall dark figure coming toward her before it closed again, she let out a blood-curdling scream and pulled the sheet over her head. "Nightmares, *signora*?" sounded the devilish voice of her captor. "With the kinds of things you have on your conscience, I can't say I'm surprised."

"Get out!" she shouted into the darkness. "The only person I'll speak to is a diplomat from the American Embassy. Do you understand me?"

"I'm afraid you're going to have a long wait."

She heard something scrape against the cement floor. She shivered to realize he'd pulled the chair next to her bed and had sat down.

"What you're doing is against the law!"

He gave a caustic laugh.

Fear of a sort she'd never known before emboldened her to say the first thing that came into her mind.

"What a tragedy that such a lovely, beautiful town produces monsters like you."

The rhythm of his breathing changed, letting her know she'd struck a nerve. Good!

"For someone in your kind of trouble," he began in a frighteningly silky voice, "I'd advise you to stop fantasizing and tell me everything before the chief prosecutor of the region gets here and you're arraigned before the magistrate."

She sat up on the cot and pressed herself into the corner of the wall, as far away from him as possible.

"Whether you believe me or not, I'm Mrs. James Parker. So far, all you've told me is that I trespassed. But I don't see how I did that when the guards wouldn't let me past the gate."

She heard him shift in the chair.

"If you're telling the truth, and you really are the hapless wife who was the last person to know what your husband was up to, explain what those pictures are doing in your laptop."

Pictures? Ally rubbed her bloodshot eyes with her palms. She was so desperately tired, maybe she was dreaming this horror story.

"I asked you a question, *signora*."

No—she wasn't dreaming. He was sitting there next to her, intimidating her by his very presence. All two hundred pounds of him, hard as steel physically and every other way.

"It's my husband's laptop. I don't know anything about any pictures."

She heard a sharp intake of breath.

"So you carried his laptop with you all the way to Montefalco for no particular reason?"

"I didn't say that!" she protested. "I told you earlier that I came to have a private talk with Mr. Montefalco and no one else."

"In order to show him the photographs and extort thousands of dollars in the process."

Thousands of dollars? What pictures would be worth that kind of money? She took a deep breath, scared of what she might discover.

"If there are pictures, I haven't seen them."

At her hotel in St. Mortiz, Ally would have looked inside the laptop, but she hadn't brought an adaptor to fit in the foreign outlet and figured she would have to wait until she returned to Portland. Part of her knew that was just an excuse. She didn't want to know.

"I planned to talk to him about things that aren't your business or anyone else's."

After a pause, he said, "You can tell me. I have his ear."

"Prove it! For all I know you're just a lowly policeman pretending to be Mr. Montefalco's bodyguard."

Suddenly he was on his feet. She could feel his rage as he pushed the chair away. She hid her face behind the sheet even though it was dark in the room.

Still bristling she said, "Now *you* know how it feels to be told you're a liar and a sleazy con artist out to cash in on someone's private tragedy. I repeat." Her voice throbbed. "I'm *not* saying another word until I can speak to someone from the Embassy."

While she waited for his response, the door opened, then slammed shut.

The next thing she knew the light in her cell went on.

She checked her watch, which she'd changed to Italian time on the train. It said 7:30 a.m.

How long were they going to leave her in here before allowing her to freshen up?

In desperation she dragged the chair over to the door so she could push the button he'd pressed earlier.

Suddenly the door swung open, almost causing her to fall.

A guard she didn't recognize waited for her to climb down, then ordered her to follow him.

She grabbed her purse and trailed him down the hall and around the corner to the bathroom. There was no sign of her captor. She sincerely hoped she would never have to see or talk to him again.

After brushing her hair and putting on some lipstick, she felt a little more human. When she emerged minutes later, the guard escorted her back to her cell where a tray of food was waiting on the chair.

Just looking at the chair reminded her how her interrogator had shoved it across the room in a fit of anger.

In spite of the precariousness of her situation, the fact that she'd been able to infuriate him caused her to smile.

The guard noted it before disappearing.

Locked in once more, her gaze fell on the sparse continental breakfast. Rolls and coffee. But she wasn't about to complain. It might be a long time before she was allowed to eat again, so she consumed everything in short order.

She kept thinking about those pictures he'd mentioned. Jim had evidently stored some in one of his files. Maybe they were photos of all the women he'd had affairs with in Europe. At this juncture she didn't put anything past him. Her husband had truly lived a double life.

Ally let out a sound of abnegation.

What a fool she'd been not to have confronted him when she'd first suspected there was another woman.

Her abductor's words stung more than ever.

If you're telling the truth, and you really are the hapless wife who was the last person to know what your husband was up to, explain what those pictures are doing in your laptop.

Ally hadn't been hapless. It was a case of not wanting to

admit something was wrong and have her mother say, "I told you so. A man with good looks and knows it can't be satisfied with one woman."

Ally didn't believe that. She knew too many attractive couples who had wonderful marriages.

Hers had started out that way, but when she saw changes happening, she should have questioned him point-blank. But she'd been scared. They could have talked things out and maybe salvaged their marriage. Now it was too late. There was no use wishing she'd acted on her suspicions a long time ago.

She looked around her claustrophobic cell. What she needed to do was get out of here.

Her abductor was waiting for her to cooperate. Maybe if she made up a lie, he'd believe her and allow her to go free with a slap on the wrist.

Without hesitation she pushed the chair over to the door and climbed up to press the button.

While she waited for a response, she put it back against the wall.

In a minute the door swung open to reveal the guard who'd brought her breakfast.

"Signora?"

"I hate it in here and I'm ready to talk."

He took the tray off her bed and started out the door.

"Did you hear me?" she cried. "I'm ready to confess!"

He shot her an oblique glance before the door closed.

"Ooh—" She pounded her fists against it. "What kind of a lunatic place is this?" she shouted.

When she realized she was only hurting herself, she gave it up and walked around her cell, trying to rub the pain from the sides of her hands.

Five minutes later she experienced déjà vu to hear the door open and see her captor enter the room. When she glimpsed the forbidding look in those fiery black eyes, she backed away from him.

"You're ready to tell the truth, *signora*?"

"Yes, but not in here. I can't abide enclosed places."

He gave an elegant shrug, reminding her what an amazing physique he had.

"It's either in here, or not at all."

"Oh all right!" She took a deep breath. "It's true I pretended to be Mrs. Parker to get the duc's attention.

"I do freelance stories for a local magazine in Portland. One of my boyfriends works for the police department and once in a while he tells me something interesting.

"A couple of months ago he told me his boss was working on a missing persons case involving a married man from Portland and another woman who died with him in Europe. Just the other day he mentioned that they'd finally identified the woman and had pictures of her.

"I asked him if he would let me see them. He did, so I scanned them and downloaded them to my laptop.

"All I wanted to do was talk to the woman's husband and ask if I could do an exclusive story on him. In case he didn't believe I was serious, I planned to show him the pictures. But I wouldn't have allowed them to be published, or have bribed him for money. I just wanted to write about his heart-wrenching ordeal. Americans love stories about wealthy, titled people with problems. It makes them feel better about their own less glorious lives.

"So now that you know the truth, please let me go. All I want is my passport and suitcase back. If you'll send for a taxi, the driver will take me to the train.

How about it? You let me out of here and I'll go straight home to Portland."

His eyes held a frightening gleam.

"You're lying through your pearly-white teeth, *signora*, but I give you credit for your amazing resourcefulness."

His wintry smile daunted her. "As it happens, I never told you the nature of those photos. If you'd known what they contained, you wouldn't have placed your source's job in jeopardy. All you've done is convince me you're a liar."

He was bluffing...

"How typical," she mocked. "If I were a man, you would have said 'good try.' But since I'm a woman, I can't be trusted."

One black brow quirked.

"Aren't you? So far you've told me two diametrically opposing lies, none of which hold water. While I'm still here, want to try for a third? I have nothing more important to do for the moment."

"Okay." She felt all the stuffing go out of her. "I'll make a deal with you. I'll give you a hundred dollars if you'll let me go. No one will need to know."

"If it were a hundred thousand dollars, I wouldn't take it."

He was impossible!

"Look— All I wanted to do was speak to Mr. Montefalco. This is between him and me, no one else."

He pursed his lips. "Why is that, *signora*?"

She lifted solemn eyes to his.

"Because it's very sad and very personal."

He put his hands on hips, the picture of the ultimate male. "I'm his closest confidant. You can tell me anything. If it will make you feel any better, you can whisper it to me. I promise it will remain sacrosanct."

Something in his tone had her halfway believing him, but it didn't matter.

"How do I know you're not wearing a listening device?"

"You don't," he clipped out. "You'll have to trust me."

She leaned close to him. "Sorry, but I have to talk to him alone."

The nearness of her heart-shaped mouth and the flowery scent her body gave off, stunned him as much as the words that fell from those enticing lips underlining her intransigence.

She couldn't be Mrs. James Parker. Any man married to her wouldn't have felt the urge to turn to Donata or any other woman for that matter.

"If you won't let me out of here," she continued in a low voice, "then bring Mr. Montefalco to me. I want to talk to him, and I believe he'll be anxious to talk to me. We might find we're a comfort to each other."

With his body still reacting to the warmth of her breath on his ear, Gino found himself reluctant to put distance between them. But he had to no matter how much the imploring look in her eyes and the haunting appeal in her voice persuaded him to believe she was finally telling him the truth.

He'd just stepped away, rubbing the back of his neck in an unconscious gesture of frustration when the door opened to reveal one of the guards. He informed Gino that Inspector Santi wanted him on the phone.

Without saying a word to her, he strode down the hall to the office, hardening himself against her sound of protest. In truth he was oddly reticent to find out she was the beautiful dust of the enemy.

He picked up the receiver, then turned his back toward the desk sergeant.

Knowing the jail phone was tapped he said, "Inspector? I'll call you back on my phone." After replacing the receiver, Gino pulled out his cell and rang him on the other man's private line.

Keeping his voice low he said, "Carlo? What did you find out?"

"She *is* Mrs. Parker, Gino."

While his thoughts took off in a dozen directions, Carlo kept talking. "I guess I'm not surprised. She's a widow grieving for her husband."

Gino had proof of that. He'd just come from her cell. She'd claimed that she'd sought out Marcello in the hope of giving and receiving comfort. But if that was true, how did she explain the laptop? Something didn't ring true.

"She said she'd been in St. Moritz to visit the scene of the accident," Gino murmured.

"It's unfortunate she chose this time to come to Italy when the press is just waiting for anything they can do to sensationalize this case. She's the last person *you* should be seen with."

Gino agreed. All it would take was a photo of the two of them together caught by one of the lurking paparazzi, and the hellish situation would escalate overnight.

"You need to leave the jail and let me handle this, Gino. I'll instruct the sergeant to free her. One of the guards will escort her to Rome by train and put her on the next plane for the States."

Gino grunted a response as he listened to his friend. Though Carlo made a lot of sense, Gino couldn't forget that Mrs. Parker had come all this way with that laptop to see Marcello for a specific reason. Since she'd put herself in jeopardy to accomplish her objective, Gino couldn't let her go until he'd found out what was so important she'd risked everything, even jail, to make contact.

"I'm sure you're right, Carlo. I'll leave it up to you."

"That's good. You need to stay as far removed from her as possible."

He would as soon as he'd had time to talk to her away from other people. "*Grazie*, Carlo. It seems that's all I ever say to you."

"Forget it. *Ciao*, Gino."

Ally had been sitting on the cot wondering what was going on when the door flew open.

It was the same guard as before.

"Come, *signora*. You've been released. Please to follow me."

Hardly able to believe it, she grabbed her purse and started after him.

"What about my suitcase?"

"It is here," he said once they'd reached the reception area of the jail.

Convinced her abductor had confiscated the laptop, she leaned over to open the catches and sure enough, she discovered it was gone.

For some inexplicable reason, which was absurd considering her circumstances, she wished he were still here so that in front of his colleagues, she could accuse him of absconding with it.

She shut the lid and lifted her head. "What about my passport?"

"You'll be given it after you board your flight for the U.S."

She almost blurted that she couldn't leave Montefalco yet,

but she stopped herself in time. All she needed was to make that mistake and then be shuffled back to her cell for defying him.

She took a deep breath to calm down. When she boarded her jet, she would claim to be ill and ask to be put on a later flight. Once she found a hotel room in Rome, she would figure out another plan to reach Mr. Montefalco.

"Very well. I'm ready whenever you are."

The jail door swung open. Another guard stood outside in front of a white police car and held the rear door open for her. Unlike her captor, he didn't help her with her luggage. No doubt he considered her a lowlife reporter who didn't deserve common courtesy.

She pushed her case across the seat and climbed in.

When their car emerged from the alley, throngs of tourists filled the walkways. The guard wound his way through the charming streets for the short ride to the depot.

She hated the thought of another hot train ride, but there was no help for it.

"Come, *signora*."

The guard had parked the car in a VIP zone. He escorted her through the crowded station and out to the quay.

After a brief talk with one of the conductors, he boarded the train with her and put her in a second class compartment already filled except for one seat in the middle. She had to put her suitcase on the shelf above without his assistance.

"I'll be in the corridor until we reach Rome, *signora*." The warning that she shouldn't try anything to escape was implicit.

Her cheeks hot with anger, she sat down, trying to avoid the interested stares of the other passengers.

No sooner had the guard stepped out of the compartment and disappeared than the train began to inch forward.

Ally was so exhausted after spending a wretched night in that jail cell, she rested her head against the back of the seat. Dispirited by everything that had happened, she closed her eyes for a few minutes, needing sleep. The first thing she would do when she could finally be alone in a hotel room was to crash.

Soon she lost track of time and was almost out for the count when she felt a hand on her arm.

"Signora?" sounded a deep male voice with a vaguely familiar timbre.

She came awake with a cry of alarm.

When she saw her striking captor still dressed in black, standing there bigger than life carrying her suitcase, the breath rushed from her lungs. She blinked up at him, wondering if he was real, or if she was dreaming.

"W-what's going on?"

His hooded eyes played over her features, awakening her senses in spite of her fatigue, or maybe because of it.

"I relieved the other guard. We're getting off at the next stop. Come with me."

Though she felt so groggy she didn't know how she'd be able to walk, she realized this man was her only chance to get Jim's laptop back, and maybe find an entrée to Mr. Montefalco.

Clutching her purse, she got up and followed him out of the compartment and down the corridor. The train had already begun to slow down.

When it came to a stop, several people were waiting to climb on board. But he stepped off the stairs first, and held out his hand to help her. Feeling distinctly light-headed from sleep deprivation, she found his strong grasp oddly reassuring.

To her surprise he kept hold of it as he led her out of the small station to a truck parked along the road. It wasn't anything like the black sedan from the palazzo she'd ridden in last night.

Heavens—was it only last night? Ally felt all mixed up and confused. She had to be confused to be happy this enigmatic stranger had rescued her from that awful train.

"Where are you taking me?" she asked once he'd turned on the engine.

"To a place where you can eat and sleep in that order."

That sounded so wonderful, she wanted to cry.

"Why would you do that for me when you had me jailed for false credentials, trespassing and impersonating someone else?" her voice trembled.

His hands tightened on the steering wheel. She could tell because his knuckles went white.

"I've found out you're who you said you were."

She jerked her head away from him so he wouldn't see her eyes smarting.

"You mean you now believe I'm Mrs. Parker…"

"Yes."

"I see. So now that you know my name, what does Mr. Montefalco call *you*?"

There was a curious silence, then, "Gino."

She stirred restlessly in the seat.

"Which may or may not be your real name, but at least it's something to call you."

"Besides bastard you mean?" he interjected in a wry tone.

Caught off guard, Ally laughed softly. She couldn't help it.

"Actually that's what I felt like calling the guard when he

wouldn't help me with my suitcase on the train. Even at your worst, you were more of a gentleman."

She heard him draw in what sounded like a tortured breath. "I owe you an apology."

She flicked him a covert glance. "If I ever get to meet your employer, I'll be able to vouch for your fierce loyalty to him. It's no wonder he keeps you on his payroll. Every man who's a target should have such a trusted bodyguard."

By now they'd left the little village of Remo and were driving through fields of sunflowers with a hot Italian sun shining down.

"How do you know so much about him?"

She studied her hands. "I know very little apart from the obvious facts."

"Which are?" he prodded.

"He's rich, titled and has lost his wife. If he loved her desperately, then my heart goes out to him."

"What about your heart?" he whispered.

"If you're asking if it was shattered by my husband's death, then yes." *If you're wondering if his probable infidelity has wounded me, then yes.* But because she'd waited too long to try to fix what was wrong between them, Jim's unexpected death had brought on guilt she couldn't seem to throw off.

Gino drove along the maze of country roads with what appeared to be long accustomed practice and expertise.

Once upon a time she would have loved traveling through the countryside, but right now she was numb to the world around her.

The next time he stopped, her bleary eyes took in a yellowed, three-story farmhouse that looked quite ancient.

"Where are we?"

"My home," he announced before helping her from the car.

He carried her suitcase and told her to follow him. She didn't question him as they entered the foyer and climbed some stairs to the next floor.

He opened a door on his left. "You'll be comfortable in here, Mrs. Parker. The en suite bathroom is through that door. I'll ask my housekeeper Bianca to bring you a tray. Sleep well. We'll talk later."

"Yes, we will. I'd like my husband's laptop back."

"All in good time."

As she was coming to find out, it was his favorite saying.

He placed her suitcase on the aged hardwood floor, then left and shut the door behind him.

Straight ahead of her was a four-poster double bed with a comfy looking white quilt. She was so tired, she removed her outer clothes and climbed under the covers. Ally didn't remember her head touching the pillow.

CHAPTER THREE

ON GINO'S WAY down to the kitchen, Sofia met him in the dining room. "Who's that lady you brought home with you, Uncle Gino?"

Gino had to think fast. "An acquaintance of mine who wanted to see the farm. She's flown all the way from the States, and is so tired, I told her to sleep before I introduced her to you."

"Oh."

"Where's Bianca?"

"Out on the back terrace with Luigi and papa."

That was just as well. He tousled Sofia's hair. "Our guest needs food. Do you want to help me fix it?"

"Yes."

She started walking to the kitchen with him.

"What does she like?"

"Can you imagine her not liking anything Bianca cooks?"

"I guess not."

His morose niece needed her friends. Now that he was home, he would arrange for it. Together they made a plate of ham, fresh bread, salad, fruit and hot tea.

"Can I go with you to take it to her?"

"Of course."

"What's her name?"

"Signora Parker."

"Does she speak Italian?"

"No." Not according to the taxi driver. "It will give you a chance to practice your excellent English with her."

"Is she a farmer, too?"

Gino was equally curious about the wife of Donata's lover. "Why don't you ask her later?" It would be interesting to hear her answer.

They went up the stairs. He tapped on the door. *"Signora?"*

"I'll peek," Sofia offered and opened the door a crack. After tiptoeing inside, she came back out again.

"She's sound asleep."

Gino wasn't surprised. "We'll fix her another plate later."

Once back in the kitchen, they worked together to clean things up while he devoured the meal meant for the intriguing woman sleeping beneath his roof.

"She has pretty hair. It looks like the color of fairy wings."

That was as good a description of gossamer as you could get. He eyed his brunette niece he loved.

"Not many people we know have hair that particular shade do they?"

"I don't know any," she declared.

Neither did Gino.

"What do you say we call Anna's mother and see if your friend can stay over with us for a few days."

"She likes me to play at her house."

He frowned. "Why not at yours?"

"I don't know."

He put a hand on her shoulder. "I think you do. Tell me what's wrong?"

Her eyes filled with tears. "I think she's scared of Papa."

Pain shot through him. "Did she tell you that?"

"No. But the last time she came to the palazzo, Papa suddenly started walking around the rooms. He kept doing it over and over again, and—" Sofia couldn't finish.

Gino crushed her in his arms, absorbing her sobs while he let her cry her heart out. Deep inside he cried with her to think of the brother he idolized reduced to this state so early in his life. But even worse, to realize Sofia had been robbed of a normal childhood. God give him the strength to help his precious niece find some happiness before her childhood was gone.

"Would you like me to drive you to Anna's?"

"No. I don't want to go anywhere. I just want to stay with you."

That's what Gino had been afraid of. Sofia was crawling deeper and deeper inside her impenetrable shell. It was up to Gino not to let that happen. But how to prevent it when he was having trouble enough holding body and soul together?

When Ally first woke up, it took a minute for her to remember where she was.

She checked her watch. It was almost 8:00 p.m. She'd slept nine hours!

Someone must have just come in the room and brought her a tray of food. She was so grateful, and so ravenous, she ate every crumb, then drained the cup of hot tea in one go.

Her suitcase was still where Gino had left it. She carried it to the bed and got out clean clothes before hurrying into the bathroom to shower.

When she walked in the bedroom ten minutes later freshly

shampooed and dressed in a clean pair of jeans and a blue cotton top, she felt a little more human again.

Delighted with her cheerful yellow room, she opened the green shutters to look outside. In the twilight she could see fields of flowers under cultivation. Incredible.

After brushing her damp hair until it formed natural curls, she applied lipstick, then left the room and went downstairs in search of her host.

A tall, slender girl about eleven or twelve with long brown hair and large, sad brown eyes met her at the bottom of the stairs. Gino's daughter?

Ally slowed down. Of course he would have a family. Why would she even question it?

"Hello."

"Hello, Mrs. Parker," the girl said.

Ally was charmed by her manners. "What's your name?"

"Sofia."

"I *love* it."

"You do?"

"Yes. There was once a very important queen ahead of her time with that name."

The girl eyed her solemnly. "What's yours?"

"It's Ally. But I like yours much better."

"What does your name mean?"

"I don't think it means anything, but I got teased a lot because of it."

"How come?"

"Do you know what a cat is?"

"Yes. Uncle Gino got me one a couple of months ago. It's black with white feet."

Uncle Gino. That explained the superficial likeness to him.

"Lucky you. What's its name?"

"Rudolfo."

"That sounds quite magnificent."

"It's Uncle Gino's real name."

How apropos. He more than fulfilled the expectation of such a name.

"I see. Well, in my case the kids called me 'alley cat'."

"What's that?"

"A cat that lives on the streets because it doesn't have a home."

"But you had a home." She sounded worried.

"Yes, darling." The endearment just slipped out. There was a wistfulness about the girl that caught at Ally's heart strings.

"Where do you live in America?"

"Portland, Oregon. Have you heard of it?"

"I think so. Uncle Gino said you came to see his farm. Are you a farmer?"

That was as good an explanation as any for Ally's presence in the home of Mr. Montefalco's bodyguard.

"Not exactly, Sofia. But my grandparents used to have a small farm at the base of Mount Hood in Oregon. It's an old volcano."

"We have volcanoes here," Sofia confided.

"I know. Very famous ones. Someday I'd like to see them."

"Is the one by your grandparents' alive?"

"I guess they can all come alive, but Mount Hood has been quiet for many years. The soil is perfect for growing lavender.

"That's one of the flowers Uncle Gino grows."

"I noticed. That's the reason I stopped by. The flower fields reminded me that my grandmother used to keep a garden and would give lavender away for gifts. One of my favorite memories was helping her separate it into bundles."

"I wish I could do that."

"Don't you get to help your aunt and uncle on the farm?"

"Uncle Gino's not married. He says girlfriends are much better."

At least Gino was honest. Bluntly so.

Having witnessed several sides of him already, she couldn't say she was surprised by his philosophy. It reminded her of her mother's attitude about handsome men making bad husbands. Maybe Gino and her mother had the right answer after all.

Ally moved closer. "Since you're family, I bet Gino would give you a special farm job to do if you asked him."

"Maybe I will." Sofia looked up at Ally with fresh interest. Do you want to meet my father? He hasn't gone to bed yet."

"I'd love to. What's his name?"

"Marcello."

"That's another wonderful name. What's your mother's?"

Her face closed up. "Donata."

Donata?

But that meant—that meant—

Fresh pain knifed through Ally.

Dear God—

Just then Gino emerged from the shadows of the corridor.

Ally wondered how long he'd been standing there. How much had he heard of her conversation with Sofia?

Their eyes met for an instant. As he hugged his niece to his side, she registered anguish in those black depths.

Ally leaned over and grasped the girl's hands.

"Gino told me about your mother, Sofia. I'm so sorry." Her voice shook.

I despise you, Jim Parker, for your part in depriving this child of her mother.

How was it possible Donata hadn't cherished her daughter

and husband enough that she would go on vacation to Switzerland without them? It made reason stare and brought a different kind of ache to Ally's heart.

She had to clear her throat before she could speak again.

"My father died a few years ago. No matter how young or old you are, I know how much it hurts."

What had hurt Ally was to learn that her father had passed away, and she'd never once met him.

Tears trickled down the girl's pale cheeks. "Uncle Gino says I have to wait until I go to heaven to see her again."

Over the last four months Ally had thought she'd cried all the tears inside her. But in the face of seeing this child's suffering, she could feel new ones threatening.

"You and your father are going to need each other more than ever. Where is he?"

"In the kitchen with Luigi drinking his tea."

"Is Luigi your brother?"

"No. I don't have any brothers or sisters. Luigi is one of the nurses who takes care of papa."

Takes care of him?

Ally darted Gino another questioning glance. She discovered a mixture of sorrow and bleakness.

"My brother was diagnosed with Alzheimer's two years ago. His was a very rare case because it hit so hard and fast."

Ally gasped. There'd been too many painful revelations at once.

She cupped Sofia's wet cheeks. "I'd love to be introduced to your father. Can he talk at all?"

"No, but sometimes he squeezes my hand. Come with me."

She grasped one of Ally's hands and led her through the spacious dining room off the foyer to the kitchen. Ally was aware of Gino's hard-muscled body following them at a short distance.

One glimpse of the black-haired fiftyish looking man seated at the oak table, and she saw the strong resemblance between the two brothers.

As they drew closer, she noticed that Sofia had inherited her father's brown eyes and widow's peak.

Two immensely attractive men in one family. How tragic that one of them had to be stricken in the prime of life.

His attentive nurse, an auburn-haired man who looked to be in his mid-thirties like Gino, kept his patient perfectly groomed.

The Duc Di Montefalco was dressed in an elegant robe and slippers, quietly drinking tea from a mug. Sofia's cat did a big stretch at the base of his chair, as if letting Ally know he was guarding Sofia's father, so be warned.

The girl drew Ally over to him.

"Papa? This is Mrs. Parker from America."

Her father took no notice. He just kept taking sips of the hot liquid.

It killed Ally to realize that this darling girl wouldn't be able to derive the kind of love and comfort she needed from her father.

The moment was so emotional for Ally, she let go of Sofia's hand long enough to clasp Marcello's arm for a brief moment.

"How do you do, Mr. Montefalco. It's an honor to meet you," she said in a tremulous voice.

Luigi smiled. "He's very happy to meet you too, *signora*. Isn't that right, Sofia."

"Yes. He likes company."

The nurse placed a hand on Sofia's shoulder. "Do you

want to help me put him to bed? I think he's still tired after our big day yesterday."

"I know he is. His eyelids are drooping." Sofia sounded way too adult for a girl her age.

Ally watched Gino kiss his niece on the cheek. "While you say good night to him, I'll be outside with Mrs. Parker. Come and find us when you're through."

"I will."

By tacit agreement Ally left the kitchen with the man she no longer thought of as her captor. Thankful he'd suggested going outside, she stepped over the threshold into the warm, fragrant night where she could breathe in fortifying gulps of air.

Gino watched her through veiled eyes. She met his glance. "Why was yesterday especially tiring for your brother?"

His features took on a hardened cast.

"The priest conducted funeral services for Donata at the church. I don't know if Marcello had any comprehension of what was going on, but Sofia insisted he did."

A sob got trapped in Ally's throat. "She's had too much grief to deal with."

"Tell me about it," he ground out. "Sofia needs her father."

Just then she heard the agony in his voice and sensed he was grieving for the loss of his brother. Any man in Gino's position would be feeling overwhelmed right now. But as she was coming to find out, Gino was no ordinary man. He had strengths she admired more than he would ever know.

Tears glazed her eyes, moistening her silky lashes. "Throughout my life I've been able to forgive those who've hurt me. But for my husband and Donata to have hurt an innocent child… Right now I'm *really* struggling."

He moved closer. "Donata was far too concerned for herself to ever consider other people's feelings, least of all her daughter's."

Ally bit her lip, realizing this man was carrying an extra heavy load now that Sofia didn't have a mother.

"I was an only child. I would have loved a sister or brother."

"Marcello and I were best friends," he whispered. "To protect him and Sofia, I've brought them to the farm where I have heavy security in place around the clock. We're safe here. No one gets in or out without my knowing about it. When the news of Donata's death is publicized, the media's going to turn it into the scandal of the decade."

Ally shuddered. Her thoughts flashed back to the night she'd spent at the jail because he'd thought she was a journalist.

"Has it always been this terrible for you?"

He nodded grimly. "Since my brother and I were old enough to go out in public with our parents, the paparazzi has dogged us. The only time I found peace or anonymity was to escape to the countryside.

"When I was away at college in England where Marcello had attended, I couldn't even look at another woman without some salacious headline showing up in the paper the next day. My every move was cataloged. The European press billed me the playboy of the decade. Perhaps some of it was deserved, but not all…

"After graduation I knew I had to end the nightmare or go a little mad. About that time tragedy struck when our parents were killed in a light plane accident.

"Marcello inherited the title, and I was left free to become a flower farmer, something I'd always wanted to do with my mother's blessing.

"So I bought property and this farmhouse. Instead of

going by the name Rudolfo Di Montefalco, I became Gino Fioretto, It's an old family name on my mother's side. Until my brother became ill, I was able to live in relative obscurity. But with Donata's disappearance and death, all hell has broken loose. I moved Marcello and Sofia out of the palazzo as fast as possible.

"You'll notice I don't have TV, radio or newspapers here."

"I don't blame you—" she cried out. "If Sofia had any idea…"

Gino studied her horrified expression. "Then we understand each other?"

"Of course."

"You forgive me for my callous treatment of you at the jail?"

"Under the circumstances, I don't know how you kept any control at all."

As she lifted her tortured gaze to him, they heard Sofia call out, "Uncle Gino?"

"We're by the fountain."

Sofia came running to her uncle. He swept her up in his powerful arms.

Ally could hear Sofia denying that she was tired. It was understandable the girl didn't want to go to bed. She was in too much pain and needed her uncle. Gino was the girl's sole source of love and safety now. They needed time to themselves.

"Gino?" Ally said. "Before it gets any later, I need to make a phone call. If you two will excuse me?"

"By all means." His sober mood hadn't altered.

She smiled at his niece to break the tension the girl must be sensing. "Good night, Sofia. I'm very happy to have met you."

"Me, too. You're not going away yet are you?" The question was so unexpected, it caught Ally off guard.

"Of course she isn't," Gino answered before she could, sounding the absolute authority. "She's here to tour the farm. That could take some time."

Ally trembled at the inferred warning that she shouldn't be planning to leave anytime soon.

"Can I come with you tomorrow?" The girl's brown eyes implored him.

"The three of us will do it together," Gino declared as if it were already a fait accompli.

"Maybe we could take Papa, too?" Sofia added.

"I'm sure your father would love it," Ally stated before Gino could say anything else. "Even if he can't talk, deep inside I'm sure he'll enjoy getting out in the sunshine with his beautiful daughter."

"I'm not beautiful."

Ally winked at her. "Then you haven't looked in a mirror lately." She kissed her cheek.

"Good night," she whispered before hurrying across the courtyard to the farmhouse entrance, away from Gino's enigmatic gaze.

Once she reached her room, she picked up the receiver of the house phone and made a credit card call to her mother.

"Mom?"

"Ally, honey— The caller ID said this was an out of area call. I was hoping it was you."

"Forgive me for phoning this early. Did I waken you or Aunt Edna?"

Ally's mother had been helping her widowed sister who'd come home from the hospital with a hip replacement.

"Heavens no. Edna and I have already had breakfast."

"That's good."

"How's the headache by now?"

"It's gone." As for Ally's emotional state, that was another matter entirely.

"Where are you and your friends staying?"

Ally bowed her head. It was time to tell the truth.

"That's what I'm phoning you about. I decided to take the doctor's advice and get away for a while by myself."

"I hate the thought of you being alone. Have you cleared it with the maestro?"

"I didn't need to. We have the month of June off, remember?"

"Of course. So where are you?"

"I'm staying at a bed and breakfast on a lavender farm."

"You always did love it at Mom and Dad's. I wish they were still alive so we could all be together."

"So do I, Mom."

"I'm sure the change will do you good. Where is it exactly?"

Her hand tightened on the cord. "In Italy, not far from Rome.

"Mom—" Ally spoke before her mother's shock translated into words. "Let me explain. Detective Davis told me the woman who died with Jim has been identified. She was Italian, so I flew to Switzerland, and now I'm in Italy to talk to the authorities."

"Oh, honey, you must be in terrible pain."

Ally had been in excruciating pain for months, but right now another emotion dominated her feelings. The compassion she felt for Gino and Sofia superseded all else.

"I need closure. This seems to be the best way to achieve it."

To prevent her mother from asking the burning question about Jim's involvement with Donata, Ally said, "This shouldn't take too long."

"I hope not. When you get back we'll find you another place to live that doesn't remind you of Jim."

No matter where Ally lived, she would always be haunted by two people's treachery to an innocent Italian girl who only asked to be loved.

"Mom? Will you do me a favor and call Carol? Since I couldn't make the concert because of my headache, she still has my violin. Tell her to keep it until I get back."

"I'll do better than that. Edna and I will drive over to her house and get it."

"Thank you. Please give Aunt Edna my love. I promise to keep you posted and I'll call you soon."

She hung up before her mother asked for a phone number where Ally could be reached in case of an emergency. That was the way Ally wanted it right now.

Too restless to sit still, she wandered over to the open window and looked out. If Gino and his niece were still walking, she couldn't see them.

"Signora Parker?"

At the sound of Gino's low male voice, she whirled around to discover him in the aperture. By now she ought to be used to him appearing as silently as a cat.

"I—I didn't realize you were there." Her voice caught.

"I knocked, but you were deep in thought."

So she was...

"Has Sofia gone to her room?"

"No. To her father's. If it's her only comfort right now, I'm not about to deny her. But as she's expecting me to join them, I'll say good night."

Ally had seen Gino at his most forbidding. But his tenderness toward his brother and niece revealed a side of him she found rather exceptional.

"Thank you for your hospitality, Gino. When I came to Italy, I had no idea I would end up here. Please know you can trust me with what you've told me."

"If I didn't, you'd be back in Portland right now," he ground out. "Sleep well."

He studied her for an overly long moment before disappearing.

Part of her wanted to call him back and ask him to return the laptop. If he had an adaptor, then she could see the pictures and read any e-mails Jim hadn't planned on her knowing about. But another part resisted because she knew Gino had too much on his mind to deal with anything else tonight. They'd only buried Donata yesterday. Tomorrow would be soon enough to ask for her property back.

This family needed sleep to help assuage their deep sorrow. As for Ally, she turned once more to the open window. After sleeping all day, she was wide-awake.

A slight breeze carrying a divine fragrance ruffled her curls. She rested her head against the frame, feeling herself suspended in a kind of limbo. It was almost as if she was standing outside herself, not belonging in the past or in an unknown future, but somewhere in between—a flowered fantasyland where she felt the unconditional love of one man for his family. In light of the tragedies that had befallen the Montefalco clan, Gino's devotion to those he loved touched her so deeply, she couldn't put it in words.

She finally went to bed with her mind full of new images. No matter the setting or situation, they all contained Gino...

* * *

"Where's Signora Parker?" Sofia asked Gino without even saying good morning. "We've been waiting for her."

For Sofia to be interested in a stranger she'd only met for a few minutes last night, it meant that Signora Parker had made a strong impression on his niece. It wasn't that surprising since Gino couldn't seem to put the American woman out of his mind, either.

He kissed her forehead. "I guess she's still asleep."

"But she slept all day yesterday."

Gino had a hunch Jim Parker's widow had lain awake most of the night just like Gino, and hadn't fallen asleep until dawn.

He knew she'd already had several months to grieve deeply, but he feared she could be in mourning for a long time to come. Why that knowledge bothered him he couldn't answer yet. He only knew that it did.

"I'll go upstairs and see if she's awake."

Before Gino could blink, Sofia ran out of the kitchen. His first inclination was to stop his niece from bothering their guest. But since he, too, had been looking forward to spending the day with her, he decided he was glad Sofia had taken the initiative.

In a few seconds his niece came running back. Her anxious expression disturbed him. "She's not in her room! I thought she came to see the farm. We were going to go around it together. Where did she go, Uncle Gino?"

The alarm in her voice echoed inside him.

He turned to Bianca who was pouring coffee into Marcello's cup. "Have you seen Signora Parker this morning?"

"No. Maybe she's outside taking a walk."

Gino jumped up from his chair. "I'll go look for her."

"I'll come with you," Sofia cried.

No sooner had they left through the side door off the kitchen than they spotted her in the distance. She was leaning over one of the rows in the special herb garden he'd grown expressly for Bianca.

It pleased Gino no end that she appeared to be intrigued by the various plants.

Sofia ran over to her. Ally raised a smiling face to his niece and put out an arm to hug her. The spontaneous gesture came naturally to her. She had a warmth that drew Sofia like a bee to the flowers growing on his farm.

"Good morning, *signora*."

Their eyes met. Hers shimmered like green jewels.

"This garden is fabulous, Gino."

"He made it for Bianca," Sofia exclaimed. "She likes everything fresh."

"Well isn't she lucky that the owner of this farm appreciates her so much."

He chuckled. "I'm the lucky one. You'll see why when you eat one of her meals."

"I'm looking forward to it."

"Come on, Ally. She has breakfast ready for us."

"I'm coming."

Gino watched her straighten. Dressed in a skirt and a peach top her curvaceous figure did wonders for, Gino found himself staring at her.

Hopefully his niece was oblivious as she pulled their lovely houseguest along. Gino hardly recognized Sofia in light of her affection for Ally whom she was already treating like an old friend.

A minute later they were all assembled at the table with Bianca fussing over them.

"I tell you what, Sofia," Gino spoke up. "On our ride we'll drop by the Rossinis'. You've never met my farm manager, Dizo. He and his wife Maria have two daughters. One of them, Leonora, is your exact age. She's a very nice girl who has been asking to meet you. You'll like her."

"Do we have to do that today? I just want to be with you and Ally."

His niece was transparent. For months she'd been so unhappy, he'd been at a loss how to help her. Now suddenly Ally Parker had come into their lives. When was the last time any of them had experienced any happiness?

Gino had to think back twelve years when both brothers had been in their prime, their parents had still been alive and all was well with their world. Until the advent of Donata…

He peeled an orange and gave a couple of sections to Marcello who automatically ate them. Gino was still incredulous that his brother would never be normal again, would never be able to make his daughter laugh and feel secure again.

In the past Marcello could always make things right for Sofia no matter how her mother neglected her. Everyone loved Marcello, especially Gino.

Sometimes like now, the pain of loss was unbearable. He could only imagine how much his niece suffered. Yet this morning she wasn't showing any signs of heartache.

"Tell you what, Sofia. I'll run over to the Rossinis' to check on business, then come back and we'll all go swimming at the river. How does that sound?"

Ally was bent over her food and didn't make eye contact with him.

"I can't wait! Don't take too long, Uncle Gino."

Maybe Leonora would return with him so the girls

could meet. He left the kitchen and went outside to start up the truck.

A few minutes later he pulled to a stop in the parking area surrounding the covered stands. The usual crowd of customers kept the staff busy. He looked around to see if Leonora was helping her mother.

Maria was in charge of the workers who ran Gino's flower market called Fioretto's. What wasn't shipped from his farm to different areas of the country by train and a fleet of trucks was sold as overflow to the local businesses who sent their buyers to his farm.

Several of the staff recognized him and waved. He reciprocated as he moved past basket after basket of flowers that would all be sold by three in the afternoon.

"Ah, Gino— Over here!" Maria called to him. She was surrounded by customers. Once she was free they talked business for a few minutes.

"Is there anything I can do for you before you go?" she asked at last.

"I need two bunches of lavender."

"Coming up." She wrapped them in paper and handed them to him. "Is Leonora around?"

"No. She's home tending the baby who has a cold."

"I was hoping she could come over and meet my niece."

Maria's eyes rounded. "She would love it! Maybe tomorrow. I could ask Dizo to drive her."

"That would be fine, Maria. I'll arrange to have her driven back later in the day. *Ciao*."

"*Ciao*, Gino."

He hurried out to his truck anxious to get back to the farmhouse. To Ally. Since finding her in the herb garden this morning, he was still so mesmerized by her femininity and shapely figure, he almost climbed into the cab of another truck before he realized what he was doing.

In point of fact, Ally Parker shouldn't be here. She shouldn't be anywhere in Italy where the paparazzi could find her. Carlo would have a coronary if he knew. But Gino couldn't think about that right now.

She was here under his roof. That's where he wanted her to stay.

He'd admired the fight she'd put up at the jail. She never once acted like a victim. Signora Parker had fire and guts, the kind you didn't often see in a man or a woman.

Jim Parker hadn't deserved a wife like her any more than Marcello had deserved Donata…

Gino gritted his teeth to think of the pain Donata had caused, but by the time he returned to the farm and saw Ally out in front with Sofia, his dark thoughts evaporated.

No sooner did he stop his truck than they walked up to him. He jumped down and handed them their gifts.

"What's this?" Ally stared at him.

"Open it and find out."

Sofia actually giggled in delight. Gino put a hand on her arm. "Why don't you take yours inside and open it with your father?"

"I will! Thank you, Uncle Gino." She kissed his cheek, then ran across the courtyard to the house.

The woman at his side was busy opening hers. "Oh, Gino— Fresh lavender. It's wonderful!"

"So are you."

She quickly lowered her eyes as a subtle blush filled her cheeks.

"Your presence has made Sofia happy. She needs people

around who care about her. An outing with you is exactly what the doctor ordered."

"No child should have to live through a nightmare like this."

"I agree, Signora Parker. That's why I'm indebted to you for staying with us."

"Please don't keep calling me Signora Parker. It makes me feel old. My name is Ally."

"I've thought of you as Ally for quite a while, but was waiting for your permission to use it."

She finally looked up at him. "Well you have it. If you'll excuse me, I'll just run these flowers in the house, then come right back."

She took a few steps then paused. "I'm afraid I didn't bring a swimsuit with me."

"No problem. I'll run you and Sofia into Remo to shop. After Sofia's growth spurt this last year, she needs a new one."

"All right. Then I'll see you in a minute."

"Bene." The Italian word slipped out of his mouth as he watched her walk away carrying the lavender in the crook of her arm. Like a bride approaching the altar with her sheaf…

Once again he was struck by how incredibly attractive she was. If he were her husband…

CHAPTER FOUR

WITH HER HEART pounding, Ally found Bianca and asked her to get a vase for the flowers she could take to her room.

The unexpected gift had whipped up her sense of excitement which was way out of proportion to the situation. The reason being that Gino was an incredible man.

Her friend Carol would call him drop dead gorgeous.

He was. But he was a lot more than that.

He had character and nobility along with those striking looks. Somehow Ally needed to forget what the combination was doing to her, how he made her feel when they were together.

Something was wrong with her to have these feelings over a man she barely knew when she'd only come here to talk to Donata's husband. It didn't make sense. She needed to get her head on straight.

But the second she walked back outside with Sofia and felt Gino's eyes assessing her with an intimacy that made her legs go weak, she realized she was in serious trouble.

His niece ran up to him. "Papa loves the lavender. He just

keeps smelling it. Bianca loves it, too. She says it's been too long since there were fresh flowers in the house."

Ally shot Gino a teasing glance. "And you, a flower farmer. Shame on you."

He broke into a full-bodied smile, turning him into the most attractive man she'd ever seen in her life. The European tabloids must have made a fortune just following him around snapping pictures.

Her heart kept rolling over on itself.

"Mea culpa. It takes a woman to civilize a man's abode."

"What's an abode, Uncle Gino?"

"A house. Come on. Up you go." He'd opened the truck door to help her inside.

Ally had purposely waited so she wouldn't have to sit next to him. But by making that decision, she'd left herself open to more scrutiny while he assisted her.

Careful to keep her skirt from riding up her thigh, she climbed in, aware of his appraising glance as she swung her legs to the floor. He seemed to pause before shutting the door.

When he finally walked around and got in behind the wheel, she exhaled the breath she'd been holding.

"Bianca has packed us a picnic lunch and some towels," he informed them. "Paolo will bring everything when he drives Luigi and Marcello to the river."

Ally eyed the girl seated next to her.

"Do you like to swim, Sofia?"

"I used to when Papa swam with me at the palazzo."

Gino's gaze met Ally's with the implicit message that his niece gauged all her happiness before Marcello had been afflicted.

Ally had no words. All she could do was put her arm around Sofia and pull her close.

An hour later while Gino and Luigi helped Marcello swim, Ally and Sofia sat huddled in huge beach towels beneath a shade tree to watch.

The river was more like a stream that broadened in parts. Near the tree it was deep enough to come up to Ally's neck. On such a hot day, the refreshing water couldn't have been more welcome.

Thankful Gino had been too occupied helping his brother to pay much attention to Ally, she and Sofia had played in the water for a while. When Ally thought it was safe from Gino's all-seeing glance she'd scrambled out, but not before he'd caught her attempting to cover her bikini clad figure with the towel. Warmth still filled her cheeks, the kind she couldn't blame on the sun.

Sofia sat next to her, eating a roll and cheese.

"I think your father is enjoying himself, don't you?"

Sofia nodded. "I wish Uncle Gino could be with us all the time, but I know he can't. He has to do Papa's business and run the farm, too."

"That's too much for any man," Ally declared. She munched on a ripe plum and looked all around them. "This is a heavenly place. I could stay here forever."

"I love it, too! But Mama would never let me come."

"Why not?"

"She said she didn't think Uncle Gino liked her very much so she preferred I stay at the palazzo. I told her Uncle Gino liked everyone and was my favorite person next to her and Papa. But she wouldn't talk about it."

Ally moaned inwardly. "Maybe your mama was a city girl."

Sofia looked at her. "Are you a city girl?"

"I like the city, but to be honest, I preferred my grandparents' farm. Unfortunately when they died, my mother and her older sister sold it so they would have money to live."

"Why didn't you all just live there?"

"Because Aunt Edna got married, and my mother was divorced. She had to raise me on her own, and she didn't like farming."

"What *did* she like?"

"Her talent was music. She could play the piano so well she gave lessons. It would have been hard to find enough students in the country, so we lived in Portland."

"Did she teach you to play?"

"Yes. Do you play an instrument?"

"I started the piano, but I wasn't very good and quit."

Ally chuckled. "I didn't like it, either, but my mother said I had to learn to play something, so I started on the violin."

"Did you like it?"

"I loved it so much, I play in the Portland symphony orchestra. It's how I earn my living, but right now the orchestra is on vacation, so I decided to come here for a holiday."

It wasn't a complete lie.

Sofia's eyes lit up. "I've been to the symphony a lot with my papa and Gino. Do you have to wear black?"

"On performance night, yes."

The girl sighed. "I wish I were good at something."

"I'm sure you're good at a lot of things. You just haven't discovered all of them yet. My husband hated piano lessons but he became an expert skier."

The observation had just slipped out.

Sofia studied her for a moment. "How come he didn't come with you?"

The question Ally had been waiting for...

"He died a while ago."

The girl looked wounded. "Do you have children?"

A pain seared Ally. "We weren't married long enough for that to happen. I always wanted a son or a daughter like you. But I have my mother and aunt, and you have your father and your uncle."

Sofia sighed. "I'm glad they're both alive."

"You're very lucky to have them."

"After we tour the farm, do you want to see where my mother is buried?"

"If you'd like me to."

"We don't have a headstone yet. Uncle Gino told me I should decide what to have engraved on it since I'm the Duchess Di Montefalco now. But I don't know what to put."

A duchess at eleven years of age. So much responsibility for a young girl. What Jim would have given…

On Ally's honeymoon he'd admitted wanting more from life than a stable job with a steady income. She heard his resentment when he spoke of people who'd been born to a life of privilege and wealth, and he hadn't.

She'd thought he was like most people who had their dream of winning the lottery or something, so she didn't place any stock in it. But over time Jim began to change into someone restless and ambitious. Before long he was willing to spend more and more time apart from her in order to get financially ahead, as he put it.

That *did* alarm her since she'd wanted to start a family.

The marriage that should have lasted a lifetime began to fall apart. Though she'd longed to have a baby, knowing what she knew now, Ally was thankful it hadn't happened.

She glanced at Gino's niece, feeling a bond with her that made her want to protect her every bit as fiercely as Gino did.

"Do you happen to know your mother's full name?"

"Yes. It's Donata Ricci-Cagliostro Di Montefalco."

"What a beautiful name. Since you know it you could say 'In memory of our beloved wife and mother,' then put her full name, and the dates."

Sofia pondered the suggestion for a minute. "I think that's perfect. I'm going to tell Uncle Gino right now."

She threw off her towel and ran toward the edge of the river where the men were just getting out.

The girl's voice carried in the light breeze.

Gino drew closer to the picnic blanket. His black eyes sought Ally's with such impact, she could hardly breathe.

"What do you girls say we go back to the farmhouse to change, then I'll drive you and Sofia around the farm."

Bemused by his unexpected aura of contentment and his blatant masculine appeal, Ally averted her eyes. The sight of Gino was too much. He put the sun god Apollo to shame.

"Let me gather up the remains of this delicious picnic first."

The rest of the afternoon turned out to be magical.

Dressed in jeans and T-shirts, Ally and Sofia rode in the back of Gino's truck. To Sofia's delight, he drove them through the colorful flower fields where they waved at the workers. She wondered which ones were the security guards Gino had posted to watch over his domain.

At different times he pulled to a stop and the three of them walked on the rich earth enjoying the fragrant air beneath a sunny sky.

A last stop at the cemetery to put some fresh flowers on Donata's grave, and they drove back to the farmhouse for dinner.

"Can we do this again tomorrow?" Sofia pled with Gino.

"Tomorrow I've arranged for Leonora to come over."

"But I don't know her. I'd rather be with you and Ally."

Gino patted her hand. "I have to do some work tomorrow, sweetheart."

Ally decided the two of them needed to be alone. While they'd been driving around, she realized it was time to separate herself from Gino and Sofia who, like her uncle, had already become too important to her.

Without hesitation Ally got up from the table. "If you will excuse me, I have to go upstairs and pack."

Two pairs of eyes swerved to hers in an instant. Sofia's were already full of tears. Gino's expression bordered on anger.

"I wasn't aware you were leaving to go anywhere," he muttered with barely concealed impatience.

"I put off my flight a day in order to spend it with you. Now that I've toured your farm, I—I have to return to Rome first thing in the morning," she stammered. "My flight to Portland leaves in the afternoon."

She hurried out of the kitchen and headed for the guest room upstairs. Ally couldn't stay here any longer. Today there'd been moments when it had felt like the three of them were a family. Sofia had already endeared herself to Ally. As for Gino...

With every second she spent in his thrilling company, she was losing her objectivity. To stay in Italy any longer would be playing with fire. She'd come to Italy to talk to Marcello, but his illness made that impossible. She had no excuse to stay any longer. She would only be intruding on Gino's personal life.

Ally hadn't missed Sofia's aside when the housekeeper told Gino that Merlina had dropped by the farmhouse while they'd been out.

"Merlina is one of Uncle Gino's girlfriends. Sometimes she used to come to the palazzo to talk to Mama about him." Hearing those words, Ally had actually experienced a stab of jealousy! Everything was getting far too complicated. She needed to go home and leave temptation behind. Back in Portland she would find herself another place to live. Keeping busy would prevent her from thinking too much. Fantasizing too much about impossible dreams.

To stay here any longer would be disastrous.

By the time she reached the bedroom, she heard footsteps behind her and wheeled around to discover Gino had followed her. With his rock-hard body filling the aperture, it prevented her from shutting the door. She had no choice but to back away from him.

"Earlier today," he began in a neutral tone of voice she couldn't help but envy, "Sofia and I had a conversation. Before you get carried away with plans, how would you like the job of teaching her the violin for the summer?"

Ally let out a soft cry of surprise. In the semidarkness his eyes glowed like hot coals. "Sofia told me that's how you earn your living. I had no idea you were an accomplished violinist. She begged me to ask you to teach her the fundamentals.

"You've sparked something in my niece I didn't know was possible. I'm indebted to you, Ally, and I'll make it worth your time financially to stay here."

Ally was stunned.

More than anything in the world she wanted to say yes, but she didn't dare. Another night under his roof and she feared she'd want to stay forever, not just for a summer.

Trying to catch her breath she said, "I'm sorry, Gino, but I can't."

I can't. Don't ask me.

"I'm under contract with the symphony. We start rehearsing again in July."

His expression darkened. "You want me to tell that to a young girl downstairs who today had her first taste of happiness in over two years?"

"That's not fair—" she cried.

His black brows furrowed. "Nothing about this situation has been fair—" he bit out.

"Even so, Gino, I—"

"Even so nothing," he cut her off without apology. "Every contract has a clause that exempts a person under extraordinary circumstances. When you explain what you've been going through, I can guarantee they'll allow you whatever time you need."

Ally knew it was true, but that wasn't what concerned her the most.

He cocked his dark head. "I don't expect you to be a babysitter, if that's what's worrying you. All I ask is that you give her an hour a day. You two can work out the time that's most convenient for you. The rest of the time you'll be free to do whatever you want.

"The farmhouse has rooms rarely used. You could choose any one of them to practice in. "You can use one of my trucks so you can drive where you want. When you don't choose to eat out, Bianca will prepare your meals."

She put up her hands. "Stop, Gino. You're making it difficult for me to refuse."

Lines marred his features. "As the acting Duc Di Montefalco, I plan to make it so damn hard, you wouldn't dare."

Acting Duc... No wonder he was given such preferential treatment everywhere he went. It explained his being able to take over at the jail as if he were in charge.

She had trouble swallowing.

"You don't understand."

"No, I don't, not after Mrs. James Parker spent a brutal night in jail insisting she needed to meet in private with the Duc Di Montefalco and no one else. That woman never once backed down.

"Your courage, like your beauty, is the talk of the Montefalco police department."

Her breathing grew shallow. "You must be talking about someone else."

"No," his voice grated. "I was there, remember? If you need reminding, take the advice you gave Sofia and look in the mirror. It will remove all doubt."

Maybe she was mistaken to think she saw a brief flash of desire in his eyes.

When she thought of the women he'd known in the past—no doubt beautiful women who'd do anything to be seen and loved by him—

All she knew was that it found an answering chord in her. She couldn't help wondering how it would feel to be kissed by him. Thoroughly kissed. Just imagining it made her so unsteady, she weaved and had to hold on to the corner of the dresser for support.

"After Leonora goes home tomorrow, I'll drive you and Sofia into town. You can pick out violins and anything else you need to get her started. Think about it. If necessary, make any phone calls you need to. Then come downstairs and give me your answer."

He disappeared too fast for her to call him back.

She couldn't.

With her senses as alive as a red-hot wire, she couldn't muster a coherent thought, let alone talk.

Four months ago she couldn't have conceived of a time when she would be so attracted to another man, she would consider staying with him. Especially when she knew she was already in emotional jeopardy.

Uncle Gino prefers his girlfriends.

Such were Sofia's words.

As if thinking about the girl conjured her up, Gino's niece tapped on the open door.

"Hi," Ally said in a shaky voice.

"Hello. Is it all right if I come in?"

"Please do." Ally tried to sound normal, but it was difficult because Sofia's unexpected visit to the bedroom had thrown her.

"Did Uncle Gino tell you I'd like to take violin lessons?"

Ally nodded.

"I know this is the country, but if you gave lessons to my friend Anna, and maybe to Leonora and her sister, that would make four students. It would give you more money. I could pay for my lessons from the allowance Uncle Gino gives me."

Ally let out a heaving sigh. "It's not the money, Sofia. I—I just wouldn't feel right about staying here at your uncle's."

"You could stay at the palazzo. Nobody's there but the staff. Paolo would drive me for my lessons."

She smothered a groan. "Your uncle wants you and your father with him for the summer. He can't be worried about you going back and forth."

They couldn't risk Ally being seen by journalists just waiting for an opportunity.

Sofia studied her. "I thought you liked it here."

"I do," she rushed to assure her. More than Sofia would ever know. But—

"This is a big farmhouse," Sofia kept talking. "And Uncle

Gino has to be gone a lot. He says you can stay as long as you want."

"That's very generous of him."

"He says if you agree, he's got a special surprise planned for us."

Ally could feel her defenses crumbling. "What kind of surprise?"

Suddenly Gino appeared in the doorway again looking devilishly handsome.

"You'll have to wait and see," he answered for his niece. "I promise it will be something neither of you will want to miss."

Ally had run out of excuses. With both of them imploring her to say yes, she couldn't take the pull on her heart any longer. Sofia needed love. As for Gino, she realized he needed someone to lean on. If she could help him through this transition with his niece, why not. Part of her felt she owed them.

"I tell you what. For the next few weeks I'd be happy to get you started on the violin. But when my vacation is over at the end of June, I'll have to go home."

I'll *have* to.

Gino put his hands on Sofia's shoulders. "We'll accept that arrangement, won't we, sweetheart."

Sofia was beaming. "Yes."

His eyes held a strange glitter of satisfaction. "Then let's say good night to our guest. In the morning we'll make our plans over breakfast."

"Good night, Ally," Sofia murmured. "I can't wait till tomorrow."

At this point Ally was a mass of jumbled emotions. Avoiding Gino's probing gaze she said, "I'm looking forward to it, too."

"We all are." As Gino closed the door, the silky timbre of his parting words almost caused her legs to buckle.

She'd done it now. There was no going back or it would crush Sofia. Even Ally could see the girl was fragile.

But no more so than Ally who would be worse off when she eventually left Italy. At least Sofia would still have Gino.

When Gino's cell phone went off the next morning, he was already up and shaved. Knowing Ally Parker was in his house, and wouldn't be leaving Italy anytime soon, had to be the reason he'd awakened with a sense of exhilaration he hadn't experienced in years.

He left the bathroom and went back to his room where he'd left the phone on the dresser.

He checked the caller ID, then clicked on.

"*Buon giorno*, Maria."

"*Buon giorno*, Gino."

"Is Dizo bringing Leonora, or do you want me to come and get her?"

"I'm calling because the children are sick. They've all come down with colds. Leonora is running a temperature. I'm so sorry, Gino. She's very upset that I won't let her leave the house."

"It's all right, Maria."

It was better than all right. She'd just given him the excuse to spend the morning with Ally and Sofia.

"Tell Leonora we'll look forward to seeing her when she's better. *Ciao*."

A few minutes later he went downstairs where he could hear female voices drifting through the rooms. The animation in Sofia's chatter when she never chattered was like a balm to his soul.

The sight of their blond guest at the breakfast table dressed in a soft yellow blouse and white skirt, was more intoxicating than his first breath of fresh air when he opened his bedroom window at sunup.

Bianca had outdone herself to make an American breakfast. She buzzed around the kitchen with new energy. Marcello appeared to have a healthy appetite. His eggs and fruit juice were disappearing fast.

As Gino and Roberto, the other nurse, exchanged a silent greeting of amusement, Sofia cried, "We thought you'd never come down, Uncle Gino."

Was she speaking for their guest, too?

His gaze flicked to Ally's. Her eyes reflected a lush spring-green in the morning light coming through the windows. With glowing skin and diaphanous hair, she didn't look a day over twenty-two.

"I had a phone call from Maria," he explained taking his place at the table across from Ally. "She told me her children are sick with colds. Leonora is running a fever and can't come over today. Maybe tomorrow."

"That's okay." Sofia didn't sound at all bothered by the change in plan. "Will you take us to get our violins this morning? Then you can do your work."

Gino chuckled. So did Ally. His niece was definitely an organizer.

"I don't see why not."

Her brown eyes sparkled, another first in several years. He saw the promise of a lovely woman inside the girl who reminded him so much of Marcello, it brought a pang to his chest.

"Ally said we should rent them and practice for a few days to see if we like them first."

His gaze trapped Ally's.

"You're the expert, so we'll bow to your judgment." Anything to prevent her from changing her mind and leaving.

His good mood had made him ravenous. He ate a double helping of everything.

After he'd praised Bianca for her cooking, he suggested they get going.

On the way out to the truck, Sofia caught hold of his arm. Ally hadn't joined them yet.

"I think we should practice in the living room because there's a piano. Is that all right with you?"

"I can't think of a better place."

"Good. Did you know Ally can play the piano, too? She says when I've learned a few songs, she can accompany me."

"That doesn't surprise me a bit, sweetheart. Signora Parker is a woman of many parts."

Gino wouldn't be satisfied until he knew all of them…

CHAPTER FIVE

ALLY CLIMBED IN the truck with an eagerness she was hard-pressed to conceal. It was because of the black-haired man at the wheel. He looked fantastic this morning in a navy polo shirt and cream trousers. Ally decided that Italian men just looked better in their clothes. Of course she'd seen him at the river yesterday when all he'd been wearing were his black trunks. The truth was, he needed no embellishment.

She'd only known him a short while, but so far she could find no fault with him.

That was the scary part. She felt she was under some sort of spell.

To be recently widowed and yet this happy when she was living on borrowed time, defied logic.

They reached Remo in no time at all. "Here we are. I made inquiries and learned that Petelli's should have everything you need."

They'd pulled up alongside an arcade with shops that had been built the century before.

Sofia followed Ally out of the truck, then ran ahead to

view the instruments displayed in the front window of the music store.

Ally glimpsed a guitar, harp, cello, viola and violin. She was no more immune to the sight of a beautifully crafted instrument than Sofia who grasped her arm.

"Let's go inside."

Gino held the door open for them. Ally's arm brushed against his chest as she trailed Sofia. The contact caused her to gasp softly.

Fearing Gino had heard her, she rushed over to the counter where a man probably in his late seventies smiled at them. She had a feeling he was the owner.

"Good morning," Ally greeted him. He nodded. "Do you speak English?"

"A little. Your husband can translate, *si*?"

"Yes," Gino responded, drawing up next to her.

She gave him a covert glance and noticed his eyes were smiling.

While heat crept into Ally's cheeks, Sofia said something to the man in Italian.

"Ah...she's the professor."

"Yes," Ally exclaimed. "We would like to rent two violins."

"For the little one and her father?"

Once again Sofia came to the rescue, obviously to Gino's delight because a rumble of laughter came out of him, deep and full bodied. The attractive sound reverberated through Ally's nervous system.

The owner eyed her with curiosity. "No violin for the little one's papa?"

The man was a huge tease. She couldn't help smiling at him. "No."

"*You* are the professor, and you need a violin?"

"Yes. I left mine in America."

"Are you good?"

"I try."

"*Momento.*" He turned behind him and reached in the case for one of the violins. Then he found her a bow from the drawer.

After tuning the instrument, he placed both items on the counter in front of her. "Play something by Tchaikovsky. Then I know which violin is for you."

Ally was more nervous than the time she had to audition in front of the maestro and the concert master. But her adrenaline wasn't surging because of the owner. She wanted to perform her best for Gino and his niece.

Once she'd fit the violin under her chin, she reached for the bow and began playing the final movement of Tchaikovsky's violin concerto.

Normally when Ally played, she receded into another world. But this was one time she couldn't forget her surroundings. With Gino's black eyes riveted on her, all she could think about was him, how loving he was to Sofia, how tenderly he treated his brother. What she couldn't tell him in words, she found herself compelled to say to him through her music. She wanted to ease the pain and suffering of this wonderful, selfless man.

"Stop—stop—" the owner cried.

Ally turned to him, surprised and confused. She saw him wiping his eyes.

"Give me the violin."

Ally handed it to him. He put it back in the case, then unlocked another one.

"Here. This is a Stradivari. Now finish, please."

Whether it was an authentic Stadivarius, or a model of one copied from the master violin maker in Cremona, Italy, Ally trembled as she fit it beneath her chin and finished the Tchaikovsky.

The difference in instruments made such a difference in the sound, she could have wept for the beauty of it. When she'd come to the end, there was silence, then a burst of applause from several people who'd come into the shop without her being aware of it.

While Gino and Sofia stared at her mesmerized, the owner clapped his hands.

"Bravo, *signora*. Bravo, Bravo."

Ally handed the violin and bow back to him. "Thank you for the privilege of being allowed to play it," she said to him.

Sofia's eyes had filled.

"I'll never be able to play like you."

Ally leaned over and kissed her forehead. "You never know until you try. Once upon a time, I was just like you. I'd never even held a violin in my hand."

She raised up and looked at the owner. "Let's fit her with one her size. I'll rent the violin you first gave me to try. We'll need a music stand, and some beginner books."

Before Ally could say she would pay for her own rental, Gino gave the other man a credit card.

As they gathered up their purchases and went back out to the truck, Gino was oddly silent. For that matter, so was Sofia. That is until they arrived at the farmhouse where she glimpsed an unfamiliar car parked near the fountain.

Roberto, another nurse she'd been introduced to, was taking Marcello for a walk in the courtyard.

The second Ally climbed down so Sofia could get out, the girl ran over to show them her violin case. "Bring Papa in the house, Roberto. He's going to love hearing Ally play. He'll think he's at the symphony again!"

While Ally watched the three of them head for the front door, she heard footsteps behind her. The next thing she knew Gino had turned her around by the shoulders.

His features solemn, he grasped both her hands and kissed her fingertips. She thought his breathing sounded labored.

"Sometimes there aren't words. Today was one of those times." His black eyes streamed into hers. "How in God's name could your husband have done what he did?"

His comment made her realize that some if not all of those pictures in the laptop were of Donata. It verified beyond any doubt that Jim had betrayed Ally. Now it meant Gino was party to her secret *and* her humiliation. Since he knew the truth, there was nothing to hide. She could be frank with him.

"That's what I ask myself about Donata every time I look into the face of her precious daughter. She's so blessed to have you to look after her and love her."

"Ally—" Gino whispered huskily before they both heard footsteps and saw Bianca hurrying toward them. Ally pulled her hands away from him in a self-conscious gesture.

The housekeeper ran up to him and said something in rapid Italian.

Though the spiel was unintelligible, Ally heard the name Merlina.

After Bianca went back to the farmhouse Gino said, "It appears I have a visitor."

"I recognized the name." The same woman had come by the day before.

Not wanting Gino to know how upset she was, Ally started for the back of the truck to get her violin.

In a few strides he'd joined her.

"How do you know about her?"

"Sofia told me she's your girlfriend."

"Was," his voice grated. "I ended it with her before Donata's disappearance."

His personal life was his own affair, yet the news set her pulse racing.

He reached in the truck bed for her instrument case and the other purchases.

"Let's go inside. While I talk to her in the study, you and Sofia can get started in the living room."

"I'll need to freshen up first." She ran ahead of him, but once again he caught up to her and held the front door open for her.

She dashed inside the foyer and up the stairs. On the way she caught sight of a lovely redheaded woman who'd come out into the hall.

Though Ally believed Gino when he said his relationship with this Merlina was over, she wished she hadn't seen her.

The presence of a former girlfriend in his house served as a wake-up call to remind Ally he preferred his single status. He could have any woman he wanted. It hardly made sense that he would be seriously interested in a twenty-eight-year-old widow who hadn't been able to keep her husband from straying.

Only one reason would bring the striking Italian woman here two days in a row. She'd come to pay her respects because she loved Gino and couldn't bear to think their relationship had ended.

It made Ally realize how futile it would be to fall in love with him.

If Ally's mother knew she'd agreed to stay with him until

July, she would say her daughter was an even greater fool than before. Ally would never hear the end of it.

"It's been all over the news for the last two days," Merlina exclaimed the minute Gino ushered her back into his study. "The police are saying that the accident that killed Donata and that American man might not have been an accident. According to them the brakes might have been tampered with and you've been named their prime suspect."

Thanks to Carlo who'd phoned him night before last, Gino already knew the worst of the lies.

"It's the usual malicious propaganda put out to sell papers, Merlina. You've wasted a trip to come and tell me something I've been dealing with for a score of years now. The media will say or do anything to create a story out of nothing. It's the way they work. If they couldn't print distortions, there would be no news anyone would want to read."

"But Gino—this time it's different because Donata was killed! Don't forget she wasn't just a local. She was the Duchess Di Montefalco."

Gino heard the envy in Merlina's voice.

"I know you could never have hurt her or anyone else. It isn't in you. But in this case you have to take this seriously."

His jaw hardened. "I don't have to do anything, Merlina."

"Please don't get angry with me. You know how I feel about you, how I've always felt. I love you, and I'm afraid for you."

"There's no need to be. This is a nine day wonder that'll pass just like all the other scandalous lies made up to try to ruin my family's happiness."

"It's so unfair to you." She pushed her hair behind her ear. "I don't have to be back in Gubbio before tomorrow.

Why don't we go someplace and I'll help you get your mind off things."

He folded his arms, resting his body against the closed door. There was only one woman who could accomplish that miracle. She was living beneath his roof.

"I'm gratified by your faith in me, Merlina. Your concern means a great deal. But to take up where we left off isn't possible. Whatever we had was over a long time ago. To pretend otherwise wouldn't be fair to either of us."

Her face closed up. "What happened to your feelings for me, Gino?"

He pursed his lips. "We've been over this ground before. We shared some good times, but that's all they were."

Her eyes grew suspiciously bright. "I was hoping if I stayed away for a while, you'd be excited to see me again."

He hated to be cruel, but she was asking for it. "I'm only sorry you made this trip for nothing."

"There's someone else, isn't there."

The salvo shot straight to his gut.

"Whatever is going on in my life is my business, Merlina. If you don't mind, I have a busy day ahead of me so I'll see you out."

"Who's that blond woman who came in with you a few minutes ago?"

Gino was stunned by her aggressiveness.

"You saw the violin cases. She's a teacher who has come to help Sofia focus on something constructive."

Merlina shook her head, causing her red hair to swish. "I saw her go up the stairs. I've never heard of you allowing another woman to live in your house."

"These aren't ordinary circumstances. Sofia just buried her mother. She's grieving."

"And you actually expect me to believe this woman has nowhere else to live while she instructs your niece? Can she actually play?"

Even as she asked the mocking question, they both heard the sounds of the Tchaikovsky. Sofia must have begged Ally to play for Marcello, and she'd chosen the first movement.

Ally didn't need the Stradivari to make her violin sing. She had the touch of an angel.

Merlina looked shocked. "Who is she?"

Time to get rid of her before she learned Ally's identity.

"Someone helping Sofia find a reason to go on living."

He unfolded his arms and opened the door. "After you, Merlina."

For a minute he thought she was going to create a scene. Finally she said, "I'm leaving."

Thank God.

He walked her to the front door and watched her drive out of the courtyard.

The difference between the women he'd known and Ally was so great, the normal comparisons didn't apply.

He moved to the doorway of the living room to listen.

Roberto and Bianca were understandably awestruck. But it was Marcello who sat in the recliner, his whole body in an attitude of being spellbound. Normally nothing going on around him fazed him.

This was different. Just by the way Marcello's hands gripped the arm rests, Gino could tell how happy it made him.

The Montefalco family had been concertgoers for years. Having heard great music before, his brother's soul recognized it.

As for Sofia, she sat on the couch, entranced.

Thankful for Ally who'd managed to captivate his entire family, Gino decided this was the best time to get a little farming business done. The sooner he got things out of the way, the sooner he'd be home to spend the evening with Ally.

One of the hardest things he had to do was tear himself away when all he wanted was to get her to himself so they could concentrate on each other. His gut instinct told him that besides her affection for Sofia, Ally didn't dislike him, even if she'd only recently buried her husband. What he needed was time to prove there was an attraction between them, even if she was fighting it. Tonight couldn't come soon enough.

Ally learned that in most Italian households, the family didn't eat supper until eight or later.

At 6:20 Gino still hadn't come home. Ally had an idea it wasn't all farm business that detained him. Even if he'd ended it with Merlina months ago, the other woman lived in denial. Ally knew all about that dangerous state of mind and was living proof of her own weakness where that was concerned.

Evidently Merlina still had the same lesson to learn and had come by Gino's house to try to stir up the old spark. Ally felt a stab of pain to think maybe it hadn't been that difficult to entice Gino after all.

Thankfully Ally had a job to do teaching Sofia about the violin. There was a lot to learn first about the various parts, how to string it and tune it.

Once immersed in showing her the proper technique of using the bow, Ally was able to separate her thoughts about Gino long enough to concentrate on her delightful student.

The girl was eager to learn. Because she'd taken piano lessons, Sofia was able to read notes which was a big help. If she could maintain this enthusiasm, she would see great results.

Before Ally knew it, the day had gone. Sofia didn't want to stop. Ally chuckled and gave her a hug.

"We've done enough for one day, but I bet your father would love to see the progress you've made."

With that suggestion, the girl ran from the room with her violin and bow.

Ally took a little walk outside to stretch her muscles.

Gino's truck was parked in the courtyard, but there was no sign of him or Merlina's car.

Deciding she wasn't about to hang around waiting for him to return from wherever, she went back in the farmhouse to find the housekeeper. Bianca was in the kitchen preparing food.

"I need to go into Remo, so I won't be eating dinner. Gino said I could use one of the trucks."

The other woman nodded. "Take his. The keys are in the ignition."

"He won't mind?"

"No, no. Before he left he said you should use it if you needed to."

Gino thought of everything.

"Thank you, Bianca. If Sofia should ask, tell her I had some errands to run."

The housekeeper smiled her assent. "She's a good student, yes?"

"Very good. In another week she'll be able to play tunes for her father."

She left the house and hurried out to the truck. Glad it wasn't dark yet, Ally started it up and headed away from the farmhouse. It gave her a secret thrill to put her hands on the steering wheel where his hands had been earlier today. Everything about him thrilled her. That was the problem.

She didn't want to be like Merlina who couldn't stay away from him.

Ally pressed on the accelerator. She had no particular destination in mind. All she knew was that he wouldn't find her watching breathlessly for him when he decided to come home.

With her mind made up to be gone for a few hours, she found her way into the small town of Remo. En route she memorized certain signposts so she wouldn't have any trouble driving back home later in the dark.

When she'd been in town with Gino, he'd pointed out various landmarks and items of interest, among them a movie theater.

It was playing an Arnold Schwarzenegger film. Ally had seen a few of them and decided it would be fascinating to watch one in Italian.

After parking the truck along the side of the street like everyone else did, she went inside and bought a ticket.

Distracted by the amount of goodies in the concession stand, she decided to try some Italian chocolate. With her choice made, she walked inside the theater. The film couldn't have been going more than ten minutes.

She found a seat in the middle of the back row where no one was sitting, then sat down to watch the screen.

There was something about the Austrian born actor trying to teach the kids in his classroom that made Ally chuckle. When he spoke in Italian, it was even funnier. She found herself laughing out loud, something she hadn't done in ages.

"Scusi, signora." An attractive guy, beautifully dressed, who looked to be about her age, sat down next to her, bumping her arm.

He'd done it on purpose of course. In fact he could have

had his pick of seats in the semifull room, but he'd claimed one next to her.

He said something else to her in Italian.

She said, "*Scusi, signore.* No Italian."

If he didn't move in about one second, she would.

Naturally he refused to budge. "You are from America. *Si*?" What an incredibly bad idea it had been to sit alone.

"You dance with me after?"

Ally started to get up when another man sat down on her other side. She panicked when he put his arm around her shoulders.

"Sorry I'm late," he spoke into her ear.

She jerked her head around, assailed by the familiar scent clinging to his skin.

"Gino—"

She'd never been so happy to see anyone in her life.

"I've missed you, too, *bellissima*," he whispered against her lips before capturing her mouth.

He drew her close like a lover who'd been anticipating this moment and could no longer hold back.

Ally had been so caught off guard, her mouth opened to the urgent pressure of his and she found herself kissing him back in a slow, languorous giving and taking she'd never experienced in her life.

The background laughter of the crowd faded. All Ally was cognizant of was the throbbing of her heart against his solid male chest. The armrest between them might as well have been nonexistent.

Incredulous when she realized the moaning sounds she heard were coming from her own throat, she finally tore her lips from his and sat back in her seat, completely breathless and ashamed she'd gotten so carried away.

"That other man has gone. Thank you for the convincing performance," she blurted when she could find her voice again. "It got me out of a difficult predicament."

"A word of warning," Gino said in a masterful tone. "Don't ever come to a place like this alone. I want your promise."

"You have it."

"Sitting back here by yourself is an open invitation."

"I know. I simply wasn't thinking." She swallowed hard. "How did you know I was here?"

"When I got home, Bianca told me you'd gone out in the truck. So I asked Paolo to drive me around until I spotted it in front of the theater. You're a fan of this film?"

"Yes."

"So am I. Let's enjoy the rest of the film, shall we?"

It was so exciting to be sitting here with him like this, she could only nod.

"How about some of that chocolate? Your mouth tasted so delicious, I've got to have more."

She thought he wanted some of her candy, but he leaned over and started kissing her again.

"No, Gino." She pushed at his shoulder with her free hand. "There's no one around me now."

"I hadn't noticed," he murmured, giving her another thorough kiss before letting her go.

Without asking her permission, he popped a piece of chocolate into his mouth.

Then he clasped her hand possessively, and sat back to enjoy the movie.

She knew what he was doing. No other man in the theater would dare approach her now. She had her own personal bodyguard to protect her.

She never watched the rest of the film. She was much too

conscious of the gorgeous man sitting too close to her. He kept caressing her palm with his thumb, filling her body with desire.

Every touch made it impossible to concentrate on anything else.

At the end of the movie, the lights went on. Gino slid his hand up her back to her neck and walked her out of the theater to the truck. He asked for the keys.

She fumbled in her purse for them. "Here."

After helping her in the passenger side, he went around to the driver's seat and started the engine.

"Do you often conduct business into the evening?"

Once they merged with the traffic, he darted her a piercing glance. "Only if I want to get everything out of the way so I have all of tomorrow off to spend with my family."

Ally bowed her head, relieved he hadn't been with Merlina for any reason.

"Sofia will be delighted."

"What about you? How does another picnic by the river sound? This time we'll take Leonora with us so the girls can get acquainted."

"I think it's an excellent idea. Sofia needs more interaction with girls her own age."

"Agreed. If you'll give her a morning violin lesson, we can leave afterward and enjoy the rest of the day."

His fingers played with the curls near her nape. His touch sent a yielding feeling of delight through her body. She was still trembling from the kisses they'd shared in the theater.

Terrified Gino would think this widow was falling in far too easily with his plans, especially after the kisses they'd just shared she decided to bring up the subject she'd been putting off.

"Gino—I wonder if you would do me a favor."

"Of course."

"I've been waiting for you to give my husband's laptop back to me."

She heard his sharp intake of breath. "If you were hoping to see the pictures, they've been deleted."

She recrossed her legs. "You had no right to do that."

"You didn't want to see them. Trust me."

Ally swallowed hard. "Were they all of Donata?"

"Yes, if that's any consolation."

"It isn't."

A sound broke from his throat. "I swear I didn't look at anything else. While you were in jail, I was so determined you were up to no good, I didn't take the time to look at the e-mails or anything else your husband might have stored in there."

"I believe you." She'd found out for herself that Gino was a man of uncommon integrity.

After a pregnant pause he said, "If you didn't know what was in the laptop, why did you bring it to Europe?"

"It's a long story…" her voice trailed.

"I'd like to hear it. We've got all night."

Since he knew her most painful secret anyway, what did it matter if she satisfied his curiosity.

"On my way out the door of my condo to drive to the airport, I listened to one of my phone messages. It was a man asking to talk to Jim." After she explained everything to Gino she said, "Since I needed to get to the airport, and Troy had just been cleaning out lockers, I couldn't very well ask him to keep the laptop until I returned. So I put it in my suitcase.

"I would have taken a look after I reached St. Moritz, but realized I didn't have an adaptor."

Gino made a strange sound in his throat. "When we get back home, feel free to use my study."

"Thank you," she whispered shakily.

"You might not thank me later if you **find anything** that could be hurtful."

"I'm past being shocked, Gino."

"Until I saw those photos, I thought I **was, too.**"

CHAPTER SIX

BEFORE LONG THEY pulled into the courtyard of the farmhouse and went inside. Without preamble he guided her into his study off the foyer. It was a cozy room with print curtains, leather chairs and couches, books and paintings.

"Sit down at my desk."

While she did his bidding, he opened the closet and pulled the laptop from the shelf.

After placing it in front of her, he opened a drawer and reached for an adaptor, then plugged the cord into the wall.

"I'll leave you to it while I say good night to my family."

His handsome features were marred by lines that made him look older. He left the room, shutting the door behind him.

Haunted by the change in his demeanor, since she'd mentioned the laptop, Ally was almost afraid to open it. Though she'd insisted that nothing could bother her now, it was obvious Gino wasn't convinced. Neither was she...

After a minute she found the courage to turn the computer on. Evidently Jim hadn't bothered with a password or Gino wouldn't have been able to see those photographs.

She booted up the system. Soon the home page Jim had created flashed on the screen.

Ally's eyes darted to the favorite pictures icon. Gino had said he'd deleted them. There was one way to find out, but something held her back and she clicked on the e-mail account.

Ally wasn't at all surprised to discover it full of messages from the same person.

She opened the top one he'd received in January before leaving for Switzerland.

I feel the same way, *amore mia*. Everything is now done.

I'll be waiting for you in our usual place with a car my husband can't trace. Once we reach the port, the family yacht will be waiting for us. We'll sail directly to Sicily where we'll be home free. Did I say that right?
Hurry!

Ally felt as if she'd just been slugged in the stomach.

She scrolled below to an earlier message he'd sent Donata.

That's how I felt the first day we met. Luckily for me Ally isn't the suspicious type. She's too into her music and has no idea I'm leaving her for good. I don't know what she'd do if she ever found out. Probably turn into a bitter woman like her mother.

It'll be much better if I disappear. She'll never know you and I are together. I live to be with you, Donata. You know that don't you? You're the fulfillment of my every fantasy.

The depth of Jim's deception left Ally speechless. Her eyes held a faraway look because she knew it was the real Jim talking.

No doubt Donata had been a true beauty, but more importantly, she'd had the right credentials Ally's husband required.

To think Ally had spent four months sobbing for her loss when Jim had been making plans to run away forever.

Compelled to read on, she opened the e-mail further down.

I've told you my husband changed into a very suspicious and calculating man. He would never allow a divorce. If he knew what I was planning, he would have me committed for insanity because he has that kind of power.

That's why I've asked you to be patient until I've made all the financial arrangements so nothing goes wrong.

Now that you've come into my life, I want only you.

Sickened by what she was reading, Ally buried her face in her hands. Though Jim and Donata might have been full grown adults, they talked like two naughty children who didn't have the emotional capacity to feel anyone else's pain.

Jim's poor parents who lived in Eugene—the knowledge of what their son had done would be so damaging, she didn't know if she could ever bring herself to tell them the truth.

Or her mother—especially not her mother who'd never trusted men since Ally's father had walked out on them when she was two.

Ally mulled over the revelations Jim never thought she'd see.

He'd met his match in Donata. If anyone was calculating, it was Sofia's mother. No wonder Gino was desperate to protect his niece from any more pain.

If Troy hadn't been super conscientious about his job, Ally would be clueless about the extent of their betrayal.

But since these e-mails *did* exist, and Ally was in possession of them, then Gino had every right to read them, too.

She was heartsick to think he and Sofia had been forced to wait *four* months to hear any news about Donata.

When he read these and found out what exactly Donata and Jim had been planning, he'd be beyond angry.

So was Ally. Enraged was more like it! Enraged over the injury they'd done to their families on both sides of the Atlantic without counting the cost.

She was appalled at their utter selfishness and cruelty.

It was one thing to have an affair. But to run away together and let their loved ones wonder what had happened? Ally couldn't comprehend it. As far as she was concerned, she and Gino's family were the victims here.

If Jim had told Ally he'd met someone else, she would have suffered, but in the end she would have agreed to a divorce. Could anything be worse than trying to hold on to a man who didn't know the meaning of love?

It had taken Jim with his blond tennis star looks, and his hunger for a woman of Donata's class and money, to charm her into disappearing with him. As long as she brought her inheritance with her, of course.

The whole thing was absurd. Outrageous!

Ally flung herself out of the chair and raced over to the door to find Gino.

She was in such a hurry, she didn't see him until they practically collided in the hallway. He put out his hands to steady her.

She tried not to be affected by his nearness, but it was impossible. The feel of his hands on her arms sent tingles of sensation through her body.

His jet-black eyes assessed her relentlessly. "I knew I shouldn't have left you alone."

"It's horrible in a way I would never have anticipated,

Gino." She tiptoed so she could whisper in his ear. "Sofia must never find out."

He relinquished his hold and rushed into the study ahead of her.

She closed the door behind her. "I made the mistake of reading the top e-mail first. If you start at the bottom, it will read in chronological order," she explained unnecessarily.

Since she already knew what was in the e-mails, there was no point in reliving something she wanted wiped from her memory, so she stood in front of the desk and waited.

An electric silence filled the room before Gino exploded with a string of expletives. Suddenly he shot to his feet. One glimpse of the wild fury in his eyes caused her to tremble.

"I knew she was capable of a lot of things," he muttered in a lethal tone, "but to forget she'd ever given birth—"

Ally rubbed her arms to try to stop the shivering. "I know," she whispered. "There's no mention of Sofia, no mention of your brother's illness. Yet she had Jim believing her husband was a cruel, calculating man."

Gino stared at her through eyes that had become black slits. "She was describing *me*, not Marcello. *I* wasn't the one blind to her faults from the beginning. She hated me for that."

His fingers made furrows through his vibrant black hair. "Ever since I repelled Donata's advances, and refused to give her money, she's been telling stories out of school about me to the tabloids."

Stunned by his words Ally said, "What kind of stories?"

His features looked like chiseled stone. "The one where I was in love with her first, but she preferred my brother. In my jealousy, I would do anything to have her for myself..."

Ally groaned.

"It's true I met her before he did. A mutual friend of our

family gave a party. Marcello had the flu and couldn't go, but I did. The host introduced me to Donata who'd come from Rome. She *was* exceptionally beautiful," Gino admitted, "but let's just say she didn't appeal to me. I left the party never expecting to see her again.

"A few months later I found out Marcello had met her at another party. He fell hard for her.

"The last thing I expected was that she would end up my sister-in-law. It was the only time I remember my brother having made a bad choice about something, or someone. Of course I wouldn't have let him know it. I loved him and wished for his happiness above all else."

She folded her arms tightly against her waist. Gino carried an even heavier burden than she'd realized.

"For what it's worth, Gino, if Donata had told my husband the truth about her family situation, Jim wouldn't have cared. He wanted Donata because she was the personification of everything he desired. After we were married I learned that he felt entitled to live a life he hadn't been born to. I'm convinced that's why he worked in Europe, so he could prey on women like your sister-in-law. As you said, she was beautiful," her voice trailed.

"She couldn't hold a candle to you."

"Spare me the platitudes, Gino."

He flashed her a rapier glance. "If you don't think I meant it, take the advice you gave Sofia and look in the mirror. It will remove any doubts."

She shook her head in denial. "This isn't about me."

He moved closer to her. "Did you know your marriage was in trouble before he was found with Donata?"

She rubbed her temples where she could feel another headache coming on.

Finally she turned to him.

"When my husband didn't get off the plane in Portland four months ago, I hired a detective to look for him.

"It took two months before I was told Jim and another woman were found dead together. It validated my suspicions that he'd been unfaithful for some time."

"How long were you married?"

"Two and a half years, but it was during the latter half that he spent longer times in Switzerland, always phoning with an excuse of some kind for not coming home sooner. Somewhere, deep down, I knew he was lying, but I wouldn't admit it to myself."

She heard a savage sound come out of her host. It made her shiver all over again.

"Donata did the same thing. She'd be gone for long periods, then call and say she'd been detained. It killed Sofia every damn time that happened."

Ally's eyes filled with liquid. "The poor darling. I'm just thankful it's over so she's not still waiting for the phone to ring, or for her mother to walk in the house."

Gino nodded, but he looked so drawn it alarmed Ally.

"Six days ago, the detective who'd worked on my husband's disappearance called me into his office. He told me about Donata. At that point I felt driven to fly to Europe to see if I could get a few more answers. How ironic to think they were hiding in Jim's computer all this time. Now that I've read the e-mails, everything is crystal clear."

She took a deep breath. "I'll leave it up to you to destroy the laptop and everything in it. Now if you'll excuse me, I'm tired and want to go to bed."

She left the room and hurried upstairs, more wounded for Sofia than anything else. Donata had planned to abandon her own daughter! Ally was so deeply hurt for that precious girl, Jim's rejection of Ally hardly made a dent.

She tried to imagine Gino going off with some woman never to be seen again, but she couldn't because he was a different breed of human being. Decent, honorable. Willing to give his all for everyone's happiness without having anyone to support him.

Marcello had been Gino's best friend. To be denied it now because of his illness while trying to be both mother and father to Sofia would place an enormous strain on Gino. Ally was glad that for a little while she could be here to ease his burden in some small way.

Before washing her face, she happened to glance in the mirror. There was a speck of chocolate on her cheek, but it appeared Gino had kissed away her lipstick. Despite the new revelations in the e-mails, just remembering the sensation of his male mouth devouring hers left her breathless and pushed everything else to the back of her mind, even after she'd turned out the light and had climbed under the covers.

Her heart did a little kick when she realized he was taking all of them to the river again tomorrow. She found herself counting the hours.

After a few minutes she turned on her side and reached for the vase of lavender, needing to breathe in its fragrance one more time. She'd never been given flowers for no reason before.

When Gino had handed them to her with that glint in his black eyes, she felt like she'd just been handed the world.

It was after two in the morning when Gino shut off the computer and went up to bed. He'd read through dozens of back pages of e-mails. There were dozens more but he didn't have the stomach for it.

He couldn't get his mind off Ally who didn't seem to know how truly wonderful she was. It explained her vulnerability, put there by a man who hadn't known how to love anyone but himself.

Unfortunately even if the fire had gone out of her marriage, Gino knew love wasn't always that cut and dried. Marcello had said as much when he'd admitted that he and Donata weren't going to make it. "I wish I were a faucet, Gino, so I could turn off certain feelings."

In Marcello's case the illness had done it for him.

Where Ally was concerned, Gino feared that deep down in her psyche, she still had some feelings for her husband in spite of what he'd done to her.

Gino couldn't fathom the other man not cherishing her, not wanting to come home to their bed every night.

He paused on the second floor, fighting the overwhelming impulse to knock on her door and ask if he could come in. He wanted to tell her how beautiful she was—show her.

Before Marcello's illness, when Gino had been playing the field with no intention of settling down, Marcello had warned him that one day there'd be a woman who would bring him to his knees. Gino had laughed at his brother, but he wasn't laughing now.

His limbs felt heavy as he climbed to the third floor. Tonight he would pray for sleep to come quickly.

When his phone roused him from oblivion at six in the morning, he realized he'd gotten his wish and cursed the person who dared to call him this early. On a groan, he reached for his cell.

It was Carlo. That brought him awake in a hurry.

"What's going on, Carlo?"

"I'm afraid you could be in trouble, Gino. I've arranged for us to meet in Rome with Alberto Toscano at nine this morning. That gives you three hours to arrange your affairs."

Gino levered himself off the bed. Toscano was one of Italy's top criminal defense attorneys.

"Don't tell me that insane story about the tampered brakes has grown legs—"

"I've just seen the forensics report on the car. There was definitely foul play involved."

Gino's eyes closed tightly as his mind grappled with the stunning news.

"It gets worse, Gino. The prosecutor has discovered that Signora Parker was in St. Moritz. He's trying to link the dots that prove she collaborated with you to carry out this crime."

A groan came out of Gino.

"I'll fill you in later. *Ciao.*"

The line went dead.

In the middle of the violin lesson, Bianca came in the living room. "Forgive me for interrupting but Leonora's papa just dropped her off and Gino's not here to make the introductions."

"No problem, Bianca. Bring her in here."

Ally sensed Sofia's disappointment, but it really was better for her to start making new friends.

"Hello," Ally said as the housekeeper ushered Leonora in the room. "I'm Ally, and this is Sofia. We're so glad you've come over."

"Thank you. I wanted to come before, but Mama said my fever had to go away first."

"Do you feel better now?" Sofia asked.

"Yes." The girl was shorter than Sofia with dark blond hair. "You're so lucky to be learning the violin."

"I think so, too. Do you want to hear Ally play?"

"I'd love it!"

The girl was so warm and natural, Ally was charmed by her.

"All right. One small piece. How about something from Peter and the Wolf?"

"What's that?" both girls asked at the same time.

"You haven't heard of it before?"

They shook their heads.

"Well, it tells a story, and each instrument represents one of the characters. The music you're going to hear is Peter's theme song."

Ally had always loved it. When she finished playing, Leonora acted as enraptured as Sofia.

"I wish I could play."

Ally looked at Sofia. "Why don't I give my violin to Leonora, and you can show her what you've learned."

Leonora's dark eyes sparkled. "You would let me?"

"Of course. Have fun you two."

Ally ducked out of the living room, delighted to realize the violins were a perfect ice breaker.

With time on her hands waiting for Gino, she walked to the kitchen to get a piece of fruit from the bowl on the table.

Bianca met her at the doorway. "I didn't want to say anything in front of Sofia, but Gino had to go to Rome on unexpected business for his brother this morning. He's not sure when he'll be back."

Ally's spirits plummeted, but she didn't dare let the housekeeper know how the news had affected her.

"That's fine. If Paolo is willing, I'll take the girls to the river as planned and have another picnic."

Bianca looked relieved. "That's good for Sofia. I'll get everything ready."

"Let me help. I don't have anything else to do."

"Bene."

They worked in harmony while sounds of a violin lesson being given drifted through the house to the kitchen.

Bianca smiled. "Sofia is very happy since you came."

"She's a lovely girl."

"Gino is happier, too. Everyone is glad you are going to stay."

Only until July, Bianca...

Ten minutes later Sofia and Leonora came running into the kitchen.

"Ally? Have you seen Rudolfo? Leonora wants to watch my cat do tricks."

"Have you checked the terrace? He likes to sun himself on the swing this time of day."

"That's right! Come on, Leonora."

They dashed out again.

The two women exchanged an amused glance.

"I'm going upstairs to change into my swimming suit."

"While you do that, I'll call Paolo and have him bring the car around."

"Thank you for making me feel so welcome, Bianca."

"It's my pleasure, *signora*."

As she left the kitchen, she turned to Bianca. "Please call me Ally." Bianca nodded and waved her off.

The trip to the river turned out to be an all day affair. Toward evening Ally asked Paolo to drive them into Remo where they enjoyed a pasta dinner al fresco before driving Leonora home.

By the time they returned to the farmhouse, Sofia looked pleasantly tired. They'd all picked up some sun.

Sofia gave Ally a hug. "Thank you for a wonderful day. Now I'd better go see how Papa is doing."

"I'm sure he's missed you."

Despite the fact that Gino hadn't been able to join them, it *had* been a wonderful day.

After reaching for the picnic basket, she started for the kitchen door. That's when she heard the sounds of a car coming into the courtyard. When she looked around she saw an unfamiliar sports car pull into the detached garage. It was Gino!

He looked impossibly attractive in a light gray suit and tie. Her heart skipped a dozen beats.

He walked toward her with his gaze narrowed on her face.

"I'm sorry about today, Ally. It couldn't be helped."

"You don't have to explain to me. It's fine."

"I called the house just now. Bianca said Sofia and Leonora had a fabulous time with you at the river."

"We did."

"Even before the violin lessons started, my niece felt a bond with you. After today her attachment to you is much stronger."

"Then it's good I'm leaving at the end of the month. I can't let her become too emotionally dependent on me."

"She already is." His voice sounded like it had come from a deep, underground cavern.

"I wish you hadn't said that. It worries me how vulnerable she is right now."

"I'm glad you recognize it because the end of June will be

here before we know it. She'll be crushed if you talk about leaving."

Ally sucked in her breath. "But that was our arrangement, Gino. If I were to stay longer, it will only hurt her more when I have to go."

"That was Donata's pattern. Come and go at will, regardless of Sofia's pain."

Heat swamped her cheeks. "How dare you compare me to Donata! I'm not Sofia's mother, but if I were," her voice trembled, "I'd love that child and do everything in my power to help her feel safe and happy for the rest of her life!"

He took a step closer. "I believe you really mean that."

"Of course I do. I already love her," Ally admitted before she realized she'd said too much. "Who wouldn't?" she cried out to cover her mistake.

"Her own mother, for one," Gino responded with bitter irony. "Her own father for another, although through no fault of his own. That leaves me, her uncle, who might not be able to protect her much longer."

Ally stared at him mystified. "Bianca said you had to leave on some urgent business for Marcello."

"I lied."

Her hands curled into fists. "If you're trying to scare me, you're doing a good job of it." He still didn't say anything.

"Gino—" she exploded. "I'm starting to get really frightened."

"That makes two of us. Give me an hour to shower and say good night to my family, then meet me on the terrace. We have to talk."

In a few swift strides he was gone.

CHAPTER SEVEN

TREMBLING WITH ANXIETY, Ally followed at a slower pace. After putting the basket on the kitchen counter, she went upstairs to shower, too. A day in the hot sun had made her messy and sticky. But Gino had upset her so much, she went through the motions of washing her hair and getting dressed without conscious thought.

He said he needed an hour. She gave him another fifteen minutes before going down to the living room.

The French doors to the terrace were ajar. With her heart pounding so hard she felt slightly sick, she stepped outside. The first thing she saw beyond the patio furniture was Gino's tall, masculine silhouette standing there in the darkness. The only light came from a slip of a moon that had just appeared above the horizon. Once again she was reminded of the way he'd looked to her the night he'd taken her to jail—like the fierce, proud falcon of his namesake.

He made an intimidating presence standing there with his legs slightly apart, his arms folded. He eyed her with frightening solemnity. She put a nervous hand to her throat.

"It's obvious something terrible has happened. Tell me what it is."

His mouth had become a tight thin line.

"So far Sofia knows her mother died in a car accident. Period. That's all I want her to know."

"I realize that. Let's hope and pray she never learns the true circumstances. At least not until she's a lot older."

"That's the idea," he bit out, "but something's come up beyond my ability to control, let alone stop."

The blood in Ally's veins started to chill. "What is it?"

"A few days ago the first stories about the accident came out in the paper with the usual sensational lies attached. This time they took the tack that foul play was involved."

She frowned. "Foul play? It was an accident! One of the Swiss authorities drove me to the bridge and explained what happened. He told me the blow to both their skulls had been caused by the bridge's beams when the car plunged into the river."

"Ally—" he said in a tortured whisper. "This is going to be hard for you to hear. The forensics report on the car came back a few days ago. It proved that the brakes had been tampered with."

She reeled. *"What?"*

"I'm afraid it means someone wanted your husband and Donata out of the way permanently."

She shook her head in disbelief. "Who?"

He drew in a deep breath. "In the words of the police, a jealous husband or wife who caught the two of them together and committed a crime of passion at the height of their pain."

"But that's preposterous! Marcello is incapacitated, and I was home in Portland when the accident happened."

"That's true," he muttered.

It took a minute for his words to sink in. When they did, her head flew back.

"They're not trying to say *you* did it?"

His face became an inscrutable mask. "Based on past lies generated by Donata herself, the prosecutor is convinced I'm guilty. He's already building his argument to present to the judge. It's a process not unlike your grand juries in the States. If the judge feels the prosecutor has a strong case, it'll go to trial. If I'm convicted by a jury, I could go to prison for life."

She couldn't credit what he'd just told her.

"On what evidence?"

"For one thing, I went on several overnight searches in January looking for Donata. I can't prove that I wasn't in Switzerland at the time the accident occurred."

"But that's not proof of anything!"

This couldn't be happening...

As her thoughts darted ahead to the possibility that he might be arrested, she clung to the side of the patio swing for support.

"If that happened, who could possibly take care of your family? It would kill Sofia!"

Silence followed her outburst. Her gaze flew to his once more.

He stared at her for a long moment.

"If anything happens to me, I only know one person beyond all else I could trust to do the right thing for both of them."

"W-who is it?" She didn't think it could be a distant relative or he would have mentioned it sooner.

"A woman I'm planning to marry in a few days."

Marry?

Ally wasn't able to hide the gasp that escaped her throat.

If she'd been shot, the pain inflicted couldn't possibly have hurt her the way this shocking piece of news did. She still hadn't recovered from being in his arms when he'd kissed her senseless in the movie theater.

For a moment she'd thought—

Oh, what a fool she'd been to think they'd meant anything to him beyond getting rid of the other man who'd been annoying her.

"I see." She struggled to keep her voice steady. "Does she know you're suspected of a crime that could put you in prison?"

"Yes."

Suddenly Ally had difficulty forming words. She swallowed a low moan.

"Does Sofia know her?"

"Yes."

It had to be one of his girlfriends. "Does Sofia like her?"

"Yes."

Ally refused to face him. "Then why haven't you married her before now?"

Her question rang in the night air. She hoped no one in the house heard her.

"The time wasn't right."

"But now it is? Just at the moment when you could be arrested and taken away?"

"Yes. There's no other way."

She forgot her promise not to look at him and swung around in his direction.

"Don't you think that's unfair to this woman?"

"Totally."

"Stop being so glib, Gino. I'm trying to have a conversation with you."

One of his black brows lifted. "I thought we were having one."

Red stained her skin. "You know what I meant. But all you do is answer in monosyllables."

Again there was no response.

"Does Sofia know what you're planning?"

"Not yet. I thought we'd tell her together in the morning."

"You mean the woman you're going to marry will be here so the two of you can talk it over with Sofia?"

"Yes. I hope that puts your mind at ease. Now you won't have to worry about my niece clinging to you."

"I was worried about it for *her* sake, not mine," she defended quietly, hurt to the quick by his comment.

"I'm well aware of that fact, Ally. So let's agree you'll go on giving her lessons until the wedding."

"But if that's only in a few days, then I'll leave at the same time, and—"

"No. You won't be going anywhere. I'm planning to take Sofia on our short honeymoon. After we get back, she'll resume her lessons."

The mention of a honeymoon tore Ally up inside.

"I—I'm sure Sofia will love being with both of you, but when you return, your wife won't want another woman in the house. I'm sure if you talk to the owner at the music store in Remo, he'll supply you with names of several violin instructors who would love to teach your niece."

He shifted his weight. "I'm afraid it's too soon to be switching teachers on her. You've become her heroine. No one else will do."

Afraid to hear anymore she said, "If that's all, then I'll say good night."

"Not yet," he muttered. "There's something important we still haven't touched on."

"What?" She needed to be alone where she could give in to this fresh new pain.

"The matter of an attorney for you."

The shocks just kept coming. "I don't understand."

"My friend Carlo informed me the prosecutor hasn't ruled you out as a coconspirator."

She blinked. "On what grounds?"

"That you conspired with me to get revenge on your husband and Donata. Maybe you didn't do the actual deed, but you'd be held equally to blame under the law. The insurance policy your husband took out on you before he left for Switzerland in January could have provided an additional motive for you to join forces with me."

She shook her head in utter bewilderment. "How did he know about the insurance?"

"Yesterday the prosecutor's office talked to the detective in Oregon who's been working with you on your husband's disappearance. The case against you isn't nearly as strong, but I'm afraid you're going to need legal counsel, too."

Ally had gone numb inside. "When I get home, I'll retain one."

"How will you do that on your salary? You won't be able to afford the kind you need."

She lifted anguished eyes to his. "What else haven't you told me about the case?"

She heard him draw in a deep breath. "My attorney, Signore Toscano, said that your appearance in Switzerland the other day would lead the prosecutor to think you'd flown over to visit the scene of the crime you and I planned. It's not unusual for a criminal to do that.

"He suggested that since you're already here in Italy, and haven't yet contacted a criminal lawyer, he believes it will be to our advantage if he represents both of us."

"But, Gino— That's impossible! Besides the fact that I could never afford him, it would be a conflict of interest. In order for him to represent both of us, I'd have to be your wife."

"Exactly."

"But you're getting married soon."

"That's right. If you'd asked me, I would have told you the name of my bride-to-be. She's an American named Allyson Cummings Parker from Portland, Oregon."

The shock of his words propelled her into the swing. She sat down with such force, it rocked back and forth.

He came to stand in front of her and stopped the motion with his hand. When their legs brushed against each other, he made no move to allow her breathing room.

"I know your heart, Ally. When you discovered what your husband had done, you felt compassion for Marcello and didn't hesitate to fly here to talk to him.

"Even at the height of your own pain, even at the risk of getting into trouble by defying me, you put Marcello's welfare ahead of your own.

"I've never known a man or woman with your kind of selflessness and courage.

"No matter how I treated you in the jail, you wouldn't break down because you didn't want to repeat anything to the wrong ears. I owe you everything for your discretion."

"No, Gino. Any woman in my position would have done the same thing."

His eyes glimmered with a strange light. "No. You're one in a million. Now I have a way to repay you.

"If we're married, then we can't be forced to testify against each other. My money will ensure the toughest defense attorney there is. Best of all, if anything happens to me, you'll be there to raise Sofia and watch over Marcello.

"Once you take my name, you'll inherit all that I possess, and you'll be given power of attorney to run my brother's affairs until Sofia turns eighteen and takes over her birthright."

He leaned closer, bringing his face within inches of hers.

"Before you come up with a dozen reasons why you can't marry me, tell me exactly what there is for you to go home to. Certainly not a husband who was unworthy of you.

"If it's a matter of leaving the orchestra, we have excellent orchestras here. Any conductor hearing you would hire you on the spot.

"Sofia told me about your mother. If you'd like her and your aunt with you, we have a whole palazzo for them to stay in.

"Sofia also told me you wanted a family, but your husband died before that could happen. I've seen the way you interact with my niece. She'll fill your heart the way she fills mine.

"If you and I have to stand trial, I'll testify that you had nothing to do with the accident, which will only be the truth. If I have to go to prison, and it's still a big if at this point, it will help me to survive knowing my brother and niece will be in your care. You'll be a wealthy woman who can do with the money as you see fit.

"Should the real culprit be apprehended and brought to justice, then we'll reassess our situation and go from there.

"Don't dismiss this out of hand, Ally. I love my family more than my own life." His voice shook. "You're the one person I trust to watch over them and see to their needs like you would your own family. There's a goodness and purity in your character that sets you apart from the other women I've known. Sofia could never go wrong under your guidance.

"As for Marcello, your gentleness to him the second you realized his condition was a revelation. Both Bianca and Marcello's nurses have remarked on it.

"They like you very much already. All the staff will be faithful to you should I have to go away.

"Think about it tonight, Ally, and we'll talk in the morning before breakfast."

He brushed her lips with his own, then left the terrace.

Ally sat stationary in the swing, unable to make a sound. She'd never heard anyone pour out their soul to her the way he'd just done.

Though Gino needed her to say yes to his marriage proposal, what he was really asking was that she enter into a sacred trust with him.

He wasn't offering his love. How could he? He hadn't known her long enough for that miracle to happen—if it could at all.

But should the unspeakable occur and he had to go to prison, she could understand how desperate he was to get his affairs in order first.

In return for becoming his wife, she would be getting something entirely different: financial security, his name and protection, a home and the chance to be a mother to a girl who needed one, the opportunity to be a caregiver to a cherished brother.

Should she marry him and he was arrested, she would have the kind of money Jim once dreamed about.

With it she could hire the manpower necessary to find the real killer and free Gino.

She sat there for a long time deep in thought.

It was well after midnight when she finally left the terrace and went up to her room.

After preparing for bed, she got under the covers, tossing and turning as her thoughts drifted back to Jim and the way they'd met.

When she'd literally run into him while they were both skiing at Mount Hood, there'd been an attraction that had led to serious dating and marriage. But after the first few months following their honeymoon, the passion didn't seem as intense. He started doing more ski shows in other parts of the country like Tahoe and Vail. The shows coincided with her concerts so they were spending more time apart. But it was the show in Las Vegas that brought about a major change in their marriage.

Jim met a Swiss promoter who offered to let him sell Slippery Slopes skiwear in St. Moritz on a trial basis. It meant being out of the country for big blocks of time.

Of course Ally had wanted him to be successful so he could realize his dream to be the owner of the company one day. But as she'd learned on her honeymoon, he'd had bigger dreams than that. Ones in which her input didn't matter to him. She'd only been a stepping stone on his way to bigger and better things.

How different in every way it was from her experience with Gino who knew his place in life and was steady as the sun coming up every morning. A man who put everyone's comfort ahead of his own and found joy being with the family he loved.

There was nothing shallow or selfish about him. Dear God how she loved him!

No one at home, not her family or friends would understand if she married Gino only four months after burying her husband.

What they didn't realize was that she'd been out of love with Jim longer than she'd been in love. But it had taken a remarkable man like Gino to remove the blinkers so she could see how empty her life had been with Jim, how barren.

Just being with Gino filled all those desolate places inside her. He was like a hot fire she rushed to embrace after coming in out of the freezing cold.

She knew that neither she nor any woman would have been his choice if the circumstances had been different.

The fact that he wasn't married yet proved it. But the precarious situation in which he found himself forced him to reach out to her because he knew he could trust her.

After her experience with Jim, she realized trust was the key element in a solid marriage if it was going to work…trust and the incredible passion she already felt for Gino.

Only time would tell if he could ever come to love her, let alone with that same intensity. But how could she compete when there'd been real beauties in his life like Merlina?

Still—Gino had turned to Ally in his darkest hour. Though he hadn't mentioned them having a child of their own, it was something she wanted with every fiber of her being. If he wanted a child, too, that would be a sign that he expected to sleep with her and make her his wife in every way.

Just thinking about lying in his arms made her breathless. She wanted to give him his answer now, but it was only four in the morning.

He expected to talk to her before breakfast. Since Bianca served it at seven-thirty, that wasn't too far off. She set her watch alarm for seven before catching a few hours sleep.

When she heard the little tinkle of the bell three hours

later, she slid out of bed to shower. Normally she would be exhausted, but with Gino waiting for her, her adrenaline was working overtime.

Once dressed, with her curls brushed and fresh makeup, she hurried downstairs. The housekeeper was already up and busy in the kitchen.

"Good morning, Bianca. Have you seen Gino yet?"

"*Si*. He's outside changing a tire on the truck."

"Thank you."

Ally left the kitchen through the side door to find him. Her heart was skipping all over the place.

A flash of pink caught Gino's attention. The sight of Ally moving toward him in a T-shirt and jeans her body filled out to perfection caused him to pause in his task of tightening the lug nuts.

If he didn't miss his guess, she hadn't been able to sleep, either. She walked with purpose, a sign that he feared didn't bode well for the desired outcome. But he was prepared for any hurdle she was determined to put in his way.

"*Buon giorno*, Ally."

"Good morning. I didn't realize we'd driven home on a flat tire the other night."

"It felt low, so I decided to change it, just to be on the safe side."

He put the wrench back in his toolbox, then dusted off his hands.

The sun had just come up over the lavender fields. Standing there in the early morning rays that gilded her hair and brought out the startling green of her eyes staring through to his soul, she looked like a piece of chocolate he would give anything to devour. But it wasn't the right time or place. Not yet...

If she was hoping he would help her find an opening, then she would have a long wait.

"After learning that someone caused that accident, I'm afraid I got very little sleep last night. I don't care how much circumstantial evidence the prosecutor says he has, I can't believe the case against either of us will go to trial. But on the outside chance that I'm wrong, I—I'll marry you provided we stay married until Sofia's eighteen."

Gino fought not to reveal his elation. He'd feared she would turn him down flat for several reasons he could think of, like the fact that she wasn't in love with him.

As for her ultimatum, there were ways around it. He'd worry about that later. All that mattered right now was her capitulation. "If some monstrous miscarriage of justice puts you in prison, Sofia will need constancy from at least one parent."

"Agreed," he murmured, still holding his breath.

"However if the person who caused that accident is caught, it would be criminal for us to suddenly dissolve the marriage, and for me to go back to the States. Sofia would grieve all over again for another loss."

Gino could scarcely control his joy. "I couldn't have said it better myself."

By the way her chest rose and fell, she still had more to say. He waited eagerly for the rest.

"To this point in time you've avoided marriage."

"I wouldn't have if the right woman had come along. I've been waiting..."

"Yes, well I thought the right man *had* come along, but

it turned out I was wrong. After the fiasco of my first marriage, I'm nervous about entering into another one."

"Then we'll both be nervous together."

"Don't tease about this, Gino. This is much too serious for that."

He took a step closer. What he wanted to do was crush her in his arms, but at this early stage it might frighten her off.

"I didn't know I was doing that. I'm only trying to say that since I've never been a husband before, I want to do it right."

"So do I," she whispered. "I want your happiness more than anything."

"You think I don't want the same for you?" he challenged.

"What you've offered me has already made me very happy," her voice throbbed. "I always wanted a family of my own. My father left when I was two. I grew up in a home without him, or siblings or cousins.

"It was hard because my mother was too immersed in her own pain to realize how lonely I felt. Don't get me wrong. She's a wonderful person in every way, but she had a warped vision of men that was hard for me to throw off. My grandparents were the bright spot in my life, but they died early.

"Mom warned me not to marry Jim. She said he was too good-looking just like my father, that he'd never stay faithful.

"I refused to listen to her. I thought—well, it doesn't matter what I thought. The truth is, I married a selfish man, so my dream of a happy home with babies didn't come to fruition.

"I'm almost twenty-nine, Gino. When I found out he'd died, I felt like I was beyond that part of life where anything and everything is possible. Mother kept saying, 'You have your music, honey. It's enough.'

"But when I met Sofia, I knew it *wasn't* enough. I saw myself in her. Because of you, I can have that family I always wanted. Sofia is a joy."

"She is that," he concurred. "As long as we're sharing let me say that any hope I had of finding the right woman and settling down pretty much died when Marcello married Donata and I saw the grief she brought to his life. Her amoral behavior was a huge turnoff. Once Marcello was afflicted with Alzheimer's, I gave up the idea of asking someone to be my wife and take on my niece and her father. It wouldn't be fair to a woman with expectations of starting out the marriage with no responsibilities except to each other.

"As you and I have discovered to our horror, your husband and Donata tried to hide their liaison from everyone, but they came to a surprise ending that caused their secrets to become public knowledge. For that reason, I have no intention of marrying anyone unless it's you. Sofia needs to believe in me, in *us*, Ally. She needs to know that what we have is real and worth imitating when she's old enough to be married. Her parents were never friends. That's what she'll see with us. Therefore there'll be no divorce when she turns eighteen. That's *my* condition."

She lowered her head, not saying anything.

"Ally?" he prodded. "Did you even have friendship with Jim?"

It took a long time before she said, "No."

He could always count on her honesty.

"Then we have more going for us than either of us has had up to now because my relationships with women to this point haven't had the depth needed to survive over a lifetime."

Slowly she raised her head. "What reason will we give Sofia why we're sleeping in separate bedrooms?"

He'd wondered how long it would take her to get around to

that question. There was a nerve throbbing frantically in her throat. It intrigued him no end. Obviously she wasn't quite ready for the big step of going to bed with him yet. He'd give her a little more time to get used to the idea.

"We won't have to tell her anything. By day we'll interact like a happily married couple. At night there's an anteroom off my bedroom. What goes on behind closed doors is our business, no one else's."

There were all kinds of side roads leading home. If necessary Gino would travel down every one of them to reach it.

"Gino?" she whispered tentatively.

"What is it?"

"I'm afraid."

"That makes two of us. But having seen the courageous Ally Parker in action, I'm willing to leap into the fire with you."

He could see her swallowing hard. "I—I'm terrified you might really have to go to prison for something you didn't do."

Deeply moved by her concern he said, "If I have my way, neither of us will be found guilty. In the meantime we have the power to make one special girl happy."

Her green eyes glistened. "If you're sure..."

His chest tightened. "I suppose everything in life is a gamble, but this time I like the odds. Shall we go inside and tell Sofia?"

She bit her lip, drawing his attention to the succulent mouth he'd wanted to taste over and over again the other night. Once he'd coaxed her lips apart, some divine chemistry had been responsible for the rest. Her passionate response had almost caused him to lose control. In a movie theater no less. It had to be a first for him.

Right now it looked like she needed a little help in the confidence department.

He reached for her left hand which was trembling. He stared pointedly at her bare ring finger.

"Where's the wedding ring you once wore?"

"Buried with my husband."

Her stunning answer pleased him in ways he didn't have the time to examine right now.

He felt in his pocket for a certain item. If she didn't fight him on this, then there'd be no going back.

"My mother gave me this before she died. It was her engagement ring. It's unpretentious, just the way she was. The way *you* are.

"She knew I loved nature and encouraged me to be a farmer if that was my choice."

One thing he did know beyond everything else. Ally Parker didn't have an avaricious bone in her gorgeous body, either.

He trapped her gaze with his. "I need you to be very sure before I slide it home on your finger. Is there anything else you want to ask me?"

She moistened her lips nervously. "I can think of a thousand things."

"But?" he prodded.

"But every time I think of what would happen to your family if you were arrested, I get so sick, I *can't* think."

"Then you agree to become a farmer's wife under the worst of circumstances? I can't promise the 'for better' part yet."

A little smile came and went as he slid the gold circle home on her finger. It happened so fast he almost missed it before she looked into his eyes with a haunted expression.

"Surely you once had dreams."

He nodded. "You've made them come true by filling this old farmhouse with heavenly music. The kind the Montefalco family has always loved. Every husband should be so lucky."

As they walked in the house, Gino had no idea Ally's heart was breaking. She'd been waiting to hear him say he wanted to fill his house with children. *Their* children.

But those words hadn't left his lips.

To her chagrin their entrance in the kitchen coincided with the rest of the family's arrival, forcing her to put on a pleasant face when she was dying inside.

While Luigi helped Marcello, Sofia ran around to hug Ally, then Gino.

He swept her up in his arms with an exultant laugh.

Sofia's intelligent eyes studied him. "You look different this morning, Uncle Gino."

"That's because I feel different."

"Why?"

"I'm happy, sweetheart."

Ally's heart plummeted to see what a brilliant performance he was putting on in front of his niece. By now everyone had settled at the table. Gino took his place across from Ally. Once Bianca served them, Gino said, "I have an announcement to make."

Ally felt close to fainting. "Is it that surprise you told me about a few days ago?" Sofia asked.

"As a matter of fact it is. I'm taking the family on a trip."

Her eyes brightened. "Where?"

"To the island of Ischia."

"I've never been there."

"You'll love it."

"How soon are we going to go?"

"On Monday."

"Why not today?"

"Because I need the next few days to get ready."

Sofia eyed Ally who was already squirming in her chair, then she looked at her uncle again. "What about my violin lessons?"

"After we get back, you can resume them."

Sofia sent Ally another troubled glance. "What will you do while we're gone?"

"Why don't you ask Ally to come with us," Gino suggested suavely.

"Would you come with us, Ally? Please say yes," she begged.

Ally wasn't immune to the pleading in her voice.

"I'd love to."

In the next instant Sofia's face lit up like a roomful of sunshine. "Have you ever been to Ischia?"

"No, but just the idea that it's an island intrigues me."

"Me, too."

"I have something else very important to tell all of you," Gino broke in. "This includes Luigi, Roberto, Bianca and Paolo."

He shot Ally a piercing black glance that defied her to say or do anything to upset Sofia now.

"On second thought," he added in a silky tone, "maybe I should let Ally be the one to explain since she's equally involved in this decision."

"What is it, Ally?" Sofia asked softly.

Ally's heart palpitated wildly because she realized he'd just thrown her in at the deep end. She had no choice but to swim.

"Y-your uncle Gino has asked me to marry him," she stammered. "How do you feel about that?"

Ally didn't have to wait long to find out. His niece bolted from her chair and came around to hug Ally's neck.

"Last night I told Papa that I hoped Uncle Gino would marry you. Papa always said Uncle Gino was waiting for the perfect woman to come along."

Gino nodded. "My brother always understood me better than anyone else."

Ally avoided looking at Gino right then. "You actually told your father that?"

"I swear it." Sofia crossed herself. "You told Uncle Gino yes, didn't you?"

Ally was in over her head now. She held out her hand for Sofia to see the gold band.

"Grandma's ring!"

"Yes," Ally whispered, but everyone in the room heard her.

Bianca clapped her hands and offered her sincere congratulations. Luigi made a little speech welcoming her to the family. If the staff was surprised by the announcement, they hid it beautifully.

"We're going to be married on Sunday at the church in Remo by Father Angelini," Gino informed them. "After the service we'll drive to Ischia and stay until we feel like coming home again."

Unless the police summoned Gino to Rome, Ally's heart cried.

Sofia kept her arm around Ally's shoulders. "Is your mama going to come for the wedding?"

"She would like to," Ally lied, "but my aunt can't travel that far with her new hip. I'm sure they'll fly over later in the year when she's better."

No way could Ally tell her mother about this yet. That would have to come later. Much later...

If or when her mother did come, she would find Ally in a vastly different situation from the one she'd been in with Jim.

"My mama won't be able to come, either, but *I'll* be there," Sofia assured Ally.

"That's all I could ask for, darling. How would you like to be my bridesmaid?"

"That's an excellent idea." Gino's black eyes gleamed. "Maybe Anna and Leonora would like to be bridesmaids, too. Ally will take you shopping for dresses when she picks out her wedding dress."

Suddenly Sofia pushed herself away from the table. "Excuse me for a minute. I have to call Anna and tell her what's happened!"

After she disappeared from the kitchen, Gino reached across the table to cover Ally's hand. He squeezed her ring finger especially hard.

"You've just seen a miracle before your very eyes. Asking her to be a bridesmaid was inspirational, but then you have all the right instincts."

Ally hoped that was true because she'd just agreed to take on a lifetime responsibility and didn't want to fail.

"I hear someone out in the courtyard," Gino said before removing his hand. "It must be Dizo. I asked him to bring Leonora over again today. Come with me, Ally. I want him to meet my future wife."

Just hearing Gino say it sent a shiver of delight through her body.

She followed him out the door to the driveway where she saw Leonora and her father get out of a truck.

The two men greeted each other warmly. Then Gino turned to Ally and put his arm around her shoulders. The gesture seemed to come so naturally to him, she could hardly credit it. "Ally? This is my friend and manager, Dizo Rossini. You've already met Leonora."

"How do you, *signore*." Ally shook his hand.

His daughter hung on to Gino's arm. "Is she your new girlfriend, Gino?"

"No." He ruffled her dark blond hair. "Ally Parker is my fiancée. We're getting married on Sunday."

The other man whooped in surprise. "You are a sly fox, Gino. Where have you been keeping this beautiful woman all this time?"

"Why don't you tell him, *bellissima*," Gino said to Ally before giving her a quick kiss on the mouth.

Gino didn't play fair, so she'd better get used to it.

"He kidnapped me off a train headed for Rome. I'm afraid one thing led to another," she said poker-faced.

"Ah, Gino. Love has hit you at last. I can see it in your eyes when you look at her."

Dizo winked at her. "He has had many women chase after him. All kinds," he chatted like the old friend he was. "Finally he found a woman *he* had to chase. That is very good."

Gino grinned. "She didn't make it easy for me."

The other man threw back his dark head and laughed. After he sobered, he waved an index finger in front of Gino. "It makes me glad this crazy business about Donata hasn't stopped you from living your life. It's your turn to have all those bambinos you've wanted to help you run the farm. To think they might all be musicians!" He nudged Gino's arm.

Ally kept the smile pasted on her face.

She turned to Leonora. "You can go in the house if you want. Sofia should be off the phone by now."

"Okay."

As she headed for the house, Sofia ran outside with a joyous smile. The difference in that face from the one Ally had seen for the first time a few nights ago almost made Gino's niece unrecognizable.

Ally was doing the right thing for Sofia. But nothing could take away the pain in her heart that Gino wasn't in love with her. It had been too much to ask, and now it was too late to change things. All Ally had to do was look into Sofia's eyes to realize there could be no going back.

Ally followed them in the house so the two men could be alone.

Sofia was full of excitement about the coming wedding and asked Leonora if she wanted to be a bridesmaid, too. While the three of them were in deep conversation in the living room, Gino entered. His dark eyes sent Ally a private message that he wanted to speak to her alone.

"Excuse me, girls. I'll be back later."

"Okay," Sofia said, but her whole attention was focused on what kind of dresses they would wear.

Gino guided Ally into the study and shut the door. She could hear his mind working.

"Tomorrow we have to meet in my attorney's office. It will take a good part of the day, so we're going to have to get a lot accomplished today."

Before he could say anything else there was a knock on the study door.

"That'll be Father Angelini," Gino explained. "Yesterday I phoned and asked him to drop by. Now that you've agreed to marry me, he needs to talk to us about the ceremony.

"After he leaves, we'll drive into Remo for the marriage license. Once that's done, we can concentrate on shopping and our preparations for the trip to Ischia."

Ally could hardly keep up with him. One minute she was

a widow. The next minute she was engaged to be married to this dynamic man who could move mountains with a snap of his fingers.

The way he was acting, there was no murder case pending that could rip her newfound happiness to shreds. Little did Gino know that his mention of an anteroom where one of them could sleep after they were married had plunged her into despair of a whole new kind. But she would hide it from him if it killed her.

CHAPTER EIGHT

"WE'RE ALMOST THROUGH, Signora Parker. This is the last document. Sign beneath Gino's signature, please."

Ally eyed Mr. Toscano. "What does this one say?"

During the lengthy process, he'd patiently translated everything from Italian to English for her.

This morning she'd thought Gino had brought her to his attorney's office to talk about the case.

Instead they'd both signed forms giving her power of attorney, not only to act in Gino's name, but to be Marcello's and Sofia's guardian if Gino were absent.

However the greater portion of the time she sat listening to a detailed explanation of the vast assets and holdings of the entire Montefalco family.

"This document will go into effect the minute you become Gino's wife. It says, 'In the event of the untimely deaths or mental incapacities of both Gino and Sofia, *you* will automatically become the Duchess of Montefalco."

Ally's gasp permeated the elegant law office. Her fingers shook so hard she couldn't hold the pen.

Beneath the conference table she felt Gino's hand slide

to her thigh. It sent shock waves through her system. He squeezed gently.

"It's just a formality," he whispered.

She jerked her head around. "Is there something you haven't told me?" she cried. "Marcello's condition isn't hereditary is it?"

She couldn't stop the tremor in her voice.

Gino's surprised expression should have told her the answer to that question. But the thought of anything being wrong with him had upset her so much, she wasn't thinking rationally.

"I swear to you there's not a thing wrong with me or Sofia," came his solemn declaration.

Though she believed him, she couldn't prevent the shiver that ran through her body.

"Sign it, Ally, then this part will be over and I'll finally have peace of mind."

Knowing how vital it was for him to get his affairs in order at such a precarious time in their lives, she managed to write her name on the dotted line one more time.

When she laid down the pen, a haunting sigh escaped his lips, reminding her this was no game but a life and death situation.

Gino handed the document back to his attorney, then turned to Ally.

"With that out of the way we can enjoy our trip to Ischia."

"Ischia?" Mr. Toscano questioned.

"That's where I'm taking the family after the ceremony."

The older man shook his head.

"I'm afraid it's out of the question now, Gino. You could be arraigned at your farmhouse as early as this afternoon."

Ally let out a cry. "Surely not this soon—"

"Anything's possible, *signora*. If they have to track you to Naples and beyond, it could be ugly for Sofia."

"I don't want my niece hurt in any way," Gino muttered grimly.

"Neither do I," the attorney said. "But if the prosecutor decides you pose too much of a threat, he can order you brought in anytime he likes."

"How long will they keep him?" Ally tried without success to keep the alarm out of her voice.

"It could be anywhere from one to three days. Depending on the judge's findings, a trial date could be set. After that Gino will be released on his own recognizance, but he'll be under house arrest. That means both of you stay on the farm."

Ally rubbed her temples where they'd started to ache. "I had no idea it could happen this fast."

Mr. Toscano eyed her with compassion. "It may not happen today or tomorrow. It might not happen for another week. But I know how this prosecutor works. He's ambitious and hungry.

"It's crucial to this case that you two keep your marriage under wraps before he makes his first official move against either of you.

"Since you took out a special license yesterday, I'd advise you to get married right now."

"You're reading my mind," Gino murmured, pulling out his cell phone.

Her adrenaline gushed. "But how can we do that?"

The attorney spread his hands in an expansive gesture.

"Very easily, *signora*. The Montefalco name opens doors. You're welcome to use this conference room. Judge Mancini is just across the courtyard. There shouldn't be a problem of his stepping over here long enough to officiate. Shall I get him on the phone, Gino?"

Gino simply nodded because he was already talking to someone.

While both men were thus occupied, Ally's thoughts reeled.

The second Gino ended his call, she grasped his arm.

"What about Sofia? She's going to be devastated if we do this without her."

"Maybe not." His black eyes flashed her a searching glance.

"Barring another emergency, Father Angelini has agreed to be available at any time. If I'm not officially served this afternoon, he'll perform the ceremony at the church this evening."

"He would do that?"

"Of course. Either way it's the only plan to stay ahead of the prosecutor."

"Y-you're right," she whispered, but he was already making another call and probably didn't hear her response.

She tried to school her feelings. Tonight would be their wedding night...

Even if they wouldn't be sleeping together, Ally's heart pounded furiously.

After a few minutes of conversation, he hung up and looked at her.

"Provided nothing goes wrong, it's all arranged with Bianca and the staff for seven o'clock. Sofia and the girls can still wear the new dresses you picked out yesterday," Gino assured her. "The few people we've asked to attend will come just the same."

"What will you tell everyone is the reason for the change?"

"That I might have to go out of town on business at a moment's notice, and didn't want to wait any longer to make you mine. Our guests will understand."

He leaned over and kissed her warmly on the mouth.

She wished he hadn't done that. The world might not know the real reason they were getting married, but Mr. Toscano did.

Bemused by the way Gino made her feel every time his hands or mouth touched her, she got to her feet.

"If you'll excuse me, I'd like to use the powder room."

The attorney nodded. "It's down the hall to your right."

"Thank you."

Without looking at Gino she left the conference room, but he caught up to her and put a detaining hand on her upper arm. Warmth seeped through the material of her cream suit jacket to her skin.

"What's wrong, Ally?"

"I'm worried about Sofia's reaction when we tell her we'll have to postpone the trip."

That wasn't all Ally was thinking about, but her other thoughts were too private to share with him. "She was looking forward to going snorkeling."

"She understands when business calls. There'll be other times, Ally. I promise you that."

If it were humanly possible, Gino would always keep his word. But because someone had intentionally caused Jim and Donata's accident, the situation was out of their control.

And what if there'd been no accident?

Ally would have lived her whole life not knowing what happened to Jim.

I would never have met Gino…

She couldn't imagine not knowing him now. Such a possibility was beyond her comprehension.

The very thought of his going to prison when she loved him so desperately— It seemed happiness was going to elude her again.

Gino eyed her with concern, obviously unconvinced she'd told him everything. But she kept on walking, not daring to tell him the truth.

Twenty minutes later the young judge who appeared to be on friendly terms with Mr. Toscano pronounced them man and wife. It was a very brief to the point ceremony because he was in a hurry.

The obligatory kiss Gino gave her was brief but thorough.

"Congratulations, Signora Di Montefalco. It was an honor to officiate for you and the Duc."

The judge appeared duly impressed by Gino's title. She supposed Gino *was* the Duc until Sofia came of age. Incredible.

"May you both be very happy in your new life.

"If you and your beautiful bride will put your signatures across from mine on the wedding certificate, my clerk will file it today."

Ally didn't think there was a wedding ceremony on record done with such dispatch.

It took family connections in high places that only someone of Gino's name and stature could arrange on a moment's notice.

When she'd signed her name, Gino put his arm around her shoulders and hugged her to him.

"Thank God for you," he whispered into her silken gold curls. "I swear on my parents' grave to do everything in my power to make certain you never regret this decision."

She lifted tremulous eyes to his. "I promise you the same thing, Gino."

"Let's go home," he murmured.

Home...

He kept his arm around her as they left the building and hurried to the parking area where Paolo was waiting.

He wasn't alone.

Ally pulled back. "What are those two men doing at your car?"

She heard Gino curse, even though he'd said it in Italian.

"Alberto must have been psychic. They've come to escort me to the magistrate's office for questioning. Poor Bianca must have been forced to tell them where I was."

No matter how much Ally wanted to scream at this injustice, she couldn't fall apart now. Gino needed her to be strong for him.

"We knew it was just a matter of time, Gino. I'm glad it happened here instead of the farmhouse."

"So am I."

"I'll take care of everything. We'll have that church service for Sofia after you return."

Gino squeezed her hand with so much force she wanted to cry out, but she didn't because she knew he wasn't aware of his own strength. Not when he'd just been plunged into hell.

"Ally—" His dark eyes stared straight through to her soul. She knew what he was trying to say.

"Don't worry about anything. Go with them. The sooner you comply, the sooner you'll be back."

"Signore Di Montefalco?" They flashed their identity cards.

"Get in the car now," he whispered to Ally.

She rushed to do his bidding. The moment she closed the door, Paolo sped away.

She turned to look out the back window. To her horror she saw some paparazzi gathered on the pavement.

Flashes went off as the man who was bigger than life to her climbed into the back of an unmarked car with both men flanking him.

"Quickly, Paolo. I need to talk to Bianca on the phone."

"*Si, signora.*"

He rang the farmhouse, then passed the cell phone to her.

"Bianca?" she cried when the housekeeper answered. "It's Ally. Listen very carefully."

She explained about them getting married in the attorney's office.

"It didn't happen any too soon. Gino has been arraigned."

The older woman's cry echoed her own.

"Whatever you do, don't tell Sofia anything. I'll talk to her myself the second I get home."

"I will say nothing, Ally. She and Anna are playing outside on the terrace with Rudolfo."

"Good. Keep them there. Thank you for everything. Paolo and I will be home shortly. Then you and I can make the necessary phone calls to Father Angelini and Gino's friends."

"*Bene.* May I say congratulations again, *signora*. I'm very happy for you and Gino. With you in the house, he won't be so worried about everything while he's gone."

"That's what I'm hoping. Bless you, Bianca."

After hanging up, she said, "Paolo? I've got lots of ideas to keep Sofia busy, but I'm going to need your help with some of them."

"I'm at your service."

"Is there a place in the garage where Sofia and I could separate some lavender into bundles to make small gifts?"

"I'll clear a place for you."

"That would be wonderful. On our way home, we need to stop at a store in Remo that sells cellophane paper and ribbon."

He gave another nod. "I know just the place where Gino has an account."

"Perfect. We also need to stop at a paint store."

"Anything you want."

Maybe it was too much to hope that she could keep Sofia in the dark while Gino was gone.

But with security in place around the farm, and help from the staff, Ally was determined that if at all possible, her new stepniece would be spared any more pain to do with Donata.

To Ally's relief, Sofia didn't see her arrive at the farmhouse when they drove in an hour later.

Bianca informed her Anna's father had come to get his daughter. For the time being Sofia was on a walk with her father and Roberto.

It gave Ally time to help Bianca make phone calls explaining that the wedding ceremony had to be postponed until Gino could get back from an important business trip.

With that done, Ally swallowed a late lunch. Before long Sofia returned with her father.

When the girl saw Ally, she put the cat down and ran over to hug her. "I'm glad you and Uncle Gino are back, Anna, and I can't wait until tomorrow."

"I know exactly how you feel." She took a fortifying breath. "Would you believe some important business of your father's came up? Gino has to deal with it, so we're going to be married in a couple of days when he gets back."

Sofia's eyes filled on cue. "But everyone is planning on it tomorrow!"

"Your uncle called Anna's parents, and the Rossinis. It's all set for a few days from now. Father Angelini is standing by."

Sofia was doing her best not to break down. "When, exactly?"

"Maybe three days at the most. In the meantime, I thought you and I would get busy on several projects I have in mind to surprise Gino."

She wiped her eyes. Partially mollified, she asked, "What projects?"

"Well for one, I need you to teach me Italian. I want to be able to say some things to Gino in his language on our wedding day. I would like to speak with such an authentic accent, he'll be shocked. It'll be our secret of course."

The girl's brown eyes suddenly sparkled. "You mean like 'I love you'?"

"Exactly. Like, 'I can't live without you.' Like, 'you're the most wonderful man I've ever known. Like, 'you're my heart and soul. Like 'I love your niece like my own daughter.'"

Sofia went perfectly quiet. "I love you, too, Ally. More than anything!"

"Then we're the luckiest people in the world."

"Gino?"

The second Gino heard Alberto's voice, he sprang from the hotel room bed where he'd spent the night going mad without a phone. His family's power may not have prevented him being investigated but did give him certain privileges.

Two security guards took turns bringing him meals, but there was no communication.

Today would be his second day before the chief judge

while he made statements and listened to the prosecutor's charges against him.

The judge would decide if there was enough evidence to call for a trial.

So far it sounded even worse than Gino had first supposed.

Mercifully Alberto had come. He was the only person allowed in to talk to Gino.

Speaking in hushed tones his attorney said, "I've talked to your wife. All is well with her and Sofia for the moment."

Gino swallowed hard. "That's the kind of news I needed to hear."

"I only have a few minutes. Thanks to the e-mails that placed Donata and her lover in the one location no one thought to look, those P.I.'s you hired to nose around Palermo, Sicily, have unearthed interesting news. It seems Donata had a great-aunt on the Castiglione side who's still alive and holds the purse strings to their family fortune."

Gino shot to his feet. "I don't think even Marcello knew about that, otherwise he would have told me."

Alberto eyed him shrewdly. "She probably kept that a secret from him like she did a lot of things. This aunt was the one who let Donata stay with her, and allowed her to use the family yacht.

"Apparently James Parker was a guest there and on the yacht several times. One of the crew let it out that the yacht picked them up in Portofino, Italy, but some members of the family weren't happy about it, particularly the great-aunt's oldest son named Vassily.

"He's next in line to inherit the money, and wouldn't stand for sharing it with a long lost family member from Rome like Donata who suddenly decided to ingratiate herself and her lover."

Gino's heart pounded like a jackhammer. His thoughts leaped ahead.

"This Vassily could have pretended to be Donata's friend by helping her procure that getaway car. All he had to do was pay off a couple of thugs to fix the brakes."

Alberto nodded. "Give the P.I.'s a little more time to investigate Vassily's activities, Gino. If everything adds up, we might well have our culprit."

Gino clapped his attorney on the shoulder. "Get all the extra help you need. I don't care how much it costs."

The other man nodded. "I'll tell your wife you're doing fine and should be home in another day or two."

"*Grazie*, Alberto."

"See you in chambers in a little while."

Ally stood in the alcove to Gino's bedroom with her hands on her hips. After dinner she and Sofia had come back with vases of fresh flowers to provide the finishing touch.

She and Sofia had spent most of yesterday painting the walls in both rooms a tan color with white trim. It covered the off-white paint which had probably been on the aged walls since the farmhouse was built.

"What do you think, Sofia?"

"Uncle Gino's going to love it!"

"I hope so. That daybed and table from the storage room are a good fit."

Sofia nodded. "It looks a lot better than an empty nook. I guess Uncle Gino didn't know what to do with it."

"If he gave up his old room for you and your father, then it makes sense he hasn't had time to worry about this suite of rooms. That's what wives are for," Ally quipped.

Sofia flashed her a mysterious smile.

"What's that look all about?"

"If you and Uncle Gino have a baby, this would make a sweet nursery."

"You're right," Ally said, trying to sound matter-of-fact.

"There's room for a crib," Sofia observed. "Signora Rossini has a new baby. Leonora tends it all the time. She says it's so much fun."

"What's so much fun?"

They both turned at the same time.

"Uncle Gino!" Sofia flew into his arms.

Ally's urge to do the same thing was so intense, she was in pain holding herself back.

He'd been gone three endless days. She'd given up hope he'd be home tonight.

He was still wearing the pale blue suit he'd been arraigned in, which meant he'd just been released and needed his suite to shower and change.

Ally thought he looked tired and leaner, yet all the more attractive for it.

"I was just telling Ally I hope you have a baby soon."

"What kind would you like? I'll see what I can do," he teased.

Heat swamped Ally's face.

"I don't care if it's a boy or a girl. Do you?"

"As long as the baby's healthy, I'll take whatever comes and be grateful."

"Me, too." She hugged Gino again.

"Do you like your surprise? Ally and I did all the painting ourselves. It's your welcome home present."

Ally saw his gaze take in the alcove's furnishings, but his eyes were hooded making it impossible to read their expression.

"I feel like I've just wandered into one of Rome's most fashionable furniture galleries."

Sofia laughed. "It was Ally's idea. Do you like the new matching bedspreads?"

They were a café-au-lait with white swirls.

He tousled his niece's hair. "I love them. They're classically modern. Did you pick them out?"

"We both thought this was the prettiest pattern. Ally said the daybed was perfect if you ever want Papa to be close to you during the night."

Gino's eyes swerved to Ally's. She noticed a strange flickering in their black depths. New sensations fired her blood.

"Ally is always concerned with everyone else's needs. That's why I'm marrying her first thing in the morning."

Sofia did a close approximation of squealing in delight.

"I made all the arrangements on the drive home from Rome. The ceremony will be at ten o'clock."

Ally rubbed her hands against her jean-clad hips, all the time aware of Gino's scrutiny.

"In that case I'll say good night to the two of you, Gino. It's already late, and I need my sleep for the big day ahead."

She sensed Gino had a lot to tell her, but now wasn't the time. She didn't want anything to alarm Sofia this close to the wedding.

Sofia ran over to her and gave her a big hug. "Good night, Ally. I can't wait for morning to come."

Neither could Ally.

"I feel the same way." She kissed the girl's cheek, then hurried out of the bedroom.

His suite was located at one end of the third floor.

She went down the stairs to her room on the second. Sofia's and her father's suite lay at the other end of the hall.

Before Gino had been forced to move his family here, he'd had the farmhouse for himself. By virtue of taking on a wife, he'd now been invaded.

She hoped he didn't mind what she'd done upstairs. They already had an understanding that they'd be sleeping apart. She just didn't want him to think she planned to turn his whole household upside down.

When she could talk to him alone, she would explain that she felt this had been a good way to keep Sofia's spirits up, and accomplish what needed to be done without anyone questioning her real motives.

But once under the covers of her own bed, her mind wouldn't shut off.

What a difference it made knowing Gino was home. His mere presence gave her an overwhelming feeling of contentment.

Growing up in an all woman household, Ally had never known such luxury.

Something about Gino engendered this marvelous feeling of well-being and security. She knew he would slay dragons for them.

How odd that Jim hadn't had this same effect on her. Physically he'd been a strong, capable man. But she must have recognized instinctively he would always put himself first. In the end, he did it to his own demise.

Gino was a different breed of man altogether. No one else measured up.

She couldn't believe she was his wife. Even if it was in name only, she vowed to be his equal in all the ways that counted.

After the ceremony tomorrow, she would call her mother on Gino's cell phone and tell her she was married.

Much as she would have liked her mother's blessing, she hadn't needed it to function.

It was all because of Gino.

As for Jim's parents, depending on many factors, she would phone to inform them she had remarried. But for the time being it would be bett—

"Ally?" Gino whispered in the darkness, jarring her out of her thoughts.

Surprised to hear his voice, she raised up on one elbow. "I didn't hear you knock."

In the next breath she felt her side of the mattress dip to take his weight.

"I hope you don't mind."

Her heart was pounding in her ears. "No. Of course not."

He was sitting so close, she could smell the soap he'd used in the shower. She started to move to give him room, but he stopped her by placing both hands on either side of her pillow, forcing her to lie back.

He was wearing a robe, and as far as she could tell, little else.

"You ran from my bedroom so fast, we didn't have a chance to talk."

Her breathing had grown shallow. "Sofia needed you."

He traced the curve of her jaw with his finger. "But my wife didn't?"

"That isn't what I meant," she whispered.

"Then what did you mean?" His fingers had trailed to her earlobe, turning her bones to liquid.

"I—I've been sick with worry waiting for you to come home and tell me everything. But I didn't want to let on in front of Sofia."

"You've done a magnificent job of keeping her occupied. I've never seen her this happy before. Now it's my turn."

"I don't understand."

"I've spent two hellish nights away from my wife. I'm not prepared to be alone tonight.

"Let me lie here. It's all I ask. I need my best friend."

She heard a strange nuance in his voice. An impending sense of dread took over.

"Something's wrong—" she cried in alarm. "What is it? Don't tell me it's nothing because I wouldn't believe you. Hasn't the investigation uncovered anything that will help our side?"

"They have several promising leads."

"But?"

His fingers tugged on one of her curls. "There's been a new twist in the case."

Moving with the stealth of a panther, he reached the end of the bed. Before she knew it, he'd come to lie on top of the comforter next to her. She felt him cover his forehead with his arm.

Making love to her had to be the furthest thing from his mind. She felt so stupid for even imagining that's what he'd had on his mind when he'd first come into her room unannounced.

They were two people intrinsically linked to a murder, fighting for survival. Gino had no one but her to turn to for the kind of mental comfort he craved. She was the only person who understood what he was going through.

Three days ago she'd vowed to comfort him for better or worse. This was definitely the worst time of their lives.

She turned so she was facing him. "Tell me what's happened," she urged softly.

In the intimacy of the darkness he began talking.

"There's going to be a trial. It has been set for a month from now."

Even though Ally knew it might come to this, the news was shattering.

"I just found out Merlina of all people is a witness for the prosecution."

Ally quivered inwardly, but she was determined to stay on an even keel for him.

"Did you meet her through Donata?"

"No. Merlina's father is a wholesale florist from Gubbio. I met her almost a year ago while she was helping her father.

"We went out several times, but I lost interest and told her it was over, By that time Donata's long vacations were starting to take their toll on Sofia. Comforting her was all I had on my mind."

"But Merlina didn't want to stop seeing you," Ally said out loud.

"No. She started coming to Remo once a month. She would show up at the flower stand waiting for me. I told her my life was complicated, and we could only be friends. I hoped she would give up without my having to spell it out to her."

Listen to what he's saying, Ally. Just listen, and learn.

"Without my knowledge, it seems she got in contact with Donata."

"Sofia told me she came to see her mother."

Gino groaned. "During those conversations Donata told lies about me. She made me out to be a dangerous man capable of committing bodily harm."

Ally was horrified. "Like what specifically?"

"According to the prosecutor, she told Merlina I used to

come to her room at the palazzo and force myself on her because Marcello could no longer protect her."

"That's sick," Ally cried.

His breathing had become labored. "Donata showed Merlina the bruises to prove it."

Ally sat straight up in the bed. "Gino—if Merlina had believed Donata's lies, she would never have shown up here in the last few days. What reason did she use for coming to the farmhouse after all this time?"

"She wanted to know why I'd really stopped seeing her. I told her what I'd said before. That it was over, and it wouldn't be fair to go on seeing her.

"But she refused to accept it. And then of course she saw you, Ally. She knew you were a guest in the house."

Ally moaned in disgust. "So she put two and two together, and in her jealous rage she decided to pay you back by running to the prosecutor with more lies."

"As Alberto keeps reminding me, her story won't be believed. Her credibility will be ruined when he gets her on the witness stand and it's learned she came to see me after Donata had warned her off. Nevertheless I have to admit I didn't see that one coming."

"Of course not. It's awful. I'd say it's a miracle you trust anyone." Her voice shook.

"You're it, Ally."

Her heart went out to him.

"You sound exhausted. Go to sleep."

After a few minutes she could tell he'd passed out from fatigue.

For the rest of the night she guarded him. When it grew cooler in the room, she stole out of bed to get an extra blanket from the cupboard. She put it over him.

Without conscious thought she smoothed the hair from his brow where his forearm had disheveled it.

Even the man she'd likened to Apollo needed respite from his burdens.

Toward morning she fell asleep and knew nothing until Sofia knocked on her door.

Ally's first thought was Gino. She opened her eyes to discover he'd left her bed already. She hadn't even noticed. Some guard she'd make.

"Come in, Sofia."

Her brunette head peeked around the door. "Uncle Gino says to hurry and get up. It's eight-thirty. Almost time to leave for the church."

"I slept that late?"

"After all the work you've been doing, he said you deserved to sleep in. He says he's so excited to get married, he can't eat."

After what he'd revealed to Ally in the darkness of the night, she wasn't surprised he'd lost his appetite.

"Have you eaten already?"

"Yes. With Papa. Now I'm going to get dressed."

"Okay. I'll hurry. Meet you downstairs in twenty minutes."

She threw off the covers and padded into the bathroom for a quick shower and shampoo.

After putting on new underwear, she went over to the closet.

For the wedding she'd picked out a two-piece suit in pale pink with a lace overlay on the short sleeved jacket.

The knee length chiffon skirt floated around her legs.

She fastened the tiny pearl buttons, before slipping into matching pale pink high heels. A pink frost on her lips, plus a poof of floral spray, and she was ready.

Gino stood waiting at the bottom of the stairs in a black tuxedo.

Once again an image flashed before her eyes of the fierce bodyguard who'd stepped from the wall into her life one dark night.

Who would have guessed the gorgeous, enigmatic stranger wearing a security guard's uniform would turn out to be her husband dressed in impeccable groom's attire?

Ally grew weak at the sight of so much male beauty.

As she reached the bottom step, he drew close. She heard him murmur something under his breath in Italian. She would have given anything to know what he said.

"A certain young, upcoming violinist told me these would match your suit."

From behind his back he produced a corsage of pink roses he pinned to her jacket.

Her heart thumped so hard, it caused the petals to rustle with each beat.

"If you hadn't been there for me last night, I swear I don't know what I would have done."

"I didn't do anything, Gino," she whispered shakily.

He kissed her forehead. "You believed in me from the beginning. Knowing that, I can get through this."

His trust in her was absolute. He didn't need anything else. Unfortunately she wanted and needed much more from him. But to behave like Donata and Merlina, neither of whom could take Gino's rejection, would be the kiss of death.

After tonight she was more convinced than ever she'd done the right thing by having a certain inscription engraved on the gold wedding band she'd bought him.

He'd wanted a best friend for a wife. That's what he was getting. She would have to find a way to live with the pain.

CHAPTER NINE

FATHER ANGELINI SMILED at both of them. "And now I pronounce you Rudolfo Giannino Fioretto Di Montefalco, and you Allyson Cummings Parker, husband and wife. May you live long and be fruitful. In the name of the Father, the Son and the Holy Ghost, Amen."

Gino didn't hesitate to give her another thorough kiss in front of the small assembly of friends. They were now officially married in the eyes of the church.

In the periphery, Ally caught sight of Sofia's shining face. She and the girls looked adorable in white lace dresses with garlands of pink roses in their hair.

Marcello might have been in a wheelchair, but he looked every inch the aristocrat in his formal attire. He wore the crest of the Montefalco family on the scarlet band stretching from his right shoulder to his left hip.

Before Ally had started down the aisle of the church on Dizo Rossini's arm, his wife Maria had handed her a sheaf of long stemmed pink roses to carry.

"Do you know how many of my country women could

claw your eyes out for getting Gino to marry you not once, but twice?" she teased.

Ally chuckled, but little did Maria know her bittersweet remark made Ally want to laugh and cry at the same time.

When the wedding party congregated on the steps of the church, one of Gino's friends took pictures for them.

Everything seemed so normal and happy, but Ally knew they were living on borrowed time. Like a bomb ticking away, their lives could be shattered by an explosion if Gino didn't win his case.

"Stop worrying," he whispered against her neck after they'd climbed in the back seat of the car.

"I'm not."

"Yes you are," came the no nonsense rejoinder. "I can tell by your eyes. They're a dark green. When you're happy, they turn a lighter shade and shimmer. Today is ours to enjoy."

She bowed her head. "I want to enjoy it, but I keep remembering those men waiting for you outside Mr. Toscano's office. If that were to happen in front of Sofia and all your friends—"

"No one's going to snatch me away again. That part is over."

Unless he was found guilty at the trial and taken away in handcuffs.

At the mere thought of it, Ally shuddered in horror.

"Where's my Joan of Arc who stood calmly before her enemies at the jail without as much as the quiver of an eyelash."

His question gave her a needed jolt. She'd better start acting the part she'd committed to play for life.

She raised her blond head. "I'm right here."

He grasped her hand. "I haven't told you how exquisite you look yet."

"Thank you."

"I'm the envy of all my friends."

"I have a few friends who would think the same about you."

When he kissed her fingers, she wanted to pull her hand away. How could she possibly remain friends with him if he kept doing things to remind her he was irresistible yet untouchable flesh and blood husband?

"I'm sorry your friends and family couldn't be here, Ally. One day our home will be open to everyone, and we'll be able to travel to Oregon."

"Sofia keeps asking me how soon you'll take us to see Mount Hood, Gino. She's fascinated by volcanoes."

"Aren't we all."

He slid his arm behind her shoulders. "I'm anxious to meet your mother and tell her what an exceptional daughter she has."

"You're going to come as a tremendous surprise to her."

"Is that good or bad," he mocked in a playful tone.

"I'm not going to bother answering that question. Suffice it to say that with my father's defection, my mother has lost her trust in men. But when she gets to really know you, her whole attitude will change."

"Trust is everything," he said in an emotion filled voice.

Ally already knew that. She stirred in place. "I agree."

Though she wanted to rest her head against his shoulder, she didn't dare for fear she'd give herself away.

"Before we left the church, Sofia told me to examine my ring carefully. I think I'll do it now."

He removed his arm in order to pull off his own ring.

Ally held her breath while she waited for his reaction.

"My kingdom for a friend," he read the words aloud.

After a breathless moment of quiet, he touched the ring to his lips, then slid it back on his finger.

By now they'd reached the courtyard of the farmhouse. Most of the guests had already arrived. More pictures were being taken.

Gino got out of the car and came around to help her. His black eyes resembled smoldering embers.

"In case you didn't know it, you've made me the happiest man alive."

Before she could take another breath, his mouth descended on hers. Like the effect of slow moving magma, it caught every particle of her body on fire.

Not until one of his friends shouted for Gino to keep on kissing her for the camera did Ally realize how carried away she'd gotten. Her husband couldn't have helped but be aware of her hungry response. She could only hope that since he was playing to the crowd, he assumed she was doing the same thing.

He pretended to be the amorous lover to such perfection, no one could have guessed the real reason for their marriage.

Everyone clapped. There were a few wolf whistles that brought a grin to Gino's handsome face. He ushered her inside the farmhouse where Bianca and some local helpers had arranged food and champagne in the dining room.

The guests filled their plates and wandered out to the back terrace where a group played music.

Without hesitation Gino pulled her into his arms and started dancing with her.

Soon others joined in. Eventually his friends broke in to dance with her, depriving her of the joy of being that close to him.

But she needn't have worried who Gino's next partners would be.

He gave each flower girl a turn around the patio before spending the rest of his time with Sofia.

Ally finally excused herself to spell off Luigi and Roberto, both of whom were there to help with Gino's brother and celebrate.

"I'll watch Marcello while you get something to eat," she told them.

When they got up, she grasped Marcello's hand in case he decided to start walking around the terrace.

Maybe it was the music, or the presence of so many people, but his thumb kept pressing the top of her hand.

She hoped it meant that in some obscure way he was enjoying himself.

The cruelty of his affliction made it hard on everyone who loved him. He and Gino had been exceptionally close.

Today should have been a time for the two brothers to rejoice.

But of course it would have been a happy time because Gino would have married someone else. A pain seared her heart to imagine missing out on marrying him.

"Ally?" Her husband appeared out of nowhere and put his hand on her arm. "What's made you go pale?"

"Did I? Maybe it's because I was wishing I'd known Marcello before he became ill."

His dark eyes flickered. "He would have been crazy about you even before he heard you play the Tchaikovsky."

"Do you know he's been pressing his thumb against my hand?"

He slanted her a mysterious glance that caused her pulse to race.

"He senses your kindness. Would you be as kind to me if I asked you to play something for our guests? I want to show you off, and I can't think of a present I'd like more on my wedding day."

"Gino—"

"Is that a yes, a no, or a maybe."

His charm made it impossible for her to refuse him anything.

When she thought of all he'd given her, it was so little to ask in return. But he had no idea how full her emotions were. They threatened to overpower her.

"Well, perhaps one piece."

"I'll ask my niece to bring out your violin."

He disappeared just as Luigi and Roberto came back on the terrace.

Soon a smiling Sofia walked over to her with her case.

The background music ended and Gino asked for everyone's attention.

"Ally and I want to thank you for sharing the most important day of our lives with us.

"Few of you know she's a gifted musician. I've asked her to play something for you as a special favor to me and my brother.

"Our parents instilled the love of music in us. Now we have Ally to fill the house with it again."

His touching words made Ally want to burst into tears.

To fight them off, she opened her case and tuned her violin until she felt she was in control once more.

"I'll play something from the Brahm's First Symphony."

Brahms was her favorite composer, whether it be piano or orchestral music.

This was the piece she'd been practicing when the migraine had hit her so hard during rehearsal in Portland. Little had she known what awaited her when she'd gone out in the hall to call the doctor and discovered there was another message waiting.

In a matter of weeks that voice mail from Troy had literally transformed her life.

Here she was in the heart of the Italian countryside, playing at her own wedding for her brand-new husband. The man she loved beyond comprehension.

For a little while she simply immersed herself in the beauty of the piece, wanting it to please Gino.

When she finished playing, there was an unnatural quiet.

Perhaps the greatest tribute to any artist was the hushed silence that followed a performance.

She looked across the patio and met Gino's gaze. Even from the distance separating them, his eyes seemed to be aflame.

Suddenly he began to applaud. Soon the others followed his lead.

"Grazie," he mouthed the words to her before she was besieged by their guests.

Sofia clung to her hand and announced she was taking lessons. That brought on requests from several parents for Ally to teach their children.

Everyone asked for an encore but to her relief Gino came to the rescue.

"I don't want my bride worn-out before the wedding day is over."

His remarks incited the men to make their little jokes. Ally didn't need a translator to know they were talking about the pleasures of the wedding night to come.

She laughed along with them because they were among

friends here and Gino needed a moment like this to get him through the dark days of the trial coming up.

While she was putting her violin back in the case, she felt a pair of strong arms slide around her waist.

"Leave the violin on the chair and dance with me again."

Ally's heart leaped in response. It was frightening how much she wanted to be in Gino's arms. But this couldn't go on much longer or he would know he'd married a woman who wanted to be much more than friends.

Avoiding his eyes, she followed his lead. He seemed determined to show his friends that he was in love with his wife. Ally had to withstand his wrapping both arms around her with his hands splayed across her back, his face pressed into her curls.

Unlike the other couples, he more or less moved them in place. You really couldn't call it dancing. She could feel every hard line and sinew of his body.

Desire like she'd never known in her life engulfed her. She felt the telltale weakness in her limbs. Her palms ached with pain only he could assuage.

She couldn't do this any longer.

Placing her hands against his chest, she pushed away a little, but not so anyone else would notice.

Still not looking at him she said, "I'm sorry, Gino, but I need to be excused for a minute."

"Of course. Hurry back." He gave her mouth a lingering kiss before letting her go.

The mere contact set off a conflagration inside her.

In a daze, she made her way through the crowded house to the hallway. As she started up the stairs she saw Bianca welcome another guest into the foyer. Ally didn't recognize the middle-aged man. He hadn't been at the church to witness the ceremony.

If the housekeeper hadn't greeted him like an old friend, Ally would have been terrified it was someone from the prosecutor's office.

She continued up the stairs to her room to freshen up in the bathroom. In truth she'd needed to get away from Gino.

Ally soaked a washcloth in cold water and pressed it to her hot face, surprised she didn't hear it sizzle.

Her biggest mistake had been to dance with him. When she went downstairs again, she would make certain it didn't happen again. That way she might just be able to make it through her wedding day without the whole world knowing how she felt about Gino.

A few minutes later she felt settled down enough to leave her room and rejoin their guests.

To her surprise she almost collided with a white-faced Sofia who'd been running from the direction of her own bedroom further down the hall.

"Sofia—what is it? Has something happened to your father?"

"No." In the next breath the girl's expression closed up. She started for the stairs, but Ally pulled her back and held on to her.

"Was someone mean to you?"

"No."

"Then what's wrong, darling? Don't you know you can tell me or your uncle anything?"

"I don't like Uncle Gino anymore," came her muffled cry against Ally's lace jacket.

Sick to the pit of her stomach, Ally drew Sofia into the bedroom and shut the door.

She walked her over to the bed and helped her to sit down next to her.

Though they had a house full of guests downstairs, this was a problem that needed to be taken care of right now.

"Why do you feel that way about Gino? He loves you so much."

"I know."

The girl was talking in riddles.

"What's upset you? Please tell me. You can trust me."

"I'm afraid to tell you." She burst into tears. "It would hurt you too much."

"Hurt me? How?"

"Because you love him. But he—" She couldn't go on.

"He what?" Ally prodded.

"It'll make you cry."

"Then we'll cry together. Tell me."

"I found out he wishes—he wishes—" She couldn't say it. Breaking into half sobs, she clung blindly to Ally who by this time feared this had something to do with Donata. Ally couldn't let this go.

"Please, Sofia. You can't keep this to yourself or it will make you ill."

Sofia finally raised her head. "He said he wished he hadn't married you, but it was the only thing he could do at the time."

It was one thing for Ally to know the truth in her own heart, but to hear Gino's niece say it was like undergoing a second death.

Fighting to remain calm Ally said, "Is that what he told you?"

"No." She kept wiping her eyes. "I heard him talking to Signore Santi."

"When?"

"Just now."

"You mean they're in your father's room?" It had to have been the man who'd come late to the reception.

"Yes. When I saw them leave the party and you weren't downstairs, I came up to see what was going on. That's when I heard Signore Santi tell Uncle Gino it was too bad he married you when it wasn't necessary."

Not necessary— Did that mean there'd been a break in the case?

"Then U-Uncle Gino said—well you know what he said. I—I couldn't believe he said that."

Sofia's shoulders shook with silent sobs. "I thought he loved you."

Poor Sofia had been caught up in the romance, but cruel reality had intruded.

"Did you hear anything else?"

"No. I didn't want Uncle Gino to know I was listening."

Thank heaven for that!

Ally's arms closed around her. "Your secret is safe with me."

The girl lifted her tearstained face. "I shouldn't have told you. Now you'll go away and I'll never see you again." Her voice throbbed.

"That's not true, Sofia. I'm going to live right here with you forever.

"The fact that he doesn't love me doesn't change my love for him or you."

"How can you say that?"

"Listen to me, darling. When your uncle proposed, I knew he didn't love me. We're friends you see? So you mustn't stop loving him. He can't help how he feels. But I know he'll always be kind to me. He wants us to be a happy family. So do I."

Sofia studied her for a long time. "I love you, Ally. Do you think someday I could call you Mama?"

The question melted Ally's heart.

She winked at her. "As long as I can refer to you as my daughter, you can start calling me that anytime you like. Now wash your face and we'll go downstairs before everyone starts to wonder what has happened to the wedding party."

Alone for a moment, Ally squared her shoulders.

Where Gino's feelings were concerned, she hadn't learned anything from Sofia that she didn't already know. The difference was, realizing Sofia knew it, too, would make things much easier around here.

When Sofia emerged from the bathroom, Ally grasped her hand.

"After we leave this room, we'll pretend we never had this conversation, agreed?"

"Yes," she answered in a sober tone.

But it was easier said than done. When they joined their guests, Gino still hadn't come downstairs. That as much as anything let her know something of tremendous import had happened, otherwise Gino wouldn't absent himself from the festivities this long.

For Gino's sake she hoped Signore Santi's arrival meant that Gino was no longer under suspicion.

How would they go on protecting Sofia if there were a trial and he had to leave the farm every day to be in court?

She was an intelligent girl and no one's fool. Ally feared it was going to be sooner than later that she learned the whole ugly truth about her mother. Then it would come out that Ally's first husband had died with Donata.

Ally dreaded the day Sofia knew everything.

After urging Sofia to be with her friends, Ally mingled with the guests who were all enjoying themselves.

Ally caught up with Maria and talked to her about the possibility of Ally and Sofia helping out part-time at the flower stand for the rest of the summer.

Maria couldn't have been more enthused over the idea. They agreed to talk about it in a few days.

"Provided Gino is willing to share you by then."

To Ally's surprise Gino reappeared. He slid his arm around her waist.

"I saw your heads together. What plot are you two hatching behind my back?"

Ally wanted to ask him the same question about his conversation with Signore Santi who was nowhere in sight.

"Your wife and Sofia are going to come to work at the stand this summer."

"Provided you agree," Ally said to him.

She felt his probing glance.

"You'd really like to sell flowers?"

"I'd love it. So would Sofia. She'll help me with my Italian."

"Leonora will be overjoyed," Maria assured her.

His arm hugged her a little tighter. "My wife lights her own fires. She's out of my sight for five minutes, and already we're a farming family."

"It's what you always wanted, Gino. I couldn't be happier for both of you."

"Thank you, Maria." He kissed her cheek. "Now if you don't mind, I'm going to whisk my bride away to a secret place."

He guided Ally toward the hallway.

"We'll slip out the side door of the kitchen," he murmured against her ear.

She swallowed hard. "What about Sofia?"

"Anna's parents are keeping her with them tonight."

"Does Sofia know that?"

"I told her before I came to find you."

"W-was she all right with it?"

"Of course. She's old enough to know a wedding couple needs time to themselves."

He swept her out the door to the courtyard where Paolo was waiting with the car.

"Where are we going?"

"The palazzo."

"I thought we couldn't leave the farm."

"Legally we're not supposed to. But Carlo Santi came to the reception with news that necessitates a visit there. Since it's our wedding night, he's taking the responsibility of vouching for us while we break the rules."

Now everything made sense. This was a charade for Gino's friends in order to perpetuate the pretense of the happily married couple going off on their honeymoon.

By the time they started to pull away from the courtyard, their guests had assembled to see them off.

Ally exchanged a soulful glance with Sofia who ran out in front of everyone who were taking pictures to wave. She was on the verge of tears.

"Gino—we can't leave Sofia behind. Look at her face."

"I've seen it, but she's better off with friends until we return."

Ally knew he was right, but it hurt to leave her when Ally knew his niece was suffering since overhearing Gino's talk with Carlo.

"We'll be in Montefalco shortly. When we start the climb up the road to the west gate, we'll lower our heads to avoid the paparazzi camped nearby. I'm phoning ahead to tell the guards to have the gate open for us. That way Paolo won't have to stop."

Ally waited until he'd used his cell phone before asking, "How long are you going to keep me in suspense about the case?"

He reached for her hand. His eyes flashed her a fiery glance. In the next few minutes he told her about the information uncovered by the P.I.'s in Sicily.

"One of the crew of the yacht has claimed that the great-aunt's grandson, Tomaso, has villas in Prague and Portofino. It seems he became friendly with Donata and your husband.

"It's possible he knows something about the accident, or even caused it. But without some sort of proof, it's the crewman's word against a wealthy member of the Castiglione family.

"In four months the authorities investigating this case haven't ever found evidence linking Donata and your husband. But you and I know the laptop exists. Which means Donata had to use some sort of computer on her end. "The fact that the authorities don't know of the correspondence between them plays to our advantage.

"Both Carlo and Alberto think she must have kept one at the palazzo, but it was hidden so well, the police never came across it.

"Naturally they went over Marcello's computer as part of the initial investigation, but nothing turned up.

"That's why I originally had my P.I.'s looking in all the coffee houses with computers in and around St. Mortiz, hoping to discover she'd used one of them. Unfortunately they never found anything."

Ally sucked in her breath. "Then let's tear the palazzo apart."

"That's the idea," Gino muttered. "Maybe we'll find it. If she had someone like Tomaso helping her, that information has to be somewhere. She couldn't have carried out everything without help from someone she thought she could trust.

"It's the kind of proof needed to take to the chief judge. It will force him to consider other suspects."

"We'll spend all night if we have to," she declared.

Not only could it mean Gino's freedom, but she'd be spared having to go to his room with him in order to fool the staff that the newlyweds couldn't wait to be alone.

She stared out the passenger window. They were near the town now. She checked her watch. It was only five in the afternoon. The sun wouldn't be setting for hours yet.

"Wouldn't it have been better to arrive in one of the estate cars with the smoked glass?"

Gino shook his head. "That's a dead giveaway. The paparazzi won't be expecting a car I use at the farm. It will buy us the time we need to make it inside the grounds."

A few minutes later Paolo muttered that they'd better get down.

Gino reached for Ally and pulled her over so the top portion of her body lay against his hard thighs.

When she was settled, he leaned over her where she could feel his heart pounding against her back.

"Am I crushing you, Ally?"

"No. I'm fine."

"I knew my beautiful bride would say that," he whispered.

"Hold on. The car's picking up speed. You won't have to suffer much longer."

That depended on the kind of suffering he was referring to. She had a lifetime of it ahead of her, but it would remain a secret between her and Sofia.

Suddenly the car came to a stop. Paolo gave the all clear.

Gino kissed Ally's brow as she raised up. "By now you have to know I'd rather be with you than anyone else in a situation like this."

She knew...

He came around to her side and opened the door. "Let's go in and get busy."

The palazzo was an eighteenth century palace so fabulous in its architectural beauty as well as its furnishings, Ally followed Gino around in awe.

He introduced her to the staff who congratulated them on their marriage. She could tell they held Gino in the greatest affection.

"We'll go to my apartment first and change."

"I don't have any of my clothes with me."

"You can wear something of mine."

He led her up marble stairs and through marble hallways to his apartment on the second floor. It was a fabulous home within a home where he could be totally self-contained.

Ally had thought his farmhouse was out of this world. But this kind of splendor left her speechless.

He pulled a pair of clean navy sweats from one of the drawers and handed them to her.

"Go ahead and use the bathroom while I change in here. Then we'll get started in Donata's dayroom where she spent a lot of time."

Once inside the large, modernized bathroom, Ally took off her wedding outfit and hung it on the door hook.

After removing her high heels, she put on Gino's clothes. They pretty well drowned her, but it was all right because she rolled up the sleeves. The elastic at the bottom of the legs kept her from tripping.

She padded back in the suite in her nylons.

He'd put on a pair of gray sweats. When he saw her he grinned.

"We look like a pair of athletes ready for a run."

Her mouth curved in a half smile. "I'm glad we'll be doing it inside here, or my poor feet couldn't take it."

His gaze traveled down her curvaceous body. "New shoes are the price of looking gorgeous on your wedding day."

"It was a wonderful day, Gino. Thank you for everything. Now let's see what we can find."

A half hour later they'd searched every square inch of the elegant dayroom on the main floor without success. Lines darkened his features. She hated to see him like that.

"I've been thinking. If I were Donata and wanted to hide something, I think I would have put it in Sofia's room."

His jaw hardened. "The police searched it thoroughly."

"But they weren't necessarily looking for a computer of some kind."

"You're right."

"Of course there's always the possibility she didn't own one, but had access through a friend."

"We'll take one last look anyway," Gino murmured.

Sofia's bedroom was across the hall from Marcello and Donata's apartment at the other end of the second floor.

"If Donata wanted to send messages, it would have been easy enough for her to slip across the hall when Sofia was at a friend's house or at school,' he said before ushering her inside his niece's room.

Ally felt like she'd entered the domain of a princess.

Her glance fell on the floor to ceiling bookcase with all kinds of books, puzzles and games.

"A laptop isn't so easily disguised, Gino. My guess is, if Donata had one, she camouflaged it in some way."

Gino shot her a piercing regard. "You're a woman with amazing instincts. Where would *you* hide it, Ally?"

She examined everything in sight.

"What's in that chest at the foot of Sofia's bed?"

"It has a lot of her toys in it. When Donata wanted to get rid of them, Marcello insisted on keeping them in case they ever had another baby."

She walked over to it. "The police probably did a cursory search, but toy boxes are notorious for holding treasures you never expect to find."

Ally opened the lid. It was a deep rectangular piece of furniture.

Gino got down on his haunches next to her and they began sifting through the jumble of items. When her hands came in contact with something about the right size, Ally let out a little cry of excitement.

But she soon groaned at the sight of a play typewriter in a plastic case.

"I was so sure—"

Gino went back to searching. She dug in at the other end and found a doctor's kit. Gino produced a makeup kit.

Starting to lose hope, she felt around the bottom. Her fingers came in contact with what she presumed was a radio in a leather case. Out of curiosity, she opened it.

A gasp came out of her. "Gino—this looks like a palm pilot! Do you think it's real?"

He took it from her and pressed the on button.

"It's real all right," his voice grated. "State-of-the-art four gig drive. Ally—" He crushed her against him. "You found it!"

She pulled away from him, unable to take much more of their physical contact.

"Get inside it quick!" she cried.

He helped her up from the floor. By tacit agreement they sat down on the side of Sofia's canopy bed.

The next five minutes felt like five hours as Gino started retrieving messages. Suddenly his tall, powerful body sprang from the bed.

"This says it all, Ally. Tomaso was the one to arrange for the car from a garage in St. Moritz. It names the place and the mechanic who let Donata buy the used car off him. Everything's there. The plan for them to drive to Portofino and board the yacht on January 25.

"Ally—" His eyes blazed with light. "Come on."

He grasped her hand. "We'll go to Marcello's study and phone our attorney."

Ally's gaze swerved to his. "If Signore Toscano needs an affidavit from Troy, I know he'll cooperate. It will prove the connection beyond any doubt."

Gino nodded. "You cracked the case wide-open, Ally. What would I have done if you hadn't come to Italy with your husband's laptop?"

Ally was euphoric to realize the horrible nightmare would soon be over. Whoever had tampered with those brakes, it wasn't Gino!

But because Ally had flown to Italy, Gino was now a married man, tied for life to a woman he would always consider his best friend.

But she couldn't imagine a virile man like him remaining celibate for that long. There was only one thing to do. She would talk to him about it after they'd returned to the farmhouse.

CHAPTER TEN

Gino got out of the car and hurried into the farmhouse.

"Ally?"

Bianca came rushing into the foyer. "She's doing errands in the truck."

He frowned. "Is Sofia with her?"

"No. She got home a little while ago and is upstairs with her father."

Gino could scarcely contain his disappointment. Not with the news he had to tell her. He'd asked Ally to be here when he got home.

Last night Alberto had told Gino to come to Rome and they'd work all night to present their case before the chief judge. Carlo had gone with him.

It was decided Paolo would drive Ally back to the farmhouse. Gino had assured her they'd celebrate today. He'd been living for it and couldn't imagine where she'd gone. But Sofia would know.

He took the steps three at a time and hurried toward Marcello's suite.

The last thing he expected to find was his niece sobbing her heart out on her father's lap.

"Sofia?" he called to her.

She lifted her head. "Hello, Uncle Gino."

Normally she came running to him.

"What's wrong, sweetheart?"

"Nothing," she answered in a dull voice.

Gino's eyes met Luigi's. The nurse shrugged his shoulders, indicating he didn't know the reason for her tears.

"Let's go in your room and have a talk."

"I'd rather not."

He felt like someone had just kicked him in the gut.

"If something happened at Anna's house, I need to know about it."

"This isn't about Anna."

"Are you upset with me for asking you to spend the night at her house?"

"No." She wiped her eyes.

"Did you and Ally have words?" He couldn't fathom it, but he had to know the truth.

"No. I love her. She said I could call her Mama."

Though those words thrilled him, he still didn't have his answer.

"Then there's something I've done to hurt you. If I did, you know I didn't mean to."

"I know."

"Then I *have* hurt you. If you don't tell me what I've done, then I don't know how to fix it."

"You can't fix it." She sounded like a woman three times her age.

He'd never seen Sofia behave like this before. His body broke out in a cold sweat.

"Why do you say that?"

"Because it's true."

"Then I've failed you, Sofia, and that devastates me."

He left the room and went upstairs. How could the joy of this day be trumped by the pain he was feeling now?

The fact that Ally wasn't here caused him to wonder if she'd left on purpose so he and Sofia could be alone to sort things out.

Was it possible his niece had learned the truth about her mother, and believed Gino was guilty of driving Donata away? The very thought made him so ill, he staggered over to his bed, wondering how in the hell to help Sofia if he was right.

He could provide the proof that he wasn't the culprit. But he couldn't do anything about Sofia's deep seated sorrow where her mother was concerned. If she knew it was Ally's husband who'd died with her, Sofia would feel so betrayed, she'd never get over it.

Ally—where are you?

In his agony, he heard a rap on the door and raced across the room to fling it open and embrace his wife.

It was his niece.

"Sofia—"

"Can I come in?"

"What do you think?"

He could thank God she was at least speaking to him.

"Ally told me not to blame you because you couldn't help it."

"Blame me for what, sweetheart?"

She stared at him for the longest time. "I heard you talking to Signore Santi in Papa's room during the reception."

Gino replayed their conversation in his mind.

"What exactly did you hear?"

"He said something about you not having to get married after all. And you said—you said you wished you hadn't gotten married, but it was the only thing you could do at the time."

Gino had been holding his breath. "And from that you deduced that I don't love Ally. Is that it?"

She nodded slowly.

"Did you tell Ally what you overheard?"

"I had to. She caught me in the hall and wanted to know what was wrong."

He closed his eyes. With those words he'd gone from joy to a new depth of despair in a matter of seconds.

"Are you angry at me?"

"No, sweetheart. But just so you know, I fell in love with Ally the moment I met her. In fact I loved her so much that when I heard she was only going to stay in Italy for one more day, I had to do something to keep her here."

"You mean like asking her to be my violin teacher?"

Gino smiled at her. "Exactly. In my fear of losing her at the end of the month, I'm afraid I rushed her into marriage before she was ready. As you know, she lost her husband a while ago and it would be understandable if she still had feelings for him. But I didn't want to wait for her to be my wife.

"I know I should have given her more time, but when you love someone as much as I love her, you're not thinking clearly.

"That's what I was telling Carlo when you happened to overhear us talking. He didn't know how I felt about Ally. All he knew was that I'd asked her to marry me because he thought I wanted you to have a mother.

"Sofia—do you know where she is?"

His niece studied him with those intelligent brown eyes of hers. "No, but you've got to find her, Uncle Gino!"

"Don't worry. I won't come back without her."

He flew out the door and down the hall to the stairs.

He almost had a heart attack when he discovered Ally coming up the stairs from the foyer.

She was composed as he'd ever seen her. Too composed.

"I was hoping you'd be here when I got back from Remo," she spoke before he could. "Tell me what I need to hear."

He knew what she was asking, but he wanted her to mean something else entirely different.

"All charges have been dropped against me. We're free, Ally."

"Thank heaven," she cried with her heart in her throat.

"It's all because of you. Now we can leave on our trip to Ischia."

"Sofia will be overjoyed."

He took another step towards her. "What about you?"

"You know I've been looking forward to it, but before we do anything, I need to talk to you."

His heart skipped several beats. "Then let's go to your room. It's closest."

He sensed her hesitation before she nodded.

Ally entered the room first and waited for him to shut the door.

"I hoped, but didn't dare to dream you'd be freed from suspicion this fast." He could tell she was breathing hard. "With this news, we can now discuss something that has been on my mind for a while."

Adrenaline riddled his body. "If it's about our marriage, you're my wife now and that's the way things are going to stay."

She eyed him with a calm that unnerved him.

"I want to stay married to you, too, Gino, but I just wanted you to know that you're free to live the way you did before we were married."

"I'm not sure I understand. I'm afraid you're going to have to spell that out for me."

She heaved a sigh. "If there's a woman you want to be with from time to time, I'll understand."

"You're talking about an open marriage?"

She averted her eyes. "Yes."

"Does that go for you, too?"

She paled. "Of course not. I plan to stay true to my wedding vows."

"But it's all right if I break mine, is that it?"

"As long as you're discreet, the eyes of the world will continue to view us as a married couple."

"So we are..."

She lifted a tremulous gaze to him once more. "I want your happiness, Gino."

"We went over all this before we got married. We agreed to stay married no matter what."

"But a lifetime is too long for a man like you who can finally stop worrying about everyone else's needs and concentrate on your own for a change.

"I have no doubts there's a remarkable, marvelous woman out there somewhere waiting to meet a man like you. If and when that time comes, you can tell her the truth about us. If you decide to act on that love, you can do it knowing we had this conversation. You're an honorable man, Gino, but you'll be carrying it too far if you have to deny yourself a full life. I can't let our marriage stand in the way of your true happiness."

His hands formed fists. "Did you make this decision before you left the palazzo? Or after Sofia admitted eavesdropping on my conversation with Carlo?"

She didn't break eye contact with him. "Before."

She was lying, just the way she'd lied to him at the jail when she'd made that ridiculous confession in order to be set free. The fact was, she didn't have a dishonest bone in her body.

"What if I told you I want you in my bed."

"That doesn't surprise me."

Her answer stunned him.

"A man can sleep with his wife and the woman he really loves without much problem."

"Your husband did a lot of damage, but don't judge every man by his behavior."

"I'm not talking about Jim."

"I think you are," he challenged her. "That's what I've been afraid of since I made up my mind I was going to marry you whether you were ready or not."

"Ready?"

He shifted his weight. "I know the kind of woman you are, Ally. You would never have married Jim if you hadn't been in love with him.

"You think I don't know that what he did has scarred you? But I was willing to take the chance that I could get you to love me like that one day.

"The only trouble is, in forcing marriage, I may have acted too soon. That's what I was telling Carlo, that I should have given you more time to get used to me.

"Unfortunately Sofia only heard the first part. If she'd stayed to hear the rest, she would know I fell hopelessly in love with you the night we met. I couldn't imagine life without you, so despite the risks, I got you to marry me first, and planned to spend the rest of my life finding ways to make you fall in love with me.

"When I repeated my vows before God, I meant every word of them, Ally. I love you more than my own life. If I can't get you to love me back, then I'd still rather live with you than anyone else. Do you understand what I'm saying?"

Her lovely body quivered in response. It defeated him more than any words she might have spoken.

"I've been a fool to hope for a miracle," his voice grated. He started for the door, needing to get out of there.

"Don't leave, darling," she called to him. But she said it in Italian, not English.

In the next minute he was treated to words in his native tongue he never expected to hear pour from her lips and heart. When he turned in her direction, she came running toward him.

"I love you, Gino Di Montefalco." She threw her arms around his neck. "I love you more than I thought it was possible to love a man."

She covered his face and hair with kisses. "When I met Jim, I fell in love, but it didn't take long to realize he didn't have the substance I'd endowed him with. Somewhere along the way my love died. Maybe he sensed it before he ever met Donata. I'll never know the answer to that, but I do know that the night I met you changed my entire life."

She cupped his face in her hands, staring up at him with adoring green eyes.

"Do you honestly think I would have agreed to marry you if I hadn't wanted it with all my heart and soul?

"Oh, Gino— Love me, darling. It seems like a century that I've been waiting for you."

* * *

Ally waited impatiently for her husband to wake up.

The sun had risen above the horizon. The birds were singing. The marvelous scent of lavender filtered through the open window of her room.

She lay facing him with their legs entwined.

They'd never made it up the stairs to his suite. In their desperate desire to love each other, they'd never come out of her room.

She knew he needed sleep. After being up all night while he'd been in Rome, only to spend all of last night making love to her, he deserved his rest.

But she was so on fire for him, it was impossible not to touch him.

He had silky black lashes she loved to feel against her cheek. Even in sleep his mouth had a sensuous curve that turned her blood molten.

He held her possessively. If she tried to move, she would waken him. Part of her was tempted. Maybe just one little kiss wouldn't hurt.

The second she pressed her mouth to his, he responded with breathtaking urgency. Then his eyes opened and she saw the flame of desire burning in their black depths.

"Buon giorno, bellissima," he said deep in his throat.

"Buon giorno, Apollo mio."

"Apollo?" he questioned, pulling her on top of him.

When she explained what she meant, he laughed triumphantly. When he did that, she thought she'd die with love for him.

He sobered for a moment. "I wish I'd met you when you were eighteen."

"Why eighteen?" she teased, tracing the line of his male mouth with her fingertip.

"You would have been old enough for me to carry you off without fear of the law coming after me."

She buried her face in his neck. "I know how you feel. So many years have already gone by. How is it you never married? You've never really told me."

He wrapped her closer in his arms. "I was waiting for you."

"Be serious, my love."

"I'm deadly serious," he came back with that hint of steel in his voice.

"In my teens and early twenties, I enjoyed women as much as the next man and didn't feel the need to settle down yet.

"After Marcello married Donata and I saw the way it was going, I thanked providence I was still a free man. That is until I met you.

"Your physical beauty attracted me immediately. Couple that with your defiance and your loyalty to my brother, a man you'd never even met, and I knew I'd met my soul mate. The trick was to get you to feel the same way about me."

She kissed him with passion, no longer afraid to express her love.

When he finally let her up for air she said, "No trick was needed. The moment I emerged from the door of the *pensione* and saw you standing there like some proud, fierce Italian prince, I felt my whole soul quake."

He chuckled before giving her a long, hard kiss she felt to her toenails. "I like the way you talk, Signora Di Montefalco. The sun god and an Italian prince. What about just plain old Gino the farmer?"

She searched his eyes. "You're so many things, there aren't enough adjectives in the world to describe you."

So saying, she switched to Italian and told him she loved him.

She heard his sharp intake of breath. "Who taught you so well, you don't sound like a foreigner."

She kissed his eyelids. "My new daughter."

"Sofia's a little monkey. She held that bit of information back from me."

"I asked her to keep it a secret."

Gino suddenly moved so she was lying on her back. He stared down at her with fire in his eyes.

"Speaking of our niece, I think it's time we concentrated on producing a male heir just to keep the balance."

Ally smiled up at him. "If it's a girl we'll call her Gina and just keep trying until we get our own little Marcello."

Gino's eyes went suspiciously bright before his mouth fell on hers. She responded with the hunger of a woman who loved her husband beyond all else.

EPILOGUE

"Can we swim a little longer, Mama?"

Ally checked her watch. "Ten more minutes. Then I need to get back to the house to feed the baby."

Two months had gone by since their precious Marcello had entered the world. Now Ally was determined to get her figure back. At this point she was within five pounds of her goal, but it was hard with Bianca's cooking always tempting her to eat more.

Gino had offered to come home at lunch to tend the baby. Father and son needed some playtime together.

If ever a man was made for fatherhood, it was her husband.

Little Marcello, who looked like his namesake, had already twisted his father around his baby finger.

The farmhouse was such a happy place, Ally felt like she was living in paradise.

When Gino had put it to a vote, no one wanted to live at the palazzo.

It would remain in the family until Sofia decided what to do with it.

The weather was already warm for the first of June. It

was hard to believe that a year ago this month she'd come to Montefalco where Gino and a new thrilling life awaited her.

With Tomaso Castiglione behind bars for his crime, the horrific trauma of the past was over. Best of all, Sofia had been spared the details.

Feeling alive and glowing, Ally got out of the river and threw on a lightweight robe over her bikini.

Sofia's naturally curly hair was cut short these days. It only needed a brisk toweling to look perfect.

In the last year she'd grown into a young teen who was starting to resemble Donata more and more.

Sofia kept pictures of her mother in her room. Donata had been a beauty all right, and her daughter was following in her footsteps.

The two of them got in the truck and headed for home. With Sofia being such an excellent tutor, they talked mainly in Italian.

It made a huge difference when Ally helped out at the flower stand. Of course it would take years to talk and sound like Gino, but that was her goal.

She loved the language and the country. She loved his family. She adored *him*.

Hoping he would be able to stay while she nursed the baby, she drove faster than usual.

"Look, Mama—there's a taxi driving away from the house."

"You're right!"

Ally couldn't imagine who'd dropped by. She slowed to a stop and parked the truck around the side, hoping their visitor wouldn't be able to see her looking like this.

They hurried into the kitchen, then stopped. Ally's mother sat at the table next to Gino, feeding the baby his bottle. Her husband trapped Ally's gaze with a silent message before she cried, "Mom—"

Her mother's dark blond head lifted. She wore a smile that transformed her.

"Oh, honey— I shouldn't have waited so long to come. My little grandson's adorable."

Though Ally had invited her mother to come many times, she'd never taken her up on it. But with a new baby in the house...

Ally's eyes filled. "He and Sofia are the light of our lives. Mom? I'd like you to meet my daughter, Sofia."

"Come around here, honey," her mother said to Gino's niece. "I need to get to know both my grandchildren."

"Just a minute, Grandma. I've got to get something for you."

"For me?"

"Yes. I made it last summer and have been saving it for you. I'll be right back."

Ally had an idea where she was going. Taking advantage of the time, she hurried around the table and hugged her mom and the baby.

Her mother studied her. "You look wonderful, honey. Obviously marriage to this man agrees with you."

With those words her mother had let her know she'd put the past behind her and was ready to move on.

"He's the most wonderful thing that ever happened to me." Her voice shook with emotion.

Gino pulled her onto his lap.

"Careful, darling, I'm wet after just getting out of the river."

"I like you exactly like this," he whispered, kissing the side of her neck.

Sofia came back in the kitchen and walked around to Ally's mother. She carried a sheaf of dried flowers wrapped in cellophane and tied with ribbon.

"Lavender—" she cried. "Just the way my mother used to preserve it for gifts."

Tears welled in her gray eyes.

Ally took the baby so her mother could hug Sofia. "Thank you, honey. This is a priceless gift."

"Mama taught me how to do it. I have my own little sticker on it. See?"

Ally's mother looked closer. "Sofia's Scents. That's brilliant." She kissed her cheeks.

"Oh, Ally—" She turned to her. "I begged Edna to fly over with me, but she said I should come alone the first time."

"There'll be other times, Mom."

Gino hugged her tighter around the waist, baby and all. At least he could reach around her now. The thought gave Ally no end of satisfaction.

"We're hoping you'll move here permanently," Gino said to her mother. "You and your sister can have the run of the palazzo if you'd like."

"I'd love it if you and Aunt Edna lived here, Mom. I've missed you so much. You're the children's only grandparents. You'd be so proud of Sofia."

She turned to Sofia. "Darling? Go get your instrument and play something for Grandma."

"Okay." She ran out of the kitchen.

"My wife's been teaching her the violin. I understand I have you to thank for Ally blessing this house with music."

Her mother was genuinely overcome. "What a beautiful thing to say."

Soon Sofia returned and played several pieces that showed she was no beginner.

When she'd finished, Ally's mother got out of the chair to hug her. "If you keep this up, you're going to be able to play like Ally."

"I hope so."

"Is there a piano in the house?"

Sofia nodded. "In the living room."

"Then let's take a look at your music and I'll accompany you."

Ally got to her feet. "While you do that, I'll put the baby back to bed and get changed."

Gino kept his arm around her shoulders as they climbed the stairs.

By the time she'd put the baby in his crib, the strains of Mendelssohn reached the third floor.

Gino had the shower ready and waiting for her.

She stepped under the spray, waiting for him to shut the door, but he kept it open and simply watched her.

No matter how intimate they'd been, she still blushed.

"You're more gorgeous than ever. I never want to go to work."

"I never want you to go."

"I'm glad your mother finally came."

"So am I."

"This house feels normal, the way my parents' once did."

"Mine never felt quite normal because Mom was so unhappy." She reached for the towel he kept just out of reach.

"Gino—" she begged.

He finally relented and wrapped it around her.

"I didn't see any shadows in her eyes just now."

"Neither did I."

"The two of them are going strong downstairs, and our son is asleep."

"The answer is yes," Ally cried, so out of breath with longing, it was embarrassing.

He picked her up in his arms and carried her to the bed.

"This is what heaven is all about," he whispered against her lips moments later. "When Marcello was diagnosed, I didn't think I'd ever be happy again."

His fingers tightened in her damp curls. "You came into my life when I least expected it."

"You'll never know how happy I was when you showed up on the train and whisked me away to the farmhouse."

"Carlo had ordered me to make you go back to the States, but I couldn't allow you to do that." He devoured her mouth once more. "I couldn't stay away from you, *bellissima.*"

"I hoped that was the reason," she whispered shakily.

"Now no more talk or your mother will think we're inconsiderate hosts."

"She knows what we're doing, Gino darling. I'm pretty sure she wants to make up for lost time, so let's give her her wish. Maybe I can grant you your wish at the same time."

"I have everything I want," he asserted.

She smiled at him. "Not everything. I was thinking we could work on another bambino to keep Marcello company and help you on the farm."

His eyes gleamed. "I believe in that kind of work. I'll give you fair warning. I'm prepared to work day and night, plus overtime."

"I think I'll put that in writing," she teased.

"You won't have to, Ally. I'll always come running home to you. Don't you know that yet?"

Oh, yes. She knew. And for the rest of their lives, she'd be waiting...

* * * * *

Australian author **Jennie Adams** grew up in a rambling farmhouse surrounded by books, and by people who loved reading them. She decided at a young age to be a writer, but it took many years and a lot of scenic detours before she sat down to pen her first romance novel. Jennie has worked in a number of careers and voluntary positions, including transcription typist and pre-school assistant. She is the proud mother of three fabulous adult children, and makes her home in a small inland city in New South Wales. In her leisure time Jennie loves long, rambling walks, discovering new music, starting knitting projects that she rarely finishes, chatting with friends, trips to the movies, and new dining experiences.

Jennie loves to hear from her readers, and can be contacted via her website at www.jennieadams.net

Invitation To The Prince's Palace

Jennie Adams

For Kara

CHAPTER ONE

'YOU'RE HERE. I expected to have to wait longer.' Melanie Watson tried not to sound too desperately relieved to see the cab driver, but she *was* relieved. She'd been saving money to try to start a new life away from her aunt, uncle and cousin. She still didn't have enough, but tonight she'd experienced very clearly just how soul-destroying it truly could be to live among people who postured rather than accepted, who used rather than loved.

The family's gloves had come off and Mel had made the choice to leave now whether she was quite financially ready, or not.

Mel had waited until her cousin had disappeared into her suite of rooms, and until her aunt and uncle had fallen into bed. She'd cleaned up every speck of the kitchen because she never left a job half done, and then she'd ordered a cab, left a note in her room, packed her life into suitcases and carried it to the kerb.

Mel tried to focus her gaze on a suburb painted in shades of silvery dawn. The sun would rise fully soon. The wispy chill would lift. Clarity and the new day would come and things would look better. If she could only stay awake and alert for that long.

She really felt quite odd right now, off kilter with an unpleasant buzzing in her head. She didn't exactly feel she might be about to faint, but...she didn't feel right, that was for sure.

'It's a nice time for a drive. It'll be really quiet and peaceful.' That sounded hopeful, didn't it? At least a little bit positive and not overly blurry?

With the kind of anonymity born of speaking to a total stranger, Mel confided, 'I'm a bit under the weather. I had an allergic reaction earlier and I didn't get to take anything for it until just now. The medication is having a lot stronger impact on me than I thought it would.'

She'd got the treatment from her cousin's stash while Nicolette had seen off the last of the wealthy guests. Maybe Mel shouldn't have helped herself that way, but she'd been desperate.

Mel drew a breath and tried for a chirpy tone that emerged with an edge of exhaustion. 'But I'm ready to leave. Melbourne airport here we come.'

'I arrived earlier than anticipated so I'm grateful that you are ready.'

She thought he might have murmured, 'Grateful and somewhat surprised' before he went on.

'And I'm pleased to hear your enthusiasm despite the problem of allergies. Might I ask what caused them?' The taxi driver's brows lifted as though he didn't quite know what to make of her.

Fair enough. *Mel* didn't know what to make of herself right now. She'd fulfilled her obligations, had pulled off all the beautiful desserts and other food for the dinner party despite harassment from her relatives and cleaned up afterwards when the party had finally ended.

Now she really needed her wits about her to leave, and they weren't co-operating. Instead, they wanted to fall asleep standing up. Like a tram commuter after a big day's work, or a girl who'd taken a maximum dose allergy pill on top of a night of no sleep and wheezing and swallowing back sneezes and getting a puffy face and puffy eyes.

'My cousin bought a new perfume. She sprayed it near me and off I went. Apparently I'm allergic to gardenias.' Mel dug for the remnants of her sense of humour. She knew it was still in there somewhere! 'Just don't give me any big bunches of those and I'm sure we'll be fine.'

'I will see to that. And you are right. It is a good time for a drive. The Melbourne cityscape is charming, even in pre-dawn light.' His words seemed so serious, and his gaze focused on her eyes, then on the spot where the dimple had come and gone in her cheek as she made her small joke. Would the dimple have offset her red nose and puffy face? Somehow Mel doubted it.

Mel focused on him, too. It was difficult not to because the man was top-to-toe gorgeous. Tall, a little over six feet to her five feet four and beautifully lean. Mel blinked to try to clear her drowsy vision.

He'd spoken in that lovely accent, too. French? No, but something European, Mel thought, to go with his tanned skin and black hair and the almost regal way he carried himself. He had lovely shoulders, just broad enough that a woman could run her hands over them to appreciate their beauty, or lay her head to rest there and know she could feel secure.

He wore an understated, expensive-looking suit. That was

a bit unusual for a cab service, wasn't it? And his eyes—they weren't hazel or brown but a glorious deep blue.

'I just want to curl up.' Maybe that explained her reaction to him because his broad shoulders looked more appealing by the moment.

'Perhaps we'd better get your luggage loaded first, Nicol—' The rest of the word was drowned by the double beep of a car's unlocking device. He reached for the first two suitcases.

She must have given her full name of Nicole Melanie Watson when she booked the taxi. Since going to live with her aunt and uncle at age eight, Mel had only been known by her middle name. It felt strange to hear the first one again. Strange and a little shivery, because, even hearing only part of the word, his accent and the beautiful cadence of his voice made it sound special.

Oh, Mel. For goodness' sake.

'It's a pretty set of luggage. I like the floral design.' Was *Mel* making sense? She'd rescued the luggage when her cousin Nicolette had wanted to throw it out, but of course this man didn't need to hear that. And *she* didn't need to be quite so aware of him, either!

'You wouldn't lose the luggage easily. The design is quite distinctive.' He cast her a sideways glance. 'You are quite decided about this?'

'I'm decided.' Had he had people try to scam him out of fares? Mel would never do that. She knew what it was like to try to live on a tight budget. Her aunt and uncle might be well off, but they'd never seen the need to do more than meet the basic costs of taking her in. Once she reached working age, they'd expected her to return their investment by providing cheap kitchen labour. For the sake of her emotional health, Mel had to consider any debt paid now. 'I won't change my mind.'

She glanced to where he'd parked and saw, rather than a taxicab, an unmarked car. The cab agency had said there was a shortage of cabs but she hadn't realised someone might come for her in their private car in their off-duty time. Wouldn't that be against company policy?

And the car was a really posh one, all sleek dark lines and perfectly polished. That didn't seem right for a cab driver, did it? How would he afford it? Mel frowned.

'Did you come straight from a formal dinner or something?' It must have been a really late night.

The words slipped out before she could censor them. The thought that followed worried her a little, but he'd have had sleep wouldn't he? He looked rested.

You'll be perfectly safe with him, Mel. It won't be like—

She cut the thought off. That was a whole other cause of pain for Mel, and she didn't want to let it in. The night had been tough enough.

'Most dinners I attend are formal unless I have a night with my brothers.' Rikardo spoke decisively and yet...his guest didn't look as he'd expected. She didn't...*seem* as he'd expected. Her openness and almost a sense of naivety...must be because she wasn't feeling well.

He tucked the odd thoughts away, and tucked his passenger into the front seat beside his. 'You may rest, if you wish. Perhaps by the time we arrive at the airport your allergy medication will have done its job and you'll be back to normal.'

'I doubt that. I feel as though I've been felled by elephant medicine.' She yawned again. 'Excuse me. I can't seem to stop.'

* * *

He'd collected a drowsy and puffy version of Sleeping Beauty. That was what Prince Rikardo Eduard Ettonbierre thought as the airport formalities ended and he carried Nicolette Watson onto the royal private jet and lowered her into a seat.

She'd slept most of the way to the airport and right through the boarding process. The medication had indeed got the better of her, but she was still very definitely...a sleeping beauty.

Despite the puffy face she seemed to have held her age well since the days when she'd been part of his university crowd during his time in Australia. She'd been two years behind him, but he'd known even then that Nicolette wanted to climb to the heights of social success.

Though their paths had not crossed since those days, Nicolette had made it a point to send Christmas cards, mark his birthday, invite him as her personal guest to various events, and in other ways to keep her name in front of him. Rik had felt awkward about that pursuit. He didn't really know what to say now, to explain his lack of response to all those overtures.

Perhaps it was better to leave that alone and focus on what they were about to achieve. He'd carefully considered several women for this task. In the end he'd chosen to ask Nicolette. He'd known there would be no chance he would fall for her romantically, and because of her ambitious nature he'd been confident she would agree to the plan. She'd been the sensible choice.

Rik had been right about Nicolette. When he'd contacted her, she'd jumped at this opportunity to elevate her social status. And rather than someone closer by, who might continue to brush constantly through his social circles once this was all over, when their agreement ended, Rik could return Nicolette to Australia.

'You should have allowed me to carry her, Your Highness.' One of his bodyguards murmured the words not quite in chastisement, but in something close to it. 'Even driving a car by yourself to get her— You haven't given us sufficient information about this journey to allow us to properly provide for your safety.'

'There is nothing further to be revealed just at the moment, Fitz.' Rik would deal with the eruption of public and royal interest in due course but there was no need for that just yet. 'And you know I like to get behind the wheel any time I can. Besides, I let you follow in a second car and park less than a block away. Try not to worry.' Rik offered a slight smile. 'As for carrying her, wasn't it more important for you to have your hands free in case of an emergency?'

The man grimaced before he conceded. 'You are correct, Prince Rikardo.'

'I *am* correct occasionally.' Rik grinned and settled into his seat beside Nicolette.

Was he mad to enter into this kind of arrangement to outwit his father, the king? Rik had enjoyed his combination of hard work and fancy-free social life for the past ten years. As third in line to the throne, he'd seen no reason to change that state of affairs any time soon, if at all. But now...

There were deeper reasons than that for your reluctance. Your parents' marriage...

His bodyguard moved away, and Rik pushed that thought away, too. He wasn't crazy. He was taking action. On these thoughts Rik turned his attention to the sleeping woman. Her hair fell in a soft honey-blonde curtain. Though her face still showed the ravages of her allergy problem, her features were appealing.

Long thick brown eyelashes covered eyes that he knew were a warm brown colour. She had soft pink lips, a slim straight nose and pretty rounded cheeks. She looked younger in the flesh than in the photo she'd emailed, than Rik had thought she would look now...

She sighed and Rik had an unexpected urge to gently kiss her. It was a strange reaction to what was, in the end, a business arrangement with a woman he'd never have chosen to know more than peripherally if not for this. A response perhaps brought on because she seemed vulnerable right now. When she woke from this sleep she would be once again nothing but the ladder-climbing socialite he'd approached, and this momentary consciousness would be gone.

The pilot commenced take-off. Rik's guest stirred, fought for a moment to wake. Her hand rose to her cheek.

'You may sleep, Nicolette. Soon enough we will take the next step.' He said it in his native Braston tongue, and frowned again as the low words emerged. He rarely spoke in anything but French or English, unless to one of the older villagers or palace staff.

Nicolette turned her head into the seat. Her lashes stopped fluttering and she sighed. She'd cut her hair too, since the emailed photo she'd sent him. The shoulder-length cut went well with the flattering feminine skirt and silk top she wore with a short cardigan tied in a knot at her waist. The clothing would be nowhere near warm enough for their arrival in Braston, but that would be taken care of.

Rik made his chair comfortable, did the same for his sleeping guest, and took his rest while he could find it. When Nicolette sighed again in her sleep and her head came to rest on his shoulder, Rik shifted to make sure she was comfortable, inhaled the soft scent of a light, citrus perfume, and put down the feeling of contentment to knowing he was soon to take a step to get his country's economy back on its feet, and outwit his father, King Georgio, at the same time. Put like that, why wouldn't Rik feel content?

'You had an uneventful flight, I hope, Your Highness?'

'Not too much longer and we'll be able to disembark, Prince Rikardo.'

Mel woke to voices, snippets of conversation in English and another language and the low, lovely tones of her taxi driver responding regally while something soft and light and beautifully warm was draped around her shoulders.

'What—?' Heart pounding, she sat up abruptly.

This wasn't a commercial flight.

There were no rows of passengers, just some very well-dressed attendants who all seemed to make her taxi driver the centre of attention in a revering kind of way.

Mel's allergy was gone. The effects of the medication had worn off. That was good, but it also meant she couldn't be hallucinating right now.

She had vague memories of sleeping...on an accommodating shoulder.

Yet she didn't remember even boarding a flight!

This plane was luxurious. It had landed somewhere. Outside it was dark rather than the sunshiny day she'd looked forward to in Melbourne, and Mel could feel freezing air coming in through the aperture where another attendant waited for a set of steps to be wheeled to the edge of the plane.

She should be feeling Sydney summer air.

Memory of that expensive-looking car rose. Had she been

kidnapped? Tension coiled in her tummy. If anything was wrong, she'd left a note saying she was moving to Sydney. Her relatives might be angry to lose their underpaid cook, but she doubted that they would go looking for her. Not at the expense of their time or resources.

Breathe, Melanie. Pull yourself together and think about this.

The driver had asked her if she was 'sure about this'. As though they already had an arrangement? That would make it unlikely that she'd been kidnapped.

But they *didn't* have an arrangement!

Mel turned her head sharply, and looked straight into the stunning gaze of the man who'd placed her in that car.

She'd thought, earlier, that he was attractive. Now Mel realised he was also a man of presence and charisma. All those around him seemed to almost feel as though...they were his servants?

Words filtered through to Mel again. French words and, among those words, 'Prince Rikardo'.

They were addressing her driver as a prince?

That was easy, then, Mel thought a little hysterically. She'd fallen down a rabbit hole into some kind of alternative world. Any moment now she would sprout sparkling red shoes. *That's two different fairy tales, Mel. Actually it's a fairy tale and a classic movie.* Oh, as though that mattered! Yet in this moment, this particular rabbit hole felt all too real. And maybe there'd been a book first, anyway.

Stop it!

'You're fully refreshed? How are the allergies? You slept almost twenty-four hours. I hope the rest helped you.'

Did kidnappers sound calm, rational and solicitous?

Mel drew a breath, said shakily and with an edge of uncertainty she couldn't entirely hide, 'I feel a bit exhausted. The allergies are gone. I guess I slept them off while we travelled between Melbourne and...?'

'Braston.' He spoke the word with a slight dip of his head.

'Right. Yes. Braston.' A small country planted deep in the heart of Europe. Mel had heard of it. She didn't really know anything about it. She certainly shouldn't *be anywhere near it*. 'I'm just not quite sure— You see, I thought I'd be flying from Melbourne to Sydney—'

'We were able to fly very directly.' He leaned towards her and surprised her by taking her hand. 'You don't need to be nervous or concerned. Just stick to what we've agreed and let me do the talking around my father, the king.'

'K-king.' As in, a king who was the father of a prince? As in, this man, Rikardo, *was* a prince? A royal prince of Braston?

Stick with the issue at hand, Mel. Why are you here? That's the question you need answered.

'You are different somehow to what I have remembered.' His words were thoughtful.

'Remembered from our drive to the airport? I don't understand.' Her words should have emerged in a strong tone. Instead they were a nervous croak drowned by the clatter of a baggage trolley being wheeled closer to the plane.

Well, this was *not* the time for Mel to impersonate a scaredy frog waiting to be kissed into reassurance by a handsome prince.

Will you stop with the fairy-tale metaphors already, Melanie!

'You're nervous. I understand. I'll walk you through this process. Just rely on me, and it will be easy for both of us to honour our agreement.'

Mel drew a deep breath. 'Seriously, about this "agreement". There's been—'

'Your Highness, if you and your guest would please come this way.' An attendant waved them forward.

The prince, Rikardo, took Mel's elbow, tucked the wonderful warm wrap more snugly about her shoulders, and escorted her to the steps and down them onto the tarmac.

Icy wind whipped at Mel's hair and stung her face but, inside the wrap, she remained warm. Floodlights lit the small, private airstrip. A retinue of people waited just off the tarmac.

Mel had an overwhelming urge to turn around and climb back onto the plane. She might not be down a rabbit hole, but she was definitely Alice in Crazyland. None of this would have happened if she'd been completely herself when she ordered that ride to the airport and believed it had arrived. Mel would never take someone else's medication again, even if it were just an over-the-counter one that anyone could buy!

'Please. Prince...Your Highness...' As she spoke they moved further along the tarmac. 'There truly has been some kind of mistake.'

What could have happened? As Mel asked the silent question puzzle pieces started to come together.

If he'd called at the right address, then he had expected to collect a woman from there.

Her cousin had been in a strange mood, filled with secrecy and frenetic energy. At the end of the dinner party, Nicolette had rushed to her room and started rummaging around in there. Had Nicolette been...packing for a trip?

Rik had said he'd arrived earlier than he'd expected to. That would explain Nicolette not being ready. Mel had thought that he'd called her by her first name of Nicole, but it could have easily been 'Nicolette' that he said. She and her cousin looked heaps alike. Horror started to dawn. 'It must have been Nicolette—'

'Allow me to welcome you on to Braston soil, Nicolette.' Rikardo, *Prince Rikardo*, spoke at the same time. He stopped. 'Excuse me?'

Oh. My. God.

He'd mistaken Mel for Nicolette. Mel's *cousin* had made some kind of plan with this man. That meant Rikardo really was a prince. Of this country! As in, royalty who had made an arrangement with Nicolette.

Mel, the girl who'd worked in her aunt and uncle's kitchen for years, was standing here in a foreign country with an heir to the throne, when it was her cousin who should be here for whatever reasons she should be here. How could the prince not realise the mistake? Surely he'd have seen that Mel wasn't Nicolette, even in dawn light and with Mel affected by allergies? Just how well did this prince know Nicolette?

Yes, Mel? And how many times has Nicolette become furious when one of her acquaintances mistook you for her when they called at the house?

'Unless we're in the public eye, please just call me Rik.' He hustled her into the rear of another waiting car and climbed in beside her. A man in a dark suit climbed into the front, spoke a few words to the prince in French, and set the vehicle in motion.

The prince added, 'Or Rikardo.'

'You probably have five given names and are heir to a whole lot of different dukedoms or things like that.' Mel sucked up a breath. 'I do watch the news and see the royal families coming and going.' She just hadn't seen this particular royal. 'The most famous ones. What I mean is, I'm not an overt royal-watcher, but I'm also not completely uninformed.'

Which made her sound like some kind of overawed hick who wouldn't have a clue how to behave in such august company. Exactly what Mel was! 'Please...Prince...Rik...I need to speak to you. It's urgent!'

'We have arrived, Your Highness.' The words, spoken in careful English, came again from the driver.

He'd drawn the car to a whisper-quiet halt and now held the door open for them to alight. Rikardo would get out first, of course, because he was, after all, a prince.

A burst of something a little too close to hysteria rose inside Mel's breast.

'Thank you, Artor, and also for speaking in English for the benefit of our guest.' Rikardo helped Mel from the car. He glanced down into her face. 'I know you may be nervous but once we get inside I will take you to our suite of rooms and you can relax and not feel so pressured.'

'S-straight to the rooms? We won't see anyone?' Well, of course they would see people. They were seeing people right now. And what did he mean by *their* suite? 'Can we talk when we get there? Please!'

'Yes, we will talk. It shouldn't be necessary at this late stage, but we will discuss whatever is concerning you.' He seemed every inch the royal as he said this, and rather forbidding.

Mel's stomach sank even further. She hadn't meant for this to happen. She hadn't meant to do anything other than take a taxi to the airport. She had to hope it would be relatively easy to fix the mistake that had been made.

Rik whisked her up an awe-inspiring set of steps that led to a pair of equally stunning studded doors. As they approached the doors were thrown open, as though someone had been watching from within.

They would have been, wouldn't they? Mel glanced up, and up again, and still couldn't see the ending of the outside of this enormous palace. Parts of it were lit, other parts melted into the surrounding darkness. It looked as though it had been birthed here at the dawn of time. Mel shivered as the cold began to register, and then Prince Rik's hand was at her back to propel her the final steps forward and inside.

Voices welcomed their prince. Members of the royal retinue of staff stood to attention while others stepped forward to take the prince's coat, and Mel's wrap.

How silly to feel as though the small of her back physically held the imprint of the prince's fingers. Yet if he hadn't been supporting her Mel might have fainted from the combination of anxiety and feeling overwhelmed by the opulence.

The area they entered was large, reaching up three levels with ornate cornicing and inlaid life-sized portraits of royal family members fixed into the walls. A bronze statue stood to one side on a raised dais. Creams and gold and red filled the foyer with warm resplendence. It would be real gold worth more than an entire jewellery store.

'Welcome to the palace.' Rik leaned closer to speak quietly into Mel's ear.

'Thank you. That is...' Mel's breath caught in her throat as she became suddenly very aware of his closeness.

She'd laid her head on his shoulder, had slept the hours of the flight away inhaling the scent of his cologne. On some level of consciousness, Mel knew the pace of his breathing, knew how it felt to have him sleep with his ear tucked against the top of her head. The feel of the cloth of his suit coat against her arm, his body warmth reaching her through the fabric.

For a moment consciousness and subconscious memory,

nearness and scent and whatever else it was that had made her aware of him even initially through a fog of medication, filled Mel. She forgot the vital need to explain to him that he'd made a mistake and she had, too. She forgot everything but his nearness, and the uneven beat of her heart.

And then Prince Rikardo of Braston spoke again, softly, for her ears only.

'Thank you for agreeing to help me fulfil my father's demands and yet maintain my freedom…by temporarily marrying me.'

CHAPTER TWO

'THERE'S BEEN A terrible mistake.' Rik's bride-to-be paced the sitting room of his personal suite. Tension edged her words. One hand gestured. 'I don't belong here. I'm not the right girl. Look at all this, and I'm—'

'You won't be staying here all that long.' Not for ever. A few months... Rik tried to understand her unease. She'd been fully willing to enter into this arrangement. Why suffer a bout of cold feet about it now? She'd stepped into his suite, taken one glance around and had launched into speech.

'This is an interlude,' he said, 'nothing more.' And one they'd agreed upon, even if she hadn't yet signed the official contract. Rik's aide had the paperwork in a safe place, but it was ready and waiting, and Nicolette had made it clear that she was, too. So what had changed?

She drew a shuddery breath. 'This is gilt and gold and deep red velvet drapes and priceless original artworks and cornices in enormous entryways that take my breath away. This is more than a rabbit hole and a golden pumpkin coach and a few other fables meshed together. This is—' Her brown-eyed gaze locked with his and she said hotly as though it were the basis of evil: *'You're a prince!'*

'My royal status is no surprise to you.' What did surprise Rik was how attractive he found the sparkle in her eyes as indignation warred with guilt and concern on her lovely face. He'd never responded this way to Nicolette. He didn't want to now. This was a business arrangement. His lack of attraction to Nicolette was one of the reasons he'd chosen her. It would be easy to end their marriage and walk away.

So no more thoughts such as those about her, Rik!

'But it is a surprise. I mean, it wouldn't be if I'd already read about you in a magazine or something and I certainly completely believe you.' Shaking fingers tucked her hair behind her ear.

She didn't even sound like the woman he remembered. She sounded more concerned somehow, and almost a little naïve.

A frown started on his brow. He'd put down her openness, the blurting of a secret or two to him when he collected her, to the influence of the allergy medication. But that had worn off now. Suspicion, a sense of something not right, formed deep in his gut. He took a step towards her, studied her face more closely and wished he had taken more notice of Nicolette's features years ago. Those freckles on her nose—? 'Why do you seem different?'

'Because I'm not who you think I am,' she blurted, and drew a sharp breath. Silence reigned for a few seconds as she seemed to gather herself together and then she squared her shoulders. 'My full name is *Nicole Melanie* Watson.'

'Nicole...'

'Yes.' She rushed on. 'I'm known as Melanie and have been since I went to live with my aunt, uncle, and cousin *Nicolette* when I was eight years old. *Nicolette* would fit right in here. I've tried to figure this out since I woke up in your private jet and realised I wasn't at Sydney airport about to get off a plane there and go find a hostel to stay in while I searched for work because I could no longer stay—'

She broke off abruptly.

Sydney airport? Hostel? Search for work? There was something else about her statement, too, but Rik lost the thought as he focused on the most immediate concerns.

'I am not certain I understand you.' His tone as he delivered this statement was formal—his way of throwing up his guard. 'Are you trying to tell me—?'

'I think you meant to collect Nicolette and you got me by mistake. I don't see what else could have happened. When you said my name before, I thought you said Nicole, not Nicolette. I thought I must have given my full name when I ordered the taxi.'

'If what you say is correct...' Rik's eyes narrowed. Could this be true? That he'd collected the wrong woman? 'I haven't seen Nicolette for a number of years, just a photo sent over the Internet. I thought when I collected you that you'd changed and that you looked younger than expected. If you are not Nicolette at all—Do you look a great deal like your cousin?' He rapped out the words.

'Y-yes, at least a fair amount. And I sound like her. It really annoys her. Acquaintances do it all the time when they come to the house. Mistake us for each other, I mean.' The woman—Melanie—wrung her hands together. 'This is all just a horrible mix-up. I was zonked out on medication, and waiting at the kerb for my ride to the airport to start a whole new life and you took me instead of taking Nicolette, who probably should have been waiting but she's never on time for anything, and you said you were early.'

Horror came over her face. 'Nicolette will be *furious* at me when she finds out what's happened.'

'It is not up to your cousin to take out any negative feelings on you if a mistake has been made.' A thought occurred to him. 'While I thought you were your cousin, you...mistook me for a taxi service?'

'I didn't know then that you were a *prince*!'

Did his lips twitch? She sounded so horrified, and Rik had to admit the idea of being mistaken for a cab driver was rather unique. His amusement faded, however, as the seriousness of the problem returned to the forefront of his thoughts. He didn't notice the way his face eased into gentleness as he briefly touched her arm.

'I'm sure there'll be a solution to this problem.' He bent his thoughts to coming up with that solution. He had planned all this, worked everything out. And after a long flight to get to Australia from Braston...he'd collected a cousin he'd never heard of, who had no idea of his marriage plans, the bargain Rik had struck with his father, King Georgio, or the ways in which Rik intended to adhere to that bargain but very much on his terms.

If he couldn't straighten this all out, his error could cost him the whole plan, and that in turn could cost the people of Braston who truly needed help. Rik held himself substantially responsible for that need.

'It's kind of you not to want to blame me.' She spoke the words in a low, quiet tone and gazed almost with an edge of disbelief at him through a screen of thick dark lashes.

As though she didn't expect to be given a fair hearing, or she expected to be blamed for what had happened whether she was in the wrong or not.

'There's no reason to blame you, Nicol—*Melanie*.' For

some reason, Rik couldn't shift his gaze from the surprised and thoughtful expression in her eyes.

She looked as though she didn't quite feel safe here. Or did she always carry that edge of self-protectiveness, that air of not knowing if she was entirely welcomed and if she could let down her guard?

Rik had lived much of his life with his guard firmly in place. As a royal, that was a part of his life. But he knew who he was, where he fitted in the world. This young woman looked as though she should be happy and carefree. She had said she'd been about to start a new life. What had happened to make her come to that decision? To leave her family at dawn with all her suitcases packed?

Had Nicolette contributed to that sudden exit on Melanie's part?

You have other matters to sort out that are of more immediate concern.

Rik did, but he still felt protective of this young woman. She'd suddenly found herself on the other side of the world in a strange place. A little curiosity towards her was to be expected, too. He'd collected a stranger. Naturally he would want to understand just who this stranger was.

He would need her help and co-operation to resolve this problem, and she would need his reassurance. 'This doesn't have to be an insurmountable difficulty. If I can get you back out of the palace, keep you away from my father and create a suitable story to explain that bringing my fiancée home took two trips...'

'It seems such a strange thing to do in the first place, to marry someone for a brief period knowing you're going to end the marriage. Why do it at all if that's the case? How well do you know my cousin?' The words burst out of Mel as she watched Prince Rikardo come to terms with the problem of a girl who shouldn't be here, and one who should be and wasn't.

She felt overwrought and stressed out. What would happen to her plans now? Mel needed to be in Sydney looking for work. Not here suffering from a case of mistaken identity.

And then she realised that she'd just questioned a prince, and perhaps not all that nicely because she *did* feel worried and uneasy and just a little bit threatened and scared about the future. 'I beg your pardon. I didn't mean that to sound disrespectful. I guess I'm just looking for answers.'

'Your cousin is a past acquaintance from my university days in Australia who has kept in touch now and then remotely over the years since.'

So he didn't know Nicolette closely, had potentially never really known her. But he'd said he intended to marry her, albeit briefly. Mel's mind boggled at the potential reasons for that. Nicolette had hugged the secret close. Maybe she'd been told she had to? What was in it for Mel's cousin?

Well, even if it were to be a brief marriage, Nicolette would for ever be able to say she'd been a princess. Mel's cousin would love that. It would open even more doors socially to her. That left what was in it for Prince Rikardo?

'This must all seem quite strange to you, to suddenly find yourself here when you thought you were headed for Sydney, wasn't it?' His voice deepened. 'To start a new life?'

'I did say that, didn't I? When I thought you were a taxi driver and blabbed half my life story at you.' She drew a breath. 'I also meant no insult by thinking that you were a taxi driver.'

'None was taken.' He paused.

Did he notice that she dodged his question about starting a new life? Mel didn't want to go into that.

'Let me get the wheels in motion to start rectifying this situation,' he said. 'Then we'll discuss how this happened.'

For a blink of time as he spoke those words Mel saw pure royalty. Privileged, powerful. He would not only fix this problem, he would also have his answers. He'd said he didn't blame her, that it wasn't her fault. But Mel couldn't be as self-forgiving. She should have realised something was amiss. There'd been signs. An unmarked car; a driver not in uniform; even the fact that he'd tucked her in the front of the cab beside him rather than expecting her to get in the back. Of course he would demand his answers. Had she really thought she would get off without having to face that side of it?

Would she in turn learn more of why he'd chosen her cousin for this interaction? 'Yes, of course you'll need to set wheels in motion, to contact Nicolette and sort out how to get her here as quickly as possible. I'm more than willing to simply be sent to Sydney. You can put me on any flight, I don't mind. I don't need to see my cousin again.' She didn't *want* to see Nicolette again and be brought to account for all of this, and for choosing to leave the family without a moment's notice, because Mel *wouldn't* go back.

What did Prince Rikardo see in Nicolette?

He didn't have to see anything.

Or maybe he liked what little he knew of Mel's cousin and they could conduct this transaction between them and perhaps even become firm friends afterwards. Nicolette could be charming when it suited her. There'd been times over the years when she'd charmed Mel. Not lately, though.

Mel searched Rikardo's gaze once more. Though his mind must be racing, he didn't appear at all unnerved. How could he portray such an aura of strength? Did it come as part of his training in the royal family? An odd little shiver went down her spine and her breath caught. What would it be like, to be a prince such as Rikardo Ettonbierre? Or to be...truly in Nicolette's shoes, about to marry him, even if briefly?

Are you sure that his strength is simply a result of his position, his royal status, Melanie?

No. There was something in Rikardo Ettonbierre's make-up that would have demanded those answers regardless, and got them whether he'd ever been trained to his heritage, or not. That would have shown strength, not uncertainty, no matter what.

'We will make all the necessary arrangements. If we do it quickly—' Rikardo strode towards a phone handset on an ornate side table. He lifted the phone and spoke into it. 'Please ask my aide to attend me in my suite as soon as possible. I have some work for him to do. Thank you.' He had just replaced the receiver when a knock sounded on the door.

'That's too soon to be my aide,' he murmured. 'It will be our dinner. You must be hungry.'

The door opened. Members of staff entered bearing covered dishes. Aromas filled the room and made Mel realise just how long it had been since she'd eaten.

'The food smells delicious.' She'd always *cooked* the meals, not had them brought to her on silver salvers. 'I have to confess I *am* quite hungry.'

'That is good to hear.'

Rather than from Rikardo, the words came in a more mature yet equally commanding voice. The owner of that voice stepped into the room, a man in his early sixties with black hair greying at the temples, deep blue eyes and the power, by his presence alone, to strike dumb every staff member in the room.

Mel hadn't even needed that impact to identify him, nor the similarities to the prince. All she'd needed was one look at Rikardo's face, at the way it closed up into a careful mask that covered and protected every thought.

The king had just walked in.

This was the worst thing that could have happened right now. They'd needed to keep her, Melanie, out of sight of this man. Mel's breath froze in her throat and her gaze flew to Rik's. What did they do now? She caught a flash of a trapped look on Rikardo's face before he smoothed it away.

Somehow that glimpse of humanness opened up a wealth of fellow feeling in Mel. She had to help Rik out of this dilemma. She didn't even realise that she'd thought of him as Rik, not Rikardo.

The king's gaze fixed on her, examining, studying. He'd spoken to her. Sort of. Mel didn't know whether or not to respond.

'Indeed, Father, and it is fortuitous that you are here.' Rik stepped forward. He didn't block his father's view of Mel, but he drew the king's attention away from her. 'I would like a word with you regarding the truffle harvest, if you please.'

The older man's eyes narrowed. He frowned in his son's direction and said: 'It *pleases me* to know my future daughter-in-law will eat a meal rather than pretend a lack of appetite to try to maintain a waif-thin figure.'

Waif-thin figure?

Mel worked in a kitchen. She might have been underpaid, but she'd never been hungry. Was it usual for kings to speak their minds like this?

There was another problem, though. Even Mel, with her

lack of understanding of royal protocols, could guess that it wasn't appropriate for Rikardo not to introduce her to his father, even if the king had surprised them in Rik's suite.

Should she introduce herself? Why hadn't Rikardo done that?

Because you're not who you should be, Melanie. How is he supposed to introduce you without either telling the truth or lying? Neither option will work just at the moment.

And anyway, why don't you interview all the kings you're on a first-name basis with, and collate the responses to discover a mean average and then you'll know whether they all speak bluntly?

She wasn't thinking hysterically exactly, Mel told herself.

Just don't say anything. Well, not anything bad. Be really, really careful about what you say, or, better still, stay completely silent and hope that Rikardo takes care of this. Didn't he say earlier if you came across his father to let Rik do all the talking?

Yes, but that was before he realised Mel wasn't Nicolette. His father didn't know that, though, and now the king had spotted Melanie. Not only spotted her but spoken to her and had a really good look at her. And if she didn't respond soon, the king might think—

'Your Highness.' Mel sank into what she hoped was an acceptable style of curtsy. She tried not to catch the older man's gaze, and hoped that her voice might pass for Nicolette's next time.

Rikardo had mistaken Melanie for Nicolette. But she'd been puffed up with allergies then. Rikardo strode towards the door of his suite.

At the door, he turned to face Mel. 'If you will excuse us? Please go ahead and eat dinner.' He asked one of the kitchen staff to let his aide know they would speak after Rikardo finished with the king. From outside, Rikardo called in another member of staff. 'Please also show my guest her rooms.'

In about another minute, the king would be out of here. Mel could stop holding her breath and worrying about what she might reveal to the king that could cause problems for when Nicolette arrived.

Mel glanced into Rikardo's eyes and nodded, acknowledging that he intended to leave.

Rikardo swept out of the room and swept his father along with him, even if he was the king.

Melanie thanked the staff for the delivery of the meal. She felt their curious gazes on her, too, and she would have liked to strike up a conversation, to ask what it was like to work in the kitchens of a palace. Instead, she kept her gaze downcast and kept the interaction as brief as she could.

The rooms she would use were lavish. Mel could barely take it all in.

And then finally she was alone.

So she could sit at the royal dining table in Prince Rikardo's suite that had its own guest suite within it, and eat royal food while she waited for the prince to have his discussion with his father about truffle harvesting. She hadn't known the country grew truffles.

But that wouldn't be all of the conversation and it would no doubt be difficult for the prince, but then Rikardo would come back here and tell Melanie his plans, and somehow or other it would all be all right.

Mel turned to the dining table, looked at the array of dishes. She would eat so at least she had some energy inside her to deal with whatever came next.

It *would* be all right. Rikardo was a prince. He would be able to make anything right.

CHAPTER THREE

RIK STOOD BY the window in the sitting area of his suite. Early sunlight filtered across the snowy landscape of mountains and valleys, and over Ettonbierre village below. Soon people would begin to move around, to go about their work—those who *had* enough work.

He had once liked this time best of all, the solitude before the day's commitments took over. Today, his thoughts were already embroiled and his aide already on his way to Rik's suite to discuss yet another matter of urgency. The past two years had been problem after problem. Rik's marriage plans had been part of the solution, or so he had believed. Now…

He had spoken to his father last night. It hadn't been the greatest conversation he'd ever had; it had taken too long, and at the end of it he had known the impossibility of trying to bring Nicolette out here now to pass her off as his fiancée.

Really he'd known that from the moment Melanie had told him he'd collected the wrong girl. Too many people had seen her. Then Rik's *father* had seen her. She had tried not to be too noticeable, too recognisable. But the king *had* noticed. Right down to the three freckles dotted across the bridge of her nose.

Rik had whisked his father out of his suite. He'd bought a little time to come up with a solution before his father formally met his fiancée. But in the end there *was* only one solution.

A soft knock sounded on the outer door of his suite. Rik strode towards it. He didn't believe in the edict that a prince should not do such menial things as open doors to his staff. He and his brothers all worked on behalf of the people of Braston one way or another, so why wouldn't they open a door?

And now you all have a challenge to fulfil. The prize is that your father will come out of his two-year disconnection from the world around him, caused by the queen moving out and refusing to return, and co-operate to enable the economy here to be healed.

'Good morning, Prince Rikardo.' His aide stepped into the room and closed the door behind him. 'My apologies for disturbing you at this hour.'

'And mine for disturbing you late last night.' Rik gave a wry twist of his lips. 'To examine an emailed photograph, no less.'

And the passport of Nicole Melanie, which had been handled by one of his retinue of attendants when they arrived at the airport with his guest deeply asleep.

Nicole, not Nicolette. Only Rik could have spotted that mistake and he'd been otherwise occupied at the time.

'But with a purpose, Your Highness. It is unfortunate that the two women do not look enough alike to ensure we could safely swap them.' Dominico Rhueldt drew a breath. 'I have carried out your wishes and transferred the funds from your personal holdings to the bank account of Nicolette Watson, and ordered the set from the hand-crafted collection of the diamond jeweller, Luchino Montichelli. It will be delivered to Nicolette within two days.'

The man hesitated. 'Your Highness, I am concerned about the amount of money going out of your holdings towards relief to the people. I know they are in need—'

'And while I have the ability I will go on meeting needs, but that doesn't fix the underlying problems.' Rik sighed. It was an old conversation. 'Nicolette. She is happy with this… buy-off?'

A gift of baubles and a cash injection in exchange for her acceptance of the changed circumstances, and her silence.

Though Rik's question referred to the woman he'd organised to briefly marry, he struggled to shift his thoughts from the one he'd carried onto a plane recently.

He glanced at the closed door of his guest suite. Last night when he'd got back, he'd tucked the covers over Melanie. She'd been curled up on the bed in a ball as though not quite sure she had a right to be there. Sleeping Beauty waiting to be woken by a kiss.

The nonsense thoughts had come to him last night. A result of tiredness and the suppression of stress, Rik had concluded. Yet the vision of her curled up there was still with him. The desire to taste softly parted lips, still there. He'd been absorbed in Braston's problems lately. Perhaps it had been too long since he took care of those other needs.

His aide rubbed a hand across the back of his neck. When he spoke again, his words were in French, not English. 'Nicolette acknowledged the payment and the order of the diamond jewellery as her due as a result of the changed circumstances. She accepts the situation but it is good, I think, that she will be unaware of any other plans you may intend to implement until such time—'

'Yes.' If 'such time' was something Rik could bring about.

'The other matter of urgency,' his aide went on, 'is unfortunately, the truffle crop.'

Rik swung about from where he'd been half gazing out of the windows. One search of Dominico's face and Rik stepped forward. 'Tell me.'

'Winnow is concerned about the soil in one of the grove areas. He feels it looks as it did last year before the blight struck again.'

'He's tested it? What is the result? We were certain we'd prevented any possibility of this happening this year. The crop is almost ready for harvest!' Rik rapped the words out as he strode to his suite. He stepped into the walk-in closet and selected work wear. Khaki trousers, thick shirt and sweater, and well-worn work boots. A very un-princely outfit that his mother would have criticised had she been here to do so. Rik started to shuck clothes so he could don the new ones.

His aide spoke from a few feet away. 'Winnow is doing the testing now.'

'I will examine the soil myself and speak with Winnow.' Rik laced his boots and strode into the sitting room.

'Your guest?' Dominico also glanced towards the closed door of the guest suite. 'Shall I wake her? Inform her of your immediate plans?'

'Allow her to sleep on while she has the chance. She had a long and difficult day before we arrived here. Please ask, though, that Rufusina be prepared to go with me to the groves.'

Melanie heard these words faintly through a closed door. She shifted in the luxurious bed, opened her eyes to a canopied pelmet draped above her head, and remembered curling up for just a moment while she waited for Prince Rikardo to return from speaking with his father. Now she was under the covers. Still in her clothes, but as though someone had covered her up to make sure she'd be comfortable. And that was Rik's voice out there, and it sounded as though he was about to go out.

Who was Rufusina?

'I'm getting up.' The words emerged in a hoarse croak. She cleared her throat, sat up, and quickly climbed out of bed. And called more loudly. 'Prince—Your Highness—I'm awake. I'm sorry I fell asleep before you got back last night. I'll be out in five minutes. I won't keep you waiting.'

Only after she called the words did Mel realise how they might have sounded to members of staff if any were out there with him, and, given he'd just spoken to someone, they probably were.

Heat rushed into her face, and then she felt doubly silly because she hadn't meant the words in that way, and the staff wouldn't care anyway, surely. And Rikardo would send her back to Australia today so none of this would be her problem for much longer.

Mel stopped in her headlong dash to the bathroom and wondered where the burst of disappointment had come from.

From being in a real live palace for a night and having to go home now, she told herself. And perhaps just the tiniest bit because she wouldn't have the chance to get to know Rikardo better.

'That's *Prince* Rikardo to you, Melanie Watson, and why would he want to get to know you? You're a cook. Not even a formally qualified one. You're not even in his realm.' She whispered the words and quickly set about putting herself together so she wouldn't keep the prince waiting.

Well, she *was* in his realm—literally right now. But in terms of having anything in common, she didn't exactly fit here, did she? No doubt he would want to speak to her sooner, rather than later, to tell her how he would get rid of her and how soon Nicolette would arrive to make everything as it was supposed to be.

That would be fine. Mel would co-operate fully. She only wanted to be sent home so she could get on with her life! Preferably avoiding contact with Nicolette in the process.

Outside in the sitting area, Rik's gaze caught with his aide's. 'I cannot be in two places at once right now. It would be rude to abandon Melanie now that she is awake, but breakfast must be offered, and I need to get to the groves.'

'Permit me to suggest a picnic breakfast for you and your guest after you have attended the groves. It would be easily enough arranged.' Dominico, too, glanced at the closed door of the guest suite. 'You might have a nice, quiet place in mind?'

Rik named a favourite place. 'That would be convenient to speak to Melanie there and see if she can find her way clear—'

'I hope I didn't keep you waiting.' The guest in question pushed her suite door open and stepped into Rik's sitting room.

Rik's head turned.

His aide's head turned.

There were appropriate words to be uttered to help her to feel comfortable, to extend grace. Rik wanted to do these things, to offer these things, but for a moment the words stuck to the back of his tongue as he gazed upon the morning face of Melanie Watson.

Soft natural colour tinged her cheeks. She'd tied her hair back in some kind of half-twisted ponytail. Straight falls escaped to frame the sides of her face. She wore a long, layered brown corduroy skirt trimmed in gold, brown ankle boots with a short heel and rubber-soled tread, and a cream cashmere sweater. In her hands she held a wool-lined coat. Her lips bore a soft pink gloss and she'd darkened her lashes with a touch of mascara.

Her clothing was department or chain store, not designer. The hairstyle had not come at the expense of an exclusive salon or stylist but thanks to a single brown hair tie and a twist of her hands. Yet in those five minutes she had produced a result that had knocked Rik out of his comfort zone, an achievement some had striven for and failed to achieve, in various ways, in decades of his life.

'You look lovely.' The inadequate words passed across his lips. A thought quickly followed that startled him into momentary silence. He wanted his brothers to meet her.

Maybe they would, if either of them were around today. And maybe Melanie would be on her way back to Australia before any chance of such a meeting could occur.

He stepped forward, lifted her right hand in his, and softly brushed her fingers with his lips. 'I hope you slept well and feel rested.' He introduced his aide. 'Dominico assists me with all my personal and many of my business dealings.'

In other words, his aide could be trusted utterly and was completely aware of their situation. At the moment, Dominico was more aware than Melanie.

Rik truly did need to speak with her, to set all matters

straight as quickly as possible. He hoped that Melanie might co-operate to help him but it was a great deal to ask.

So much for your arrogant belief that you could outwit your father, still get all that you want, and not have to pay any price for it aside from the presence of a fiancée here for a few months.

Rik had collected the wrong woman and created a lot of trouble for himself.

So why did he feel distracted by the feel of soft skin against his lips? Why did he wish that he could get to know Melanie?

He pushed the thoughts aside. There was work to do. A truffle crop to bring to fruition disease-free, and a woman to take to breakfast. 'Will you join me for a walk outdoors? I need to attend to some business and then I thought we might share a picnic breakfast. I know a spot that will be sheltered from wind and will catch the morning sunshine. We can speak privately and I can let you know the outcome of my discussion last night with my father.'

'A—a picnic breakfast would be lovely, but is it all right for people to see me?' Her balance wobbled just enough to make him think she might have been about to curtsy to him. 'I'm sorry I wasn't still awake when you finished speaking with your father last night. It would have been okay to wake me up. I must have crawled under the covers.'

She hadn't. Rik had tucked her in. Had paused to gaze at a face that seemed far too beautiful. He suspected it had occurred to her that he might have tucked her in. The flush in her face had deepened.

Rik realised he still had hold of her hand. He released it and stepped back. 'It will indeed be fine. You are dressed well for the conditions. Shall we?'

Rikardo led Melanie through corridors and along passageways and past vast rooms with domed ceilings. Everywhere, staff worked with silent efficiency, going about their day's tasks.

Without making it seem a big deal, he explained that she never needed to curtsy to anyone but his father or mother, and to them only in certain formal circumstances.

'Am I likely to meet your mother this morning?' Mel glanced about her and tried not to let an added dose of apprehension rise.

Rikardo shook his head. 'No. The queen is away from the palace.'

'Well, thank goodness for that, anyway,' she blurted, and then grimaced.

But Rikardo merely murmured, 'Indeed,' and they fell silent.

In that silence, Melanie tried not to let her mind boggle at the thought that she was walking through a palace beside a prince, and feeling relieved not to be about to meet a queen, but it all did feel quite surreal. Rikardo nodded to a staff member here or there. He'd said it was fine to be seen out with him by anyone they came across, so Mel would take that at face value. He'd obviously come up with some explanation for her presence.

'The kitchens here would be amazing.' She almost whispered the words, but she could imagine how many staff might work there. The amazing meals they would prepare. Mel felt certain the royal staff wouldn't have cake plates thrown at their heads as her cousin had done to her that final night.

Rikardo turned to glance at her. 'You can see the kitchens later if you wish.'

Before she left for the airport. Mel reminded herself deliberately of this.

'I didn't know that Braston grew truffles. I probably should have known.' She drew a breath. 'I've never cooked with them. My relatives loved throwing dinner parties but they were too—'

She bit the words back. She'd been going to say 'too stingy' to feed their guests truffles.

'Truffles have been referred to as the diamonds of the kitchen. Along with tourism they have represented the main two industries for Braston for some years now.' Rik stepped forward and a man in liveried uniform opened the vast doors of the palace and suddenly they were outside in the morning sun with the most amazing vista unfolding all around.

'Oh!' Melanie's breath caught in her throat. Everywhere she looked there were snow-capped mountains on the horizon. A beautiful gilded landscape dotted with trees, hills and valleys and sprinkled with snow spread before them. 'I didn't see any of this last night. Your country is very beautiful. I'm sure tourists would love to see it, too.'

'It is beautiful, if small.' Pride found its way into Rikardo's voice. 'But much of Europe is, and there are countries with more to offer to travellers. I would like to see an improvement in the tourist industry. If my brother Anrai has his way that will also happen very soon.'

Melanie liked his pride. Somehow that seemed exactly as it should be. And also the warmth in his tone as he referred to a brother. That hadn't been there when he'd spoken about the king or the queen, and, even if she'd only met the king briefly and had tried not to catch his attention too much, Georgio did seem to be a combination of forthrightly spoken and austere that could strike a girl as quite formidable.

You could handle him. If you managed yourself among

your aunt and uncle and cousin for that many years and held onto your sense of self worth, you can do anything.

It hadn't hurt that Mel had set up a back-door arrangement and sent lots of cakes and desserts and meals out to a local charity kitchen to be shared among the masses. Her relatives never had caught on to that, and Mel had had the pleasure of giving away her cooking efforts to people who truly appreciated them.

Well, that life was over with now. Over the past year or so the family had forgotten to give her the kind moments that had balanced the rest. They had focused on the negative, and Mel had started saving to leave them. Now she just had to get back to Australia and to Sydney so she could start afresh.

It would be all right. She'd get work and be able to support herself. It didn't matter if she started out with very little. She pushed aside fears that she might not be able to find work before her meagre savings ran out.

Instead, she turned to smile at Rikardo. He looked different out of doors and in profile in these surroundings, more rugged somehow.

Face it, Mel. He looks attractive no matter what light you see him in, and each new light seems to make you feel that he's more attractive than the last one. And that moment of shared consciousness when she first stepped into his sitting room this morning. Had she imagined that?

Of course she'd imagined it. Why would a prince be conscious of...a kitchen hand? *A cook.* Same difference. They were both worlds away from being an heir to a kingdom.

'We commercially grow black truffles here.' Rikardo spoke in a calm tone. 'If you are not aware of it, truffles have a symbiotic relationship with the roots of the trees they grow under.'

'In this case oak trees,' Melanie murmured while she tried to pull her thoughts together. *Was* he calm? If so, his threshold for dealing with problems must be quite high. 'That's what they are, isn't it?'

Her glance shifted below them to the left where grove upon grove of trees stood in carefully tended rows. 'I'd heard that truffles could be grown commercially in that way. I think in Tasmania—'

'That's correct, and, yes, they are indeed oak trees.' He'd taken her arm, and now walked with her towards a grouping of ...

Outbuildings? Was that a fine enough word for buildings within the palace grounds? There were garages with cars in them. Sports cars and other cars. Half a dozen at least. They all looked highly polished and valuable. They would go very fast.

Did the sun go in for just a moment? Mel turned her glance away. A man drove past them in one of the vehicles. Rik raised an arm as the driver slowed and tooted the horn before driving on. 'That is Anrai.'

'I thought he resembled you in looks.' Except Rikardo was far more handsome. And having her arm held by him made Mel way too conscious of him.

Small talk, Mel. You're supposed to be indulging in polite, get-to-know-you-but-don't-be-nosy-about-it small talk. 'How many brothers do you have?'

'Just the two, both older than me and busy trying to achieve their own plans—' He broke off.

A worker walked towards them, leading...a pig with a studded red collar around its neck. When the animal saw Rikardo, it snorted and almost pulled the worker over in its enthusiasm to get to the prince.

Rikardo looked down at the animal and then turned to Mel. 'This is Rufusina. She is a truffle hog and will be coming to the groves with us this morning.'

'*This* is Rufusina?' For some reason Melanie had pictured a gorgeous woman in an ankle-length fur-lined coat with long flowing brown hair. Maybe the woman had known Rikardo for ever and had secretly wanted to marry him herself.

Can we say overactive imagination? Well, this was the perfect setting for an imagination to run wild in! Mel tried to refocus her thoughts. 'She's a very interesting-looking truffle hog. She looks very...'

Porcine?

'Very intelligent,' Mel concluded.

'I am sure that is the first thought that comes to all minds.' For the second time since they'd met, Rikardo's lips twitched. Though his words laughed at Mel just a little, they laughed at Rufusina, too, for there was a twinkle in his eye as he watched the hog strain at her leash to get to him, and succeed.

Rikardo then told the hog to 'sit' just as you would say to a dog. The pig planted her haunches and cast an adoring if rather beady gaze up at him. She got a scratch behind each ear for her trouble. Rikardo took the lead.

They were at the groves before Mel had come to terms with her prince having a pet pig, because, whether he'd said so or not, this animal had been raised to his hand.

Mel would guarantee it. She could *tell*. They arrived also before Mel could recover from the beauty of Rikardo's twinkling eyes and that hint of a smile.

And what did Mel mean by '*her*' prince' anyway? He certainly wasn't! She might have him for a few more hours, if that, and all of which only by default anyway because she'd been silly enough to think he was a cab driver.

Later, after she'd been returned to Australia, she could write her story and send it in to one of those truth magazines and say she'd spent a few hours with a royal.

She wouldn't, of course. She wouldn't violate Rikardo's privacy in that manner.

Today, in the broad light of Rikardo's...kingdom, Mel couldn't imagine how she'd mistaken him for anything other than what he was, whether she'd been overtired and overwrought and under the influence of an allergy medication or not.

It wasn't until they reached the actual truffle groves that Mel started to register that Rikardo seemed to have somehow withdrawn into himself as they drew closer to his destination. She wasn't sure how to explain the difference. He still had her arm. The pig still trotted obediently at his side on its lead. Rikardo spoke with each person they passed and his words were pleasant, if brief.

But Rikardo's gaze had shifted to those rows of oak trees again and again, and somehow Mel *felt* the tension rising within him as they drew nearer.

'Winnow.' Rik greeted a spindly man in his fifties and shook his hand. 'Allow me to introduce my guest, Miss Watson.'

So that was how Rik planned to get around that one. But would that be enough? Because for all the people that mistook Mel for her cousin, plenty more...didn't.

'Do you have the results of the soil test, Winnow? Are we infected again with the blight?'

This time Mel didn't have to try to hear the concern in Rikardo's tone.

'The test shows nothing, Prince Rik.' The man stopped and glanced at Melanie and then back to the prince. 'I beg your pardon. I mean, Prince Rikardo.'

'It's fine, Winnow. We are all friends here.' Rik dipped his head. 'Please go on.'

Winnow pulled the cap from his head and twisted it in his hands. 'The test shows nothing, but last year and the year before...'

'By the time the tests showed positive, it was too late and we ended up losing the crop.'

'Yes. Exactly.' Winnow's face drew into a grimace. 'I cannot prove anything. Maybe I am worrying unduly but the soil samples that I pulled this morning do not *look right* to me.'

'Then we will treat again now.' Rikardo didn't hesitate. 'Yes, it is expensive and a further treatment we hadn't planned for will add to that expense, but our research and tests show that enough of the treatment will keep the blight at bay. If you have any concern whatever, then I want the treatment repeated.'

The older man blew out a breath. 'I am sorry for the added expense but my bones tell me—'

'And we will listen.' Rikardo clapped the man on the back. 'Order the treatment. I will draw funds for it.'

From there Rikardo examined the soil samples himself, and took Rufusina into one of the groves to sniff about. Mel didn't fully understand the process. The older Winnow kept lapsing into the beautiful local dialect as he spoke with Rikardo.

It was worth not being able to understand, to hear Rikardo respond at times in kind. She felt as though she'd heard him speak to her in the same language but she must have imagined that. In any case it was very lovely, a melodious harmony of tones and textures.

'We will take breakfast up there, if you are agreeable.' Rikardo pointed to a spot partway up a nearby mountainside. He'd handed the truffle hog over to Winnow, who was about to put her to good use in the groves before seeing her returned to her home. And with an admonishment to ensure the pig didn't run off, as she was apparently wont to do on occasion.

But right now...

There was a natural shelving of rock up high where a bench seat and table had been set into it. The view would be amazing. 'Oh. That would be lovely.'

They began the climb. 'The truffles. Will they be okay?'

'I hope so. We've had two years of failed harvests. That has resulted in a devastating financial blow to the country's economy while we searched for a preventative treatment that would work without affecting the quality of the truffles.' He led her to the bench seat and table.

Opposite was a mountain with large sections covered in ice. Mel sat, and her glance went outward and down, over groves of trees and over the village named after the royal family. 'There must be so much rich history here. I'm sorry that there have been difficulties with the truffle industry. From Winnow I gather you play a key role in this truffle work?'

'I run the operations from ground level to the marketing strategies.'

Mel's gaze shifted to the village below. 'You must care about the people of Braston very much.'

'I do, and they are suffering. Not just here and in Ettonbierre village, but right across the country.' He drew a breath. 'I had planned that we should eat while I led up to my request but perhaps it is best to simply state it now and then explain.'

Mel's breath locked in her throat. Rikardo had a request of her? She glanced again at the scene below. Rikardo led a privileged life compared to the very ordinary ones playing out down there. There was a parallel to her life with Nicolette and her cousin's parents. But there was also a difference.

Rikardo seemed willing to go to any lengths to help those who depended on his family for their livelihoods. 'What can I do to help you? To help...them?'

'You are kind, aren't you?' It wasn't a question, and he seemed as concerned by it as he was possibly admiring of it. 'Even though you don't know what I may want.'

Mel lowered her gaze. 'I try to be. What is it that you need?'

'If it is at all possible, if it's something you can do without it interfering unreasonably with your life or plans and I can convince you that you will be secure and looked after throughout the process and after it, I would like to ask you to take Nicolette's place.' Blue eyes fixed on her face, searched.

'T-take her place?' She stuttered the question slightly.

If Mel had peered in front of her in that moment, she felt quite certain she would have seen a hole. A rabbit hole. The kind that Alice in Crazyland could fall down.

Or leap into voluntarily?

'Just to be clear,' Mel said carefully, 'are you asking *me* to be the one to temporarily marry you?'

CHAPTER FOUR

'I KNOW A marriage proposal must seem quite strange when you expected to be sent back to Australia today.' Rik searched Melanie's face.

He felt an interest and curiosity towards her that he struggled to explain.

And an attraction that can only get in the way of your goals.

He couldn't let that happen. And right now he needed to properly explain his situation to her. That meant swallowing his pride to a degree, something he wasn't used to doing. Yet as he looked at the carefully calm face, the hands clenched together in the folds of her skirt as she braced herself for whatever might come next, it somehow became a little easier.

At worst she would refuse to help him.

That would be a genuine 'worst', Rik. You need her help, otherwise you'll end up locked into a miserable marriage like that of your parents, or unable to help the people of Braston at all because this plan of yours has failed.

'May I be plain, Melanie?'

'I think that would be best.' She drew an uneven breath. 'I feel a little out of my depth right now.'

She would feel more so as he explained his situation to her. He had to hope that she would listen with an open mind.

'The arrangement that I made,' he said carefully, 'was to bring your cousin over here and marry her a month later.'

Melanie responded with equal care. 'You indicated that would be a temporary thing?'

'Yes.' He sought the right words. 'The marriage was to end with a separation after three months and Nicolette would then have been returned to Australia and a quick divorce would have been filed for.'

'I see.' She drew a breath and her lovely brown eyes focused on his blue ones and searched. 'You didn't intend to let your father know those circumstances until after the marriage, I'm guessing? What did you hope to gain from that plan?'

'Aside from my brothers, Nicolette, and my aide, no one was to know of the plan.' He'd intended to outplay his father, to get what he wanted for the people without having to yield up his freedom for it. 'This plan probably sounds cold to you.'

'It does rather reject the concept of marriage and for ever.' Melanie sat forward on the bench seating and turned further to face him. Her knee briefly grazed his leg as she settled herself.

The colour whipped into her cheeks by the cold air around them deepened slightly. That...knowledge of him, that awareness that seemed to zing between her body and his even when both of them had so much else on their minds...

Is something that cannot be allowed to continue, Rik, particularly if she is willing to agree to the business arrangement you're asking for with her.

'In my family, many lifelong marriages have been made to form alliances or for business reasons.' He hesitated, uncertain how to explain his deep aversion to the idea of pursuing such a path. 'That doesn't always result in a pleasant relationship.'

Melanie's gaze searched his. 'It could be quite difficult for children of such a marriage, too.'

'It's not that.' The words came quickly, full of assurance and belief as though he needed to say it in case he *couldn't* fully believe it?

Rik had his reasons for his decision. He was tired of butting heads with his father while the king tried to bully him to get whatever he wanted. His father needed to acknowledge that Rik would make his own decisions. That was all. 'There have been myriad problems in the past couple of years.

'The first year the truffle crop failed it was difficult.' People relied on the truffle industry for their survival. 'Around that same time, my mother, the queen, moved out. That was an unprecedented act from a woman who'd always advocated practical marriages and putting on a good front to the public, no matter what.'

Melanie covered her surprise. 'That must have caused some complications.'

'It did. For once my father found himself on the back foot.'

'And you and your brothers found yourselves without a mother in residence. I'm sorry to hear that. It's never pleasant when you lose someone, even if they choose to leave.' A glimpse of something longstanding, deep and painful flashed through her eyes before she seemed to blink it away. 'I hope that you still get to see her?'

'I see my mother infrequently when there are royal occasions that bring us all together.' Would Mel understand if he explained that his contact with his mother hadn't changed much? That the queen had never spent much time with her sons and what time she had spent had been invested in criticising their clothing, deportment, efforts or choices in life? Better to just leave that alone.

'My parents died years ago.' She offered the confidence softly. 'I went to live with Nicolette and my aunt and uncle after that happened.'

He took one of her hands into his. 'I'm sorry for your loss.'

Dominico had informed him of some of these things this morning after the security check the aide ordered on her came through. The invasion of Melanie's privacy had been necessary, but Rik had refused to read the report, asking only to be told 'anything that might matter'. Though he had to protect himself, somehow it had still felt wrong.

'Thank you.' She gently withdrew her hand, and folded both of them together in her lap.

She went on. 'You've explained about the truffle crops failing, how that's impacted on your people. One year is a problem but two years in a row—'

'Brought financial disaster to many of our truffle workers.' And while Rik pursued every avenue to find a cure for the blight to the truffle crops, his father had denied the depths of the problem because he was absorbed in his anger and frustration over his queen walking out on him.

'On top of these issues, the tourist industry also waned as other parts of Europe became more popular as vacation destinations. Tourism is Anrai's field. He has the chain of hotels and the country certainly still gets a tourist market, but when there is so much more to do and see just over the border…'

'You have to have something either comparable, or totally

unique, to pull in a large slice of the tourist market.' Melanie nodded her head.

'Exactly. Our country needs to get back on its feet. My brothers and I have fought to get our father to listen to the depth of the problems.' They'd provided emergency assistance to the people out of their own pockets as best they could but that wasn't a long-term solution. None of them had endless supplies of funds.

In terms of available cash, nor did the royal estate. It had what it had. History, a beautiful palace and the means to maintain it and maintain a lifestyle comparable to it for the royal family. Their father oversaw all of that, and did not divulge the details of what came and went through the royal coffers. It was through careful investment of a shared inheritance that Rik and his brothers had decent funds of their own.

'Despite these difficulties you came up with a plan.' Mel searched Rikardo's face. Her heart had stopped pounding in the aftermath of his remarkable request, though even now she still couldn't fully comprehend it, couldn't really allow herself to consider it as any kind of reality.

It was Alice down that alternative universe hole again, yet it wasn't. He truly wanted her to marry him. For practical purposes, to outwit his father, and just for a few months, but still…he wanted her to marry him.

She started to find it hard to breathe again. 'And somehow your plan involved trading off a brief marriage for sorting out the country's economic troubles.'

'Yes. My father has pushed all three of us to marry. I think we all have expected that Marcelo would have to do that whether he wanted to or not because he is the eldest. It is part of his heritage.'

Mel nodded. 'I thought when I came here, well, I guess

I was so overwhelmed by it all that I didn't stop to think that everything might not be rosy just because there's a palace filled with amazing things. Just because you're a prince doesn't mean everything is easy for you. Or for your brothers, either.'

'My brothers and I went to our father in a concerted bid to get him to listen to the seriousness of the problems the people are facing and with our plans for addressing those problems. Leadership reform is also desperately needed, and that is something Marcelo has been working to achieve for some years now.' Rikardo drew a breath. 'Our father finally did listen. We got our concessions from him.'

His tone became even more formal as he went on. 'But that agreement came at a cost. In return for agreeing to requests that will help us protect Braston's people from further financial hardship, his demand was that we each marry within the next six months.'

'To ensure that the family carries on?' Mel asked the question and then wondered if she should have.

Even as a king, did Georgio have the right to push his sons to marry if they didn't feel ready? If they didn't want to? For Rik to go to such lengths to avoid the institution, he must have some deep-seated reasons. Or did he just not want to be bullied? That was reason enough, of course!

Mel might not ever fully understand, and for some reason she felt a little sad right now. Her gaze shifted to the cliff face opposite. Two men were near the top, tourists or locals with rappelling equipment.

Mel had to navigate *this* discussion. And Rik's explanations did help her to start to understand what was at stake, at least for the people of Braston.

Could she decide to just walk away when the futures of so

many people hinged on Rik meeting his father's demands? When him bringing her here by mistake could have ruined those plans? If she hadn't been on the street filled with allergy medication…

Whether she'd meant it or not, her actions had contributed to this current problem, and if there was no other way to fix it…

But it's such a big undertaking, Mel. Marriage, even if it is only for a few months! And there'd be publicity and a dress and so much else, and you'd be fooling Rik's father the whole time and then he'd realise he'd been fooled and be very angry.

Yet Mel knew that Rik would protect her; that he would make sure his father didn't bring any of his wrath down on Mel's head. Rik wouldn't *allow* that anger to have its head. 'When it ended you would send me back to Australia, to Sydney. I wouldn't be exposed to the aftermath here.'

'And because we'd give an interview when we dissolved the marriage and let the magazines and tabloids have that, I would hope you wouldn't attract much media interest when you went home.' His gaze searched hers. 'I would direct them towards me and ask you to do the same. At worst there might be some photographs and speculation about you in the newspapers over there for a brief time.'

That was to be expected when such an event had happened, but if all the information were already given, surely the papers wouldn't care much once they realised Mel wasn't going to talk to them, and the split had been amicable? 'That shouldn't be so bad.' The whole thing wouldn't be too scary if she decided to do it. Would it?

She reached for the picnic basket that sat ignored on the table before them, and hoped that Rik couldn't see the tremble in her fingers. 'Would you like coffee? Something to warm your hands around?'

'Thank you.' His gaze, too, shifted to the men on the nearby mountain peak before it returned to Mel. 'I should have unpacked the basket and made it all available to you the moment we got up here.'

The thought of a prince unpacking breakfast for her horrified her but she bit back her words about it and instead, served the food and coffee for both of them.

When she set his plate in front of him, he caught and held her gaze.

'I know what I'm asking isn't easy. I made this plan because I do not feel I can marry, truly…permanently.' He hesitated. 'The demonstration of that institution within my family—'

'Has been about as warm as what I've seen in Nicolette's family.' Mel bit her lip, but that was her truth and there didn't seem to be much point in avoiding saying it now.

They started on their food. There were eggs cooked similarly to a quiche but without the pastry base. Small chunks of bread dipped in fragrant oil and herbs and then baked until they were crisp and golden. Grilled vegetables and fruits and a selection of pastries.

'What you've asked me to do *is* unexpected.' Stunningly so. 'But I ended up here, you can't swap me for Nicolette, and if I don't agree, the game is up with your father and you either have to marry someone for real and stay married to her, or your father won't grant you the "concessions" you asked for.'

'I'm afraid I didn't allow for collecting the wrong woman outside Nicolette's home, but that is not your fault.' He frowned and sipped his coffee. 'It's important you don't make your decision based on guilt. A mistake happened that was out of my control, and yours.'

She did feel at least partially responsible, but Mel kept that thought to herself and instead took a small bite of a tasty grilled vegetable before she went on. 'I'd like to know what the concessions are that your father has agreed to.'

'I am determined that the truffle crop this year will not fail.' Rikardo set down his knife and fork and turned to face her. 'When it flourishes, I'll need a spectacular marketing idea to get buyers back onside to buy our product. Many of them have lost faith because of the blight that struck our crop two years running.'

Mel, too, set down her utensils. 'What is this marketing idea?'

'On the palace grounds there are truffles that grow naturally.' Rik's gaze shifted to where the palace sat in splendour in the distance. 'For centuries those truffles have been eaten only by royals. It probably sounds rather archaic but—' He shrugged and went on.

'These truffles are particularly fine. If buyers are given the chance to obtain small quantities of them in exchange for purchasing commercial quantities of our regular truffles, I believe they will jump at the opportunity.'

'What a clever idea.' Melanie spoke without hesitation. 'People will go nuts for a chance like that. I can also imagine that you might have had a job on your hands to get the king to allow you to use those truffles.'

'Correct. My father tends to adhere to a lot of the old ways and does not want to consider change.' Georgio was strong, stubborn, unbending. Rik preferred to take the strengths he'd inherited from his father, and turn them to better purpose.

As for Melanie, she looked beautiful and innocent and

wary and uncertain all rolled into one as she sat beside Rik on the bench. Yet she also seemed well able to think with a business mind, too, and her eyes shone with genuine encouragement for him as she heard his plans for the truffle marketing.

Would she agree to help him out of the corner he'd got himself stuck in? Did he even have the right to ask that of her?

'I don't want to harm you through this agreement, Melanie.' That, too, had to be said. 'I have asked for your help, but if it is not something you can do, you do not have to give it.'

'But you want to help your people.' Her gaze turned to meet his, and held. 'You chose Nicolette because you weren't...romantically attached to her or anything like that, didn't you?'

'I did. That allowed the situation to remain as uncomplicated as possible.'

'It would be easy to end the marriage and get on with what you really wanted to do with your life afterwards.'

He dipped his head. 'Yes.'

'I'm not ready to consider marriage yet. The real thing, I mean.' Even as Melanie spoke the words, a part deep inside her whispered a question. Did she believe she would ever be ready? Did she even feel she had the right—?

What did she mean by that? Of course she had the right, and she would still have the right if she married Rikardo and they then divorced. Melanie pushed the strange question aside.

And she thought about all those people subject to circumstances beyond their control, just trying to get on with their daily lives. People in a lot of ways who would be just like her. Not royal people, but everyday people who simply needed a bit of a hand up.

Mel could do this. She could be of help. She could make it so Rikardo didn't have to lock himself into a long-term marriage he didn't want. Maybe later he would find someone and be able to be happy. The little prick she felt in her chest must have been hope that he would indeed find that happiness.

'I'll do it.' Melanie spoke the words softly, and said them again more forcefully. 'I'll do it. I'll marry you so you can make your plan work. I want to help you.'

'You're quite certain?' Rik leaned towards her as he spoke.

'I am. I'm totally sure.' And in that moment, Mel was. She could help him. She could do this to make up for him not being able to marry her cousin.

'Thank you, Melanie.'

'You're welcome.' Her face softened and the beginnings of a smile came to her lips. Her gaze moved to *his* lips and suddenly she had to swallow because something told her he was going to kiss her as part of that thank you.

She thought it, and her breath caught, and then he did.

Rik's lips brushed hers in a soft press. His hand cupped her shoulder, and even through layers of cloth Mel felt that. Registered that as she received a kiss from a prince.

That was why it felt so remarkable. It had to be the reason—a kiss from a prince to thank her for agreeing to help him out of a tight corner.

Yet Melanie didn't feel as though a prince was kissing her. She was being kissed…by a man, and it felt wonderful in a way no kiss had before.

In that moment her response was completely beyond her control. Her mouth softened against his, gave itself to his ministrations before her thoughts could catch up or stop her. If those thoughts had surfaced, would the kiss have ended there, with a simple brushing of lips against lips? A simple "thank you" expressed in those terms? Because that was indeed what Rik had set out to do.

It had to have been and yet somehow, for Mel at least, it had become something very different.

Mel closed her eyes. For a moment she forgot she was on a mountainside in Europe with a royal prince, seated at a table with a picnic breakfast spread before them and the most amazing scenic vistas on all sides.

She forgot that it was chilly here but that the sun shone and they were sheltered from the wind. A man was simply kissing her and she was kissing him back and that man had a pet truffle hog he'd named and whom he doted on, even though he tried very hard to hide the fact. He cared for his brothers and for the people who lived in his country, and she'd liked him from the moment she'd thought he was a gorgeous cab driver come to take her away to the airport so she could make her way to Sydney.

'Rik.' She'd slept on his shoulder and blabbed at him when she wasn't quite sensible, and, despite all the smart things she should be thinking right now, the kiss felt right.

'Hmm?' He whispered the half-question against her lips.

Mel didn't know whether she said it, or thought it. She simply knew the words.

Kiss me again.

CHAPTER FIVE

I WOULD KISS you for ever and it would not be enough.

Rik thought the words inside his mind, thought them in his native language. Thought them even though they could not possibly be true and he must simply be swept up in gratitude and relief.

Yet deep within himself he knew that now, in this moment, Melanie would welcome the prolonging of this kiss. His instincts told him this. The way she yielded petal-soft lips to him told him this.

It was that thought of her willingness that finally prompted him to stop something that he should not have started in the first place, and that he hadn't expected would make his heart pound. He, who rarely lost his cool over anything, had been taken by surprise by kissing a slip of a girl up high on a mountainside.

'Thank you...' Rik released Melanie and drew back, and for a moment couldn't think what he was thanking her for.

For rescuing him. The prince was being rescued by the same generosity that he'd felt in Melanie's soft lips.

You are on dangerous ground with this thinking, Rikardo.

If she is kind, then she is kind and that is something indeed to be appreciated. But the awareness of each other—that cannot be, and it cannot go on.

He shouldn't have touched her. Arrogantly, he hadn't known that doing so would be such a stunning thing.

The kiss had been startling in its loveliness. It wasn't a manly description. But with Melanie it felt exactly right to describe it in this way.

Melanie was startling in her loveliness, and that came from the generous way she gave of herself.

He'd meant only to touch her lips with his, should perhaps not have considered even that much. Rik would like to say that he'd expected not to feel any attraction to Melanie, that he had expected to feel as indifferent towards her as he had felt towards Nicolette, but he'd known it would be different.

Yet he had kissed her, and had ended up shocked and a little taken aback by just how much he had enjoyed that kiss. Her response to him had felt unrehearsed and open. That, too, had added to her appeal.

Maybe she had simply wanted to kiss a prince.

In many other circumstances, Rik would have accepted the thought and yet Melanie had agreed to help him for no reason other than out of generosity to try to help others. She hadn't asked him what she would get out of the arrangement. She'd wanted to hear the problems and then she'd made a decision based on what she felt she could do to help.

'I guess we just sealed the bargain.' Her words held a tremor. She turned to the picnic basket and started to carefully repack it. 'We should probably get back. Now that we've made this decision, your father will want that official meeting. That's assuming he can fit me into his schedule. I imagine royal families are very busy and I certainly wouldn't presume—'

'It will be all right, Melanie.' She was fully back into 'dealing with a prince and a promise and a royal family' mode and in feeling out of her depth, though she had valiantly jumped into this for his sake.

And for the sake of the people of Braston.

Did that mean she *hadn't* thought of Rik in that light as they kissed? That he had simply been a man kissing a woman, and she a woman kissing a man? Had his impact on her come completely from Rikardo the man, not from him being the third prince in line to the throne of Braston?

It wasn't a question that should even have mattered. Rik had accepted that women were attracted to his title first, sometimes to the man within, second, but always that first was there.

Perhaps some of his questioning came from the relief of knowing he hadn't blown his chance of avoiding being locked into a miserable marriage as part of his bargain with his father.

Melanie's gaze meshed with his. 'Are *you* quite sure you want to do this? I want to help you and help the people of Braston, but in the end what you do has to be really what you want.'

'I'm sure.' He got to his feet and lifted the picnic basket. 'We may not get much done today other than the meeting with my father if he is available, but Dominico will want to get the ball rolling on a few things.'

Melanie agreed. Now that she had committed to marrying Rikardo, she wanted to get things moving.

She didn't want to stop and give herself too much time to think about the next month and the three that would follow it.

That might have been rather easier for her before they shared that kiss. Mel stumbled slightly on the uneven ground. She didn't want to think about the kiss, either! Her heart still beat hard from its impact.

'I have you.' Rik's hand shot out and grasped her arm.

And I have received the most moving kiss I've ever experienced.

Not that Mel *had* a great deal of experience. Her life with the family had kept her busy. Oh, she'd dated here and there with men that she met out in her 'normal' world. At the fresh produce store, or once it was the delivery guy from the local butcher's shop. There hadn't been a lot of time or opportunity.

There is always the time and the opportunity if you want it enough.

Well, now there was a prince.

No, there wasn't. Not like that. She wasn't dating Prince Rik. She *was* going to marry him, but that was for an agreed purpose that had nothing to do with romance. Right. So she was safe from getting any of the wrong kind of ideas about him or anything like that.

Why then, with Rik's hand on her arm, and the memory of a kiss still fresh in her mind and stamped on her lips, did Mel feel anything *but* safe?

From what? Falling for him? That would be insane. Much more than falling down a rabbit hole or wearing sparkling magic shoes that would take her anywhere.

So focus on getting back to the palace to start this process that will help lift the country's economy. Rather than thinking about kisses, you should think of how you can find out as much as possible about truffle crops so you really can be of help to Rik for the short time you're here.

'Do you have books about truffle cropping in the palace?' She glanced towards the prince.

Yes, *the prince*! That was what Rik was, and Mel mustn't forget it. And since when had she started to think of him as Rik?

He said you could.

And if you have a shred of self preservation left, then you should address him as 'Your Highness' or something equally distancing, in person and in your thoughts.

'I have books at the palace and also at my personal home up in the mountains.' He glanced at her, and then up and beyond her to where those two tourists had found their way to what to Mel looked like a sheer wall of ice.

Rikardo had a second home in the mountains?

Well, duh, Mel. He's got to be about thirty and he's a prince. Did you think he'd still live permanently in a couple of rooms in the palace? Even if those rooms were quite glorious and added up to more like a small house. 'I'd like to look at the books, if that would be okay. I'd like to learn more about the industry.'

She might not be able to do anything to help with the problems they'd had, but if Rik planned to harvest truffles from the royal grounds that, too, would be rather special. Maybe there were records about that, as well.

'The kitchen staff would have special truffle recipes, wouldn't they? Maybe handed down through the centuries? I'd love to see those!' Mel tried hard to walk normally and not lean into him. He still had hold of her arm and her silly response receptors wanted to melt into his side as though they had every right just because he'd kissed her.

He might be marrying Mel, but he was doing that to help him *avoid* a committed relationship.

And Mel was marrying him to help him out, and she didn't need to add the complication of being attracted to him to *that* mix. So it was just as well they'd shared that kiss and put it behind them. They could get on with the business end of things now.

As if it will be that easy, Mel. What about the wedding preparations? The fact that his father will think the two of you want to marry for real?

'I need to have the right things to say to your father!' The words blurted out of her with a panicky edge she didn't anticipate until it was too late to cover it up. 'That is, I don't want to be unable to answer any questions he might ask about how we met, how long we've known each other, that kind of thing.'

'We met through your cousin Nicolette when I was at university in Australia. Six months ago we came across each other on a computer forum and we've been chatting online and on the phone ever since.' He turned his head and deep blue eyes looked into hers. 'I wanted you for my princess. You are calm and pleasant and I felt I could spend the rest of my life with you. It's not the entire truth, but it's as close as we'll get.'

'Okay. That will work. I know the years that Nicolette was at university, though I didn't attend myself.' There was one other issue, though. 'What's my story? Why did I say yes?'

Before he could answer, she shook her head. 'If your father asks me that question, I'd rather tell him that I will do everything in my power to be as supportive of you as I possibly can in all the time we're together.'

He dipped his head. 'Then stick to that. Commitment to me is implied in such statements. My father should find that more than acceptable.'

'Wh-what will be expected…otherwise?' Mel asked the question tentatively, and she didn't want to be tentative. She needed to know, therefore she was asking. She straightened her spine. 'When we're married, will we be in your suite as we are now, or…?' Despite the straighter spine she couldn't quite bring herself to put it into words.

His gaze met hers. In it was steadiness. 'For the sake of appearances we would be sharing my room and…bed at first. This is something that can be managed with a little creative imagination without needing to cause you undue concern. Just for the look of things, you understand?'

'Just—just part of our overall practical arrangement. Yes. I understand totally. That's very sensible.' Mel tried not to stutter the words, tried to sound mature and au fait with the situation and what it might entail. They might be sleeping together at the start—her mind tried to boggle and she forced it not to—but they wouldn't be *sleeping together*. Not, well, you know. Not like *that*. She drew a breath. 'Right. That's okay, then. We can make that work.'

'We will, Melanie, so do not worry.' His words again held reassurance.

And Mel…relaxed into that reassurance.

They were at a turn in their downward descent where the two mountainsides faced each other when a cry ripped through the air, shattering her composure and bringing Rikardo to an abrupt stop.

'Damn. What's the man doing? He's tangled in his equipment!' Rik dumped the picnic basket and strode towards the source of the cry.

Mel followed, and after a few moments managed to spot what Rik had already seen. A man dangled against that icy outcrop. It was one of the two men she'd seen earlier. The other—Mel couldn't see.

'Stop, you fool!' Rik spoke the words aloud but they were too far away for any hope that the man might hear them.

Even so, Mel echoed the sentiment.

The prince let out a pithy curse. 'If he keeps trying to get loose, he'll drop to the bottom.' He didn't slow his pace, but he turned to glance at her. 'There's no one anywhere near except us. I've rappelled that section many times. I have to see if I can help while we wait for a rescue team to get here.'

He already had a cell phone out, and quickly called for assistance and explained the situation and that he would see what he could do until the rescue team arrived.

Mel could hear someone at the other end insisting the prince must not go anywhere near the dangerous situation, before Rik said, 'Get help here as quickly as possible' and ended the call.

She bit back the inclination to ask him if he *would* be safe enough. 'What can I do, Rik?'

'Keep yourself safe. Do not follow the path I take. Follow the path that's cut into the mountain and you'll reach the same destination. It will take longer, but I'll know you are not at risk. When the rescue team starts up the mountain, point them to where I am.' He strode ahead confidently.

Mel followed at the best pace she could manage. Each moment counted and Rik quickly got ahead of her, and then cut a different path towards the ice-bound cliff. After a few minutes she could hear him shout to the man first in English, and then in French. The conversation continued in French, and Mel could only guess what was being said.

She struggled on, determined to reach Rik and be of help if she could. She was within shouting distance herself when she looked back and saw the rescue team starting up the mountain. Mel waved to them and pointed to Rik's location, and got a wave back from the leader of the team.

Mel kept going, and then there was the man, dangling in mid-air, and Rik saying something sharp and hard to a second man at the top of the cliff before taking that man's unused equipment and kitting up.

The third prince of Braston was over the edge in a breathtakingly short time. Mel didn't go any further, then. She wasn't sure she could have if she tried. Instead she stood frozen in place, completely unable to breathe as all the concern for his safety that she'd pushed back rushed to the surface and threatened to overwhelm her.

She bit back the instinct to call out, 'Be careful.' Considering what he was doing, he would already be at the bottom of the cliff if he weren't taking care.

Nevertheless, what followed made Melanie's blood chill. She'd never watched ice rappelling. It looked risky, and it was obvious from the way he tried to control his slip that Rik didn't have the right boots on his feet for the job.

The stranded man, despite Rik's instructions that even Melanie could tell were to stay still and wait whether they were in French or not, continued to tug and pull at the tangle he was in. Did he *want* to end up at the bottom of the mountain?

'Your Highness, you must wait for us!'

'Please, Prince Rikardo, you must come away from there!'

The words were called as the rescue team came close enough to see what was happening, but it was too late. If Rik didn't do something about this man, he would kill himself. Panic had the man in its grip. The second man showed no apparent interest in proceedings, sitting there with a blank look on his face.

Had Melanie looked like that when she'd taken that medication and faded into sleep?

He's taken some kind of illicit drug, Mel. You've seen enough of that in Melbourne to recognise it. No doubt Rik recognises it, too.

'You have to make sure that second man doesn't interfere with what Rik's doing or do anything stupid himself.' She spoke the instruction to the head of the rescue team as they drew close. 'He's under the influence of something. It's likely that both of them are, because Rik's struggling to get the stranded one to listen and stop fighting to get free.'

Rik had rappelled out beside the man. He couldn't untangle him, but he was trying to calm him. At his own risk! Even now the man reached for Rik with clawing hands!

'Oh, please, be careful,' she whispered.

She didn't notice that she'd called him Rik as she spoke to the rescue team, or that she'd spoken as though she had every right to that authority. Mel didn't care.

The next ten minutes felt like a lifetime. When the man was hauled up, Rikardo followed. He moved with confidence. Mel had made her way to the top and wanted to grab him once he got up there and...

Shake him? Check that he was unharmed?

Kiss him a second time?

'All is well, though I have asked the team to take both men to the nearest hospital and have them checked over, drug tested and, if need be, charged by the police.' Rik's words were spoken across a very calm surface.

But beneath that calm must be all the anger over the stupidity of those two men.

'Your Highness…' One of the rescue team approached.

'I am well and unharmed but you must excuse me now,' Rikardo said with respect, and firmness.

And then he stripped out of the equipment he'd commandeered, took Mel once again by the arm, and started down the mountain with her.

Mel walked at his side. 'I'm so glad you knew what to do up there. I'd like to see you do that properly one day, with all the right equipment, because I think you would be amazing at it.'

I'd like to see you do that properly one day…

Melanie's words rang in Rik's ears as he put his Italian sports car through its paces on the way to his mountain retreat home.

Her words were a salve to the anger he'd bitten back over the stupidity of those two men. Had they *wanted* to get themselves killed? The other one, when questioned, had said he was waiting for his turn to go out 'alone' and that ice rappelling was 'easy, man'.

The man had been so far gone that he hadn't even comprehended the danger his friend was in. Well, they were both safe now.

Rik let the thoughts go and turned his attention to his driving. He'd held back until he reached the private road that led to his home. This road, he knew better than the back of his hand, every turn, just how much he could give behind the wheel to release the pent-up energy that came from that stressful rappel in someone else's untested equipment. He'd needed this.

He's going too fast. Mel couldn't get the thought out of her head. Her logical mind understood that Rik had control of the car. It was clear he knew this road well. The road itself was wide with plenty of room for dual traffic and yet it was a private road. They hadn't seen any other cars and she guessed they were quite unlikely to do so.

All of this made infinite sense. The paralysing fear inside Mel did not make sense. Her fingers curled into the edges of her seat. Her heart pounded with a mixture of apprehension and the need to get out of this situation at any cost.

'Please stop.' The words whispered through her clenched teeth, whispered so quietly that she didn't know how Rik could have heard them.

All Mel knew was that she wanted out of this car. Now.

'Melanie.' A voice tinged with remorse broke through her fear. The car began immediately to slow and Rik said, 'I'm sorry. I didn't realise you were uncomfortable.'

It's all right. I'm fine. There's no need to slow down or stop.

In her mind, Mel entertained these polite thoughts. But her instincts were in a very different place. She struggled to breathe normally, to not throw her door open and try to get out. The reaction was so intense and so deep that it completely unnerved her. She couldn't speak, couldn't think clearly, didn't know what to say to him, didn't understand why she had ended up feeling like this.

Within moments the car moved much more slowly and fingers wrapped firmly around the hand nearest to him. 'Do you need me to stop the car completely, Melanie? My house is less than a minute away and I'd rather get you there if possible.'

The roaring in her ears started to recede but Mel was still a long way from calm. Her fingers tightened around his. 'I don't know what came over me. I feel stupid for the way I've reacted.'

'You are certainly not stupid.' Rik spoke these words softly as he drew the car to a stop in front of his mountain home. The place was maintained for him, but did not have permanent staff. They would be alone here, and he was glad for that now to give Melanie a chance to recover.

Whatever had happened during the trip had affected her deeply, and he felt she would benefit from space and not having to deal with anyone new just for the moment.

Had the panic come on because of all the pressure he'd put on her? It was a lot to ask a woman to become his temporary princess, to work with him to fool his father into believing the marriage was intended to last a lifetime.

It was a lot for her to find herself here under confused circumstances let alone the pressure Rik had added to that load for her.

You must take care of her. Give her time to calm down.

He got out of the car, opened her door for her and took her hand to help her out. His home was chalet-style, built of log and with a sharply pitched roof. Large windows gave beautiful views from every part of the home and were one-way tinted for privacy. Rik doubted that Melanie noticed any of it. Her face was sheet-white and the hand he held within his trembled.

'Let me get you a hot drink, Melanie.' He led her inside and to a comfortable leather sofa in the living room.

'Thank you. It is a bit chilly, isn't it?' Melanie sank onto the sofa and didn't argue about who should be preparing the beverages.

Rik didn't waste time, and quickly returned with coffee for both of them. He took his seat beside her. 'This will take the chill away.'

The rooms were centrally heated, but she'd clearly had a

shock. It would take time for her body to return to a normal temperature.

Rik had brought that shock about. He had put too much on her. Bringing her to Braston with her waking up from a long sleep to discover she was in the middle of Europe instead of in Sydney. He'd asked her to replace her cousin and briefly marry him. Had piled all the worries about the country onto her, and then had left her to cope with her concern for him while he rappelled onto an icy cliff in dangerous circumstances to deal with a man who didn't want to hear reason, and another who could have added more trouble to the mix.

To cap it off, Rik had come up here to get away from things, and the speed of his driving had frightened her enough that she hadn't been able to even tell him what was wrong.

As Melanie sipped her coffee and colour began to come back into her face Rik set his drink down and turned to her. 'I am sorry that you were afraid during the drive up here.'

'You weren't to know that I would react like that. I didn't know it myself.' She forced her gaze about the room before meeting his eyes. For the first time since leaving the car, she seemed to see her surroundings.

Maybe that, too, helped her, because she said valiantly, 'It was worth the trip. This is a lovely home and the views are amazing. And I feel much better. I'm sure I won't have that kind of problem again.'

'I am pleased that you're starting to feel better. What happened to you? Do car trips always make you uneasy?'

Back in Australia, she'd checked when he collected her from outside Nicolette's home that he felt fresh enough to drive. Rik hadn't thought anything of it.

'That's the first time I've been in a sports car. They go

very fast.' As she seemed to consider what had happened she frowned. 'I don't understand this myself. I don't drive, but I'm not usually the type to panic unnecessarily, and with hindsight I *know* that you had control of what you were doing.

'I'm just sorry that I spoiled the drive for you,' she said. 'You obviously needed an outlet after dealing with those two foolish men and keeping your calm so well, both before and after.'

Rik *had* needed that outlet. Sometimes keeping his cool came at a cost to his blood pressure!

'I felt like telling them off myself for being so stupid,' she added hotly, 'and I wasn't the one who had to risk life and limb to go out and stop that first man from falling to his death!'

Maybe if she learned to drive herself, she might feel better informed and more confident to assess the skill of other drivers when they were behind the wheel.

They were side by side on the sofa, and Rik became very conscious of that as they fell silent and gave their attention to their drinks.

After a moment, she spoke with a slight teasing tone in her voice. 'You make very good coffee. Is it allowed, for a prince of the realm to do such tasks as make coffee?'

'And do them well?' He shrugged his shoulders. 'I think in today's world it is, and I would go hungry and thirsty up here if it weren't.'

She was a plucky girl. Resilient. The thoughts came to Rik and lodged. He couldn't help but admire her for that.

'Do you think I could have a tour while we're here?' she asked. 'I'd love to see the rest of your home.'

'Absolutely.' Rik got to his feet and held out his hand to help Melanie rise.

He was getting in the habit of that, of reaching for her hand far too often...

But you will need to do things like that to make the upcoming marriage plans seem realistic to your father.

Even though Georgio would not expect it to be a love match, he would still expect such demonstrations.

'The meeting with my father has not yet been arranged. I think it can wait for a little longer yet.' Rik drew a breath. 'I'd like some time to restore a better mood before I tackle that talk, to be honest.'

'Then I'm glad I asked for the tour.' Mel melted the moment Rik confessed his need to prepare for the talk with his father. And she truly did feel so much better now. 'We can stay here as long as you want. It's a beautiful place.'

Rik was good company and they'd just sort of got engaged, so why shouldn't they stay here for a bit, if they wanted to? She could use the time to ask a few questions about how they would work their way through the next few months, too.

'I'll need a wedding dress.' Visions of past royal marriages scrolled through her mind. 'Something very simple that won't cost the earth.' She turned to Rik. 'How do we pull off a wedding in a month?'

'With a really good wedding planner, and, as you've already realised, with the most simplified plans possible.' He started towards the rear of the house and said firmly, 'Now let me show you the rest of my retreat, and all the views. I think they're worth seeing.'

They were, and Mel looked out of floor-length windows at some very lovely scenery before Rik toured her through the rest of his home. It was surprisingly humble. Well, not humble. It was a delightful four-bedroom chalet-style home but it certainly wasn't, well, a palace.

'I love this place,' she blurted. 'If it was me I'd be up here all the time. Normal-sized rooms, calm atmosphere, no one to tell you what to do.'

'You've just worked out the secrets of my attraction to this home.' He smiled and led her into the final room.

It was an office, with a desk and computer and shelves of books about... 'Oh. Can I look at some of those? Do you have ones that show what the truffles look like when they're harvested? History books? Anything about the *royal* truffles? Cooking? The growth process from beginning to end and the uses of truffle hogs?'

'Yes to all of that. And I trained Rufusina under the tutelage of Winnow. There is a photo album.' Rik brought out the photo album and a selection of books and before Mel knew it she was nose down in some gorgeous pictures, and some very interesting information. He didn't have cookbooks, but he told her that some of the old recipes were still produced at the palace and described some of the dishes.

'Truffled turkey. I'd like to cook that.' Mel thought back through her cooking career. 'The closest I've come to cooking with truffles is using truffle-flavoured oil a few times.'

Rik's brows lifted. 'You had a career as a cook?'

'Yes, working for my aunt and uncle.' Mel glanced at him through her lashes. She'd thought he would have known that already.

They were seated with her on the swivel chair, and him leaning back against the corner of the desk in his office. It wasn't a large room, and as she let herself register the cosiness, his closeness, Mel suddenly became breathless. 'I cooked for them for years. Cakes and desserts were my speciality, but I cooked all the meals, including for dinner parties. They liked to schmooze wealthy—'

She coughed and turned her attention back to the books. 'These are wonderful resources. It's an intricate industry. You've done well to get the black truffles growing commercially here.'

'Not so well in the past two years.' Rik glanced up and towards the windows.

The frown that came to his face made Mel follow his glance.

She hadn't noticed the change in atmosphere, but now she saw it. 'I didn't know it had started snowing.'

'Yes.' He got up from the desk. 'Why don't you select what books you'd like to bring back to the palace when we return, while I see what's in the kitchen that we can have for our lunch?'

Not that Mel minded either way and it wasn't as though Rik were trying to trap her into spending time with him here. He'd probably enjoy the time away from the palace while he could, but would have been just as content to be up here by himself.

Something in his expression still made her ask. 'How long do you think it will snow?'

CHAPTER SIX

IT SNOWED ALL that day. When darkness fell, Rik closed the curtains throughout his chalet home and turned to face Mel.

While Rik appeared completely calm Mel couldn't say the same. She stood rather uncertainly in the middle of the living room.

With the prince. Up here in his chalet where he'd just made the decision that they wouldn't be leaving until morning. So they would be here. All alone. Together. For all that time.

'It won't matter too much?' She asked the question in a deliberately businesslike tone that somehow managed to emerge sounding chatty and confiding and breathless all at once. Mel forged on. 'That you can't get back tonight, I mean?'

Even despite the tone, Mel would have said she did well, that the question was at least focused on whether he might have problems because he couldn't attend to duties at the palace tonight.

Yes. That was a good way to put it. 'Your duties—?' Really, she felt quite relaxed about this whole situation.

After all they were just staying in a different location for a night. She'd slept in a bedroom within Rik's suite of rooms last night, which was rather intimate when you thought about it, and that hadn't bothered her.

Not even when you leapt out of bed the next morning because you could hear him speaking just outside your closed door? Because you wanted to get through the shower and look your best for him before he saw you? Because you hadn't been entirely certain whether he'd pulled the covers over you the night before when you might not have looked your best?

'It won't matter at all. I gave Dominico another quick call while I was outside checking the snowfall. He'll take care of anything urgent until I get back tomorrow morning.' His cheek creased as he gave a lopsided and quite devastating smile. *He* didn't seem at all concerned or put out by their circumstances.

Which was great, of course.

That was exactly how Mel would feel in a moment when she finished pushing away these silly thoughts about being up here alone with him and how that might impact on the rest of the evening. It must be because he had kissed her on the mountainside earlier. Or because they'd spent the afternoon poring over truffle books and photo albums that showed many shots of Rufusina being trained by Rik and Rik laughing in some of the shots.

Perhaps it was also because she would be pretending to be engaged and then married to him.

'We'll end up holding hands and kissing...' Somehow the words were attached to the blood vessels in her face. Heat swept upwards from her neck and rushed into her cheeks.

'Yes,' Rik said in a deep voice. 'At times we...will.'

Rikardo. Prince Rikardo. You'll end up holding hands and kissing Prince Rikardo.

Oh, as though putting it in the correct words made it any better!

Even the reminder didn't hold the weight it should have, and Mel just didn't know what to do about that. Something had happened when he took her hand and got her out of the car and brought her inside and made her a hot drink and set to work to help her get past the ridiculous fear she'd experienced.

He acted just like your dream idea of a very ordinary man, showing a sensitive side while still being very, very strong and being wonderful and appealing and all the things you might want—

But Mel didn't want a man. Well, not for a long time. Not like that in the way of settling down together and falling in love so she ended up vulnerable. She wasn't ready for that! The thought burst through, and was somehow linked to her earlier panic while trapped in the speeding car with Rik.

Maybe she just felt panicky at the moment, full stop.

Maybe she needed to focus on right now because this was enough of a challenge, thanks very much!

Rikardo wasn't an ordinary man anyway. Mel couldn't afford to forget that.

Not while reading truffle books and smiling over Rufusina photos. Not while kissing him on a mountainside because that had been a kiss to seal a bargain. It might have blown her away, but he'd just kissed her and that had been that. Probably checking to make sure he could make it look believable any time they had to repeat the exercise over the next month and the months after that.

How many times might they…?

Mel's heart tripped.

She contemplated turning into a contortionist so she could

kick herself for being so silly. The next months would be businesslike as often as possible. That was what they would be. Now what had they been saying? 'Evening in. Yes. That'll be fine. The only thing that matters is that it doesn't interfere with other plans of yours. The treatment in the truffle groves—has that been done today or do you need to be there to supervise it? That's the one thing I didn't ask about while we studied those books.'

'Winnow has supervised the treatment today. He knows what to do, and Dominico organised payment to cover it.' He brushed this aside as though it were irrelevant.

Not the treatment part, the money part. Was it? Mel hadn't got the impression that the money would come out of some endless royal coffer. If that could happen then Rik wouldn't be stressing over getting the people out of financial trouble to the degree that he was. He'd said that there needed to be reform.

Her eyes narrowed. Had he paid for that treatment himself somehow? Out of money that perhaps shouldn't be invested in that direction because it was for his personal use or he'd earned it himself? She knew so little about him and she wanted to know…everything?

Purely because Mel preferred to understand the people she dealt with!

'We'll treat tonight as an evening off,' he declared. 'If the remainder of this month is very busy, we can remember that we at least had a few hours to—how do you say it? "Veg out and do nothing."'

'Why, yes.' A delighted laugh escaped Mel. She couldn't help it. The sound just flew out. Mel also couldn't drag her gaze from that crease in his cheek, or from the sparkle in his deep blue eyes.

So she gave in and let herself enjoy the moment. It wasn't as though Rik would want to spend the entire night kissing her senseless just because they were alone.

Just because he'd kissed her once already. Just because he was the best kisser she'd ever been kissed by and there would be times in the public eye, at least, when he would kiss her again. Just because he made her want to don sparkly shoes *and* leap into a rabbit hole.

'If we're having a night in,' a night of not kissing each other, 'then I guess we just need to work out how we want to spend our time.'

'Not reading about truffles.' This too was said with a smile.

Oh, she could fall heavily for that smile. She wouldn't, though. Not when she'd reminded herself that she was doing this to help him, and help the people of Braston, and because she'd ended up here by mistake and there weren't a lot of other options for him now, like none at all really, and she could afford the time and effort to help. Did it really make any difference whether she started her new life in Sydney this week or four months from now?

'I think I've taken in as much information about truffles as I can manage for one day, but I'm pleased to know more about the industry. It's obviously really important—to—to people here.' She'd almost said that it was important to Rik, and that was why she'd wanted to understand.

That wouldn't be the key reason, of course. She wanted to be supportive of Rik's efforts. She'd made the commitment to marry him for that reason. But she wasn't obsessing over learning all about his life and work or anything like that.

Are you sure about that, Melanie? Because you seem mightily interested in him, really.

Yes, she was sure! And no she was not ridiculously interested! She was helping to fix a problem that she was partially responsible for creating in the first place. She was no more interested than she should be.

'It's a fascinating industry,' she said in the most dampening tone she could muster. 'The truffle industry. But perhaps we could pass the time this evening some other way?'

Like snuggling on the sofa?

No. Like…well, she didn't know. Cooking? Playing on the Internet?

'How do you feel about television?' Rik indicated the large screen in the corner of the room. 'I have a selection of DVDs I've not yet got around to watching.'

'Watching DVDs would be…' *Smart. Sensible. Safe? Better than thinking about kissing the whole night?* 'A good idea. I don't mind a good comedy, but I'll watch most things.'

They sat on the floor in front of the DVD cabinet going through choices until she found episodes of an Australian comedy show she hadn't yet watched. 'Oh, you have this series! I've only ever seen a few episodes but it's supposed to be brilliant!'

So they sat side by side on the sofa with popcorn that Rik made in the microwave, and sodas from his fridge, and watched comedy episodes until Mel had giggled so many times that she'd forgotten to feel self-conscious at all in Rik's presence. Instead she had become totally enamoured of the rich, deep rumble that accounted for *his* laughter.

And she forgot to guard against letting herself be aware of him as an attractive appealing man and not a prince who should be held at arm's length because she was only here for a few months and he was marrying her so he could avoid any kind of commitment to a woman, even if Mel didn't know why he seemed to need to do that as much as he needed to. They were almost through the evening, anyway.

So why are you almost holding your breath, Mel, as though waiting for something to happen?

'Goodnight, Mel.' Rik walked Melanie to the opened doorway of her bedroom.

They'd watched their comedy episodes. Mel had paid more attention than he had. Did she feel it the way that he did? This compulsion that ate at him to draw closer, know her, use every avenue and every moment to learn more of her and to let her learn more of him? And a coinciding physical consciousness that seemed to fill the air around them with a charge of electricity just waiting for one small spark to set it ablaze?

Why did this woman make him feel this way more than any other had? Rik didn't want to admit that to himself, but he forced the acknowledgement.

Then admit that you desire her, and that the desire is as much about her personality as it is about her physical appeal.

He'd spent this evening with her and he'd thought about how different their lives were and mad thoughts had come through his mind about bridging the gaps.

Look how well longevity and sticking together had worked for his father and mother. The queen had walked out, had done the one thing Rik and his brothers had never expected. She had turned her back on what she had treated as the core of her duty. And now neither parent would discuss the matter with their sons.

Rik turned his thoughts back to the present.

At times today Mel seemed to have almost forgotten that Rik was a prince. He'd…liked that. But now was not a good time for him to forget the arrangement they'd made. He needed this to work. To be distracted by her beauty and appeal was not the right thing for him to do, to be distracted mentally and in *liking* her so much, even less smart because it spoke of an emotional awareness that couldn't happen. Rik could never trust...

'Good—goodnight, Rik.' She said the words quietly, almost tentatively.

With a question in their depths?

Her small hand came to rest on his forearm and she reached up and briefly kissed his cheek. 'I'll see you in the morning and I'll be ready for whatever needs to be done to help get your temporary marriage plans started, or just to keep out of the way if you need to work in the truffle groves tomorrow.'

Rik searched her face and saw the determination to do the right thing, to dismiss him and her awareness of him at one and the same time. To remain Melanie here and Rikardo there and never the two should cross over their lines.

He saw all that, and he *felt* what was inside her. A very different compulsion that he felt, too, that made him want to lean in and replace that pseudo-kiss with the real thing. To know for himself if the last kiss had been some kind of strange fluke. If her lips would taste as good a second time.

'Sleep well.' He turned and started for his room at the end of the short corridor. 'I will see you in the morning. Thank you for your company this evening. I...really enjoyed it.'

And with that, Prince Rikardo Eduard Ettonbierre of Braston went to his room, stepped inside and shut the door firmly behind him.

Only then did he lift his hand to allow his fingertips to lightly trace where her lips had pressed to his cheek.

It was perfectly fine for him to find Melanie likeable,

and to still marry her, end the marriage short months later, and get on with the single life that he wanted, and *needed* to maintain.

He *would not* be marrying for real.

Rik sighed and dropped his hand. For now he needed to prepare for bed.

Tomorrow was a new day and no doubt a new set of challenges.

CHAPTER SEVEN

'I WOULD LIKE to present to you my fiancée, Nicole Melanie Watson.' Rik spoke the words to King Georgio formally, and as though the other impromptu meeting had never occurred. 'My fiancée is known by her middle name of Melanie.'

If the occasion had been less formal, Mel might have smiled at Rik's tweaking of history to suit himself. But this was not that kind of moment. Mel curtsied.

'I am pleased to meet you, Melanie.' Georgio took her hand and air-kissed above the fingers and, while doing so, searched her face. After a moment he gave a slight nod and indicated a setting of leather lounges and chairs to the left.

They were in what Rik referred to as one of the 'great rooms'. It was a large area, and could have felt intimidating if Mel hadn't walked in here determined *not* to be intimidated.

Mel and Rik had made their way down the mountain this morning. He'd driven at a gentler pace and Mel had remained calm until they were almost at the palace. Nervous anticipation had set in then but Mel felt that was justified.

'Let us get to know one another a little, Melanie,' Georgio said as they all took their seats.

Rik sat on one of the sofas beside Mel. He seemed deeply resolved this morning. Last night, when she'd thought he would kiss her at her door, kiss her *properly*, Melanie had thought he might feel as confused and tempted and aware of her as she did of him. But of course that was quite silly. He might have wanted to kiss her. But that didn't mean his emotions were engaged.

Not that Mel's were!

Concentrate on the king, Mel. This is not the time for anything else.

'Melanie and I first met through a cousin of hers.' Rik added a few details.

When the king nodded, Mel bit back the urge to heave a sigh of relief. But she also had to handle her share of the conversation. 'I admire Rikardo, and the work that he does for the people of Braston. I want to be as supportive of that as I possibly can.'

'That is good.' Georgio's glance shifted from Mel to Rik and back to Mel again. 'And what did you do before you agreed to marry my son?'

'I worked as a cook.' It might not have been a glamorous job. It would probably sound even less glamorous if she admitted she had done that for little money, working for her relatives to earn her right to a sense of belonging.

Note to self, Mel. You never did earn that right and you waited too long to get yourself out of that situation.

A similar set of rites was being played out in this room between Rik and his father.

She turned the highest wattage smile she could muster towards King Georgio. 'My history is humble, I suppose, but there's nothing to be ashamed of in coming from everyday stock.'

'If that "stock" has an appropriate history attached to it.' Georgio's eyes narrowed. 'My son will run a check. I will see this report for myself.'

Like a police-record check or something?

No, Mel, it will be a lot more detailed even than that.

She tried not to bristle at the thought, and at the king's emotionless declaration. As though he did this all the time and would have no hesitation in eliminating her like a blot from Rik's radar screen if she didn't come up to standard.

It didn't actually matter whether Georgio liked her or approved of her or not, provided she could marry Rik so that Rik could carry out his plans.

I still don't like it. My family history is my business. I don't want it exposed to all and sundry.

'Dominico already ran the check.' Rik clipped the words off. 'You may take Melanie at her word, Father. There is nothing in her history to justify the need for you to view the report.'

Mel stiffened inwardly for a second time.

Rik leaned close to her and said softly, 'I'm sorry. It was necessary. Dominico gave me a very light summary of the report.'

Much of Mel's agitation subsided. 'I don't have anything to hide. I just don't like the idea...'

'Of your privacy being invaded.' The twist to his lips was ironic.

Somehow that irony helped Mel to let the matter go.

Georgio straightened slightly in his chair. 'I could order a search of my own.'

A chill formed in the edges of Rik's deep blue irises. 'But I think you will agree there is no need.'

For a moment as father and son locked gazes the room

filled with the powerful clash of two strong wills. It occurred to Mel then that there were matters within such families that were very different from 'regular' life. Yes, Rik had ordered a search of her life and history. No, she hadn't liked hearing that. But if Rik hadn't done the search, his father would have ordered it. At least this way Mel wasn't exposed to Georgio reading the entire report.

A moment later Georgio glanced away. Rik had won that round, it was done and the conversation moved on to more general topics.

Rik raised the matter of the truffle harvest. Mel sat quietly listening, but she remained aware of Georgio's examination.

No way would he have accepted a switch between her and her cousin. He was too observant.

So you've done the right thing, Mel, by agreeing to help Rik. And Georgio is a strong-willed man and very set in his attitudes. You're helping Rik to avoid being pushed into a long-term loveless marriage for the wrong reasons, too.

'You have done well this morning, Melanie. I'm proud of you.' Rik spoke the words and then realised it perhaps wasn't his place to feel such an emotion in the rather personal way that he did towards his fiancée right now. She wasn't marrying him for real reasons. She was doing this to help him and she understood that it would all end a few months from now.

Tell her what the buy-off will be in exchange for her assistance.

The thought came, and Rik...pushed it aside once again, for later. He would take care of Melanie, would ensure that she got good assistance to start her on her way with her new life in Sydney when she returned to Australia. When the moment was right to bring the topic up, he would do so.

He…felt that she would know inherently that he would… take care of her.

Rik used a key to unlock the door to a small room. 'There will be a number of rings you can choose from for your engagement ring.'

'From the family h-heirlooms?' Mel's footsteps faltered in the doorway.

For a moment Rik thought she might back out of the room, refuse to enter. 'They are not all heirlooms,' he said, 'but yes.'

She drew a deep breath, threw her shoulders back and continued into the room. 'It's probably a good idea to use something from the family's stock of jewellery. The ring can be given back when we're finished, and it won't have cost you anything. We need to find one that fits and doesn't need adjusting, and that you wouldn't choose if you were—'

Doing this for real.

The words echoed unspoken in the room.

The practicality of her determined attitude made Rik want to smile, and yet when they stepped fully into the room and he saw the spread of jewellery that Dominico had laid out for them, a strange feeling swept over him. His gaze shifted from piece to piece until he found a ring that he felt would suit Mel. A ring that he would have chosen for her if their circumstances had been different?

There *were* no different circumstances possible, either now or in his future. Yet to Rik in this moment—

He lifted a ring with a platinum band. The three diamonds were Asscher cut to reflect light off the many facets. The stones were perfectly round, and set with the larger of the three diamonds raised higher than the two to its left and right. Because the ring was simple and the setting not as high as some, the size of the diamonds did not leap out as it might have.

The platinum band would suit Melanie's colouring; the setting would look beautiful on her finger. It was a ring he could enjoy seeing on her for decades.

Well, it would do for the time being. He lifted the ring. 'This was not an engagement ring, but a dress ring of my grandmother that she had fashioned for her later in her life. Her fingers were small and delicate as yours are. I do not know if she ever even wore it. She was rather indulgent when it came to such creations. I...feel the ring may suit you.'

'Oh.' Melanie didn't even glance at the remaining jewellery. And when Rik took her hand gently in his and slipped the ring onto her finger, she caught her breath. Her gaze flew to his. 'It—it fits perfectly. Just as though—'

'Just as though,' he murmured, and there, in the quiet of a small room filled with valuable jewellery that Melanie had been hesitant to go anywhere near, Rik lifted her hand and kissed the finger upon which his engagement ring now rested.

'Just as though we were a real engaged couple, I was going to say.' She whispered the words and glanced down at the ring. 'I didn't expect it to look—'

Right. She hadn't expected it to look right. Rik didn't need her to finish the sentence to know that was what she'd meant to say. He hadn't expected it either. Nor had he expected the sudden sense of well-being and destiny that swept over him when he placed the ring on her finger.

Was he getting in over his head with her somehow despite his determination to treat this as a business transaction? Had he allowed some attitudes and thoughts to slide in wrong directions because, if he hadn't, then how had he ended up with such unexpected feelings in the first place?

Rik should have been sorting out the answers to those questions. Instead he leaned towards her and somehow his arm was around her, drawing her close.

This time when he kissed her it was he who lost himself in a moment that should not have been, lost himself in the taste and texture and the giving of Melanie's lips as he kissed her until he had to break away or—

It would all feel far too real?

You cannot let it become that way, Rikardo. Melanie is a sweet girl, but she never will be more than a means to an end. You will never marry permanently, not for real and not for love, and not to lock yourself for ever into a loveless marriage.

He would never trust such an emotion as 'love' within that institution. Not when his parents hadn't managed even to love their sons let alone each other.

'I have something else that I wish to show you this morning.' Rik escorted her from the room, Away from a room full of the beauty that should go with emotion and dreams and the love of a lifetime, but had it ever existed within his family? There was that old legend, but...

Rik increased his pace.

'Th-thank you for the beautiful choice of ring, Rik,' Mel said softly as they stepped out of doors and started along an outside pathway that led between vast stretches of snow-covered grounds.

On her finger, the ring felt light and comfortable. It fitted perfectly and maybe that was what disturbed Mel so much. That and the fact that *Rik* had chosen it out of a dazzling array of royal jewellery. Rik had wanted her to wear *this* ring, and then he'd kissed her. It was the second time they'd sealed their agreement with a kiss, and each time became more difficult to treat as just a meeting of lips against lips.

What kind of state would she be in by the time he kissed her on the wedding day?

'I should not have kissed you like that.' His glance meshed momentarily with hers.

Had he read her mind? Considering the messy confused state of the thoughts in there, she hoped not!

Rik went on. 'Our arrangement is not for…that kind of purpose and I should have remembered.'

'Well, it was probably because we'd just been with your father and working so hard to make sure that all went well.' She gave a laugh that sounded just a bit forced. 'We got a little too carried away in our roles but it was only for a moment. It probably barely left an impression, really.'

Her words were just making this worse! She bit her lip. Mel glanced about them and her gaze fell on a small piece of machinery ahead. 'That's an interesting-looking vehicle.'

Rik followed Melanie's gaze.

She was wise to change the topic. He was more than happy to work with her in that respect, though his glance did drop again to her hand where the ring sat as though it belonged there, and then to her soft lips, which had yielded so beautifully beneath his just moments ago. He wanted to kiss her again. Kiss and so much more.

Not happening, Rik.

And yet his instincts told him that the kisses they'd shared had been far more than instantly forgettable to her.

To him, too, if he were honest.

'This is an all-weather buggy.' He explained that Winnow had taken the vehicle out of storage and made sure it was in working order. 'In first gear it doesn't drive any faster than a person can walk. It's easy to handle. All you need to do is steer and make it stop and start. It will drive on snow and it can handle rough terrain but there are plenty of paths here to drive it on. Our appointment with the wedding planner is not for another hour. I thought I might show you how to work this while we wait.'

Her gaze flew to his. 'You want me to drive it?'

'I thought it might be a good way for you to start to be able to get around more while you're here.' In truth there were a dozen ways he could ensure that Melanie could move around the area, and for the most part Rik expected to be with her anyway. Even so...

'I don't drive cars.' She said it quickly, and then tipped her head to the side and looked at the buggy, and back at Rik. 'I've never really had any interest in learning.'

'This is not a car.' He watched her face, and took a gamble. 'But if you don't feel that you can try it—'

Her chin went up. 'Of course I'll try it. That would be like saying I didn't want to try riding a skateboard or making some new dish in the kitchen.'

She was a plucky girl, his Melanie, Rik thought. Before he could pull himself up on the possessive manner of wording that thought, Melanie stepped forward and did an at least passable job of feigning delight at the idea of learning all about the buggy.

'First I will demonstrate.' Rik sat in the driving seat with Melanie beside him and showed her the controls. They were on castle grounds in an area where the worst that could happen was they ended up off the path. He got the buggy moving, explaining as he drove, and then, when he felt Mel was ready, Rik simply got out of the seat and started walking beside her. 'Slide into the driver's seat.'

Mel slid over and gripped the wheel. A moment later she was steering the buggy grimly.

He guided her along, helping her to master steering around corners and stopping and starting. After a few minutes Mel didn't need his help, and even asked if he would get back in with her so she could increase speed to a higher gear.

Finally her hands unclenched and she gave the first hint of a smile before she stopped the buggy and turned to look at him.

'Well done,' he praised. 'I am glad you have been able to do this, Mel.'

'It was fun. It's such a long time since I've completely enjoyed anything that resembled vehicle travel. All the way back to when my parents used to take me every Sunday and we'd go...' Her expression sobered and she frowned as though trying to remember something.

Though she tried to conceal it, sadness touched her face. She climbed out of the buggy. 'I don't remember what we used to do. They...died in a car crash.'

His hand wrapped around her fingers, enclosing her. He wished he could warm her heart from that chill. He wanted to do that for her so much. 'I am sorry—'

'It's all right. It was a long time ago.' Her words relegated her pain to the past. But her fingers wrapped around his...

A member of the palace staff approached to let Rik know that the wedding planner had arrived. The moment ended, but the tenderness Rik felt for Melanie grew inside him.

Duty. He had to attend to his duty.

Rik dipped his head. 'Please tell the planner we will be with her shortly.'

'Yes, Prince Rikardo.' The man walked away.

Melanie turned her gaze towards Rik and drew a deep

breath. 'This is the next phase, isn't it? We have to convince this planner that we're doing this for real, even if we do want a simple, quick, trouble-free arrangement.' She seemed to think about what she'd just said, and a thoughtful expression came over her face. 'You must have chosen a great planner, if the woman believes she can achieve that, in a month, for a royal wedding of any description.'

Rik drew a slow breath as his gaze examined her face, flushed with the success of learning to drive the buggy, and her expressive eyes that had clouded when the topic of her parents had come up.

Perhaps he should ask Dominico for a proper look at that report after all. It might tell Rik more about Melanie's background.

Only to help understand her, he justified, and then frowned because, of all reasons he might read the report, wasn't that the most personal and therefore to him, at least, the most unacceptable? 'Dominico seems to believe this planner will be up to the task. Let us go see how she fares with our requests.'

CHAPTER EIGHT

'You have made very rapid plans, Rik.'

'Are you sure you want to marry so quickly? Our father might still have given us what we wanted if we all became engaged and then spoke to him again about the arrangement. That way you could have held off from actually marrying until closer to the six-months mark. Things might have changed by then.'

The words came to Melanie in two different male voices as she went in search of Rik. It was four days later and she'd woken to find her breakfast waiting for her, and Rik already gone to the palace grounds to oversee the harvesting of the first of the special truffles.

'It won't make any difference whether I marry soon, or marry after many months. You know this. Our father will not change his mind or soften his expectations.'

Rik didn't explain the reason for his statement—the brief nature of the intended marriage—and Mel didn't know if he'd told his brothers the truth about it as yet or not. But did his voice sound oddly flat *because* he knew this fact?

She must be imagining it.

You and your over-inflated ego are imagining it together, Mel.

'Good—good morning, Rikardo.' Mel spoke to make her presence known. Not because she minded her impending marriage to Rik being discussed, but because it wasn't right to eavesdrop, even if she hadn't meant to.

'Melanie. I am glad you're awake and have found us.' Rik stepped forward. He touched her hand and gestured to the two men standing to their left. 'These are my brothers, Marcelo and Anrai.'

'Hello. I'm pleased to meet you both.' The words emerged in a calm tone before Mel stopped to remember that she was being introduced to two more princes.

Rabbit hole. Sparkly shoes. Do I look good enough for this occasion, and why didn't I address him as Prince Rikardo or Your Highness?

She drew a breath.

'It is a delight to meet you, Melanie. Our brother has told us about you.' The older man bowed over her hand and managed to make the gesture seem relaxed and European rather than princely and...royal. 'I am Marcelo.'

The first in line to the throne. The brother who would most of all be expected to marry and stay married, whether he wanted to or not. He was dark like Rik, a little taller, and his eyes were such a deep inky blue, they were almost black.

'I am Anrai.' The second brother smiled a killer smile, shook her hand, and stepped back as though content to observe proceedings from this point. His hair was a lighter brown, thick and with a slight wave. It flopped over his forehead and drew attention to sparkling pale blue eyes.

Mel had dismissed him as not as handsome as Rik. She could now see that he would actually be a quite stunning lady-killer, but he still didn't appeal to *her*. She only had eyes for—

'Hello.' Mel tried to smile naturally and not feel overwhelmed by being surrounded by these three very royal men. It wasn't until she glanced at Rik's face that she realised she'd placed herself so close to his side that they were almost touching. Not because she felt intimidated but because…

Well, she couldn't explain it, actually. What she did realise was that she'd been allowing herself to think of Rik more as a man, and less as a prince. At least this meeting had given her that reality check. And it was nice to meet his brothers. 'Have any of the truffles been dug out yet?'

A snort from behind them drew Mel's attention. She turned her head and there was Rufusina. The pig had a quilted coat on and a keen look in her eyes, as though she was sitting in apparent obedience waiting for something.

'Rufusina's obviously champing at the snout,' Mel observed. 'What's the hold-up?'

'There's no hold-up—' Rik started.

'We were just deciding how best to go about the extraction,' Anrai added.

Marcelo's brows formed a vee. 'It is the most stupid thing to wait for a sign from—'

Rufusina lifted her snout, sniffed the air once, and then again.

Rik said under his breath, 'Wait for it.'

Anrai's shoulders stiffened.

The truffle hog sniffed the air a third time and trotted to a group of trees.

'*Now* I will go in there.' Anrai followed Rufusina's rapidly receding form. 'But only because I think she knows where the best truffles are. It has nothing to do with anything else.'

'Marcelo?' Rik turned to his older brother.

'I was not concerned in the first instance.' The oldest brother followed Anrai. 'All the truffles on the palace grounds are exceptional, as has been proved in years past. That is all that matters.'

Rik turned to Mel. 'Would you care to be present while Rufusina does her work and finds us the choicest truffles?'

'I would love to be there.' Mel's curiosity was tweaked. Just what had that "rite of passage" been about? And to be present while such wonderful foods were lifted from their resting places? Imagine *tasting* such a wonderful, rare indulgence!

Rik took her arm and started towards a grove of trees that looked very old. 'It is an exciting moment.'

'Apologies, Melanie, for walking away.' Anrai rubbed the back of his neck with his hand. 'Once the pig sniffs the air three times—'

'It will guide the prince to truffles that are the choicest, and that are possessed of the power to make his deepest hopes come true.' Marcelo said the words with a dismissive twist of his lips. 'You must forgive us, Melanie. We are being foolish this morning, but Rikardo—'

'Asked nicely if you would both like to be present for this event.' Rik jumped in with the words that were almost defensive.

Mel thought about her rabbit hole and the sparkly shoes and how out of place she'd felt when she arrived here, and how different this world was from anything she had ever known. And she looked at three big, brave men who had hovered at the edge of a grove of trees and refused to shift until...

'A magic truffle hog unlocks the key to safe passage, and perhaps to the granting of your wishes?' The words came with the start of a smile that spread until it almost cracked her face in half.

She could have laughed aloud. Mel could have done a lot of things. But then she looked properly at the grove of trees and thought about age and history. Three princes *had* all come to participate in this ritual. Rufusina *had* lifted her nose and sniffed three times and then trotted over here with purpose. Mel sobered. 'How old is the legend? Are there bad aspects attached if you don't do things the right way?'

'Centuries. None of us have ever come near the harvesting of these truffles until now. It's usually left to our staff, but I wanted to oversee it this time.' Rik didn't seem offended by her initial amusement. He did seem a little uncomfortable having to explain the situation. 'The legend is more to do with prosperous lives, and making the right choice of marriages and so on. But I am only concerned with getting good truffles for my overseas buyers.'

'Yes. That is no doubt the priority.' Mel bit back any further smiles. She turned to the others and said to all three of them, 'I'm grateful to have the chance to see this, and I hope to get a good look at the truffles themselves when they're harvested.'

Winnow approached as Mel made this statement.

The three princes were all about business after that. It was strange to stand back and watch these three privileged men go about digging bits of fungus out from beneath beds of rotting leaves. Rufusina did her thing, and Rik praised her for being a good hog, at which the pig sort of…preened, Mel thought fancifully, and checked her own feet to make sure they hadn't sprouted those sparkly shoes while she was daydreaming.

'This one looks good, brother. And smell the pungent odour.' Anrai handed a truffle to Rik.

Rik examined the truffle. 'It is good. Take a look at it, Melanie.'

Before Mel could blink, the truffle had been dumped into her hands. She didn't know much about truffles. Not in this state, but that didn't stop her from wanting to cook with them, to discover if they were indeed as fine as it was claimed, to revere the opportunity to hold this piece of life and privilege and history. 'Will they be enough for your marketing plans, Rik?'

She didn't notice the softness in her tone, didn't see the look exchanged between Rik's brothers as Rik bent his shoulders to protect her from the wind that had sprung up as he answered her question.

'I hope so, Mel. I very much hope so.'

They gathered the truffles. Some were sent with Winnow to be prepared for travel. Rik placed the others in a basket, thanked his brothers for their presence and saw them on their way, and then turned to Mel. 'Shall we have that peek at the kitchen that you mentioned?'

'Y-yes. I'd like that.' Mel liked it even more that Rik had remembered that small comment of hers from days ago.

They made their way to the kitchens. Rik introduced Mel to the staff and somehow, even though she'd always been on the other side of things in this environment, he made it comfortable and easy. Enough that when he had to excuse himself to attend to other matters, Mel accepted the invitation to remain behind and observe as the staff prepared the midday meals.

'I'm almost afraid to taste,' Melanie murmured as Rik removed the cover from the last dish.

They were in his suite. He'd asked for their meal to be sent here, and wasn't that what people would expect of a newly engaged couple—to want every moment alone? Yet Rik knew that he'd chosen to dine with Melanie here because *he* wanted to keep her to himself more than he perhaps should.

The legend talked of sharing the first meal prepared with the truffles, that the prince must share the tasting process...

He pushed the fanciful thoughts aside. This was a matter of practicality. And perhaps of giving Melanie a moment that she might not otherwise experience. 'Each of the dishes have been enhanced with the addition of the truffles.'

'The kitchen staff said there are different opinions about actually cooking the truffles.' Mel had listened with interest to the discussion about that in the kitchens earlier. She'd learned so much! 'The risotto and the duck dishes both smell divine.'

'Before we start on those, I would like to give you the chance to sample the first truffle in very simple form.' Rik lifted a single truffle from a salver. His fingers shook slightly. He steadied them and lifted his gaze to hers.

It was just a legend. Foolish stuff.

The prince prepares the truffle and offers it to his bride.

Mel drew a shaky breath as though she perhaps, too, felt the air change around them, almost as though it filled with anticipation as she yielded her palate to his ministration...

He shaved transparent slices of truffle onto the pristine white plate. The butter knife slid through creamy butter. Just the right smear on each sliver, a sprinkle of salt crystals.

Rik held the first slice out to her. Soft pink lips closed over it, just touched the tips of his fingers as her eyelids drifted closed and she experience her first taste of...a legend.

'It's almost intoxicating.' Her words whispered through

her lips. 'The permeation of the scent, the beautiful texture. I can't even describe how amazing...I feel as though I've tasted something sacred.'

She couldn't have rehearsed those words if she'd tried. Rik took his own slice of truffle, unbelievably pleased in the face of *her* pleasure.

They moved on to eat the other dishes. Melanie experienced each new taste with curiosity and perhaps with a little awe. Rik shared her pleasure and knew that it renewed his own. He couldn't take his gaze from her mouth. He wanted to lean forward and taste the flavour of the truffle, of salt and butter, from the inside of her lips.

It was just a legend.

But Melanie Watson was not a legend. She was a very real woman, and Rik...desired her in this moment, far too much.

They left for France that afternoon. Mel settled into her seat on the family's private plane and observed, with some wonder, Rik's calm face. 'I don't know how you do it.'

'Do what?' He glanced out of the window at the scudding clouds beneath the plane's belly before he turned his gaze to her and gave her all of his attention.

'Remain so calm in the face of being chased all the way to the plane by a wedding planner waving colour swatches and bits of lace and begging for fittings and a decision on the choices for the table settings.'

'We gave her the answers she needed.' A slight smile twitched at the corners of Rik's mouth. 'And perhaps next time she won't wear those kinds of heels for running.'

'I could learn a thing or two.' Melanie had taken to the wedding planner. 'She's doing her best to make things easy for us while we fly all over Europe showing buyers what they'll be missing out on if they don't make an order this year for Braston truffles.'

'In truth we're only going to Paris.' There was a pause while Rik looked into her eyes, and while he registered how committed she had sounded to his country's industry as she spoke those words.

'It's still more exciting than almost anything I've done.' Melanie returned his glance.

How did he do that? Make it seem as though the whole rest of the world suddenly faded away and it were just the two of them? Mel would be hopeless at truly being married to him. There'd be photos through the tabloids all the time of her making goo-goo eyes at him when she didn't realise she was doing it.

Um, where was she?

She would not, anyway. An unguarded thought here or there, or coming to realise that he was a good man and one she could admire, hardly equated to a Rufusina-like devotion to the man.

And you just compared yourself to a truffle hog, Mel. I don't think pigs wear magic slippers. 'Magic trotters, maybe,' Mel muttered, and snapped her teeth together before anything even sillier could come out.

'I hope the marketing trip is successful.' For a moment Rik dropped his guard and let her see the concern beneath the surface. 'There's no room for failure in my plans, but I still...'

Worry?

'All the kitchen staff said the truffles were the best ever. I have nothing to compare to, but I thought they were stunning.' Mel was glad she'd spent the time in the kitchen while Rik finalised plans for their trip.

He'd sprung it on her just as though they were taking a

walk around the corner. "Oh, and by the way we're leaving for Paris this afternoon, I'll have the staff pack for you."

She'd let that happen, too, and hadn't even tried to oversee what got put in the suitcases. Melanie Watson, cook, had stayed clear and let the palace staff pack her things for a trip to Paris.

'I'll help you in any way I can, with the marketing efforts.' Mel didn't know if she could do anything. Did being his fiancée count?

Her glance dropped to the ring on her finger. Every time she looked at it, it seemed to belong there more than the last time. It had seemed to be made for her from the moment Rik lifted it from a bed of black velvet and placed it on her finger.

What was happening to her? She was losing the battle to keep her emotional distance from him, that was what. There was no point saying she only cared about the people of Braston, or only admired him because he cared about their futures. Mel did feel all those things, but they were only part of what she felt for him.

Face it, Mel. Somehow you got caught in your own feelings towards him and, instead of getting them under control or stopping them altogether, they've grown more and more with each passing day.

CHAPTER NINE

'I AM INTERESTED, you understand. Braston black truffles have been a high-standard product.' The owner of the group of elite Parisian restaurants spoke the words to Rik with a hint of regret, but as much with the glint of good business in his eyes. 'It is just with your truffles being totally off the market for two years I have found other supply sources.'

This was the fourth restaurant owner they'd seen since they arrived in Paris. The others had come on board, but something told Mel this one might be a harder sell.

They were inside the man's home, seated at a carved wooden dining setting. At the end of the table, a wide glass vase held a bunch of mixed flowers. The moment they walked into the room, Rik's gaze had examined the arrangement.

He'd been checking for gardenias, Mel had realised, and her heart had been ridiculously warmed by the gesture on his part. There were none, but that bunch of flowers looked particularly pretty to her now.

'The blight to our crops was tragic, but we are back on our feet and, as you can see, the commercial truffles are the same high standard.' Rik lifted one of the truffles he had placed on an oval plate in the centre of the table, took up a stainless-steel shaver and shaved thin slices from the black shape.

As the older man examined the truffle slices, and Mel recalled the almost spiritual moment of trying her first truffle with Rik, he went on.

'I know at this time of year you would be sourcing truffles. I'd like to see Braston truffles back on the menu at your restaurants.'

At his feet was a travel carrier containing more truffles, and from which he had unpacked the plates and shaver as well as a beautiful small kitchen knife with a gold inlaid handle.

'And I'd like to put them there, but—'

'I have an added incentive that may sweeten the deal for you, Carel.' Rik spoke the words quietly.

'And that is?' Carel was the last on their list.

It was almost nine p.m. now and they had been fortunate that the man rarely worked in any of his kitchens these days, preferring to visit as suited him, so he'd been more than happy to meet with Rik at his home.

The incentive of the truffles harvested from royal grounds had worked well with the other restaurant owners. They'd all placed orders for commercial truffles so they could also obtain some of the other truffles. Mel wondered if Carel would be as willing to be convinced. Middle-aged, and ruthlessly business focused, this man was much harder to read than the others.

A surge of protectiveness of Rik rose in Mel's breast. He shouldn't have to beg for anything. He was, well, he was a prince! And yet that description was not the first one that had come to Mel's mind. Rik was good and fair and hardworking and dedicated and his care for the people of his country ran so deep that she knew it would never leave him. He deserved to be respected because of what was inside him.

Carel tipped his head slightly to the side. 'We have already discussed pricing and you certainly do not plan to give away—'

'Braston's truffle crops at a price that won't help my people get back on their feet?' Rik said it softly. 'No. And deep down I know you would not respect such a gesture if I made it.'

The older man was silent for a moment before he dipped his head. 'You are correct.'

'How would you feel about a complimentary gift of some of the truffles grown on the palace grounds?' Rik watched Carel's face for his reaction. 'To go with your order, of course.'

Mel watched both their faces.

'There are legends surrounding those truffles.' The older man's glance moved to Mel before it returned to Rik and he asked with the hint of a smile, 'Do I need to ask whether you harvested the truffles yourself? I am assuming you have brought them with you to show?'

'You do not need to ask, and I have brought them.' Rik's answer was ironic and guarded all at once.

Before Mel could try to understand that, Rik drew another white rectangular plate out and placed just one truffle on it.

Carel leaned forward to look.

Rik shaved the truffle, allowing the wafer thin slices to fall onto the plate and the pungent aroma to rise.

What exactly did that legend stand for? Mel made a note to find out when they got back to the palace.

'The aroma is muscular with a particular rich spiciness I have never encountered.' Carel lifted one of the slices to examine the texture, and colour.

He looked, he inhaled, and after a long moment he put the truffle slice down. 'I do not know. I'm not convinced that the royal truffles will equate to anything exciting enough on the plate. If I agreed to your offer, I would want to be sure that the truffles were a good enough selling point in terms of taste, not only legend.'

'And yet they *are* the stuff of legends,' Rik said with a hint of the same spark.

This was the business dance, and both men were doing it well.

'Indeed.' The older man dipped his head. 'That is undeniable and an excellent marketing point. But I would be using them at my restaurants for the most expensive dishes only on a very limited basis. They would have to live up to and beyond expectation in all ways.'

'They do. They would!' The words burst out of Mel. She touched the edge of one truffle slice with the tip of her finger and caught and held Carel's gaze. 'These truffles have a flavour and scent you'll never find anywhere else. The texture is beautiful. They provide the most stunning enhancement to the dishes they're used in or when eaten by themselves.'

'This is quite true.' Rik's gaze softened as he glanced at Melanie's face. She wanted so desperately for this trip to be successful, for him to obtain all the markets for his truffles that he had set out to recapture. 'But I understand Carel's point, too.'

Rik appreciated Mel for that investment in him. It seemed a bland way to describe the warm feeling that spread through his chest as he acknowledged Melanie's fierce support of his efforts. It *was* a bland description, but Rik wasn't at all sure he wanted to allow himself to examine that warmth, or try to know exactly what it might mean.

'For me, I do not have the evidence of this truth.' Carel again smelled and examined the truffle and its slices. 'I am sure my chefs would like to try cooking with these, but they are busy at the restaurants—'

'*I'll* cook them for you!' Melanie got out of her chair. 'Right here and now.'

If Carel had given any indication that he wouldn't allow it, no doubt Melanie would have immediately stopped. But the older man simply watched with a hint of appreciation on his face as Melanie fired up on Rik's behalf. Carel waved a hand as though to say: By all means go ahead.

Rik had to push back a bite of possessive jealousy as he realised the older man was…aware of his fiancée as a woman.

Surely this doesn't surprise you, Rik? Every man would notice her beauty. How could they not?

Melanie stepped into Carel's open-plan kitchen. It was immediately apparent that she was at home in this environment. A chopping board sat on the bench.

She glanced towards the refrigerator. 'May I use anything, *monsieur*?'

Carel smiled. 'Yes. Anything.'

Mel took chicken breast, salad greens and dried raspberries, and then selected a bottle of red wine. Finally she retrieved salt and pepper and cashews and a long thin loaf of bread from Carel's pantry.

Rather than the kitchen knives available to her, Mel walked back to where Rik sat at the table. She took the gold-handled knife from where it rested near Rik's right hand.

As she did so she touched his shoulder briefly with her other hand. 'For luck.'

He didn't know whether she meant the knife, or the touch. Perhaps both.

'Your fiancée has pluck.' The Frenchman spoke the words quietly as he sat back to watch Melanie take control of his kitchen. 'I shall eagerly observe this.'

A half-hour later, Mel drew a deep breath and carried the chicken salad to the table. The meal looked good on the plate, colourful and versatile, full of different textures with the thin slices of truffle heated through and releasing their gorgeous aroma. The wine reduction made a beautiful sauce. The thick slice of bread coated with beaten egg yolk, the lightest combination of chopped herbs and grated sharp cheese and lightly toasted made a perfect accompaniment.

Even so, the proof would be in the taste, not only the visual appeal. Mel placed the dish before her host and brought the other two servings for Rik and herself.

Minutes later, Carel put down fork and knife and lifted his gaze. He spoke first to Rik. 'The truffles are better than anything I have ever tasted. Cooked in the right way, and served with a little royal legendary on the side, these will be highly sought after at my restaurants this season. I am happy to place my order with you.'

'Thank you.' Rik dipped his head and cast a smile in Mel's direction. 'And thanks to you, Melanie, for this meal. You are a wonder in the kitchen. I did not realise just how skilled you are.'

'I would have you in any of my kitchens, Melanie.' Carel's statement followed Rik's.

And while Mel basked in Rik's surprise and the fact that he'd obviously enjoyed the meal, she had to be judicious about it. 'I have to confess that I watched the truffles being prepared at the palace today and learned all I could from the process.'

She turned to smile at the Frenchman. 'Thank you for your compliment.'

'In truth it is a job offer.' The man's gaze shifted between Mel and Rik. 'Any of my restaurants, any time. Permanent work, good wages and conditions. You would be more than welcome. Not that I suggest you would be available…'

Mel was more "available" than the man realised. She said something that she hoped was appropriately appreciative but non-committal. Carel didn't know that she and Rik wouldn't remain together as a couple, so she couldn't exactly have asked the man to hold that thought for a few months.

Plus there'd be work permits and all sorts of things, and when this was all over Mel would need to be back in Australia. She tried valiantly not to let those thoughts spread a pall over Carel's acceptance. Conversation moved on then. Mel sat back and let Rik lead those topics with their host. And *she* tried to gather her calm, and not think too much about the future. Not tonight. Not here in Paris. Not while she felt…vulnerable in this way.

'I hope you will excuse us if we leave you now,' Rik said twenty minutes later.

They had shared a second glass of wine with Carel but it was getting late. 'It is time for us to return to our hotel.' He thanked the man again for his business, and then he and Melanie were outside.

'I would like to stroll the streets before we go back to our hotel.' He turned to examine her face. 'Are you up to a walk?'

'That would be…I would like that.' Her response was guarded. She hoped he couldn't hear that within her words. Beneath it there was too much delight, and that made her feel vulnerable. 'I'd like to see a little more of P-Paris by night.'

'Then I will get our driver to drop us a few blocks away

from our hotel.' Rik did this, and they made their car trip in silence before they got out to walk the rest of the way.

The hotel Dominico had booked for Rik was in a beautiful part of the city. At first Melanie felt a little stilted with Rik, but he linked his arm with hers and told her the history of the area, pointing out buildings. And using the night and this moment to enjoy her closeness?

Dream on, Melanie Watson!

'I never thought I would see places like Paris, and Braston.' Melanie turned her face to look into his. 'It's very beautiful on your side of the world.'

'It is...' His gaze seemed to linger on her eyes, her mouth, before he turned his glance back to the buildings around them. 'We have some time in the morning. Is there something you'd like to do?'

'I would love to see some markets.' Mel tried to keep her enthusiasm at a reasonable level. She did. But the chance to explore Paris, even a small portion of it. How could she not be excited? 'A peek at some local colour?'

'Then we shall find markets tomorrow,' Rik said and tucked her more closely against his side. For a moment he felt, not resistance, but perhaps her effort to maintain what she considered to be an appropriate mental and emotional distance?

He should resist, too, but tonight...he did not want to. And so he walked calmly until he felt her relax against his side, and then he took the pleasure of these moments with her in peace, away from expectations and work commitments and other things that went with being...who he was.

'I am enjoying being anonymous with you right now, Melanie.' His voice deepened on the words, on the confession. He couldn't hold the words back.

'Sometimes I forget that you're a prince.' She almost whispered the words in response, as though they were a guilty secret. 'You make extraordinary things seem everyday and normal. Then I forget who you are and just—' She broke off.

Treated him as a man?

Dangerous territory, Rik. The next step is to believe she likes you purely because of you and not your title, and then there would be a woman seeing the man first.

If Rik allowed himself to form any kind of attachment to that woman it could be difficult to let her go when the time came.

He had to do that, and he had no proof that she liked him in any way particularly. Other than kisses, and could he really say those kisses meant all of these things?

You don't have the faith to look for anything else. You've allowed your upbringing to taint your outlook, to stunt what you will reach out for.

In an attempt to refocus his thoughts, he turned his attention back to their visit to Carel. 'You said you'd been a cook, but I did not know you had such skills as you displayed tonight. You won Carel over to placing that order.'

Rik's compliments warmed Mel. 'I enjoyed cooking with the truffles tonight, and I'm so relieved that Carel liked the dish. I took a risk. I wondered if you might have felt I stepped out of line.'

Mel searched his face. 'I—I could just as easily have *lost* you that deal!'

'I do not think so.' Rik gave a slight shake of his head. 'He was too enamoured of you from the first moment. The job offer he made...'

'Was flattering but it's out of the question, isn't it?' She didn't make a question out of it. Well, it wasn't one! 'I've signed on to help you, not to try to set myself up to cook in a Paris restaurant the day after our m-marriage ends.' Mel crossed her fingers and prayed that Rik hadn't heard that slight stumble when she'd referred to that last bit.

'You are very faithful, Nicole Melanie Watson.' Rik shifted his arm and instead caught her hand in his.

His fingers were strong and warm and familiar, and Mel couldn't stop from curling hers around them.

Rik's eyes softened as he smiled at her. 'That is rare and I admire you for it very much.'

They continued their walk in silence, just strolling side by side as though they had all the time in the world. As though they didn't have a *care* in the world.

But underneath, tensions simmered. If everything were so comfortable and unthreatening, why did Mel's heart beat faster with each step they took? Why did a sense of hope and anticipation mix with her awareness of Rik and make her want their walk never to end, and yet at the same time make her want to return to the hotel because she hoped against hope...

That he would kiss her goodnight again? That this night would never end? That it would end for her in his arms? All such foolish thoughts!

'Here we are.' Perhaps he felt it, too, because he swept her into the hotel without another word.

And it seemed as though time warped then because they were at the door of their suite before she could draw a breath, and yet she remembered the endless silent moments in the lift, just the two of them, wishing she could reach out to him, wishing she had the right...

Face it, Mel. You're starting to care for him. To care for

Prince Rikardo Ettonbierre of Braston. Caring as though you might be...

Caring for a man who was a good man, but also a prince, and that meant he was not any man for her because she was an everyday girl.

Mel didn't know what she was thinking, what she hoped for!

Except for a kiss from...a prince?

No. A kiss from Rikardo. That was what she wanted and needed. He *was* a prince, but he could have been the boy next door and she would have wanted that kiss just as much.

You are in trouble, Mel. Big, big trouble because you can't fall for him!

The scent of brewed coffee met them as they entered the suite. A glass bowl with fruits, a bottle of wine and chocolates sat on the low coffee table near the sofa and chairs, and, in the small kitchenette, a basket held fresh baked croissants. The lights were turned down. The suite looked ready to welcome lovers.

Mel's breath caught in the back of her throat. They weren't, of course. There were two bedrooms. It wasn't as though she and Rik—

'The coffee smells good. Just the ticket after that walk in the night air.' Mel stripped off her coat and followed her nose to the kitchenette. She felt she did really well at acting completely normal and unconcerned.

Except she should have dodged the idea of coffee altogether, said goodnight and headed straight for her room rather than prolonging this. What if Rik thought she'd done that so they could take advantage of this romantic scene? What if he thought she was angling for more of his company for that reason?

'You don't need to have any, of course,' she blurted, and then added, because that could have been taken as rather ungracious, 'but I'll pour you a cup if you like, and if you're hungry I can get you a croissant.'

'Coffee would be welcome.' He briefly glanced at the food items and away again. 'I do not think I will spoil the memory of that meal just now.'

Mel found two cups. She got them out of the cupboard and filled them with steaming liquid, and was proud that her fingers didn't tremble.

There was an enclosed balcony, beautifully warm and secluded with stunning views. They took their drinks out there and stood side by side soaking in the ambiance of the city lights.

They weren't touching and yet Mel felt so close to him, so aware of him. How was she supposed to walk away at the end of this arrangement without…looking back and wishing?

If wishes were horses then beggars would ride. Wasn't that the saying? She wasn't a beggar, but she was also not the princess who lived around the corner from the prince. She and Rik weren't on an even playing field; they never would be. Mel needed to remember that. She had to remember who he was, and who she was.

'I am pleased with this evening's efforts.' Rik set his empty coffee cup down on the ledge, took hers and placed it beside it. 'I've regained four key markets. There are others to chase but those are smaller and can be done out of Braston over the next couple of weeks.'

'You've taken a big step towards getting the people back on their financial feet.' There was pride in her voice that she couldn't hide. In the soft night light Mel looked into his face and knew that her happiness for him must show. 'You've earned the right to feel some peace.'

'You have played a part in my peace.' He spoke softly, with a hint of discovery and perhaps acceptance in his voice. 'And I should keep my distance from you. I know it, but I do not want to do it.'

Her breath quivered in her throat. 'What is it that you want to do?'

'This.' Rik leaned in and claimed her lips with his.

'Melanie.' Rik breathed her name into her hair. Her face was pressed against his chest. He had kissed her until they were both breathless with it. He wanted to kiss her again, and with his fingertips he gently raised her chin.

Her eyes glowed, filled with softness and passion for him. She'd told him there were times when she had thought of him as a man, not a prince. Rik wanted that acceptance from her now, for her to see him as Rikardo, regardless of what else there might be in his life. For once he simply wanted to be a man to a woman.

He drew her soft curves more securely into his arms and breathed the scent from the side of her neck and let his mouth cover hers once again. Tongues caressed and a low moan sounded. His, and a warning bell began to register in the back of his mind not to do this because there was naivety in the way she yielded to him, as though she was new to this, as though perhaps she wasn't particularly experienced…

'What are we doing?' Melanie spoke in a low tone. She drew back. Shields rose in her eyes, concealing her reaction to him, protecting her. 'This—this isn't the same as before when there was a reason to kiss me. It doesn't matter about

Paris, about the romance of being here. I shouldn't have let myself be tempted. I shouldn't have looked for that—'

Her words were disjointed. Discomfort filled her face, and Rik...wished it didn't have to be that way, but hadn't he set them up for exactly this? He'd made his choices. 'I should not have stepped over this line, either. It was not a smart thing to do.'

He wrestled with his own reactions. He'd wanted to take, conquer, claim—to stamp his ownership on her and possess her until she was his and his alone. That urge had bypassed all his usual roadblocks.

'I have never—' He stopped himself from completing the sentence. Instead he tried to turn his attention to tomorrow. 'You must go to bed now, get some sleep ready for our visit to the markets.'

Her eyes still held the glaze of the moments of passion they had shared, but they also held confusion, uncertainty, and unease. She searched his face and Rik saw each emotion register as she found her way back to here and now and... to who they were and to remembrance of the arrangement they shared. *He* should have never forgotten that arrangement, yet when he was near her he couldn't seem to remember even the most basic of principles, of sticking to his word and to their goals.

'Thank you for showing me a little of Paris this evening, and for allowing me to take part in your talks with the restaurateurs.' Her chin tipped up. 'Goodnight, Rikardo. I hope you sleep well.'

CHAPTER TEN

'THANK YOU FOR finding these markets for me to see.' Mel let her gaze shift from one market stall to the next as she and Rik walked through them. Somehow that felt much easier than looking the prince in the eyes.

They'd kissed last night and she'd withdrawn. Did he know how far she had stepped over the line within herself by entering into that kiss? Mel was too close to falling dangerously for...a prince. She couldn't do that. She had to be businesslike about her relationship with Rik, even if their surroundings or circumstances felt very romantic or extraordinary.

No matter what, Mel. You have to keep your distance inside yourself no matter what. So treat this outing as an outing. Nothing more and nothing less.

She drew a breath and forced her gaze to his. 'Thank you for making time for us to come here.'

'You are welcome, Melanie.' His tone, too, sounded more formal than usual.

And were his shoulders held a little more rigidly?

Mel tried very hard after that, to focus only on the moment. The markets were a treasure trove of local clothing, some new, brand name and quite expensive but with equally much vintage and pre-loved. It was the latter that appealed to Mel.

'You are sure you don't want to look at the branded items?' When they arrived here Rik had pressed what felt like a very large bundle of currency into Mel's hands, and instructed her that she was not to leave empty-handed.

That, too, had felt awkward. Ironically, not because he had wanted to give her this gift but because they had both let their fingers linger just a little too long, and then quickly withdrawn.

Mel's thoughts started to whirl as they had last night in the long hours of courting sleep that wouldn't come. A part of her wanted to find a way to get him to care for her truly. *That* was the problem.

He didn't, and he wouldn't. Not today, not tomorrow or next week or next month or in any number of months. At the end of their time together he would send her away from him fully. How much more did she need to think about it before she accepted that fact? Accepted that a few kisses in the heat of the moment in a beautiful city didn't mean all that much to a man who could kiss just about anyone, anywhere and any time?

Mel drew a slow breath. She forced air into her lungs, forced calm into her inner turmoil. And she cast her glance once more about the market and kept looking until the blur of colours turned once again into garments piled on tables, and she spotted a pretty skirt and moved closer to look…

'I'd like to buy this one.' It wouldn't break the bank. In fact, it was ridiculously cheap. But it was exactly what Mel would wear, a long, beautifully warm tan suede that fell in an

A-line cut. A memento of Paris. That thought, too, was bittersweet. 'It should fit me, but even if it doesn't I can take it in.'

She held out the rest of the money. 'Thank you for giving me this gift. I'd like to browse a little longer and then I'll be ready to go.' She hoped her words were convincing and didn't sound as strained as she felt.

'You must keep that to spend any time you wish.' Rik pressed the money back into her hands, and waited for her to tuck it away in her purse.

As the days passed after Paris, Melanie showed her strength by being the perfect fiancée to Rik. No one, not his brothers and not his father, could have said that she wasn't fully supportive of him, utterly committed to him.

Not in love with him, perhaps. That kind of acting would be a stretch, but the rest yes. She maintained her role beautifully. She showed no stress. She seemed perfectly content as she forged ahead making plans for their marriage, liaising with all those involved in the preparations as the days slid closer to the first of the three wedding rehearsals. But beneath the surface…

Rik was not content. He couldn't forget holding her in his arms in Paris. He, who had grown up trained to live by his self-control, had felt that night as though he teetered on the brink of losing it. He had longed, *longed deep down inside*, to make love to her but Melanie had broken away.

'You behaved like some smitten, lovelorn—' He bit the words off before he added fiancé. It was already bad enough that he was talking to the walls as he walked along. He *was* Melanie's fiancé. Just not in any normal sense of the word.

Their first rehearsal was tomorrow and he did not feel prepared. Perhaps things were just moving too quickly for his comfort, for him to feel that he possessed that control that he needed to have. All would be safe in Melanie's capable hands. Instinctively he knew this. Provided the actual marriage day went ahead, anything else would not overly matter anyway...

Rik made his way to the kitchen. The palace always had kitchen staff on call. He could have got one out of bed to make him a cup of coffee or a sandwich or to bring him pickings from the refrigerators, but he would rather forage for himself. At least it would pass some time until he managed to nod off, and Mel would be safe and sound asleep in *her* bed while Rik wrestled his demons.

That was part of his insomnia problem, knowing Mel was so close and he couldn't touch her. Mustn't touch her. He strode to the double doors of the palace kitchen and pushed with both hands. Before he even opened them, the scent of fresh baking hit him.

Why would anyone be baking at this time of night? Baking up a storm, he realised as his gaze lit on an array of cakes and cookies spread on the bench.

Something tickled the back of his mind, and was lost as he realised *who* was doing the cooking. 'Mel—'

'Rik! Oh, you startled me.' The cake plate she held in her hands bobbled before she carefully set it down and placed a lid over it.

'I had permission.' Her words were almost defensive. 'I needed some time in the kitchen. It's what I do when I need—' She cut the words off, waved a hand. 'Well, never mind. I'm almost done here, anyway. All I need to do is leave the kitchen sparkling. It's almost there now.' Mel turned to wipe down a final bench top.

She had dark smudges under her eyes. Was Melanie, too,

more disturbed than he'd realised since their trip to Paris despite her valiant efforts to support him? Was she also feeling tortured and struggling with her thoughts?

Leave the cleaning up for the staff.

Rik wanted very much to say the words. He bit them back because it seemed important to her to leave the kitchen as she had found it. Aside from those cakes and cookies.

'The staff told me these could be used tomorrow.' Mel gestured towards the food items. She went on to mention some need for the foods.

Rik only half heard the explanation, because he was looking at those smudges beneath her eyes.

'I don't suppose you're hungry?' She gestured towards a chocolate cake covered in sticky icing. 'It's probably the worst thing to do, but I thought I'd eat a piece and maybe—'

'Relax for a while?' He didn't know what she'd planned to say, but to Rik, standing in the kitchen in the middle of the night unable to sleep, with Melanie obviously also unable to sleep, it made perfect sense to use his insomnia to try to at least help *her* to relax. 'Why don't we take it back with us?'

Mel hadn't expected Rik to walk in on her cooking splurge. He was the reason for it, so maybe it would be good to spend that time with him. Perhaps then she would be able to shake off the feeling of melancholy and impending loss that had become harder and harder to bear as each day passed.

You'd better smile anyway, Mel. He doesn't need to see your face and start wondering what your problem is.

In truth Mel didn't *know* what the problem was. She'd hoped that cooking would shake the answer loose but it hadn't.

'I guess we can make coffee in our suite?' It was only after she said the words that she realised she'd referred to the suite as theirs as though she had every right, as though she had as much ownership of it as Rik did.

'I put a pot on before I left.'

His words made her realise that, while he'd caught her cooking in the middle of the night because she couldn't sleep, he must have had similar problems otherwise he wouldn't have been wandering the corridors and making pots of coffee when normal people would be asleep in their beds.

Mel put pieces of cake onto plates and loaded them onto a tray, which Rik promptly took from her hands. One final glance around the kitchen showed that the staff would have nothing more to deal with than delivering the goodies tomorrow morning, and Mel would try to be available to help with that.

The smell of brewed coffee met them as they stepped into the suite. It reminded Mel of Paris, of being held in his arms and kissed.

'Did the suede skirt fit, or did you have to alter it?' Rik's words made Mel realise that he, too, was remembering.

Her breath hitched for a moment. She forced her thoughts away from the reaction. She'd got through day after day doing the same. Each time any unacceptable thought tried to raise its head, Mel pushed it away. Surely no one would be able to tell just how often she thought about Rik, about those moments? How she longed for them all over again? 'The skirt fits perfectly. I'm planning to wear it tomorrow, actually.'

For the festival being held in the town. Rik hadn't spoken of it, so Mel didn't know what his role of involvement would be, if any. And the kitchen staff had told her that the event itself would be a low budget affair.

That didn't mean it couldn't be fun, though, and it was an unusual theme. Mel at least wanted to take a look. All of which was trivia, really, and yet there were times when trivia felt a little less emotionally threatening than the rest of life!

They sat side by side on the sofa eating cake and sipping coffee. A very ordinary, normal thing to do except for the fact it was after midnight, and this was Rik's suite of rooms, and they were engaged and yet in the truest sense they really weren't.

She blurted out, 'The wedding planner supervised a fitting of the gown this afternoon. I won't wear it to the first rehearsal tomorrow, of course, but…'

How did she explain what she couldn't understand herself? Just how much that fitting had taken from her emotionally and she couldn't say why because it was just a dress in the end, and the wedding wasn't going to be real, and Mel *knew* all of this.

Mel didn't want to think about why. 'Well, it's a beautiful gown. I'm amazed at how quickly it's being created.' She drew a breath and tried to make light of it as she went on. 'Have you been fitted for your suit?'

'Yesterday.' He glanced towards her. 'I've left you to handle the bulk of the work for this wedding while I attended to other things. I should have supported you better.'

She leaned towards him, shook her head. 'You've been all over the country checking on the truffle harvesting, making sure the orders are going out in perfect condition. That's so important.'

'And that's your generosity shining again.' He lifted his hand to the side of her face. 'You have a tiny dot of cake batter right there.' His fingertip softly brushed the spot.

Mel closed her eyes. Oh, it was the stupidest thing to do but it was what his touch did to her. She melted any time they were close.

'It's there, isn't it?' The feather-light touch of lips replaced his fingertip against her cheek. He kissed the spot where her cooking efforts had made their way onto her face, and then he sighed softly and pressed his cheek to hers. 'All the time that need is there. I do not know why.'

That was as far as he got, because he turned his head to look into her eyes, and Mel turned her head to look into his eyes, and their lips met.

The fire ignited. Immediately and utterly and Rik's arms closed around her and Mel threw hers around his neck and held on. She didn't know if she could have let go if she'd wanted to. This was what had been troubling her. This was what she'd tried to think about and figure out.

Her thoughts formed that far, and then they became action. Her mouth yielded to his, opened to him even as she took from him. She sipped from his lips and ran her tongue across his teeth.

Everything was pleasure, and somehow all of those feelings seemed to have caught themselves in a place deep in her chest where they swirled and twined and warmed her all at once. Rik was the warming power. Everything about him drew her. Mel didn't want to resist being drawn.

'I don't want to leave this, Mel.' His words echoed her thoughts, and he used the diminutive of her name, and Mel loved that.

'I don't want to leave it, either, Rik.'

'Do you understand what will happen?' His words were very deep, emotive and desirous and almost stern all at once.

'I do.' If there was any hesitation in her words it was not because of uncertainty in that decision. 'This—this is new for me.'

Please don't stop because I've admitted that.

'But it's what I want, Rik. I—I have no doubts.'

'I do not want to consider doubts, either.' Rik's words were strong, and yet the touch of his hand was so gentle as he stroked the side of her face, her neck. 'I will cherish you, Melanie. I will cherish you through this experience.'

That made it right for her. It just…did. The tiny bit of fear that had been buried deep down, that she might not know what to do or how to please him, evaporated. He would guide her. Mel could give this gift and share the gift of his intimacy in return. She wanted that. She *needed* it, though she did not understand why that need held such strength.

Rik took her hand and led her to his bedroom. Mel managed to register that the room was similar to her own but with a more manly tone, and then Rik drew her into his arms and kissed his way from the side of her neck to her chin and finally to her lips as their bodies pressed together and Mel didn't notice anything more about the room.

This felt exactly right. That was what Mel thought as her hands pressed against his chest, slid up to his shoulders and she let herself touch his muscular back through the cloth of his shirt. Yet that was not enough. 'I want—'

'What do you want, Melanie? Tell me.' He encouraged her to put her need into words.

And maybe he needed to hear that, too, for her to tell him.

'I need to touch you. I need to feel your skin beneath my fingertips while you're kissing me.' She almost whispered it, but he heard and he guided her hand to the buttons of his shirt.

It was all the permission that Mel needed, and, though she trembled inside, her fingers slipped each button free until his chest was revealed and she could touch his bare skin. 'You're so warm.'

'That is because you are in my arms.' He shrugged out of the shirt and then he gave all of his attention to her and to this exploration that they shared moment-by-moment in giving and receiving and discovering and finding.

When he laid her on the bed, Mel looked into his eyes and though her thoughts and feelings were blurred by passion, impossible to define, every instinct told her. 'This is what I've needed. I know it's right. I want you to make love to me, Rik. Just to share this together, the two of us without thinking about anything else.'

Rik cupped her face in his palm. 'And so it will be.'

Melanie blossomed beneath Rik's ministrations. She was beautiful in every way, and he told her in English and French and told her in the old language of Braston, words that he had never uttered to another woman as he led her forward on this journey.

He hesitated on the brink of claiming her. 'I am sorry that there will be pain. If you want me to stop—'

'No.' Mel let the word be a caress of her lips against his. A sigh inside her. A whisper of need that she gave from her heart, and that was terrifying because Mel couldn't bring her heart to this. That was far too dangerous a thing to do. 'Please don't stop, Rik. I...don't think I could bear it if you did.'

There *was* pain, but she held his gaze and the tenderness in his eyes, the expression that seemed akin to awe as he bent to kiss her lips again, allowed her to release that pain, to let it pass and to trust in him to lead her forward.

He did that, and then there was only pleasure and she crashed suddenly over an incredible wave and he cried out with her, the most amazing experience Mel had ever experienced, and the most powerful, knowing that she, too, had brought *him* to *this*.

Afterwards he held her cuddled against his chest as their breathing slowed. A deep lethargy crept up on Mel. She tried to fight it, to stay alert, to even *begin* to figure out what happened now or what she should say or do. There was so much and she didn't know how to find understanding but she knew she didn't regret this, could never regret it.

But what did it mean to him, Mel? What did it mean to Rik? Is there any possibility now—?

Mel could have been embarrassed, but they had shared this. How could she now feel anything that even resembled such an emotion? There was no room inside her. She was filled with other emotions, inexplicable to her right now, and overwhelming because what they had shared had been overwhelming. She shivered, wishing for his warmth, and then he was there, drawing her close.

He tucked her chin into his chest and she felt tension drain from him, too, and wondered what his thoughts might be.

'Sleep, Melanie. You need it right now more than you know.' He stroked his fingers through her hair.

Mel slept.

CHAPTER ELEVEN

'If I'd remembered this festival was on today I'd have left the country.' Marcelo's face pulled into a disgruntled twist.

'Oh, I don't know. Is it so horrible having the opportunity to flirt with lots of lovely local women?' Anrai dug his brother in the ribs.

Marcelo didn't crack a smile. 'It is if they then want to marry you!'

Anrai, too, now grimaced. 'I forgot that from last year.'

'And the year before and year before and year before,' Marcelo said beneath his breath. 'You need to stop being such a flirt, Anrai. It will catch up with you one day. Anyway, we had to be here. Rik's first wedding rehearsal is later today.' Marcelo turned to Rik. 'Can you believe the marriage is only a week away?'

'No.' Rik glanced at his brothers, heard the sibling teasing. He might even have wanted to join in, if there'd been any space left in his thoughts or emotions right now for anything other than the woman he'd held in his arms last night.

It was just one week before their marriage.

They had spent just one night in each other's arms.

He should not have let that happen but it had and now he did not know what to do, how to go forward. So many thoughts and emotions swirled, and Rik...did not like to feel out of control, confused, uncertain of his path and yet all he could do was continue because...nothing had changed when in a way...everything had. But nothing at the core of him, nothing of how he was. Of his parents' traits within him.

Nevertheless, Rik needed to find Melanie. The marriage *was* only a week away. They did have a rehearsal this afternoon and...he didn't know if he had irreparably messed things up with Melanie.

And even now you wish you could take her again into your arms.

Rik tried to force the thoughts aside. They were of no use to him, a line crossed that must not be crossed again. He glanced around him. He and his brothers were in Ettonbierre village, and, yes, there was a festival on today.

Rik had forgotten all about it. So had Anrai and Marcelo who'd both only arrived back at the palace late last night and had walked out with him this morning intending to meet a man to discuss tourism plans for the region.

All three brothers had plans and goals. All three relied on the success of each other to allow them to achieve those goals. The prize was recovery for a struggling country, the cost to be their freedom if Anrai and Marcelo could not also figure out ways to avoid their father's insistence that they lock into lifetime marriages.

Rik tried to dismiss the thoughts. He looked around him. This festival was what Melanie had cooked for in the middle of the night. Just a few hours ago, and then Rik had found her in the kitchen and taken her back to his suite. She'd mentioned the wedding rehearsal. She had probably been worrying about it and that had prompted her cooking spree. And then perhaps other thoughts had pushed those worries aside for a time as they...made love.

And those thoughts had now given her new concerns? Of course they would have. They had given Rik fresh concerns, fresh questions. He had to keep her with him and keep both of them to their agreement. He hoped last night would not have undermined that goal. That was the only *clear* path Rik could define. Surely the only one that mattered, so why did reminding himself bring a sense of loss rather than the sense of eventual freedom it should?

Every thought brought Rik back to the same thing. He and Melanie had made love. That *had* changed things. He'd felt as though his world had shifted alignment and Rik couldn't figure out why he felt that way or what it meant.

He'd woken at dawn with Melanie curled in his arms and a sense of rightness that had quickly changed when the reality of what they had done stabbed him in the chest.

How could that have been a smart decision on his part? Melanie had been innocent and had allowed passion to sway her judgement, but Rik was experienced and should have known not to let this happen.

Not when there was no future for them, no future when their involvement was based on a situation that he had set up to avoid becoming tied down in a relationship. He couldn't bear to perpetuate his family's emotional freeze-out into another generation, to be the one turning the cold shoulder to his partner and receiving the same in return. To have his children asking themselves why they were not fit to be loved.

No. He could not carry that legacy forward.

When he woke this morning and thought of all that, remorse and confusion and a lot of other emotions had set in.

Melanie was a giving girl. She would be kind. She would definitely care for her children.

But Rik…could not match those traits. He'd eased away from Melanie and got up. Showered, dressed, told himself he needed to think and that he would wait for her to wake and then they would…

What? Somehow sort themselves out so that last night didn't have the impact on them that it already had done?

She'd been a virgin. She'd given him a beautiful gift. That could never be undone now and even with all his concerns, Rik felt that he *had* been given that beautiful gift, the gift of Melanie in all of who she was, and he didn't begin to know what to do now because he hadn't planned for this and he had nothing to give in return of equal or acceptable value.

A confronting thought for a man who always set out to be in charge of his world, who had been raised into position and privilege and must now acknowledge that in this, he lacked.

'I just want to find Melanie.' He frowned. 'There are a lot of people around. She is the fiancée of a prince now, and shouldn't be unattended without at least two bodyguards with her.'

Rik totally overlooked the fact that he had encouraged Melanie to move about the palace grounds and surrounds using the small buggy vehicle, and had believed she would be perfectly safe where members of the palace staff would never be too far away or the villagers would know she was a guest at the palace.

But the festival would bring tourists and strangers. Anything might happen.

And your protectiveness of her is out of proportion to your ability to let her into the core parts of you that you withhold from the world.

But not from his brothers?

That was different. It was all that he had. Care for his brothers and for the people of Braston. He could not bring normal love and caring feelings to a marriage.

'Hate to point it out to you, brother, but *we* don't have any bodyguards with us.' Anrai raised his brows. 'You're sounding very serious considering the temporary nature of your arrangement with Melanie. Much as I think she's a wonderful girl,' his brother added.

'She is.' Rik didn't notice the tightening of his mouth as he spoke, the flash of warring emotions that quickly crossed his face. Instead his gaze scanned the crowds, searching as he missed the surprised and thoughtful gazes his brothers exchanged before they gave nods of silent decision, told him they needed to find their contact and get on with their meeting, and gave him the space to make his search.

Rik glanced around the crowded village square. There were colourful rides for children to play on, stalls out in the open selling home produce and hand-sewn items. A kissing booth, another to have your romantic future read, another for chemistry tests to find potential matches.

The fair had started out as a proposal day centuries ago as a means for men to woo their potential brides with offers of a fowl or a pig as a dowry. Today it had turned into an opportunity for the folk of Ettonbierre village to let their hair down for a day, for children to play and young men and women to flirt with each other, ask each other out.

He didn't want Melanie anywhere near this.

The jealous, protective thought came from deep within Rik. He had no right to it but still it came. A moment later he spotted her and he strode towards the small group gathered outside the food marquee at the edge of the town square.

***

'It's very flattering of you to say that to me, and yes I guess it would be fair to say that I am a guest of Prince Rikardo at the palace at the moment.' Mel spoke the words as she tried to edge away from the small crowd that had gathered outside the food tent.

She tried to sound normal, polite and not as deeply confused and overwrought as she felt this morning. Pretending calm until she started to feel it was a method that had worked for her after their trip to Paris. Surely it would work again now?

After Paris you were recovering from a kiss. Last night you made love with Rik. The two aren't exactly on a par. 'I'm really not at liberty to discuss that any further at this time.'

Though Rik had assured her none of the villagers would recognise the ring she wore as her engagement ring, Mel tucked her hand into her skirt pocket just in case, and was proud that she'd managed to think clearly enough to consider that need.

In that same thrust to find some sliver of normalcy in the whirl of her emotions she'd delivered all the cakes she could carry to the fair. She had stepped outside the catering tent intending to take a quick look at the festival before heading back to the palace.

Rik had been out on the grounds somewhere when she had first woken up. She probably could have gone looking for him, but what would she have said? She'd needed a moment to try to clear her head before she faced him.

You wanted more than a moment. After all that you shared with him last night you had no idea how to face him. Why downplay it, Mel, when it's all you can think about and every time you do think about it, you can hardly breathe for the mix of feelings that rushes through you?

She'd fallen asleep in his arms, more drained emotionally and in every way than she had understood. And had woken alone, only to realise she was not alone because doubt had come to rest on her shoulder to whisper in her ear. Doubt about his feelings in all of this. Doubt that she had any right to expect him to *have* any feelings about it. Just above the other shoulder lurked despair. Mel didn't want to acknowledge that, but…

She and Rik had shared something. It had been stunningly special to Mel, but that didn't mean it had been any of that to Rikardo. To the prince. How could it have been?

You managed to forget that little factor last night, didn't you? That he's a prince and you're a cook and his path is carefully set and doesn't include any kind of emotional commitment to you.

'If you change your mind while you are here…' The man in front of her gave an engaging smile and handed her a piece of paper with his phone number on it.

Proposal Day. The festival had a history. Mel had heard it all from the kitchen staff. But nowadays it was a chance for people to get to know each other, date or whatever. Mel wouldn't have been interested before. Now that she'd made love with Rik, she felt she could never be interested in any other man, ever again.

The man turned away. There were two others. Mel managed to quickly send them both on their way. She needed to get out of here, to make her way back to the palace and maybe during that solitary walk she would gather up all the pieces of herself and get them back into some kind of working order. Maybe she could hole up in her room for the entire day to complete that task. Would that be long enough?

It will never be long enough, Mel. You know what's happened.

The thought was so strong, so full of conviction. It forced her hand, and realisation crashed over her, then, whether she was ready for it or not.

She'd fallen in love with Rik. It was the answer to why last night had moved her emotions so deeply that she had wondered if she would ever be the same. The answer was no, she never would.

Because "everyday girl" Melanie Watson had fallen in love with Prince Rikardo Ettonbierre of Braston.

It should have been a moment of wonder, of anticipation and happiness. Instead, devastating loss swept through her because last night had been the total of any chance to show her love to him in that way. A moment that shouldn't have happened.

In return, Rik had made no promises. Not at the start of their marriage agreement, and not last night. He'd given in to desire. That wasn't the same as being bowled over by love so that expressing those feelings was imperative.

Mel was the one who had foolishly given her heart. Well, now she had to get back on her feet somehow. She had to get through marrying him and walking away, to do all that with dignity when all she would want to do was beg him to keep her, to want her, to not reject her or abandon her or punish her for—

What did she mean, punish?

And today there was the first wedding rehearsal. How could she get through that?

'Melanie. What are you doing here? Why were you talking to those men?'

Rik's words shook her out of her reverie, stopped a train of thought that had started to dig into a place deep down where she had hidden parts of herself. But the interruption did not save her from her sense of uncertainty and panic. That increased.

She glanced at him. Oh, it was hard to look and to know what was in her heart.

Please don't let him see it.

That one glance into his face showed austerity, as though he had stepped behind shields, had taken a fortified position.

In that moment he really resembled his father...

Rik had told her he couldn't buy into a cold relationship. He'd been so against the institution of marriage. He...hadn't believed in love.

Mel had thought that was because he'd been hurt, had seen his parents in a loveless relationship. But looking at him now, seeing that capacity to close himself off when she needed so very much for him to...let her in...

Last night was not the same for Rik, as for you. And whether or not he is like his father, you have to accept what he told you at the start. He won't ever love you, Mel. Not ever.

That attitude must make it much easier for Rik to deal with things like arranging this marriage and knowing he would be able to walk away from it later. It wasn't his fault that he'd asked her to help him. He had the right to try to protect his interests, and he'd wanted to help the people of Braston. His father had put him in an impossible position.

And now you have allowed yourself to end up in one, by falling for him.

All she could do was try to match his strength. She stared

at the face she had come to cherish far too much in the short time she had known him, and prayed for that strength.

'Rik. I…' She didn't know what she wanted to say. What she should try to say.

'I was concerned. You may not be safe here, Melanie.'

If his frown showed anything but attention to her presence here at the fair, Mel couldn't discern it.

He went on. 'You are all on your own.'

Oh, she knew that more than well, though she realised that Rik meant it literally in this case.

A thousand moments of trying to escape wouldn't have got her any closer to feeling ready for this. For facing the feelings that had overcome her, and for facing him. She loved him. Deep down in her heart and soul, all those feelings had formed and intertwined and she had no choice about it.

How could Mel combat that? How could she take what had happened last night, and put it in some kind of perspective somehow so that she could contain these feelings, get them under control and then somehow make them stop altogether when it just wasn't like that now?

How could she marry him, live as his…princess but secretly in name only, let herself become more and more familiar with him with the passing of each day and then leave at the end of a few short months and get on with her life as though none of this had happened?

Those pretty, sparkly shoes were nowhere to be found right now.

'I came out to deliver some of the cakes that I baked last night for the festival.' Her words held a tremor and she cleared her throat before she went on. She didn't want that tremor. She couldn't allow it. She just couldn't. He mustn't detect how shaken she felt and perhaps figure out why.

Rik wanted a single life, not to be bound in the very relationship that he'd asked her to help him avoid. The knowledge lanced through her, of how utterly useless it would be to hold out any hope that their circumstances might change.

So press on, Mel. You can do it. One step after another until you get there.

'I wanted a look at the festival.' There. A normal tone, a normal topic of conversation.

A bunch of unspoken words filling the air between them.

She tightened her lips so they wouldn't tremble. 'I thought it might be interesting, and I didn't want the kitchen staff to have to bring all the cakes and cookies themselves.'

'And you had men lined up to ask you out.' His words held no particular inflection.

So why did Mel believe she could hear possession in them?

Because you are engaged to him, but for a purpose, Mel. That's all it is.

They might have been keeping their marriage plans secret from the masses for as long as they could possibly manage, but that wouldn't mean he would be happy to see her out being asked on dates by local men. 'I didn't expect that to happen. I just stepped out of the food tent.'

'I know. I saw.' Rik suppressed a sigh as he searched his fiancée's eyes, her face. She looked overwhelmed and uncertain, shaken to the core.

He blamed himself for that. And into that mix he had brought a burst of jealousy that was completely inappropriate.

'I should have waited for you this morning.' Whether he'd known what to say to her, or not, Rik should have waited. A prince did not avoid facing something just because he did not know how to manage a situation. 'Winnow called early and I went—'

'It's all right.' She touched his arm, and quickly drew her hand away as though the touch had burned her.

Remorse pricked him afresh. Remorse and a confusion of feelings? He pushed the impression aside. There were no warring feelings, just resolve and the need to try to ease them through this so they could go forward. Rik straightened his shoulders.

Melanie gestured in front of them. 'I've probably wasted your time, coming to look for me, too. Let's head back. I'm sure you have a lot of things that you need to do before the—the rehearsal later.'

'There is nothing that cannot wait until then.' But it was good that Melanie would come back with him now. For the first few minutes until they got free of the fair and started on the path back to the palace, Rik let silence reign.

Once they were alone, he slowed his pace. 'We need to talk, Melanie. About last night.'

'Oh, really, I don't think there's any need.' Every defence she could muster was immediately thrown up. She tipped her chin in the air. 'It's just—it was—we have our arrangement! Last night wasn't—it happened, that's all but it doesn't need to make any difference to anything. Nothing needs to change. Really I'd prefer to just forget all about it.'

'But that is not possible.' And even though he knew it should not have happened, Rik did not want...to deny the memory or to let her think— 'I don't want you to imagine that I took what we shared lightly,' he began carefully. 'It was—'

'Lots of people sleep together for lots of different reasons.' She drew a shuddery breath. 'We did because we did. We were...a little bit attracted to each other and maybe we were...curious. Now that curiosity is set to rest it doesn't have to happen again.' Her words emerged in stilted tones but with so much determination.

She was saying all the things that Rik himself believed about their situation. Not dismissing what they had shared, but doing all she could to put it in an appropriate context. This was what he would have tried to do himself, so why did her response make his chest feel tight? Make him want to take her in his arms again and try to mend them through touch when touch had brought them to this in the first place?

They rounded a bend in the road. The palace came into view.

Rik barely looked ahead of them. He could only look at Melanie. Guilt that he had caused her this unease vied with feelings of…disappointment and…loss within him. How could that be so? He must only feel relief, and…the need to reassure her.

So get your focus back on the goal, Rik. It's as important now as it was at the start.

It was. In her way, Melanie was right. Nothing about any of that had changed. Nothing at the core of him, either. Nothing of what he needed, of what he could give and…what he could not give.

So do what you can to reassure her, Rik, both for now and for later.

'I will look after you for the short term of our marriage, Melanie.' A rustle sounded around a bend in the path and he briefly wondered if Rufusina had got loose again before the thought left him for more important ones. 'You will lack for nothing. I will provide everything you might want, and when you go back to Australia afterwards—'

'I don't need anything extra from you. I still have all the money you gave me while we were in Paris. That's more than enough to see me back to Australia.' Her words were protective, proud. 'I can take care of myself once I've finished being your temporary princess. All that matters is that you've held onto your freedom, and you've got the things you needed—'

'What is this? What is going on here?' King Georgio appeared before them on the path.

Not Rufusina on the loose and foraging.

But Rik's father, becoming angrier by the moment as what he had just heard sank in.

'What trickery have I just heard, Rikardo? I did not say that you could marry temporarily. You must marry permanently!' His gaze shifted to Melanie and further suspicion filled it.

Before the king could speak, Rik took a step forward, half shielding Melanie with his body. 'This situation is of my making, Father. You will not question Melanie or accuse her about any of this.'

'Then you will explain yourself.' Georgio's words were cold. 'And this will not be done standing in the middle of a walkway.'

Security people had gathered in the king's wake.

'You will attend me appropriately, inside the palace. You will not keep me waiting.' Without another word, the older man walked away.

Rik turned to Melanie.

'All your plans, Rik.' Concern and unease filled her face. 'He looked so angry.'

'I must speak to him now, try to get him to understand.' He hesitated. 'You will wait for me?'

'I'll wait in our—in the suite until you can let me know what happened.'

With thoughts churning, Rik took one last look at the woman before him, and turned to follow his father.

CHAPTER TWELVE

I AM STUNNED.

Rik thought the words silently as he walked towards the grand historic church where he and Melanie were to today rehearse the marriage ceremony. Stunned almost to the point of numbness by what his father had just revealed.

He needed to speak to Melanie now more than before, and when he stepped through the doors of the church, she broke away from the small group of people gathered near the front of the large ancient building, and rushed to his side.

'I couldn't wait for you any longer.' She said the words in a hushed whisper. 'Dominico came to get me and I couldn't tell him anything was wrong. Is—is the wedding off now? What happened? What did your father say?'

Beyond them, Anrai and Marcelo waited, along with the priest and various others expecting to participate in this marriage ceremony next week.

Another brother could be standing there.

'This will shock you, as it did me when my father revealed it, and I would ask that you not tell anyone until I can speak to Anrai and Marcelo.' Rik drew a slow breath. 'The reason that my father pushed so hard for marriages is because there is an older brother, a love child to a woman in England. Two years ago this man discovered his true identity. He's been trying to gain a position in the family through my father since.'

'Is—? That isn't sounding like good news to you?' Melanie's hand half lifted as though she would press it over her mouth before she dropped it away again.

'His existence is the reason my mother left, and he has now gained access to copies of our family law and worked out that he can try to claim ascendancy and, with it, Marcelo's position, rights, and work. If Marcelo is married, his position is safe, but until we are also married, Anrai's and mine…are not.'

'In other words he doesn't really belong within the family.' She said it quietly. 'He's not wanted.'

'He is not royal born.' Rik said it carefully. 'Whether he will find a place within the family, at this stage I do not know. I would like to meet him and discern for myself what manner of man he is and go from there. I would not reject a brother, but I also would not welcome a threat to the security of my country and people.'

'That's fair.' She seemed to relax as she said the words.

Rik went on. 'The old laws—this is part of why Marcelo wants to bring change. This is not merely so we can all maintain our positions. It is to keep the people of the country safe as well.'

'Why would this man push for a position that shouldn't rightly be his? Surely he must realise that he can't just walk in and take someone's place?'

'My father has no doubt contributed to the man's anger and frustration by refusing to acknowledge him at all when he should have done so many years ago.'

'Well, you can take care of your part in it. You're marrying me. You can say you've been married then. Your position will be safe!'

All but for one vital thing. 'I must *remain married*, Melanie. My plan to marry you and then end the relationship afterwards will not work for this.'

'What—what will you do?' She searched his face and her eyes were so deep and so guarded as she began to realise how this new situation had raised the stakes. 'You'll need to find someone else. You'll need to start looking right away. Someone you can make that kind of commitment with. There must be *someone* you could accept in that way.'

The priest cleared his throat noisily at the front of the church.

Rik's brothers cast glances their way that were becoming more than curious.

Of all settings and times, this had to be about the worst but at least as Rik had informed Melanie of the basics of the issue his thoughts had cleared. He knew exactly what he needed, now, and from whom, but could he yet again convince her?

'You want me to be the one, don't you?' The words came from between lips that had whitened with shock. 'You want me to be married to you permanently?'

'We are already together. I would provide for your every need. You would live a privileged life, want for nothing.' It would resolve problems, not only for Rik, but also for Melanie. 'You would never again have to fend for yourself, and later if you wanted a child I would...allow it.'

There were other words that tried to bubble up, but Rik needed to protect himself in this—

Her glance searched his face before it shifted to take in the church, the people waiting for the rehearsal to start. 'I can't do it. Not even for the people.' She whispered the words before she added more strongly, 'I've tried hard in my life and I've never rejected people even when they've rejected me, but I won't line up for another lifetime of that.

'I blamed myself for losing my parents in that car crash. I thought after that I didn't deserve happiness, to be alive when they weren't, but that was grief talking. I do deserve happiness. I deserve better from you.'

Melanie turned on her heel and ran from the church.

CHAPTER THIRTEEN

'I'VE MADE THE biggest mistake of my life.' Rik spoke the words to Marcelo as his brother drove them towards the country's small international airport. He felt sick inside, close to overwhelmed and very, very afraid that he might have lost his chance with Melanie for ever by stupidly trying too hard to protect himself and by being too slow to realise…

Rik had lost valuable time searching for Melanie out of doors. He'd thought she must have run to their spot on the mountainside, or perhaps back to Ettonbierre village to lose herself in the crowd there.

As he'd searched, knowing his brothers were also looking, Rik had begun to panic. In her distraught state, what if something happened to Melanie? And all that he had locked down inside him and tried to deny since he and Melanie made love had begun to inexorably make its way to the surface and demand to be known.

'She will not leave the airport.' Marcelo offered the assurance without taking his glance from the road. 'If need be, the flights will all be delayed until we get there. Dominico will take care of it.'

That was a privilege of position that, in this moment, Rik was willing to exploit without compunction. It was Melanie's reaction when he caught up with her that concerned him.

'I have used Melanie without considering how she might feel. Not respected her rights and emotions.' He shook his head. 'I asked her to remain permanently married to me as though she should be grateful for all the privileges she would receive as part of the family.'

'Such as being in a loveless marriage for life?' Marcelo's words were not harsh, neither teasing, but a statement of understanding of things that he and Rik had never discussed about their upbringing.

'I wanted to avoid that at all costs.' Why hadn't Rik understood sooner that his drive to pull Melanie into exactly that long-term relationship had not been fuelled merely by the need to protect his position and that of his brothers, in the knowledge of this unknown brother? It had been driven by need of *Melanie*. And yet he felt no warmth towards this unknown man. 'I cannot find soft emotion in my heart for him, Marcelo. Even now when I realise how I feel about Melanie—'

'One thing at a time,' Marcelo advised. He drew the car to a halt in a no stopping zone in front of the airport. 'We all need to get to know this man. Good luck, brother.'

Rik met Marcelo's gaze as he threw the car door open. 'Thank you.'

Rik drew a deep breath and strode quickly into the airport terminal.

I'm not going to feel guilty about the money.

Melanie thought this as she twisted her hands together in her lap. She'd packed all her luggage, half dreading that Rik might appear at any moment. Then she'd summoned palace staff to carry it all downstairs and put it in the cab she'd ordered. A real cab this time, with no mix-ups.

She'd bought an airline ticket to get back to Australia. The flight wasn't going directly there. She'd asked for the first one that would get her out of the country and she'd used the money Rik had given her that day in Paris, to pay for it.

It was almost time, just a few more minutes and she would be able to board the plane, and...fly away from Braston, and from Rik, for ever.

Her heart squeezed and she forced her gaze forward. Other people in the boarding lounge talked to each other or relaxed in their chairs, at ease with themselves and their plans. Mel just wanted to...get through this. She felt she was letting down the people, but Rik would find someone else. Prince Rikardo Eduard Ettonbierre of Braston would not struggle to find a woman willing to marry him for life.

Mel couldn't be that woman. Not without love.

'Melanie!'

At first she thought she'd imagined his familiar voice, a figment within her mind because her heart hurt so much. It was going to take time to get past those raw emotions and begin to heal.

Could she heal from falling in love with Rik?

'Mel. Thank goodness you're here.' Rik appeared in front of her. Ruffled. Surprisingly un-prince-like with his tie askew and his suit coat hanging open. *Real.*

Mel shot to her feet. She wasn't sure what she intended to do when she got upright. Run? Faint? Throw herself at him and hope against hope that he would open his arms and his heart to her?

Get real, Melanie Watson. You're still a cook and he's still a prince and he doesn't love you and that's that.

'I don't have a glass slipper.' His words were low.

And confusing. 'I—I don't understand.'

Words came over the airport speaker system. French and then English. Her flight was being called. Mel had to get on the flight. She glanced towards the gate, to people beginning to go through. Her heart said stay. Her survival instincts said go. Go and don't look back because you've done that "love people and not be loved in return" thing and it just hurts too damned much to do it again. 'I have to go, Rik. I paid all your money to buy the ticket. I can't buy another one.'

'I will buy you another ticket, Mel.' He lifted his hand as though he would take hers, and hesitated as though uncertain of his welcome. 'If you still want to go.'

Oh, Rik.

'Please. I left out something very important when I asked you to marry me.'

'Another bargaining chip?' She hadn't meant to say it. She didn't want to spread hurt, or reveal her heart. Mel just wanted…to go home and yet, where was home now? Could home be anywhere when her heart had already decided where it wanted to be? 'I didn't mean that.'

'You had every right to say it.' Rik gestured to a room to their left. 'There's a private lounge there. Will you give me a few minutes, Mel? Please? You will still be able to make this flight if you want to, or a next one. Anything you want, but please let me try—'

'All right.' She led the way to the room, pushed the door open and stepped inside. Somehow it felt important to take that initiative. To be in charge even if she was agreeing to stall her plans to speak with him.

It was a small room. The lounge suite was quintessential airport "luxury". Deep red velvet with large cushions all immaculately kept. There were matching drapes opened wide and a view of runways with planes in various stages of arrival and departure.

All Mel could see was Rik's blue eyes, fixed on her brown ones, searching as though there was something that he desperately needed to find.

'This isn't a fairy tale, Rik. I know you're a prince but to me you'll always be a man first. You'll be Rik, who I—' Fell in love with. She bit back the words.

'No. There is little of the fairy tale about current circumstances and I confess I was shocked by my father's announcement of a secret brother.' Rik did take her hand now, and led her to a lounge seat.

Somehow they were seated with her hand still held in his and far too much of a feeling of rightness inside Mel's foolish, foolish heart. 'I hope that situation can be worked out so that nobody loses too much.'

'I do not know what is possible. I have not had time to get all the facts together, let alone think of how to act on any of them.' For this moment Rik brushed the topic aside. 'Melanie, I asked you to marry me permanently—'

'But deep down even though you have to do it, you don't want to be tied in a relationship like that, and I…can't do it when—' She ground to a halt.

'When I offered all those things that don't matter to you, and nothing else? They never have.' One side of Rik's mouth lifted in a wry, self-mocking twist. 'Everything that makes me a prince, that might appeal, doesn't matter to you. I was too slow to think about that, and too slow to understand why I needed so much for you to agree to help me anyway.'

Was it care that she saw in his eyes? Mel didn't want to hope. Not now. Not when she'd made up her mind to go and that was the only solution. 'You'll find someone, Rik. You'll be able to marry and hold onto your job. I'm sorry it will have to be for all your life. I'm sorry for that.'

Each word tightened the ache in her chest. Each glance at him made it harder to keep the tremor out of her voice.

'The thing is, all that has changed for me, Melanie. It has changed because I fell in love with you.' His words were low. Raw.

Real? Mel frowned. Shook her head. There was no allergy medication to blame now. Nothing but a hope and sense of loss so deep that she was afraid she'd heard those words only inside her, afraid to hear them at all, and so she denied. 'No.'

'The moment I took you into my arms and made love to you, I fell in love with you.' This time when he said it, emotion crowded *his* face. 'Please believe me that this is true.'

Mel had never seen that emotion, except…lurking in the backs of his eyes when he held her last night…

Could she believe this? Could Rik truly have fallen in love with her? 'You're a prince.'

'As you said when we first met.' He inclined his head. His eyes didn't twinkle, but memory was there.

'I'm a cook. From Australia.' A commoner with no fixed abode. 'I didn't even know how to curtsy properly.'

Do you really love me, Rik?

Could he really love *her*, Nicole Melanie Watson? 'You said you would never love.'

'I didn't know there would be you, and that you would come to live, not only at the palace, but that you would move into my heart.' He took both her hands into his.

She glanced down. 'The ring! I meant to leave it in the suite.'

'*Our* suite. I am glad you didn't take it off.' He touched the diamonds. 'It is made to be there.' His gaze lifted to hers. 'I know I am asking for another leap of faith, and if you cannot find anything in your heart for me then I will accept it, but I am hoping against all hope that you will agree to give me a chance to show you how deeply I have come to love you.'

'I want to, Rik.' Oh, she wanted to do that with all of *her* heart. 'If you truly love me—'

'I do.' He didn't hesitate. Conviction filled his tone. 'If you can learn to love *me*, I will be the happiest man in the world.'

'That was what you meant about the glass slipper.' She hadn't realised that he wanted to make her his princess truly, in every way. 'I'm a practical girl, Rik. I like cooking and I lost my parents and grew up trying to be loved and my aunt and uncle and Nicolette didn't, and I promised myself I would never be hurt like that again.'

But she'd opened her heart to Rik and he…loved her. 'Are you sure? Because I don't know how you could have overcome all that. You were so firmly fixed that you wouldn't be able to have that kind of relationship.'

'I thought I was incapable of experiencing those feelings. Love, commitment.'

'Your upbringing harmed you.' Mel didn't want to hurt him with the words, but they were part of *his* history, of who he was.

'We have both experienced hurt at the hands of family.' There was regret and acknowledgement, and love shining in his eyes openly for her now. 'But you have set all of my love free.'

Mel believed it then. She let go of the last doubt and took her leap of faith. 'I fell in love with you, too, Rik. I thought I was going to help you to solve a problem and then go back to Australia. Instead I wanted to stay with you for ever, but when you asked me—'

'I stupidly didn't realise what those feelings inside meant.' He drew a breath that wasn't quite steady. 'I thought I'd lost you. I couldn't bear that thought.' Again his fingers touched her ring as he drew her to her feet with him and held both her hands. 'Will you marry me next week, Mel? Give me a chance to show you every day for ever how much you mean to me?'

'Yes.' Melanie said it and stepped into his arms and, oh, it felt right. So, so right, to be in Rik's arms, in the prince's arms, where she belonged. There were no sparkly shoes. She wasn't down a rabbit hole. She had simply…come home to this man of her dreams. 'Yes, I will marry you next week and stay married for ever, and love you every single day while you love me every single day.'

Mel knew there would be hurdles. She was marrying a prince! But she would give all of her heart to him and now she knew that she could trust it into his love and care.

He glanced out of the window and smiled. 'You've missed your flight. Let's go…home and start counting the days until next week.'

'The wedding planner is going to be relieved that she doesn't have to start all over again.' A smile started on Melanie's face and she tucked her arm through Rik's and they left the room and made their way out of the airport to a car parked and waiting for Rik. The keys were in it, just as though it had been brought for him and left specially.

Well, it would have been, wouldn't it? Mel thought. After all, he was a prince.

And Melanie Watson, cook, was marrying him.

For now and for ever.

And that seemed exactly right.

EPILOGUE

'There is nothing to be nervous about.' Anrai spoke the words to Melanie as they made their way towards the rear-entry door of the church. 'And thank you for allowing me to be the one to escort you for this occasion.'

Melanie drew a deep breath and glanced at her soon-to-be brother-in-law from beneath the filmy bridal veil. Excitement filled her. This was the moment that she and Rik had worked towards, and that now would be the fulfilment of very new and special dreams for them. 'You know that I love him.'

'Yes. He is lucky. I do not profess to hold similar hope for myself, but I am glad that you have found each other.' Anrai's words were warm, accepting, and then the doors were thrown open and music started and they began the long walk to the front of the church.

Soft gasps filled the air as guests saw the beautiful gown, the train that whispered behind her. A hint of lace. Tiny pearls stitched in layers. A princess neckline for an everyday girl about to become that princess.

Mel's glance shifted to one row of seats in the church. To

her uncle, and aunt, and her cousin. Her gaze meshed with Nicolette's for a moment. Nicolette looked attractive in a pale pink chiffon gown. But today the attention was all for Melanie.

For a moment Mel felt a prick of sadness, but she couldn't make her cousin see that love came from within, was a gift so much more important than any material thing.

It was Nicolette who looked away, who couldn't seem to hold her cousin's gaze any longer.

And then there was Rik at the front of the church, waiting faithfully without glancing back until Anrai arrived with Mel on his arm and passed her hand to Rik's arm, placing it there as Mel's father would have done if he'd been here.

Warmth spread through Mel's chest as she looked into her prince's eyes and saw the love and happiness there and somehow she thought her parents might have been watching. She felt their love and warmth, too.

'Dearly beloved...' The priest began the service.

And there before God and his witnesses, Nicole Melanie Watson married Rikardo Eduard Ettonbierre, third prince of Braston.

He *did* have several titles and various bits of land.

His wife-to-be *was* a wonderful cook.

And they were still working on the agreement about who got ownership of any of Rufusina's offspring should the hog ever choose to bless them with a litter.

But Rik and Mel were happy today, and they would remain happy. And Rufusina's offspring were a whole other legend...

* * * * *

With a degree in mechanical engineering from Stanford University, the last thing **Melissa McClone** ever thought she would be doing was writing romance novels. But analysing engines for a major US airline just couldn't compete with her 'happily-ever-afters'. When she isn't writing, caring for her three young children or doing laundry, Melissa loves to curl up on the couch with a cup of tea, her cats and a good book. She enjoys watching home decorating shows to get ideas for her house—a 1939 cottage that is *slowly* being renovated. Melissa lives in Lake Oswego, Oregon, with her own real-life hero husband, two daughters, a son, two loveable but oh-so-spoiled indoor cats and a no-longer-stray outdoor kitty that decided to call the garage home. Melissa loves to hear from her readers. You can write to her at PO Box 63, Lake Oswego, OR 97034, USA, or contact her via her website: www.melissamcclone.com

Not-So-Perfect Princess

Melissa McClone

For Tom

Special thanks to:
Elizabeth Boyle, Terri Reed,
Schmidt Chiropractic Center
and the Harlequin Romance team
for letting me tell Julianna's tale!

CHAPTER ONE

"Three arranged marriages and not one has made it to the altar. That is unacceptable!" King Alaric of Aliestle's voice thundered through the throne room like a lion's roar. Even the castle's tapestry-covered stone walls appeared to tremble. "If men think something is wrong with you, no amount of dowry will convince one to marry you."

Princess Julianna Louise Marie Von Schneckle didn't allow her father's harsh words to affect her posture. She stood erect with her shoulders back and her chin up, maximizing her five-foot-eight-inch-stature. The way she'd been taught to do by a bevy of governesses and nannies. Her stepmother didn't take a personal interest in her, but was diligent in ensuring she'd received the necessary training to be a perfect princess and queen.

"Father," Jules said evenly, not about to display an ounce of emotion. Tears and histrionics would play into her country's outdated gender stereotypes. They also wouldn't sway her father. "I was willing to marry Prince Niko, but he discovered Princess Isabel was alive and legally his wife. He had no choice but to end our arrangement."

Her father's nostrils flared. "The reason your match ended doesn't matter."

Jules understood why he was upset. He wanted to marry her off to a crown prince in order to put one of his grandchildren on a throne outside of Aliestle. He was willing to pay a king's ransom to make that happen. She'd become the wealthiest royal broodmare around. Unfortunately.

He glared down his patrician nose at her. "The result is the same. Three times now—"

"If I may, Father." Indignation made Jules speak up. She rarely interrupted her father. Okay, never. She was a dutiful daughter, but she wasn't going to take the blame for this. "You may have forgotten with all the other important matters on your mind, but you canceled my first match with Prince Christian. And Prince Richard was in love with an American when I arrived on San Montico."

"These failed engagements are still an embarrassment." Her father's frown deepened the lines on his face. The wrinkles reminded Jules of the valley crags in the Alps surrounding their small country. "A stain on our family name and Aliestle."

A lump of guilt lodged in her throat. Jules had been relieved when she found out Niko wouldn't be able to annul his first marriage and marry her. From the start, she'd hoped he would fall in love with his long-lost wife so Jules wouldn't have to get married.

Oh, she'd liked Vernonia with its loyal people and lovely lakes for sailing. The handsome crown prince wanted to modernize his country, not be held back by antiquated customs. She would have had more freedom than she'd ever imagined as his wife and future queen. But she didn't love Niko.

Silly, given her country's tradition of arranged marriages.

The realist in her knew the odds of marrying for love were slim to none, but the dream wouldn't die. It grew stronger with the end of each arranged match.

Too bad dreams didn't matter in Aliestle. Only duty.

Alaric shook his head. "If your mother were alive…"

Mother. Not stepmother.

Jules felt a pang in her heart. "If my mother were alive, I hope she would understand I tried my best."

She didn't remember her mother, Queen Brigitta, who had brought progressive, almost shocking, ideas to Aliestle when she married King Alaric. Though the match had been arranged, he fell so deeply in love with his young wife that he'd listened to her differing views on gender equality and proposed new laws at her urging, including higher education opportunities for women. He even took trips with her so she could indulge her passion for sailing despite vocal disapproval from the Council of Elders.

But after Brigitta died competing in a sailing race in the South Pacific when Jules was two, a heartbroken Alaric vowed never to go against convention again. He didn't rescind the legislation regarding education opportunities for women, but he placed limitations on the jobs females could hold and did nothing to improve their career prospects. He also remarried, taking as his wife and queen a proper Aliestlian noblewoman, one who knew her role and place in society.

"I'd hope my mother would see I've spent my life doing what was expected of me out of respect and love for you, my family and our country," Jules added.

But she knew a lifetime of pleasing others and doing good works didn't matter. Not in this patriarchal society where daughters, whether royal or commoner, were bartered like chattel. If Jules didn't marry and put at least one of her children on a throne somewhere, she would be considered a total failure. The obligation and pressure dragged Jules down like a steel anchor.

Her father narrowed his eyes. "I concede you're not to blame for the three matches ending. You've always been a good girl and obeyed my orders."

His words made her sound like a favored pet, not the beloved daughter he and her mother had spent ten years trying to conceive. Jules wasn't surprised. Women were treated no differently than lapdogs in Aliestle.

Of course, she'd done nothing to dispel the image. She was as guilty as her father and the Council of Elders for allowing the stereotyping and treatment of women to continue. As a child, she'd learned Aliestle didn't want her to be as independent and outspoken as her mother had been. They wanted Jules to be exactly what she was—a dutiful princess who didn't rock the boat. But she hoped to change that once she married and lived outside of Aliestle. She would then be free to help her brother Brandt, the crown prince, so he could modernize their country and improve women's rights when he became king.

Her father eyed her speculatively. "I suppose it would be premature to marry you off to the heir of an Elder."

A protest formed in the back of her throat, but Jules pressed her lips together to keep from speaking out. She'd said more than she intended. She had to maintain a cool and calm image even if her insides trembled.

Marrying a royal from Aliestle would keep her stuck in this repressive country forever. Her children, most especially daughters, would face the same obstacles she faced now.

Jules fought a rising panic. "Please, Father, give me another chance. The next match will be successful. I'll do whatever it takes to marry."

He raised a brow. "Such enthusiasm."

More like desperation. She forced the corners of her mouth into a practiced smile. "Well, I'm twenty-eight, father. My biological clock is ticking."

"Ah, grandchildren." He beamed, as if another rare natural resource had been discovered in the mountains of Aliestle. "They are the only thing missing in my life. I shall secure you a fourth match right away. Given your track record, I had a backup candidate in mind when you left for Vernonia."

A backup? His lack of confidence stabbed at her heart.

"All I need to do is negotiate the marriage contract," he continued.

That would take about five minutes given her dowry.

"Who am I to marry, Father?" Jules asked, as if she wanted to know the person joining them for dinner, not the man she would spend the rest of her life with in a loveless marriage negotiated for the benefit of two countries. But anyone would be better than marrying an Aliestlian.

"Crown Prince Enrique of La Isla de la Aurora."

"The Island of the Dawn," she translated.

"It's a small island in the Mediterranean off the coast of Spain ruled by King Dario."

Memories of San Montico, another island in the Mediterranean where Crown Prince Richard de Thierry ruled, surfaced. All citizens had equal rights. Arranged marriages were rare though the country had a few old-fashioned customs. She hadn't been allowed to sail there, but the water and wind had been perfect.

Longing stirred deep inside Jules.

Sailing was her inheritance from her mother and the one

place she felt connected to the woman she didn't remember. It was the only thing Jules did for herself. No matter what life handed out, no matter what tradition she was forced to abide by, she could escape her fate for a few hours when she was on the water.

But only on lakes and rivers.

After Jules learned to sail on the Black Sea while visiting her maternal grandparents, her father had forbidden her to sail on the ocean out of fear she would suffer the same fate as her mother. Two decades later, he still treated Jules like a little girl. Perhaps now he would finally see her as an adult, even though she was female, and change his mind about the restrictions.

"Am I allowed to sail when I'm on the island?" she asked.

"Sailing on the sea is forbidden during your engagement."

Hope blossomed at his words. He'd never left her an opening before. "After I'm married…?"

"Your husband can decide the fate of your…hobby."

Not hobby. Passion.

When she was on a boat, only the moment mattered. The wind against her face. The salt in the air. The tiller or a sheet in her hand. She could forget she was Her Royal Highness Princess Julianna and be Jules. Nothing but sailing had ever made her feel so…free.

If La Isla de la Aurora were a progressive island like San Montico, she would have freedom, choice and be allowed to sail on the ocean. Her heart swelled with anticipation. That would be enough to make up for not marrying for love.

"Understand, Julianna, this is your final match outside of Aliestle," he said firmly. "If Prince Enrique decides he doesn't want to marry you, you'll marry one of the Elder's heirs upon your return home."

A shiver shot down her spine. "I understand, Father."

"You may want to push for a short engagement," he added. A very short one.

Jules couldn't afford to have Prince Enrique change his mind about marrying her. She had to convince him she was the only woman for him. The perfect princess for him. And maybe she would find the love she dreamed about on the island. Her parents had fallen in love through an arranged marriage. It could happen to her, too.

She'd avoided thinking about tomorrow. Now she looked forward to the future. "When do I leave for the island, sir?"

"If I complete negotiations with King Dario and Prince Enrique tonight, you may leave tomorrow." Alaric said. "Your brother Brandt, a maid and a bodyguard will accompany you."

This was Jules's last chance for a life of freedom. Not only for herself, but her children and her country. She couldn't make any mistakes. "I'll be ready to depart in the morning, Father."

Lying in bed, Alejandro Cierzo de Amanecer heard a noise outside his room at the beachfront villa. The stray kitten he'd found at the boatyard must want something. He opened his eyes to see sunlight streaming in through the brand-new floor-to-ceiling windows. Most likely breakfast.

The bedroom door burst wide-open. Heavy boots sounded against the recently replaced terra-cotta tile floor.

Not again.

Alejandro grimaced, but didn't move. He knew the routine.

A squad of royal guards dressed in blue and gold uniforms surrounded his bed. At least they hadn't drawn their weapons this time. Not that he would call another intrusion progress.

"What does *he* want now?" Alejandro asked.

The captain of the guard, Sergio Mendoza, looked as stoic as ever, but older with gray hair at his temples. "King Dario requests your presence at the palace, Your Highness."

Alejandro raked his hand through his hair in frustration. "My father never requests anything."

Sergio's facial expression didn't change. He'd only shown emotion once, when Alejandro had been late bringing Sergio's youngest daughter home from a date when they were teenagers. In spite of the security detail accompanying them, Alejandro had feared for his life due to the anger in the captain's eyes.

"The king orders you to come with us now, sir," Sergio said.

Alejandro didn't understand why his father wanted to see him. No one at the palace listened to what Alejandro said. He might not want to be part of the monarchy, but he wasn't about to abandon his country. He'd founded his business here and suggested economic innovations, including developing their tourist trade. But his ideas clashed with those of his father and brother who were more old-fashioned and traditional in their thinking.

A high-pitched squeak sounded. The scraggly black kitten with four white paws clawed his way up the sheet onto the bed. The thing had been a nuisance these past two weeks with the work at the boatyard and renovations here at the villa.

"I need to get dressed before I go anywhere," Alejandro said.

"We'll wait while you dress, sir." Sergio's words did nothing to loosen Alejandro's tense shoulder muscles. "The king wants no delay in your arrival."

Alejandro clenched his teeth. He wanted to tell the loyal

captain to leave, but the guards would use force to get him to do what they wanted. He was tired of fighting that battle. "I need privacy."

Sergio ordered the soldiers out of the room, but he remained standing by the bed. "I'll wait on the other side of the door, sir. Guards are stationed beneath each window."

Alejandro rolled his eyes. His father still saw him as a rebellious teenager. "I'm thirty years old, not seventeen."

Sergio didn't say anything. No doubt the captain remembered some of Alejandro's earlier...escapades.

"Tell me where you think I would run to, Captain?" Alejandro lay in bed covered with a sheet. "My business is here. I own properties. My father's lackeys follow me wherever I go."

"They are your security detail, sir," Sergio said. "You must be protected. You're the second in line for the throne."

"Don't remind me," Alejandro muttered.

"Many would give everything to be in your position."

Not if they knew what being the "spare" entailed. No one cared what he thought. Even when he tried to help the island, no one supported him. He'd had to do everything on his own.

Alejandro hated being a prince. He'd been educated in the United States. He didn't want to participate in an outdated form of government where too much power rested with one individual. But he wanted to see his country prosper.

"Guard the door if you must." Alejandro gave the kitten a pat. "I won't make your job any more difficult for you than it is."

As soon as Sergio left, Alejandro slid out of bed and showered. His father hadn't requested formal dress so khaki shorts, a navy T-shirt and a pair of boat shoes would do.

Twenty minutes later, Alejandro entered the palace's reception room. His older brother rose from the damask-covered settee. Enrique looked like a younger version of their father with his short hairstyle, tailored designer suit, starched dress shirt, silk tie and polished leather shoes. It was too bad his brother acted like their father, also.

"This had better be important, Enrique," Alejandro said.

"It is." His brother's lips curved into a smug smile. "I'm getting married."

About time. Enrique's wedding would be the first step toward Alejandro's freedom from the monarchy. The birth of a nephew or niece to take his place as second in line for the throne would be the next big step. "Congratulations, bro. I hope it's a short engagement. Don't waste any time getting your bride pregnant."

Enrique smirked. "That's the plan."

"Why wait until the wedding? Start now."

He laughed. "King Alaric would demand my head if I did that. He's old-fashioned about certain things. Especially his daughter's virginity."

"Alaric." Alejandro had heard the name. It took a second to realize where. "You're marrying a princess from Aliestle?"

"Not a princess. *The* princess." Enrique sounded excited. No wonder. Aliestle was a small kingdom in the Alps. With an abundance of natural resources, the country's treasury was vast, a hundred times that of La Isla de la Aurora. "King Alaric has four sons and one daughter."

"Father must be pleased."

"He's giddy over the amount of Julianna's dowry and the economic advantages aligning with Aliestle will bring us. Fortunately for me, the princess is as beautiful as she is rich. A bit of an ice princess from what I hear, but I'll warm her up."

"If you need lessons—"

"I may not have your reputation with the ladies, but I shall manage fine on my own."

"I hope the two of you are happy together." Alejandro meant the words. A happy union would mean more heirs. The further Alejandro dropped in the line of succession, the better. He couldn't wait to be able to focus his attention on building his business and attracting more investors to turn the island's sluggish economy around.

"You are to be the best man."

A statement of fact or a request? "Mingling with aristocracy is hazardous to my health."

"You will move home until the wedding."

A demand. Anger flared. "Enrique—"

"The royal family will show a united front during the engagement period. Your days will be free unless official events are scheduled. You'll be expected to attend all dinners and evening functions. You must also be present when the princess and her party arrive today."

Alejandro cursed. "You sound exactly like him."

"They are Father's words, not mine." Rare compassion filled Enrique's eyes. "But I would like you to be my best man. You're my favorite brother."

"I'm your only brother."

Enrique laughed. "All the more reason for you to stand at my side. Father will compensate you for any inconvenience."

Alejandro's entire life was a damn inconvenience. Besides, he would never be able to get the one thing he wanted from his father. "I don't want *his* money."

"You never have, but when Father offers you payment, take it. You can put the money into your boats, buy another villa, donate it to charity or give it away on the streets," Enrique advised. "You've earned this, Alejandro. **Don't** let pride get in the way again."

He wasn't about to go there. "All I want is to be left alone."

"As soon as Julianna and I have children, you will no longer be needed around here. If you do your part to ensure the wedding occurs, Father has promised to let you live your own life."

Finally. "Did you ask for this or did Father offer?"

"It was a combination, but be assured of Father keeping his word."

"When am I to move back?"

"After lunch."

Alejandro cursed again. He had a boatyard to run, investment properties to oversee and the Med Cup to prepare for. Not to mention the kitten who expected to be fed. "I have a life. Responsibilities."

"You have responsibilities here. Ones you ignore while you play with your boats," Enrique chided.

Seething, Alejandro tried to keep his tone even. "I'm not playing. I'm working. If you'd see the upcoming Med Cup race as an opportunity to promote—"

"If you want to build the island's reputation, then support this royal wedding. It'll do much more for the economy than your expensive ideas to improve the island's nightlife, build flashy resorts and attract the sailing crowd with a little regatta."

"The Med Cup is a big deal. It'll—"

"Whatever." Enrique brushed Alejandro aside as if he were a bothersome gnat. Like father, like son. "Do what you must to be here after lunch or Father will send you away on a diplomatic mission."

The words were like a punch to Alejandro's solar plexus.

Not unexpected given the way his father and brother operated sometimes. The threat would be carried out, too. That meant Alejandro had to do as told to secure his future. His freedom.

"I'll be back before your princess arrives."

But he would be doing a few things his way.

Once the black sheep, always the black sheep.

And let's face it, Alejandro didn't mind the title at all.

A helicopter whisked Jules over the clear, blue Mediterranean Sea. The luxurious cabin with large, leather seats comfortably fit the four of them: her, Brandt, Yvette her maid and Klaus their bodyguard. But even with soundproofing, each wore headsets to communicate and protect their ears from the noise of the rotors.

Almost there.

A combination of excitement and nerves made Jules want to tap her toes and twist the ends of her hair with her finger. She kept her hands clasped on her lap instead. She wanted to make her family and country proud. Her mother, God rest her soul, too. Presenting the image of a princess completely in control was important, even if doing so wasn't always easy.

She glanced out the window. Below, on the water, a Sun Fast 3200 with a colorful spinnaker caught her eye. She pressed her forehead against the window to get a better look at the sailboat.

Gorgeous.

The crew sat on the rail, their legs dangling over the side. The hull planed across the waves.

Longing made it difficult to breath.

What she wouldn't give to be on that boat sailing away from the island instead of flying toward the stranger who would be her husband and the father of her children… But she shouldn't wish that. Jules had a responsibility, a duty, the same that had been thrust upon her mother so many years ago. Marrying Prince Enrique had to be better than being stuck in patriarchal Aliestle for the rest of her life. At least, she hoped so. If not...

Jules grimaced.

"You okay?" Brandt's voice asked through her headset.

She shrugged. "I think I'm cursed. When my godparents offered gifts at my christening, one of them must have cursed me to a life of duty with no reward. A loveless arranged marriage."

And an unfulfilled yearning for adventure and freedom.

"Look out the window," Brandt said. "You're not cursed, Jules. You're going to be living on a vacation paradise."

Crescents of postcard-worthy white sand beaches came into view. Palm trees seemed to stand at attention, except for the few arching toward the ground. The beach gave way to a town. Pastel-colored, tiled roofed buildings and narrow streets dotted the hillsides above the village center.

She glimpsed rows of sailboats moored at a marina. The masts, tall and shiny, rocked starboard and port like metronomes. Her mouth went dry.

Perhaps cursed was the wrong word. All these sailboats had to be a good sign, right? "Maybe life will be different here."

"It will." Brandt smiled, the same charming smile she'd seen on a cover of a tabloid at the airport in Spain. "Your fiancé will be unable to resist your beauty and intelligence. He'll fall head over heels in love with you and allow you to do whatever you wish. Including sailing on the ocean."

She wiggled her toes in anticipation. "I hope that's true."

"Believe," he encouraged. "That's what you always tell me."

Yes, she did. But this situation was different. Jules knew nothing about Prince Enrique. She'd been so busy preparing for her departure she hadn't had time to look him up on the internet. Not that she had a choice in marrying him even if he turned out to be an ogre.

For all she knew he was old with one foot in the grave. Okay, now she was overreacting. Her father had always matched her with younger men because he wanted grandchildren. This match shouldn't be any different.

Jules hoped Enrique was charming, handsome and would sweep her off her feet. She wanted to find him attractive and be able to love him. She also wanted his heart to be free and open to loving her in return.

Her concern ratcheted. Prince Richard and Prince Niko had been in love with other women. If Enrique's affections were attached to a girlfriend or mistress that wouldn't bode well for their match reaching the altar or, if it did, love developing between them.

Jules shifted in her seat. "I do hope this island has up-to-date ideas about women."

"It has to be more contemporary. Aliestle has been asleep since the Middle Ages." Brandt cupped one side of his headset with his hand. "Listen, I hear Father snoring now. The tyrant could wake the dead."

A smile tugged at the corners of Jules's mouth. "Too bad we can't wake him."

"Along with the entire Council of Elders."

Nodding, she stared at her brother who was more known as a playboy crown prince than a burgeoning politician and ruler. "When you're king, you'll change the way things are done."

Brandt shrugged. "Being king will be too much work."

"You'll rise to the occasion," she encouraged.

He gave her a look. "You really think so?"

"Yes." Her gaze locked with his, willing him to remember their previous discussions and their plan. Okay, her plan. "You will bring our country into the twenty-first century. If not for our younger brothers and subjects, then for your children and theirs. Especially the daughters."

"I don't know."

"Yes, you do. And I'll help." The bane of his existence was being crown prince. Brandt wanted all the perks that went with being royalty without any of the responsibility. One of these days he was going to have to grow up. "Once I marry someone outside of Aliestle, Father's reign over me ends. I'll be able to represent our country to the world and gain support to help you enact reforms when you are king, even if the Council of Elders is against them. We must change Aliestle for the better, Brandt."

He didn't say anything. She didn't expect him to.

"We are approaching the palace," the pilot announced over the headsets.

Goose bumps prickled Jules's skin.

Full of curiosity at her new home, she peered out the window. A huge white stucco and orange-tile roofed palace perched above the sea. The multistoried building had numerous balconies and windows.

But no tower. Another good sign?

A paved road and narrower walking paths wove their way through a landscape of palm trees, flowering bushes and manicured greenery. Water shot at least twenty-five feet into the air from an ornately decorated fountain.

The Mediterranean island and palace were a world away from Aliestle and the stone castle fortress nestled high in the Alps. Living somewhere lighter and brighter would be a welcome change from the Grimm-like fairy-tale setting she called home.

"Father may have finally gotten this right," Brandt said.

Jules nodded. "It's pretty."

"At least on the outside."

She sighed. "Don't forget, dear brother, you're here for moral support."

"And to make sure the honeymoon doesn't start early," Brandt joked.

As if she'd ever had that opportunity present itself. She glared at him. "Be quiet."

"Sore spot, huh?"

He had no idea. Engaged three times, and she'd never come close to anything other than kisses. Besides making out with Christian while a teenager, she'd been kissed once as an adult. Prince Niko's kiss while sailing had been pleasant enough, but nothing like the passion she'd overheard other women discussing. Perhaps with Prince Enrique…

The helicopter landed on a helipad. The engine stopped. The rotor's rotation slowed. Her hand trembled, making her work harder to unbuckle her harness. Finally she undid the latch. As they exited, a uniformed staff member placed their luggage onto a wheeled cart.

"Welcome to La Isla de la Aurora, Your Royal Highness Crown Prince Brandt and Your Royal Highness Princess Julianna." An older man in a gray suit bowed. "I am Ortiz. Prince Enrique sends his regrets for not meeting you himself, but he is attending to important state business at the moment."

"We understand." Brandt smiled. He might not be the typical statesman, but no one could fault his friendliness. "State business comes first."

Jules looked around at the potted plants and flowering vines. A floral scent lingered in the air. Paradise? Perhaps.

"Thank you, sir." Ortiz sounded grateful. "I am in charge of the palace and at your service. Whatever you need, I'll see that you have it."

Jules glanced at Brandt, whose grin resembled the Cheshire cat's. She would have to make sure he didn't take advantage of the generous offer of hospitality.

"The palace grounds are lovely, Ortiz," she said. "Very inviting with so many colorful flowers and plants."

"I am happy you like it, ma'am." His smile took years off his tanned, lined face. "Please allow me to show you and your party inside."

Klaus nodded. Her bodyguard, in his fifties with a crew cut and a gun hidden under his tailored suit jacket, had protected her for as long as she could remember.

"Lead the way, Ortiz," she said.

As they walked from the helipad to the front door, Ortiz gave her a brief history lesson about the palace. She had no idea the royal family had ruled the island for so long. No doubt the continuous line of succession had impressed her father who would want to ensure a long reign for his grandchildren and the heirs that followed.

"Prince Enrique has done so much for the island," Ortiz said. "A finer successor to King Dario cannot be found, ma'am."

If only Jules knew whether the compliments were truthful or propaganda. She knew little about her future husband besides his name. "I'm looking forward to meeting Prince Enrique."

Ortiz beamed. "He said the same thing about you at lunchtime, ma'am."

A third good sign? Jules hoped so.

When they reached the palace entry, two arched wooden doors parted as if by magic. Once the heavy doors were fully open, she saw two uniformed attendants standing behind and holding them.

Jules stared at the entrance with a mix of anticipation and apprehension. If all went well—and she hoped it did—this palace would be her new home. She would live with her husband and raise her children here. She fought the urge to cross her fingers.

With a deep breath, she stepped inside. The others followed.

A thirty-foot ceiling gave the large marble tiled foyer an open and airy feel. Stunning paintings, a mix of modern and classical works, hung on the walls. A marble statue of a woman sitting in the middle captured Jules's attention. "What an amazing sculpture."

"That is Eos, one of the Greek's second generation Titan gods," Ortiz explained. "We are more partial to the Latin name, Aurora. Whichever name you prefer, she'll always be the Goddess of the Dawn."

"Beautiful," Brandt agreed. "Eos had a strong desire for handsome young men. If she looked anything like this statue, I'm sure she had no trouble finding willing lovers."

"Close the front doors," a male voice shouted. "Now."

The attendants pushed the heavy doors. Grunts sounded. Muscles strained.

"Hurry," the voice urged.

The people behind Jules rushed farther into the foyer so the doors could be shut. The momentum pushed her forward.

A shirtless man wearing shorts ran toward the doors. Something black darted across the floor.

Yvette screamed. "A rat, Your Highnesses."

"There are no rats in the palace," Ortiz shouted.

The ball of black fur darted between Jules's legs. Startled, she stumbled face-first.

"Catch her," Klaus yelled.

Too late. The marble floor seemed to rise up to meet Jules though she was the one falling.

She stopped abruptly. Not against the floor.

Strong arms embraced Jules. Her face pressed against a hard, bare chest. Her cheek rested against warm skin. Dark hair tickled her nose. The sound of a heartbeat filled her ears. He smelled so good. No fancy colognes. Only soap and water and salty ocean air.

She wanted another sniff.

Ortiz shrieked. "Your Highnesses. Are either of you hurt?"

Highnesses? The man must be a prince. Her father had only spoken of the crown prince. No other brothers had been mentioned. Oh, if this were Enrique…

CHAPTER TWO

"Jules?" Brandt sounded concerned.

"I'm fine," Jules said quickly, more interested in the man—the prince—who saved her from hitting her face on the floor and still held her with his strong arms. Such wide shoulders, too.

Awareness seeped through her.

"My apologies." His deep, rich voice and Spanish accent sent her racing pulse into a mad sprint. "The kitten darted out of the room before I could grab him."

Ortiz raised his chin. "As I said, there are no rats in the palace, Princess."

The prince inhaled sharply. She found herself being set upon her feet. But he kept hold of her, even after she was standing.

"Stable?" he asked.

She nodded, forcing herself not to stare at his muscular chest and ripped abs.

He let go of her.

A chill shivered through Jules. She wasn't used to being in such close contact with anyone, but she missed having his nicely muscled arms around her.

She studied him, eager for a better look.

Over six feet tall with an athletic build, he looked more pirate than prince with shoulder-length dark brown hair, an earring in his left ear, khaki shorts and bare feet.

His strong jawline, high cheekbones and straight nose looked almost chiseled and made her think of the Eos sculpture. But his full lips and thick eyelashes softened the harsher features. The result—a gorgeous face she would be happy to stare at for hours. Days. Years.

Jules's heart thudded. "Thank you."

Warm brown eyes met hers. Gold specks flickered like flames around his irises. "You're welcome."

Everyone else faded into the background. Time seemed to stop. Something unfamiliar unfurled deep inside her.

He swooped up a black ball of fur with one hand. The look of tenderness in his dark eyes as he checked the kitten melted her heart. She would love for a man—this man—to look at her that way.

The kitten meowed. As he rubbed it, he returned his attention to her. "You're Princess Julianna from Aliestle."

It wasn't a question.

"Yes." Jules had never believed in love at first sight until now. She hoped their children looked exactly like him. A smile spread across her lips and reached all the way to her heart. Her father *had* gotten this right. She would realize her dream of marrying for love. A warm glow flowed through her. "You must be Enrique."

"No." His jaw thrust forward. "I am Alejandro."

Alejandro held on to the kitten as confusion clouded Juliana's pretty face. He was a little confused by his own reaction to this so-called ice princess. She had practically melted against him, and he'd yet to cool down from the contact. The woman was gorgeous, with a killer body underneath her coral-colored suit, long blond hair and big blue eyes a man could drown in.

She smelled sweet, like a bouquet of wildflowers. He wondered if her glossed lips tasted...

Not sweet.

He forced his gaze off her mouth. Julianna's marriage to Enrique and the children she conceived would remove Alejandro from the line of succession. She was his ticket out of his obligation to the monarchy. He couldn't think of her as anything other than his future sister-in-law.

That shouldn't be difficult since she wasn't his type.

Beautiful, yes, if you liked the kind of woman who knew how to apply makeup perfectly and could give any supermodel a run for her money. But he wanted a woman who didn't care about the trappings of wealth and royalty. A woman who was down-to-earth and didn't mind the spray of salt water in her face.

"Alejandro," Julianna repeated as if he didn't know his own name.

He couldn't remember the last time anyone had mistaken him for Enrique. Polar opposites didn't begin to describe their differences. But the fact Julianna didn't know what her future husband looked like surprised Alejandro more. Arranged marriages were still a part of royal life in some countries, but agreeing to marry someone without seeing their photograph struck him as odd. "Yes."

She stiffened. The warmth in her eyes disappeared. The expression on her face turned downright chilly.

Ice princess?

He saw now why she'd been called that. The change in

her demeanor startled him, but he shouldn't have been surprised. Alejandro had dated enough spoiled and pampered royals and wealthy girls to last a lifetime. This one, with a rich-as-Midas father, would most likely rank up there with the worst. He almost pitied Enrique. Emphasis on almost.

She drew her finely arched brows together, looking haughty not curious. "That makes you...?"

The kitten chirped, sounding more bird than cat. Alejandro used his thumb to rub under the cat's chin.

Impatience flashed in Julianna's eyes.

He took his time answering. "Enrique's younger brother."

Alejandro waited for her look of disdain. No one cared about the second in line for the throne, especially a woman meant to be queen.

"Oh." Her face remained expressionless. But royals were trained to turn off emotion with the flick of a switch and not display their true feelings. "I didn't realize Enrique had a younger brother."

That Alejandro believed. "My family prefers not to talk about me."

Ortiz cleared his throat.

"The princess will be family soon enough, Ortiz." Alejandro would be counting the days as soon as the official wedding date was set. He couldn't wait to live his own life without interference from his family. Of course, an heir or two would need to be born until he would be totally free. He shifted his gaze to the princess. "She'll hear the stories. Whispers over tea. Innuendos over cocktails. Nudges during dessert. No sense hiding the truth."

Tilting her chin, she gave him a cool look. "What truth might that be?"

"I'm the black sheep of the family."

Julianna pursed her lips. "A black cat for the black sheep."

"Not by choice," he admitted. "The cat chose me."

She stared at the kitten, but didn't pet him. Definitely ice running through her veins. "Such a lucky kitty to be able to choose for itself."

"It's too bad royalty doesn't get the same choices," Alejandro said.

He waited for her to reply. She didn't.

"Eat, sleep, play." A man in his early twenties with dark, curly brown hair stepped forward. He had rugged features, but his refined demeanor matched his designer suit and Italian leather shoes. "The life of a cat seems perfect to me. Much better than that of a prince."

"Well, the kitten is a stray," Alejandro said. "Caviar isn't part of his diet."

The man grinned. "It's only part of mine on occasion."

Julianna sighed. "Prince Alejandro, this is—"

"Alejandro," he corrected. "I don't use my title."

"Wish I could get away with that," the other man said. "Though the title does come in handy when it comes to women."

"That is the one benefit I have found," Alejandro agreed.

Julianna rolled her eyes. "The two of you can compare dating notes later. Now it's time for a formal introduction."

The princess's words told Alejandro she was cut from the same cloth as Enrique. Both seemed to hold an appreciation for royal protocol and etiquette. Something Alejandro saw as a complete waste of time. The two stuffy royals might live happily ever after.

"Alejandro," she continued. "This is His Royal Highness Crown Prince Brandt. One of my four younger brothers."

Brother? Alejandro studied the two. He couldn't believe

they were so closely related. Brandt was as dark as his sister was fair.

"Half brother," Julianna clarified, as if reading Alejandro's thoughts.

That explained it. But nothing explained why his gaze drifted to the curve of her hips. A nice body would never make up for an unpleasant personality that was the female version of his older brother. Maybe he'd been spending too much time working at the boatyard and not enough time out partying with the ladies. Perhaps later...

Right now he wanted to return to his room. Being surrounded by royalty was suffocating.

"It's been nice meeting you." His obligation to be here when the princess arrived had been met. He cradled the now napping kitten in the crook of his arm. "I'll see..."

Julianna stroked the kitten. The move took him by surprise. The soft smile on her face reached all the way to her eyes and made him do a double-take. His pulse rate shot up a few notches.

He'd always been a sucker for a pair of big baby blues. "Would you like to hold him?"

She drew back her hand. Her French manicured nails had no cracks or chips. "No, thank you."

Alejandro didn't know whether to be intrigued or annoyed by the princess. Before he could decide which, a cloud of strong aftershave hit him. He recognized the toxic scent, otherwise known as the expensive designer brand of cologne his brother wore.

Enrique turned the corner. He strode across the floor with quick steps and his head held high. Whereas Brandt looked regal, Enrique came across as pompous.

He stared at Julianna as if she were a red diamond, a rare

gem meant only for him. Dollar signs shone in his eyes. Enrique's priority had always been La Isla de la Aurora. Women were secondary, which was why an arranged marriage had been necessary.

After an uncomfortable moment of silence, Enrique glared at Ortiz, who introduced everyone with lofty titles and more middle names than Alejandro could count.

Enrique struck a ridiculous pose, as if he were at a photo shoot not standing in the foyer. "I hope you had a pleasant journey from Aliestle."

"Thank you. I did." Julianna's polite smile gave nothing away as to her first impression of her groom. "The palace is lovely."

Leave it to Enrique to turn meeting his future wife into such a formal event. Alejandro couldn't believe his brother. Didn't he remember their charm lessons with Mrs. Delgado? If Enrique had a clue about women, about Julianna, he would kiss her hand and compliment her on her shoes. He would make her feel as if she'd arrived home, not treat her like a temporary houseguest. But Enrique only did what he wanted, no matter how that affected anyone else.

"Alejandro." Irritation filled Enrique's eyes. "What are you doing with that animal?"

"He's a kitten. And I'm only following your instructions, brother," Alejandro explained. "I'm here, as requested, to meet your lovely bride."

Enrique's face reddened. "You could at least have taken the time to dress."

"He escaped while I was changing." Alejandro petted the sleeping cat. "I assumed Father wouldn't want a kitten tearing through the palace unattended."

Enrique started to speak then stopped himself. Their

guests must be keeping his temper in check. At least the princess and her entourage were good for something around here.

"I'll take him to my room," Alejandro added. "See you at dinner."

"Formal attire," Enrique reminded, his voice tight. "In case you've forgotten, that includes shirt and shoes."

Alejandro rocked back on his heels. "I know how to dress for dinner, bro, but thanks for the reminder."

The air crackled with tension.

Twenty years ago, they would have been fighting while Ortiz called for the palace guards to separate them. Ten years ago, the same thing might have happened. But Enrique would never lower himself, or his station, to that level now. Even if his hard gaze told Alejandro he wanted to fight.

"At least your younger brother knows how to dress, Enrique. Not all of mine do." Julianna sounded empathetic. "I don't know about you, but sometimes it's hard being the oldest."

Her words may have been calculated, but they did the trick. Enrique's jaw relaxed. He focused his attention on Julianna.

Alejandro was impressed. Diffusing the situation so deftly took skill. And practice.

"It can be difficult." The corners of Enrique's mouth lifted into a half smile. "Younger siblings don't take things as seriously or have the same sense of duty."

Idiot. Alejandro wondered if his brother realized he was also slamming Brandt, another crown prince, with his words.

"Some don't," Julianna agreed. "But others just need to understand their responsibilities a little better. Isn't that right, dear brother?"

Brandt nodded, looking more amused than offended. Alejandro liked the guy already.

Enrique's mouth twisted, as if he finally understood how his words could be construed. "I was talking about Alejandro."

Julianna smiled at Enrique. "Of course, you were."

The woman was smooth. Alejandro had no idea if her skills came from dealing with her brothers or boyfriends, but he'd never seen anyone handle Enrique so well. Not even their mother who had separated from their father years ago. Maybe Julianna could rein in the future ruler's ego and temper. If she had a brain in that pretty head of hers, as she seemed to, she could stop him from making bad decisions, like focusing on projects that aggrandized himself, but did nothing to help the island.

The ice princess might be exactly what Enrique needed.

Alejandro would have to make sure his brother didn't blow this engagement.

For both their sakes. And the island's.

"Thank you for escorting me to my room." Standing with Enrique, Jules glanced around. The pastel pink and yellow decor was bright and cheery. Maybe some of it would rub off on her because right now she was feeling a little…down. She forced a smile anyway. Replacing Enrique's aftershave and teaching him a few manners wouldn't be difficult. It could be much worse. "The suite is lovely."

"I asked Ortiz to put you in this room." Enrique pulled back a curtain. "I thought you might like the view."

She stared out the window at rows of colorful flowers below. A burst of hot pink. A swatch of bright yellow. A patch of purple.

Another wave of disappointment washed over her. The

same way it had when she'd discovered her hottie rescuer wasn't going to be her husband, but her brother-in-law.

Don't think about that. About him. Otherwise she might find herself back in Aliestle.

"A garden." She hoped she sounded more enthusiastic than she felt. A bush of red roses captured her attention until she noticed the large thorns on the thick stems. Ouch, that would hurt. "How nice."

"The garden is the closest thing I have to a hobby now. A majority of the flowers are in bloom," Enrique explained. "When you open the window, the breeze will carry a light floral scent into your room."

"Picking out this room for me is so thoughtful of you." Even if she would have preferred the smell of salt water, a view of the sea, Alejandro.

No, that wasn't fair.

Enrique was handsome. He looked more like a fashion model from Milan than a crown prince in his designer suit, starched shirt, silk tie and leather shoes. If he'd been shirtless and she found herself pressed against his hard chest...

She tried to imagine it. Tried and failed.

He wasn't Alejandro, who had appeared in the foyer like the Roman god Mars come to life and looking for a fight. Well, until he held the kitten in his hand, and then he'd looked...perfect.

Not perfect. No one was perfect.

But the two brothers were tall, dark and handsome. They shared the same brown eyes, but the similarities ended there. One was sexy and dangerous, the black sheep. The other was formal and Old World, the future king.

Jules might be inexperienced when it came to men, but she wasn't stupid. Even if thinking about Alejandro made her pulse quicken, Enrique would make the better husband and father. He was the logical choice, the smart choice.

The only choice.

She was here to be Enrique's bride and his alone. She would be his wife and one day a queen. Whatever she may have felt in Alejandro's arms didn't matter. No one could ever know she found him attractive. As for her fiancé…

So what if he had similar mannerisms and speech as her father? Perhaps Enrique's formality stemmed from nervousness. Crown princes were human, even if few would admit it.

He had selected this room for her. Granted, the view wasn't the one she would have preferred, but he'd had his reasons for choosing it. And he was still better than marrying anyone from Aliestle. Jules smiled genuinely at him. "Thank you for welcoming us into your home."

"It'll be your home soon enough."

She nodded, trying to muster a few ounces of happy feelings and peppiness. She hoped they would come.

"I look forward to seeing you at dinner," he said.

"As do I."

He took her hand and raised it to his mouth. He brushed his lips over her skin.

Jules wanted to feel the same passion and heat she'd felt in Alejandro's arms. She would settle for a spark, tingles, warmth at the point of contact, even a small shiver. But she felt…nothing.

Enrique released her hand. "Until later, my princess."

Later. The word resonated with her.

As he left and closed the door behind him, she remembered what she'd told Izzy, Princess Isabel of Vernonia.

Remember, just because you don't love someone at the be-

ginning doesn't mean you won't love them in the end. Love can grow over time.

Jules needed to listen to her own advice.

My princess. She would be Enrique's princess. She needed to act like it, too.

Just because she didn't feel anything with him now, didn't mean she wouldn't ever. Physical attraction and chemistry weren't the same as love. Passion could be fleeting, but love remained. Prevailed. This first meeting was only the beginning.

Love could grow between her and Enrique.

She had to give the relationship time, keep an open heart and remember how love had blossomed with her parents.

But to be on the safe side until love bloomed with Enrique, Jules realized with an odd pang, keeping her distance from Alejandro would probably be a good idea.

Dinner was exactly what Alejandro thought it would be—a total drag. Each course of the gourmet meal took forever. He enjoyed good food, but by the time the meal finished, he'd be falling out of his chair sound asleep. The conversation about international trade agreements would make a rabbit in heat want to nap.

Across the table, Julianna sat next to her brother, Brandt. She looked stunning in a blue evening gown that matched the color of her eyes. The dress didn't show a lot of skin, but the flowing fabric gave enough of a hint of what was underneath to make a man want to see more.

He tried not to look at her.

Enrique was doing enough staring for both of them.

But Alejandro heard her voice drone on. She tried to sound interested in what others were saying, but her tone lacked warmth. Yes, she was going to be an excellent match for his superficial brother.

Five formally dressed staff members set plates of pan-seared sea scallops in front of each of them at the exact same time. Two wine stewards circled the table filling wineglasses from bottles of Pinot Gris.

What Alejandro wouldn't give for plates of tapas and a pitcher of sangria right now.

Enrique laughed at something Julianna said. So did his father.

"Who knew your bride would be an expert in trade?" Dario said.

"Thank you, sir." Julianna's smile didn't reach her eyes the way it had when she'd petted the kitten. "But trade is a hobby."

A hobby? Maybe a geek lived inside the beauty's body. Or maybe she was trying to impress her future father-in-law. Either way, Alejandro wanted nothing to do with her.

"Now that is a worthy hobby." Enrique pinned Alejandro with a contemptible look. "Unlike *some* of the hobbies others of us have."

He stared over the rim of his wineglass. "Care to wager how my hobby turns out during the Med Cup, bro?"

Julianna's fork clattered against her plate and bounced off the table. Her cheeks turned a bright shade of pink. "Excuse me."

Alejandro studied her. Strange. The stumble in the foyer aside, Julianna didn't seem like a klutzy princess. It was unusual for someone as elegant as her to drop her fork in the middle of dinner and make a spectacle of herself.

Two servants rushed to her side. One picked up the fork from the ground. The other placed a new fork on the table.

"Thank you." She raised her half-filled water glass. "So you sail, Alejandro?"

"I sail. I also build boats. Racing sailboats." He noticed the glance exchanged between Julianna and Brandt. "Do either of you sail?"

She looked again at her brother.

"We sail," Brandt answered. "On local lakes and rivers. For pleasure. Unlike many of our royal compatriots who enjoy the competitive side of the sport."

Alejandro couldn't understand why Julianna needed her brother to answer such a simple question. She'd had no problem talking about trade.

Enrique swirled the wine in his glass. "Some royals take sailing too seriously. I enjoyed the few regattas I competed in, but I no longer have time to sail with so many other obligations."

"Horse racing may be the sport of kings," Brandt said. "But many royals have sailed for their countries in the Summer Games. I'm sure more would have liked to."

Dario nodded. "I've always preferred the water to horses."

"As have I," Enrique added hastily.

Julianna leaned forward. The neckline of her gown gaped, giving Alejandro a glimpse of ivory skin and round breasts. He forced his attention onto the sea scallops instead.

"Will one of your boats be entered in the Med Cup?" she asked, as if trying to draw him into conversation.

He appreciated her taking an interest. "My newest design."

"A bit risky, don't you think?" Enrique asked.

Alejandro shrugged. "You never know until you try."

A smug smile curved Enrique's lips. "I may take you up on that wager."

"My sons take the opposite sides on everything," King

Dario explained. "And if they can figure a way to bet on the outcome…"

"They sound like my brothers, sir." Julianna's smile lit up her face. The result took Alejandro's breath away. She looked more like the woman he'd held in his arms, not the cool, proper princess. "Brandt isn't as bad as the younger three. At least not any longer."

Brandt raised his glass to her. "Thanks, sis."

"So will you be sailing in the race, Alejandro?" She sounded not only interested but also curious.

"Possibly." The change in her intrigued him. "I'm trying to find the right mix of crew. But the boat can be sailed single-handedly, too."

"Doesn't sound like much of a racing boat," Enrique said.

"The best boats can perform with varying numbers of crew." Her eyes became more animated as she spoke. "I'm sure it'll be an exciting race."

Alejandro thought he heard a note of wistfulness in her voice. "Racing is always exciting. I'd be happy to take all of you out sailing. You could see the boat for yourself."

Julianna straightened.

Brandt smiled. "Thanks, that sounds like fun."

"Yes, but a sail isn't possible right now." As Enrique spoke, Julianna leaned back in her chair with a thoughtful expression on her face. "I don't need to sail on your boat to know what the outcome of the race will be."

Alejandro didn't know why he tried.

"Enough sailing." Dario gave a dismissive wave of his hand. "We have more important things to discuss, like wedding plans. King Alaric says there is no need for a lengthy engagement."

"Our father is satisfied with the marriage contract,"

Brandt said. "Whatever wedding date you decide upon is fine with him."

"Outstanding. A short engagement, it'll be." Dario beamed. "How quickly do you two want to get married?"

Enrique and Julianna smiled at each other, but neither said a word.

"If I might make a suggestion, Father," Alejandro offered.

"Go on."

"Set the wedding date a week after the Med Cup, sir."

"That would be a short engagement. Why then?" Dario asked.

"Because two people have never seemed more perfect for each other." Oddly, the words felt like sandpaper against Alejandro's tongue. But the sooner the two were married, the sooner he would be free. "Having the wedding after the Med Cup will allow me to focus all my attention on my responsibilities as best man."

"Excellent suggestion," his father said. "Enrique, Julianna. Do you agree?"

"I do." Enrique stared at Julianna. "I can't wait to marry."

"Neither can I." Julianna sounded like she meant it.

Dario clapped his hands together. The sound echoed through the large dining room. "I'll call King Alaric in the morning."

"I'll start planning our honeymoon," Enrique said.

The thought of Julianna in his brother's bed left a bad taste in Alejandro's mouth. But heirs were necessary if he wanted to be left alone by his father.

Julianna didn't seem to mind. A charming blush crept up her long, graceful neck.

He remembered what Enrique had said about King Alaric's daughter being a virgin. That didn't seem possible unless he had used his wealth to protect her virtue. But was the seemingly in-control princess ready for some passion?

Alejandro couldn't forget the way she'd pressed into him and how her heart pounded against his chest when he'd held her in his arms or the excited tone of her voice and the gleam in her eyes when she talked about sailing. Only a talented actress could feign that kind of interest.

Maybe there was more to her than Alejandro realized.

Not that it mattered. He picked up his wineglass and sipped. Not much anyway.

CHAPTER THREE

After dinner, Jules stood out on the terrace alone. Cicadas chirped. A breeze rustled through the palm fronds. The temperature had cooled, but no jacket was required.

She glanced inside through the open terrace doors to see Brandt having a brandy with King Dario. Enrique must still be on his telephone call with the ambassador to the United States.

Jules enjoyed the moment of solitude, a break from the endless conversation at the dinner table. At least the topic had finally turned to something interesting.

With her hands on the railing, Jules gazed up at the night sky. The stars surrounding the almost full moon winked at her. A smile graced her lips.

Perhaps she wasn't cursed.

Enrique hadn't said yes to the sailing invitation, but his words "right now" filled Julianna with hope. He'd raced sailboats. Alejandro built racing sailboats. Her wedding date was a couple of weeks away.

What were the odds of so many things working out so well? Not only was she marrying into a family of sailors, she would soon be Enrique's wife. She could say goodbye to being submissive for the rest of her life.

On La Isla de la Aurora, she would be able to do what she wanted. Personal freedom, yes, but she could also help Brandt to show the world Aliestle was more than an eccentric, backward country. Maybe by doing that, Jules would be able to live up to the spirit of her mother.

Laughter bubbled up inside her.

Oh, she'd visit her homeland, but she would no longer be expected to live by all the restrictive laws and traditions.

The only thing missing was falling in love, but given how well everything else was turning out she believed it would happen. She would fall in love with Enrique and he with her. The same way her parents had fallen in love after their arranged marriage.

It was all going to work out. "I know it will."

"Know what will?" a male voice asked from the shadows.

Jules jumped. "Who's there?"

"I didn't mean to startle you."

She squinted. She couldn't see anyone, but recognized the voice. "Alejandro."

He ascended the staircase leading to the terrace where she stood. "Good evening, Julianna."

Her heart lurched. She fought against the burst of attraction making her mouth go dry. It wasn't easy.

The stubble on his face made him look so much like a sexy pirate. She could easily imagine him standing behind the wheel of a sailing ship trying to capture a vessel full of gold or pretty wenches.

He'd removed his jacket, tie and cummerbund. The neck of his dress shirt was unbuttoned, the tails hung out of the trousers and his sleeves were rolled up. The high rollers decked out in the finest menswear on the Côte d'Azur had nothing on Alejandro. Even with his bare feet.

"How long have you been lurking in the shadows?" she asked.

He moved gracefully like a dancer or a world-class athlete. "Long enough to hear you laughing."

Heat enflamed her cheeks. "If I'd known you were there…"

Alejandro crossed the terrace to stand next to her. "No need to apologize for being happy."

Maybe not for him. But happy wasn't an emotion Jules was used to experiencing let alone expressing. Sharing that moment embarrassed her. Still she owed him for what he'd said at dinner about sailing and the wedding. But one was more important than the other. "Thank you for suggesting a short engagement."

"Afraid you'll change your mind?" he asked.

"Worried Enrique will."

"Not going to happen."

Jules wished she shared Alejandro's confidence. "I've heard that before."

"He'd be a fool, a complete idiot, if he didn't marry you."

His compliment made her feel warm all over. His opinion shouldn't matter, but for some reason it did. "Well, intelligence has never been a requirement to be a crown prince."

The deep, rich sound of his laughter seeped into her and raised her temperature ten degrees. "You're a contradiction, Julianna."

"How so?"

"Your dress and demeanor present the image of a proper, dutiful princess, who dots her I's and crosses her T's. Yet you show glimpses…"

No one had ever looked beneath the surface or beyond the

label of dutiful princess. She wouldn't have expected Alejandro to, either. Full of curiosity, she leaned toward him. "Of what?"

"Of being a not-so-perfect princess."

It was her turn to laugh. That wasn't who she was. Oh, well...Perhaps Enrique would recognize the real her. "You're reading too much into my words and deeds. Women are second-class citizens in Aliestle. We must obey the men in our lives or deal with the consequences. Duty becomes our way of life. But that doesn't mean we don't have the same hopes and dreams, the same sense of humor, as women in more contemporary lands such as this island."

"As I said, a contradiction."

She eyed him warily. "Thank you, I think."

"It's a compliment." He glanced back toward the sitting room. "Your groom has returned."

Jules looked behind her to see Enrique holding a brandy and talking with the others.

"I should leave you." Alejandro took a step toward the staircase. "I don't want my brother to think I'm trying to steal his princess bride."

Would Alejandro do that? Her pulse skittered thinking he might.

Stop. Now. She couldn't allow herself to be carried away with girlish fantasies. She raised her chin. "Enrique wouldn't think—"

"Yes, he would."

"Have you stolen his girlfriends in the past?"

His eyes raked over her. "No, we have different taste in women."

Alejandro's stark appraisal should have made her feel uncomfortable, but he also made her feel sexy, a way she'd never felt before. She wet her lips. "Would your being the black sheep and all the gossip have something to do with Enrique feeling this way?"

Alejandro grinned wryly. "Possibly."

"So the rumors and stories are true."

"Some are," he admitted. "Others are exaggerations."

He was a gorgeous prince. That often led people to act out of…"I'm sure a few tales are due to jealousy."

He eyed her curiously. "Has this happened to you?"

"Oh, no. I'm about as proper a princess as you'll find."

"Proper with obvious skills of manipulation."

"Proper with practiced social skills and manners that help others get along."

"Yet you downplay your intelligence by saying your knowledge about international trade is nothing but a hobby."

His perceptiveness made her feel like a mouse caught in a trap. He might be a black sheep and prefer to go barefoot, but he was sharp. She'd have to watch herself. "Education opportunities for females in my country exist, but are limited. Women are allowed to hold only certain jobs. We must work within the system. I've been more fortunate than others and able to use my time traveling abroad to…expand my knowledge base. But the last thing my country wants is their princess spouting off how smart she thinks she is."

Laughter lit Alejandro's eyes and made her temperature rise ten degrees. "You'll be good for Enrique. Keep him on his toes. But he won't mind."

"I hope not. What about you?" Jules liked the easy banter between them. Earlier when she'd arrived, she thought Alejandro didn't like her. "Will you mind not being second in line for the throne after Enrique and I have children?"

He glanced inside once again. "I can honestly say the more

children you and my brother are blessed with, the happier I'll be. I've been hoping to be made an uncle for years."

His words sounded genuine. She ignored her disappointment that he wouldn't want her himself. That was stupid. Her father would never approve of a man like Alejandro, and she needed to be a queen to best help Brandt and Aliestle. "That's sweet of you."

"The kitten is sweet. I'm not." He took two steps down the stairs. "Enrique's on his way out here. That's my cue to fade back into the shadows."

Alejandro's cryptic words intrigued her. "Do you usually hang out in the shadows?"

"Yes, I do."

She watched him disappear into the night.

Behind her, footsteps sounded against the terrace's tile floor. A familiar scent of aftershave enveloped her. She didn't like the fragrance. Still better than the alternative, she reminded herself.

Jules leaned forward over the railing, but couldn't see Alejandro. "I hope your call went well.

"It did." Enrique stood next to her. "But you needn't worry about state business. The wedding should be your focus."

"I've been thinking about our wedding." She wondered if Alejandro was listening from below. Not that she minded if he eavesdropped. A part of her wished he was here with her instead of his brother. "And children, too."

"We are of like minds." Enrique placed his hand over hers. His skin was warm and soft. His nails neatly trimmed. Not the hands of a sailor or gardener. "Heirs would please my father."

"Mine, too." Her duty was to extend the bloodline. But Jules also wanted babies of her own. She remembered helping the nurses with each of her brothers. She wanted to be more involved with raising her children than her stepmother.

Enrique's eyes darkened. "Once we are married we shouldn't waste any time starting a family."

His suggestive tone made her shiver. Not a surprising reaction given she'd never discussed sex with any of her matches before. Offspring had always been assumed. "I would like a big family. At least four children."

He tucked her hair behind her ears. "I hope they all look like you."

His compliment was nice, but the words didn't make her feel warm and fuzzy the way Alejandro's had. "Thank you."

"My brother will be pleased to know you want so many children," Enrique said. "He can't wait to fall lower in the line of succession. I believe if he could give away or relinquish his title he would without a second thought."

"I can't imagine anyone wanting to do that," she admitted. "But Alejandro does have his boats."

She envied his ability to follow his dreams.

"Nothing matters but those damn boats. Sailing has consumed him. He works as a manual laborer, a commoner, refusing to take advantage of the free publicity being a royal engaged in business always brings."

Enrique's critical tone didn't surprise Jules. The two brothers seemed to always be going at each other. But sometimes that might keep them from seeing a situation more clearly. "If Alejandro wins the Med Cup, he'll earn respect. New customers."

"He won't win with a new design," Enrique said. "Competition is fierce. The best crews are going to be on well-known, tested designs. Too bad my brother is too stubborn to use the same boat as last year. But he always wants something newer, better. That's one reason I doubt he'll ever marry. He upgrades the women in his life like they were cars."

The picture Enrique painted of his younger brother was not flattering. Jules wondered if this was one of the stories Alejandro had mentioned. The two brothers needed to get along better. That gave her an idea.

"Sail his other boat for him," she said. "The one he sailed last year."

"I haven't raced since my duties became expanded. State business takes up the majority of my time."

His curt tone rebuked her. "It was only a suggestion."

"Racing in open water isn't without risks."

"I've never sailed in the ocean." Just dreamed about it.

"Your father told me he's forbidden you to sail on the sea. That's why I didn't accept Alejandro's invitation to go sailing."

"You and Brandt can go."

"Not without you," Enrique said, and she appreciated his courtesy. "Your father mentioned your mother's accident. So tragic."

Jules knew information would be exchanged during the marriage negotiations, but she'd never been privy to it. "My mother's death was an accident, a freak occurrence."

"No matter the circumstances." Enrique's voice softened. "Your father said he was deeply affected by the loss."

"I've been told he changed after she died. He loved my mother very much."

"He loves you, too."

Hearing the words from someone outside her family made Jules feel as if all the sacrifices she'd made to live up to the expectations of her father, family and country had been worth it. Her tongue felt thick, heavy, so she nodded.

"A lesser man might not have recovered from such a tragedy," Enrique continued.

She appreciated the admiration in his words. "My father is a king. He is a strong man. He mourned my mother's death, but he remarried less than a year later. He needed a male heir. I was a young child who needed a mother."

"Understandable."

Jules wondered if that meant Enrique would do the same should she die. Probably. "La Isla de la Aurora seems more progressive than Aliestle."

"It is, though we are a little old-fashioned about a few things," Enrique said. "Do not worry. I intend to make sure you like it here, Julianna."

His words fed her growing hopes. She gathered her courage. "My father said you would decide whether I could sail on the ocean after we are married. You told Alejandro we couldn't sail right now. Does that mean you've given some thought to my sailing after our wedding?"

"Your father also discussed this with me. I've already made my decision."

Her heart raced. She held her breath.

Please, oh, please. Say yes.

Enrique squeezed her hand again. "Sailing on the sea is too dangerous."

Jules felt as if someone had wrapped a line around her heart and pulled hard. She had to make him understand, to see how important this was to her. "I am a careful sailor. I would never take undue risks."

"You are on the ocean. Weather can change. No one, not even the best sailors in the world, can remove all the risk."

She understood that. She wasn't a complete idiot.

Desperate to make this work she sought another test. "Sailing is a pleasurable leisure activity. Something we could do together in our free time."

"I don't have a lot of free time."

"It wouldn't have to be that often. Only once in a while."

"We may have just met, but I must admit I understand your father's concerns." Enrique spoke to her as if she were a child. "You are to be the mother of my children, my wife, my queen. I wouldn't want anything to happen to you as it did your mother."

Disappointment settled in the center of Jules's chest, but she didn't allow her shoulders to slump. Being here was still better than Aliestle. "So I'm only allowed to sail on lakes and rivers?"

"I've seen what sailing has done to my brother. The sport killed your mother. Once we are married, I do not want you to sail again."

The air rushed from Jules lungs. Tears stung her eyes. She clutched the railing. "But I've always been able to sail. Just not on the ocean."

"That was your father's decision. This is mine."

No! Her chest tightened. This was so much worse than she imagined. It wasn't only the sailing. The tone of Enrique's voice told her she would be exchanging her controlling father for a controlling husband. Her freedom would be curtailed here, too.

"Don't look so disappointed," Enrique chided. "This isn't personal. I'm not trying to be cruel."

"What are you trying to do then?"

"Be honest and help you," he said. "It's time for you to grow up and put childish things aside, Julianna. You may believe sailing is good for you, but it's been brought to my attention that sailing brings out a wilder side in you."

She drew back. "What have I done?"

"Kissed Prince Niko."

"One kiss. We were engaged at the time."

"There have been other reports," Enrique said calmly, as if they were discussing business and not her life. "Such a pursuit is inappropriate for a future queen. You must embrace the bigger duty you'll now have."

Jules forced herself to breathe. Carving a new life for herself and helping Aliestle would be an uphill battle. She would be constrained here on the island, too. "What is to be my role here? My bigger duty?"

"You are to be my wife. You will provide me with heirs."

Both of those things she'd known about. Accepted. But she doubted that was all Enrique would want from her. "And?"

"You will be a conventional princess and queen the people can respect. It's in your best interest to do what I say and not bring any embarrassment to our name."

Her best interest? What about their best interest? Enrique seemed to want to tell her what to do, not have a real relationship with her. How could love grow out of that?

Emotion clogged her throat.

What was she going to do?

Returning to Aliestle in disgrace and marrying a nobleman would be the worst choice for her, Brandt, her country and her future children. Doing something more drastic didn't appeal to her, either.

Other women might run away. But if she turned her back on her responsibilities she would be exiled. Her father would keep her brothers from seeing her. Not only that, her father would also denounce her. Conditions would worsen for the women in her country. She couldn't give up on everything she'd sacrificed her whole life for and her family.

That left one choice—going through with the wedding. Her stomach churned.

Think of the bigger picture, the future, others.

Jules would be able to help Brandt and Aliestle. Her children would have a better life and more choices on the island. Those things would make up for everything she was giving up. In time, Jules would see she made the right decision.

But right now, it still…hurt.

In an apartment on the ground floor, Alejandro tried to relax. But being back at the palace made him antsy. So did something else. Someone else…

Julianna.

Maybe she wasn't as bad as he originally thought. She seemed different tonight, warmer and more genuine. But if that were the case, he couldn't understand her icy facade earlier.

Not that he should be thinking about his brother's fiancée at all.

Alejandro sat on the floor and used a laser pointer to play with the kitten. This was the same room he'd had as a teenager, though the furniture had been replaced, the floors refinished and the walls painted. The decor wasn't the only change. Back when he'd been a teenager, a guard had always been stationed outside the back door that led to the beach path to keep him from running away. Not that a guard had been able to stop him. At least his father hadn't posted anyone there tonight.

The kitten sprinted across the hardwood floor after the red dot, pawing and pouncing until he plopped onto a handwoven rug and purred. His eyes closed.

As Alejandro moved from the floor to a chair, a flash

of blue passed outside the window. The same blue as Julianna's gown.

He stood to get a better look.

Silky fabric and blond hair billowed behind her as she hurried down the path leading to the beach, making her look almost ethereal with the starry night sky as her backdrop.

Not his type, Alejandro reminded himself.

He glanced at the clock. Eleven o'clock. A little late to go beachcombing. Not that what she did was any of his business.

But no one seemed to be with her. Not Enrique. Not her bodyguard.

That didn't sit well with Alejandro.

She shouldn't be alone. It was dark. She could lose her way.

On a lighted path, an inner voice mocked.

Something could happen to her. Alejandro ignored the fact that he could find his brother and send him after Julianna.

Alejandro stepped outside onto the patio. The tile was hard beneath his bare feet. Planters full of fragrant flowers lined the edge. Lanterns hung from tall wrought-iron poles.

Maybe Julianna wanted a closer look at the water, or to dance on the beach under the moonlight…or skinny-dip.

As his blood surged at the thought, he quickened his pace. Now that he would like to see. Ice princess or not.

The lighted path stopped at the beach. Alejandro's bare feet sunk into the fine sand. Thanks to the moonlight, he saw Julianna standing at the water's edge holding her high heels in one hand. The hem of her gown dragged on the sand. Wind ruffled her hair and the fabric of her dress. Waves crashed against the shore, the water drawing closer to her. She didn't move.

Mesmerized by the sea or thinking? About him?

He scoffed at the stupid thought. She would be thinking about Enrique. Her fiancé. Alejandro should leave her alone.

Yet he remained rooted in place, content to watch her.

Being here had nothing to do with the way her dress clung to her curves or the slit that provided him with a glimpse of her long, smooth legs. He was here for her protection. Even though this strip of white sand was private, reachable only from the palace or by water. He didn't see any boats offshore, only silver moonlight reflecting off the crescents of waves.

Still he stood captivated by the woman in front of him. The individual, not incarnations of women she would become. Future sister-in-law, mother of his nieces and nephews, queen.

He longed to go to her, pull her into an embrace, taste her sweet lips and feel her lush curves pressed against him.

What the hell was he thinking?

Disgusted with the fantasy playing in his mind, Alejandro turned to leave. Julianna moved in his peripheral vision. He looked back. She sat on the sand, resting her head in her hands. Her shoulders shook as if she were crying.

A sob smacked into him. His gut clenched.

The instinct to bolt was strong. Tears made him uncomfortable. He'd been in enough short-term relationships to know crying women were to be avoided at all costs. He never knew what to say and feared making a situation worse.

Yet he walked toward her anyway as if pulled by an invisible line. Compelled by something he couldn't explain. "Julianna."

She didn't look up. "Go away, please."

Her voice sounded raw, yet she was polite, always the proper princess. He saw her behavior wasn't an act like his brother's. His respect inched up for her. "I'm not going away."

"I'll pretend you aren't here then."

"It won't be the first time that's happened." He plopped onto the sand next to her. "I've been becalmed many times. Having the boat bob like a cork while waiting for wind to return used to drive me crazy, but I've learned to enjoy the downtime."

She remained silent.

As waves broke against the shore, Alejandro studied the stars in the sky. He drew pictures in the sand. A boat. A crab. A heart. He wiped them away with the side of his hand.

Julianna raised her head. "You're still here."

"Yes." Tears streaked her cheeks. The sadness in her swollen eyes reignited his desire to take her in his arms and kiss her until she smiled. "I may have some of the same stubborn streak shared by other members of my family."

She sniffled.

He wished he had a tissue for her. One of those handkerchiefs his brother and father carried in their pockets would come in handy. "When you're ready to talk…"

A new round of tears streamed down her face. She looked devastated, as if someone she loved had died.

Her vulnerability clawed at his heart, made him feel useless, worthless. He couldn't sit here and do nothing.

Alejandro turned toward Julianna and lifted her onto his lap.

She gasped. Stiffened.

A mistake, probably, but he'd deal with that later. He needed to help Julianna.

The moment he wrapped his arms around her something seemed to release inside her. She sagged against him, rested her head on his shoulder and cried. He rubbed her back with his hand, the same way his mother used to do whenever he'd been hurt by something Enrique did or his father had said.

Julianna's tears didn't stop, but that didn't bother Alejandro. She felt so perfect nestled against him. Her sweet scent enveloped him. He would have preferred to be in this position under different circumstances, but he knew that wasn't possible. She had a fiancé—what she needed tonight was a friend.

He could be a friend. That was all he could ever be to her.

Her tears slowed. Her breathing became less ragged.

"Thank you," Julianna muttered. "I'm sorry for inconveniencing you. This is so unlike me."

Alejandro brushed the strands of hair sticking to her tearstained cheeks. "You're in my arms and on my lap. Formalities and apologies aren't necessary."

She stared up at him. Even with puffy, red eyes she was still beautiful.

But she was almost family. She would be his sister-in-law.

Julianna scooted off his lap. "I'm better now."

He missed the warmth of her body, the feel of her curves against him. "Tell me what's wrong."

She looked at the water. "It's nothing."

"Let me be the judge of that."

A beat passed. And another. "Did you hang around after Enrique joined me on the terrace?"

"No." Maybe Alejandro should have.

She took a slow breath. "I thought coming here and marrying Enrique would be so much better than staying in Aliestle. I believed things would be...different."

"I don't understand."

"It's difficult to explain. Do you recall at dinner when you asked if we sailed, and Brandt answered?"

Alejandro nodded. He'd thought that odd.

"Brandt spoke because he knows how much sailing means

to me, and I would've gotten carried away. I love it. I'd rather sail than do anything. Being on a boat is the only time I can be myself. Not a proper princess or a dutiful daughter and sister." She gazed at the water. "It's heaven on earth for me."

The passion in her words heated the blood in his veins. The longing for independence, for a freedom from all the expectations of being a royal matched the desire in his heart. This perfect princess was as much a black sheep as him. She just kept the true color of her wool hidden. "I know exactly how you feel."

She studied him. "I thought you might. My father has never allowed me to sail on the ocean due to my mother dying during a race. That's why Enrique turned down your invitation to go sailing. My father said once I married, Enrique could decide whether I could sail or not."

"You'll be living on an island," Alejandro said. "Why wouldn't you sail?"

"That's what I thought. After you left the terrace, I asked Enrique about being able to sail." Her lower lip quivered. "He has forbidden me to sail. Not only on the ocean, but ever again. He says sailing brings out a wildness in me that's not appropriate for a future queen. I'm to be a conventional wife and princess."

Tears gleamed in her eyes.

Damn Enrique. His brother was a complete moron. A total ass. As usual. "He has spoken without thinking."

"He was quite serious about his expectations of me."

"My brother might be a cad, but he isn't a monster. He'll come around."

Tears slipped from the corners of her eyes. "I don't think he will."

Alejandro's chest tightened. "I'll talk to Enrique. Make him see how much sailing means to you."

"No," she said. "He might change his mind about marrying me."

Not likely given her dowry. But Julianna was so much more than the money she brought to the marriage. She might act like a cold, dutiful princess, but underneath the perfect facade was a passionate woman looking to break free of the obligations that came with her tiara and scepter. La Isla de la Aurora deserved a queen like Julianna. Too bad Enrique didn't deserve a woman like her.

"Ask to be released from the marriage contract." Alejandro couldn't believe those words had come from his lips.

"I can't."

"You won't."

"If I don't marry Enrique, I'll be sent home to marry one of the sons of our Council of Elders." The way her voice cracked hurt Alejandro's heart. "In Aliestle, it's against the law to disobey your husband. I'd rather raise my children in a country that is more progressive. At least in principle. This is my fate. I must learn to accept it."

Alejandro hated seeing her so distressed. She deserved to be happy, to have the freedom to do what she wanted to do.

"Not so fast," he said. "In spite of a few traditional mindsets here, La Isla de la Aurora is a progressive country. That includes our laws. Enrique can't throw you in prison or lock you away in a tower if you disobey him and go sailing."

"This isn't only about my sailing."

"I'm not only talking about sailing. My mother left the island fifteen years ago." Alejandro had learned an important lesson the day his mother left. Never rely on anyone but yourself. "Separation is an option here, even for royals."

"That's very modern compared to where I come from." She wiped her eyes. "You see, I'd hoped to use my position as future queen to effect change back home without embarrassing my country and family."

Alejandro remembered what she'd told him. "Working within the system."

She nodded. "Royals can't be selfish and ignore the people who look up to them."

"That's noble of you," Alejandro said. Too bad most royals didn't feel that way. "But you shouldn't be too upset. My brother's pulling one of his power plays with you. He's done it to me many times and will change his mind. Your life will be better here than in Aliestle. You'll have royal obligations, but you'll also be able to do what you want to do, including help your country and sail."

Her shoulders remained slumped. "Enrique could annul the marriage if I defy him. I'd have to return to Aliestle."

"I don't see a ring on your finger."

"Not yet anyway." She glanced at her left hand. Straightened. "No ring."

"What?" Alejandro asked.

Her gaze met his. "Maybe Enrique will change his mind about things or maybe he won't. I can't change anything that will happen once I marry. But if I go sailing now, I wouldn't be disobeying my husband since Enrique is only my fiancé."

Her tone sounded different. Not as distraught. "You lost me."

Julianna's gaze met Alejandro's with an unspoken plea.

Understanding dawned. He leaned away from her. "No. No way. I can't get involved in this."

"You're already involved." She scooted closer. "All I need is a boat for one sail."

The flowery scent of her shampoo filled his nostrils and made him waver. He leaned backed to put some distance between them. "If you're caught disobeying your father..."

"I'll make sure I'm not," she said. "You believe Enrique will change his mind, but you didn't see the look in his eyes. It's worth the risk for one last hurrah before I get married."

"Maybe to you, but not to me." Alejandro would be in deep trouble. That had never bothered him in the past. But the stakes were higher this time.

"What do you have to lose?" she asked.

His chance at freedom. He hated the way Enrique was treating Julianna, but Alejandro didn't want to cause an even bigger problem between the couple. He needed the two to marry and have children.

A deep shame rose up inside him. He was thinking of himself while Julianna was trying to do her duty even if it made her unhappy.

"I'm sorry," he said. "But I won't be the reason you get in trouble."

Disappointment shone in her lovely eyes.

"Fine." She flipped her hair behind her shoulder with a sexy move. "I'll find a boat myself."

She would, too. He pictured her heading to the marina and going out with anyone who'd take her. That could end in disaster. If he helped her...

Alejandro couldn't believe he was contemplating taking her out, but he didn't want to think only of himself. "Sailing is that important to you?"

"Yes."

The hope and anticipation in the one word made it difficult for him to breath.

"Please, Alejandro." Julianna stared up at him with her wide, blue eyes. "Will you please help me?"

A long list of reasons why he shouldn't scrolled through his mind. But logic didn't seem to apply in this situation. Or with Julianna.

He thought about it a minute. Taking her sailing wasn't that big a deal. "I suppose it would be against my character and ruin my bad reputation if I turned down an opportunity to do something Enrique was against."

She leaned toward him giving him another whiff of her enticing scent. "So is that a yes?"

CHAPTER FOUR

Yes. I'll take you sailing tomorrow night.

Jules fell asleep thinking about Alejandro's words. She woke up with them on her mind, too.

Sunlight streamed through the windows. Particles in the air gave the rays definition, as if a fairy had waved her magic wand to make the sunshine touchable. She reached out, but felt only air.

With a laugh, she rolled over in the queen-size bed eager to start her day. She couldn't wait to go sailing tonight. Of course if she was discovered...

Don't think about that.

She needed to do this. Everything else in her life, from her education to her marriage, had been determined for her. Not out of love, but because of what tradition dictated and what others believed to be best for Aliestle.

Going sailing tonight was the one decision she could make for herself. She was desperate enough for this one act of disobedience. A secretive rebellion of sorts, the kind she never did as a teenager.

Jules tossed back the luxurious Egyptian cotton sheet and

climbed out of bed. Her bare feet sunk into a hand-woven Persian rug. Only the finest furnishings for the grand palace.

She entered the large bathroom. Yvette had set out her toiletries on the marble countertop. The gold plated fixtures reminded Jules of every other castle she'd stayed in. Gold might be considered opulent, but didn't any of the royal interior designers want to be creative and try a different finish? Then again, royalty could never be too creative or different. The status quo was completely acceptable.

Jules stared at her refection in the mirror. Today she would maintain that status quo. People would look at her and see a dutiful princess. Even if she would be counting down the hours until her first and last taste of...

Freedom.

Her chest tightened. She had no idea what true freedom would feel like.

So far, Jules's choices in life had been relegated to what she wanted to eat, if it wasn't a state dinner, what books she wanted to read, if she'd completed all her assigned readings, and what she purchased while shopping. Perhaps that was why she'd become a consummate shopper.

Choosing what she wanted to do without having to consider the expectations of an overprotective father and a conservative country would have to feel pretty good. She couldn't wait to experience it tonight.

Jules had thought about what Alejandro said about the island not being Aliestle, about the legal rights she would have here and about his mother leaving his father. Those things had led her to devise a new plan.

She would sail tonight, then return to being a dutiful princess in the morning and marry Enrique after the Med Cup. Once they had children, she would work to improve her position, get Enrique to be more cooperative and try to change things.

Thirty minutes later, Yvette clasped a diamond and pearl necklace around Jules's neck. "Excellent choice, Yvette. You have quite an eye when it comes to accessories."

"Thank you, ma'am." The young maid stared at their reflection in the mirror. "You look like a modern day Princess Grace."

Jules felt a little like Princess Grace, who had been forced to stop acting because someone said the people of Monaco wouldn't be happy if she returned to making movies. Life for many royals didn't always have a happy ending.

"Thank you, Yvette." The retro-style pink-and-white suit had been purchased on a recent trip to Paris. Jules tucked a strand of hair into her French roll. "I'm sure the hairstyle helps."

"Prince Enrique will be impressed."

"Let's hope so." Jules tried to sound cheerful, but her words felt flat. She doubted Enrique would be impressed by anything she did. He was nothing like…Alejandro.

She couldn't imagine Enrique cradling her in his arms and offering sympathy while she cried. He would have cursed her tears, not wiped them away as Alejandro had.

A black sheep? Perhaps, but he was taking her sailing. She guessed he was more of a good guy than he claimed to be.

She smiled. "Perhaps I'll make an impression on the entire royal family."

"Not Prince Alejandro." Yvette sounded aghast. "I've been told to stay away from him."

The words offended Jules. She would rather spend time with Alejandro than Enrique. "Who said that?"

"One of the housekeepers. She's young. Pretty," Yvette

explained. "She said Prince Alejandro has a horrible reputation. Worse, his taste in women is far from discriminating. Royalty, commoner, palace staff, it doesn't matter."

Alejandro had warned her about the gossip. But the words stung for some reason. "That could be a rumor. The press loves to write about royalty whether it's true or not. People will believe almost anything once it's in print or on the Internet."

"The housekeeper sounded sincere, ma'am," Yvette said. "She's especially concerned about you."

"About me?" Jules remembered the warmth of Alejandro's body and the sense of belonging she'd felt in his arms. He could have taken advantage of the situation and her emotional state last night, but he hadn't. He'd acted like a friend, not a man who wanted some action. She'd actually been a tad bit disappointed he hadn't found her desirable.

Silly. Pathetic, really. She straightened. "I appreciate the warning, but I'm going to be Alejandro's sister-in-law. He doesn't see me in the same way as he sees other woman."

Doubt filled Yvette's eyes. "I hope you're correct, ma'am."

Jules didn't. She wouldn't mind being wrong about this. Alejandro was...attractive, but the way he'd made her feel on the beach—understood, accepted, safe, ways she'd never felt before—intrigued her the most. After tonight, following the housekeeper's advice and staying away from him would be the best course of action. No matter how much a tiny part of Jules wished he were the one she was marrying.

Better squelch that thought. Alejandro was going to be her brother-in-law. Nothing else.

"Don't worry." She raised her chin. "I'm not about to risk my match with Enrique for a fling with a self-avowed black sheep."

Even one who was gorgeous and sailed and sent tingles shooting through her. More reasons to keep her distance.

After tonight.

Tonight would be her first chance to experience freedom. The initial step in figuring out how to be an influential princess and her own person.

"That is smart." The tight lines around Yvette's mouth relaxed a little. "Being matched to a man outside Aliestle would be a dream come true for most of our countrywomen, ma'am."

Be careful what you wish, or in this case, ask for.

Jules recognized the maid's wistful tone. She'd sounded the same way on more than one occasion. The weight on her shoulders felt heavier. She wanted life to be different for her countrywomen. "Has a match been secured for you?"

"Yes, ma'am. A very good match." Yvette gave a half smile. "One that will be advantageous to my family."

"That's excellent."

"Yes, ma'am. We marry in two years, after I complete my obligations on the palace staff." The look in Yvette's eyes didn't seem to agree with her words. "I am…most fortunate."

Most likely as fortunate as Jules. Her heart ached. She wanted men to treat the women of Aliestle with respect, consideration and love. Not like commodities.

When Brandt became king…

Yvette adjusted her starched, white apron. "I transferred the contents of your handbag into the purse, ma'am."

"Thank you, I'll…"

A high-pitched noise sounded outside the bedroom door. Not quite a squeal, but not a squeak, either.

Yvette's forehead creased. "It sounds like a baby, ma'am."

Jules hurried to the door and opened it. The noise sounded

again. She glanced around the empty hallway. A black ball of fur scratched at the door across the hall.

"You're correct, Yvette. It is a baby. A baby cat." Jules picked up the kitten who pawed at her. A long, white hair above his right eye bounced like an antenna in the wind. "I can't imagine someone let you out into this big hallway on purpose. Did you escape again?"

The kitten stared up at her with clear, green eyes.

Her heart bumped. She'd always wanted a pet. This one was adorable.

"I can see where he belongs, ma'am," Yvette offered.

"I'll return him." The kitten wiggled in Jules's hands. She cuddled him closer in hopes of settling him down. He rested his head against her arm and purred. "I know where he belongs."

With Alejandro.

Anticipation spurted through her. She wanted to see him. Because of the sailing, she rationalized. That was the only reason. Anything else would be too…dangerous.

"Cat?" Alejandro checked the closet, the bathroom, under the bed and beneath the other furniture. No sight of the furball anywhere.

The kitten didn't come running as he usually did.

Maybe he was locked in the bathroom? Alejandro checked. No kitty.

The last time he'd seen the kitten was before his shower. He glanced around the apartment again. A vase with colorful fresh-cut flowers caught his eye. Those were new.

Only Ortiz knew about the kitten. If whoever delivered the flowers had left the door to the apartment open, the kitten could have gotten out.

Alejandro ran to the door and jerked it open.

Julianna stood in the doorway.

He froze, stunned to see her.

A smile graced her glossed lips. Clear, bright eyes stared back at him. Her pastel-pink suit made her look like the definition of the word princess in the dictionary.

She was the image of everything he didn't like in a woman—royal, wealthy, concerned with appearances. He shouldn't feel any attraction toward Julianna whatsoever. But he couldn't stop staring at her beautiful face.

Awareness buzzed through him. Strange. Alejandro didn't usually go for the prim and proper type. But this wasn't the time to examine his attraction to her. He needed to find a kitten. "I—"

"I was about to knock," she said at the same time. "Look who I found."

Alejandro followed her line of sight. The kitten was sound asleep in her arms.

Relief washed over him. "I was on my way out to look for him. Where did you find him?"

"In the hallway trying to squeeze under the door across from mine. A futile effort given his size, but he made a valiant attempt." She smiled at the kitten. "I figured he must have escaped and you'd want him back."

"Yes." Alejandro tried focusing on the cat, but his gaze kept returning to her. He wanted to chalk his reaction to her up to gratitude but knew better. "Thanks."

"You're welcome."

Alejandro waited for Julianna to hand over the cat. She didn't. He needed to go to the boatyard, but he wasn't in that much of a hurry. He motioned into the apartment. "Please come in."

Julianna looked to her left and then to the right. "Thanks, but I'd better not."

He gave her a puzzled look. "You have plans."

"No," she admitted. "I don't want to upset Enrique."

Alejandro ignored the twinge of disappointment. He understood her concern. "You're right. We don't want to add fuel to the fire."

"Especially with tonight," she whispered. Excitement danced in her eyes.

He was looking forward to the sail. He wanted Julianna to like it here. For his sake as much as hers. She'd realize she wouldn't be a prisoner on the island. Enrique didn't know how to treat women properly; a combination of selfishness and lack of experience. His brother would settle down eventually.

"Rest up today or you'll be exhausted," Alejandro said.

"Like the kitten. He fell asleep on the walk over here. He must have tired himself out during his adventure."

Alejandro wouldn't mind tiring himself out with Julianna. He imagined her beautiful long hair loose and spread across his pillow, her silky skin against his, the taste of those lips...

His blood heated and roared through his veins.

He pushed the fantasy out of his mind. Thinking of Julianna in a sexual way was wrong and dangerous. They both had too much to lose.

"I've been wondering what the kitten's name is," she said.

Good, he could think about something other than her in his bed. "Cat."

"Cat is the kitten's name?"

"Yes."

Julianna drew her delicately arched eyebrows together.

Her pretty pink mouth opened then closed, as if she thought better of what she wanted to say.

"What?" he asked.

"It's nothing."

Alejandro recognized the look in her eyes. "Tell me."

Julianna hesitated. "You're doing me a favor taking me sailing. I shouldn't criticize."

He'd been criticized his entire life by his father and by his brother. He never could live up to what the people wanted him to be, either. The bane of being the spare. Nothing he did was ever good enough. Alejandro had grown immune to the put-downs. "I want to know."

"You might get mad."

He didn't want her to be afraid of him. "Enrique might get a little heated at times. You don't have to worry about that with me."

She squared her shoulders, as if preparing for battle. A one-hundred-eighty-degree difference from her sobbing on the beach last night. "Cat isn't a proper name for a pet."

That was what this was all about. Alejandro almost laughed. He thought it was something serious. "Cat doesn't seem to mind the name."

"That's because he loves you."

The warmth in her voice wrapped around Alejandro like a soft, fluffy towel. He couldn't remember the last time anyone had made him feel so good. But he knew better. The feeling was as fleeting as the love she spoke about. "Love has nothing to do with it. He's a cat. He comes because he's hungry."

"He'd come no matter what you call him," she continued.

"Cat isn't a child."

"No, he's your pet."

Children and a family weren't something he'd considered

before. Saying he had a pet was pushing the level of commitment he was comfortable with. Love and commitment didn't last so why bother? His mother had claimed to love him. But she'd abandoned him to a father who disapproved of him and a brother who antagonized him. Alejandro rocked back on his heels. "Cat's a stray."

"Living in a palace."

Her voice teased. Okay, she had a point. "If I give the cat a proper name, I'll have to keep him."

She pursed her lips. "Do you plan on releasing him when he gets bigger?"

Alejandro fought the urge to squirm under her scrutiny. He hadn't done anything wrong or irresponsible. At least not yet. "I haven't thought that far ahead. But cats take off when they get tired of you."

She peered around him and motioned to the sock tied in a knot, piece of rope and empty boxes strewn across the floor. "You're going to need to buy a suitcase when he goes so he can take his toys with him."

"I just had that stuff lying around." Alejandro shoved his hands in his pockets. "I'll probably keep him. At the boatyard when he gets older," he clarified.

"Then you might as well come up with a more original name for him."

"He's a cat. The name fits."

"True, but look at his green eyes. His handsome face. The white boots on his paws." She held the kitten up as if he were a rare treasure. "He is so much more than a generic cat."

Alejandro laughed, enchanted by her tenacity. "If you ever get tired of being a princess, you should become a trial lawyer."

She scrunched her nose. "I've never considered such a

career, but I would be happy to provide more evidence for changing the kitten's name."

"For someone who wants *me* to take them sailing," he lowered his voice, "you're not very agreeable."

Her eyes widened. Her complexion paled. "Oh, I'm—"

"Kidding." Alejandro didn't think she would take him seriously. But he could make it up to her. He thought about her description of the kitten. One word popped out at him. "Boots."

A line creased above her nose. "Excuse me?"

"Cat's name is now Boots. Satisfied?"

"Very." She smiled, visibly relieved. "Thank you."

Pleasing her felt better than it should. Just trying to make her happy so she'd want to marry Enrique.

Yeah, right. Alejandro leaned against the doorjamb. "It's the least I could do after the way you argued for his rights. Perhaps you should do the same for your own. And your countrywomen."

Her smile disappeared. So did the light from her eyes. He didn't like the change in her.

"I would if I could, but that's not the kind of princess Aliestle or your brother wants." She touched one of the kitten's small paws. Her expression softened. "The least I could do was support a fellow underdog."

"I don't think Boots would like to be associated with anything having to do with a dog."

The corners of her mouth slanted upward. "You're probably right about that."

Alejandro reached out to pet the kitten. His fingers brushed against the bare skin on Julianna's arm. Tingles shot outward from the point of contact. He jerked his hand away.

She didn't seem to notice.

Good. He didn't want her to know she had an effect on him. "You like cats."

"I do, but I've never had one." She rubbed the top of the kitten's head. "My father didn't want any animals in the palace. He claimed they were too dirty and too much trouble."

Alejandro hadn't expected to have anything else in common with her except sailing. "We had a dog growing up, but after she died my father didn't want another one. He said dogs were too much trouble."

Julianna eyed him with curiosity. "Yet you have Boots."

But Alejandro didn't live in the palace. He doubted his family would want Julianna to know he was here for appearance sake and would be departing after the wedding. "Black sheep, remember?"

"I haven't forgotten. I hope your reputation means you're an expert at subterfuge and not getting caught."

He winked. "You're in experienced hands, Princess."

"Excellent." The sparkle returned to her eyes. She glanced behind her as if to make sure they were still alone. "Have all the arrangements been made?"

The princess's hushed voice made it sound as if they were going to undertake an important, secretive mission. Alejandro realized in her mind they were. The least he could do was play along.

"Almost," he whispered back. "Check your closet this afternoon. Everything you need for tonight will be in there."

Her mouth formed a perfect O. "My closet? You're going to go into my room. Isn't that risky?"

"No one will see me."

"You can't be certain. My maid might be—"

"There are secret tunnels and passageways throughout the palace." He didn't want her to worry. "You access them through hidden latches in the closets."

"Oh."

The one word spoke volumes of her doubt.

"Do you trust me?" he asked.

She handed the kitten to him. "I don't have a choice if I want to go sailing."

"No, you don't."

Alejandro felt like a jerk. He was the last person she should be putting her faith in. He had the most to gain by her marrying Enrique. She had the most to lose by saying "I do." Okay, his brother wasn't that bad. But she was still sacrificing for the marriage.

"Not many people would understand how important tonight is to me," she said. "I trust you won't let me down."

He appreciated her earnest expression and words. He was used to those in the palace being unable to see past his rebellions as a teen and his wanting to change the monarchy from the archaic monolith it had become.

But Julianna was far too trusting. She must have lived a sheltered life in Aliestle. Things would be better for her on the island. "You're the perfect fairy-tale princess."

Defiance flashed in her eyes, but disappeared quickly. "A princess, yes. Perfect, not so much. Though I try my best."

"Trying is an admirable trait, but not if it makes you unhappy."

"Doing what is expected of me is all I know."

Julianna was nothing like he imagined she would be. She wasn't jaded in spite of being a royal prisoner her entire life. She was the closest thing to perfection he'd ever met. Alejandro would make sure Enrique treated her fairly. "You do a good job."

She rewarded him with a closemouthed smile. He would

have preferred to see one with her straight, white teeth visible. "I plan to continue to do so."

Except tonight.

Crossing the line had become second nature to him growing up. Alejandro didn't do it as often now. Still he didn't care what anyone thought about him. The lovely princess did care. The way she dressed, spoke and acted made it clear. She might feel the need to rebel in this one-time act of defiance. A brief escape from an impending arranged marriage and a curtailed freedom. But he didn't want Julianna to have any regrets over what they were going to do.

"Are you certain you want to go against your father and sail tonight?" Alejandro whispered.

"Most definitely.

"You may regret—"

"I'll regret not doing so more," she interrupted. "This is the right thing to do. Even if I'm caught."

Julianna was saying the right words. Alejandro hoped she meant them. Because if she got caught, the price she would pay might be higher than either of them imagined.

That evening, the hands on the clock in the dining room moved slower than the Council of Elders. King Dario sat at the head of the table. His two sons sat on his left with Jules and Brandt on the king's right.

She tapped her foot, impatient the meal was taking so long. Servers scurried about with wine bottles and platters. She wanted dinner to end so she could excuse herself and prepare for the sail with Alejandro.

He sat across the table from her. No tuxedo, but a designer suit and dress shirt sans tie. He looked more like a CEO than a boatbuilder. Well, except for his hair. The dark ends brushed his shoulders. She preferred his casual, carefree style to Enrique's short, conservative cut.

She kept hoping Alejandro would say something to turn the dinner conversation away from the upcoming royal wedding and onto something more interesting.

He didn't. He barely spoke or glanced her way.

No doubt trying to keep anyone from guessing about the rendezvous later. Jules suppressed the urge to smile about her impending adventure.

King Dario yawned. "I'm going to skip having a brandy."

Alejandro straightened. "Are you feeling okay, Father?"

The king waved off his son's genuine concern. "I'm fine. Just tired."

"Dealing with the demands of the island takes a lot out of a person." Enrique narrowed his gaze as he spoke to Alejandro. "Something you would know little about, brother."

Jules waited for Alejandro to fire back a smart-assed comment. He took a sip of wine instead. When he finished, he wiped his mouth with a napkin. His dark eyes revealed nothing of his thoughts. "Sleep well, Father."

With that, King Dario departed.

Silence filled the dining room. The servers seemed to have vanished along with the king. Jules counted to one hundred by tens in Japanese. When could she say good-night without drawing suspicions to herself?

"I have work to attend to." Enrique scooted his chair away from the table. "If you do not mind," he said to her as if an afterthought.

Perfect! Her entire body felt as if it were smiling. "I don't mind."

"I was planning to hit the clubs," Brandt said with eager anticipation in his voice.

Yes! She couldn't have arranged this any better if she'd planned it. "Take Klaus with you."

Brandt rolled his eyes.

"Listen to your sister," Alejandro suggested. "You'll be thankful you have a bodyguard should things get out of hand."

"My brother knows the island's club scene intimately." Derision dripped from each of Enrique's word. "He's often at the center of the melees."

Jules didn't like his tone. She often gave her four brothers a hard time and teased them, like any big sister, but she never spoke with such disrespect.

"Please, Brandt," she said. "Father would never forgive me if something happened to you."

"And vice versa." Brandt directed a warm smile full of love her way. "I'll have Klaus accompany me."

Relieved, she smiled at him. "Thank you."

Enrique remained seated in his chair, but he looked ready to bolt out any minute. She wished he'd go.

"What will you do tonight, Julianna?" he asked.

"Oh, I don't know." She forced herself not to look at Alejandro. "Read. Watch TV. I'll find something to do."

She wiggled her toes in anticipation of what she would actually be doing.

Enrique rose from the table. "Then I'll bid you good-night and see you tomorrow."

Jules watched him exit the dining room. The atmosphere seemed less stuffy with Enrique gone. Her uncharitable thought brought a stab of guilt. He was her future husband. She'd best accept him as he was.

Alejandro rose. "I'm going to say good-night, also."

"Will I see you later?" Brandt asked.

"Not tonight," Alejandro said. "I have a prior engagement."

Yes, he did. She bit back a smile. In two hours and twenty-two minutes she would meet him at a private dock. The map, a headlamp and everything else she needed were sitting inside a duffel bag she'd found in her closet this afternoon.

"Blonde or brunette?" Brandt asked.

Alejandro laughed at the innuendo. "I wish I could say differently, but unfortunately it's not that kind of...engagement."

Jules tried to figure out what Alejandro meant. That he wished he were seeing a different woman or he wished he were meeting her under different circumstances? Not that he would or she could. But still...

"You can meet me at a club later," Brandt said.

Alejandro glanced her way. "Maybe I will."

"No." The two men looked at her with surprised expressions. Jules's heart dropped to her feet. She hadn't meant to say the word out loud. "I mean, do you know how long you'll be, Alejandro? Brandt might not want to stick around one club waiting for you to show up."

Brandt shook his head. "Stop being such a big sister, Jules. He can text me when he arrives."

"Oh, right," she said. "You know how often I go clubbing."

"You've never been to a club," Brandt said.

She'd never been allowed to go. She always wondered if her bodyguards were more concerned protecting her or ensuring she remained a virgin so her father could use that in marriage negotiations. "Exactly."

"Your sister's correct, though," Alejandro said. "I have no idea how long I'll be. I may not make it."

Brandt shrugged. "More lovely ladies for me."

"Save some for us tomorrow night."

Her brother grinned. "You're on."

Jules didn't want to think about tomorrow and the life waiting for her as Enrique's bride and future queen. She wanted tonight to last forever. She wanted it to start now.

She rose from the table. "Good night, gentlemen. I hope you enjoy the rest of your evening."

"I hope you're not too bored here alone," Brandt said.

"Don't worry. I won't be bored at all." Her gaze met Alejandro's for a moment. "Tonight is exactly what I need."

CHAPTER FIVE

Two hours later, Jules stood in the walk-in closet in her room. The headlamp she wore illuminated the dark space. She wore sailing clothes two sizes too big, a short, dark wig and a cap. She clutched a map in her left hand. With a steadying breath, she searched for the hidden latch with a trembling right hand.

She'd never disobeyed her father or anyone else for that matter. She'd never come close to doing anything illicit unless you counted eating an entire bag of chocolate in one sitting. But this...

Her heart pounded against her chest.

You're in experienced hands, Princess.

Alejandro's words gave her a needed boost of courage.

Jules's fingers brushed across something. She sucked in a breath. The latch. She pressed the small, narrow lever. Something squealed. She stepped backward. A secret door opened to reveal a staircase.

Her insides quivered with a mix of nerves and excitement and a little fear.

She stood at the threshold and glanced down the pitch-black stairwell. The headlamp illuminated the narrow steps.

Jules ventured forward onto the first step with a slight hesitation. Nerves bubbled in her tummy. She found a latch on the inside of the passageway and closed the secret door.

The steep staircase led to a tunnel that looked as if it had been there for decades, possibly a century or more. She wondered what the tunnel had been used for in the past. Had other princesses used it to escape?

Her feet carried her across a packed dirt floor. Weathered, thick wood beams reinforced the walls and ceiling. The map said the tunnel was two kilometers long. The distance felt longer with the inky shadows stretching out in front of her.

Something gray darted across the floor at the edge of the headlamp beam.

Her breath caught in her throat. She shivered with a sense of foreboding. Nothing like being in an underground tunnel with rodents for companionship.

Not rodents, she corrected. Mice.

"No rats in the palace," she muttered. "No rats in the palace."

With the words as her mantra, Jules continued forward. Adrenaline quickened her pace. More creatures scurried across the floor or ran along the walls. Her nerves increased. She wanted out of here. Now.

She came to a wrought-iron gate secured with a combination lock. She pulled the lock toward her and dialed in the digits written on the map: 132823. The lock clicked open.

The sound of freedom.

Jules opened the gate and stepped through with all the excitement of Christmas morning back when she was a child. She exited the tunnel and found herself in a grotto. No one would ever guess inside one of the rocks was a secret tunnel. She memorized the spot where she'd come out.

Following a paved path, her apprehension rose. She had no idea where she was. Insects chirped and buzzed. But she saw no people, no other lights.

Keep going.

Alejandro had planned the outing so she wouldn't get caught. A good thing, Jules knew. She trusted him for the reason she'd told him. She had no other choice if she wanted to sail. She couldn't have pulled this off on her own in spite of her bravado on the beach last night.

She continued walking, unable to shake her uneasiness at being out here secluded yet exposed. Not that she was about to turn around. This opportunity was too important.

Being out here alone, without servants, bodyguards, chaperones or family, was something she rarely got to do. She might be fighting nerves, but the experience gave her a little thrill.

The canopy and walls of rocks gave way to a large field of grass with gardens on either side. The moonlight eased some of her anxiety.

The path led her up a rise. She heard the sound of waves crashing against the shore. At the top, she stopped, mesmerized by the sight of the sea. The beach had to be below her somewhere, but she focused on the water. Light from the full moon shimmered like silver on the crests of the waves.

Jules's breath caught in her throat.

So beautiful.

As she descended the path toward the water, she noticed a light shining. A lone lamppost stood on a short dock with a sailboat moored at the end.

Her pulse rate quadrupled, as did her excitement. She'd found the place without getting lost or caught.

Jules hurried down the path, eager to hop onboard and set sail.

A figure stood in the cockpit of the boat. A man. Alejandro. Her heart gave a little lurch of pleasure.

He waved.

Jules waved back.

Alejandro reached below deck. The running lights illuminated—red on port, green on starboard and white on the stern.

Exhilaration shimmied through her. She could forget about duty and obligation tonight. She could be herself and sail on the ocean like a bird set free from its cage.

With Alejandro.

He motioned for her to join him in the boat.

Shoulders back. Chin up. Smile.

This time it came naturally. No effort required. Jules turned off her headlamp. She no longer needed the light with the lamppost on the dock.

Tingles filled her stomach. She couldn't imagine sharing tonight with anyone else.

As Julianna walked along the private dock with a clear spring to her step, the tension in Alejandro's shoulders eased. He'd planned her escape from the palace with the precision of a military operation. His efforts had seemed to work. With one foot in the cockpit and the other on the rail, he waited for her to come to him.

She stopped two feet away from the boat. "Your map was spot-on, Alejandro."

He liked the way his name rolled off her tongue. She might

sound like the same elegant princess he'd met yesterday, but she looked nothing like the woman who had stared down her nose at him, cried in his arms on the beach and prompted him to rename his cat. The disguise had completely changed her appearance.

He looked beyond her to the path leading up to the cliff, but only saw a few trees. Anyone who ventured out here on this late night would be trespassing. He'd picked this secluded spot for that reason. "Were you seen?"

"Not that I know of," she said. "Though I doubt anyone would recognize me if they saw me."

A satisfied smile settled on his lips. "You're right about that."

Baggy clothes covered Julianna's feminine curves and round breasts. A short, brown wig and America's Cup baseball cap hid her luxurious blond hair. With all the makeup scrubbed from her face, no one would mistake the fresh-faced kid for fashion icon Princess Julianna of Aliestle.

"You look like a teenager," he added.

"A teenage boy," she clarified. "You picked an excellent disguise for me."

She sounded appreciative, not upset. That surprised him a little. Most women wouldn't want to look like a boy. But then again, she hadn't wanted to get caught. A good disguise had been necessary.

"I had no problems, except Ortiz might want to reconsider his claim about no rats in the palace. I saw mice, and something…larger in the tunnel."

"Ortiz doesn't know about the tunnels. Only the royal family knows of their existence and an architect long dead," Alejandro explained. "The tunnels were built by pirates to hide treasure. When the king had them attached to the palace, a hand-selected crew was used. They were blindfolded and had no idea where they were working."

"How did the royal family find out about the tunnels?"

He grinned. "Supposedly my great-great-great grandfather was a king and pirate."

She laughed. The intoxicating sound floated on the air and made him want to inhale.

"You think that's funny."

"A little," she admitted. "But I'm not surprised you come from a line of pirates."

"Not a line," he clarified. "One pirate."

Amusement gleamed in her eyes. "If you say so."

"I do."

"Aye, aye, Captain," she teased.

It was his turn to laugh. Alejandro liked knowing he wasn't the only black sheep in his illustrious family line. He'd embraced the fact he had a pirate ancestor and thought others might, too. The island could capitalize on the colorful past except his father and brother didn't want the knowledge made public. "Ahoy, matey."

With an eager smile, she inspected *La Rueca* from bow to stern. "Lovely boat."

"I'm pleased with how she turned out." Alejandro touched the deck. He'd put everything he knew about boats and a fair share of money into her design. "Though she is untested in an actual race. The Med Cup will be interesting."

"You don't sound concerned."

"I'm not." If he were, he wouldn't have entered *La Rueca* in the race. "I'm confident she can perform and be competitive with the right wind and crew."

Julianna looked at the boat's name written in script on the stern. *"La Rueca."*

"The Spinning Wheel."

"Interesting name."

He stared at her slightly annoyed. "I already caved on the kitten. Are you going to challenge me on my boat's name, too?"

"No, but I'm curious if it has a special meaning."

"Most boat names do."

"What's the meaning behind yours?"

Alejandro remembered how persistent she'd been about the kitten's name. He had to tell her something. "*La Rueca* is a reminder that I haven't been spinning my wheels when it comes to boatbuilding."

"Spinning your wheels?" she asked.

Wanting to put an end to this topic of conversation, he lowered his one foot to the floor of the cockpit, reached back and started the outboard motor. He left it running in neutral. "Now is not the time."

"Later?"

"Do you always pester so much?"

"I'm sorry." Julianna raised her voice to talk over the idling motor. "Occupational hazard."

"Of being a princess?"

"Of having four younger brothers who never tell me anything unless I pester and pry. They are the only males, men, I'm allowed to be alone with for any extended period so they get the brunt of my curiosity." She looked around, not meeting his eyes. "Being out here with you like this…"

His annoyance disappeared. He appreciated her honesty. He also acknowledged the risk she was taking.

"It's okay. I'm not used to having a sister around." Though he didn't feel brotherly toward Julianna at all. "This is new for both of us."

She smiled softly. "I hope *La Rueca* turns out to be everything you wish for."

"Thanks. It's looking pretty good." And it was. A new sailboat design, a full moon and a beautiful woman to share a sail with tonight. She was so easy to talk to. He liked how she laughed.

Remember, sister-in-law. Julianna belonged with Enrique, not Alejandro. The realization left him feeling adrift.

Time to set a new course. They'd spent enough time talking. The longer they were out here, the more likely they were to be caught.

Alejandro extended his arm from the cockpit. "Climb aboard."

Julianna's hand clasped and melded with his. Heat shot up his arm. The reaction startled him, but he didn't let go. Truth was, he liked how her hand fit in his.

Her disguise might fool others, but not him. He knew she wasn't a teenager but a grown woman with lush, feminine curves. He'd held her in his arms and smelled the sweet fragrance of her shampoo. He wouldn't mind doing that again.

She stepped onto the boat and released his hand. As Alejandro flexed his fingers, she inhaled deeply. "I love the salty air."

"Wait until you get a taste of the sea spray."

"I'm looking forward to it." Gratitude shone in her eyes. "Thank you for going to so much trouble. Not many people would do this for a total stranger."

"It's my pleasure." And it was. Julianna looked so young, eager and pretty. Very, very pretty. "Besides you're not a stranger. You'll be family soon. My sister-in-law."

Alejandro said the words more for his benefit than hers. He waited for her to respond, but she didn't.

Julianna stared up at the clear, starry sky. The moonlight made her ivory complexion glow. Enrique didn't seem to understand the lovely princess from Aliestle. She was more than a showpiece, more than her dowry. She was a stunning, intelligent woman...Alejandro wondered why King Alaric had picked Enrique to be her husband. His brother had some admirable qualities, even if they disagreed over how best to help their country. But Julianna could do so much better.

"The weather is cooperating with us tonight." Her voice sounded lower, a little husky...sexy. Desire skimmed across his skin. "Lucky," she added.

Getting lucky tonight would be the perfect end to a midnight sail. Not that she would. Or he...

Yes, he would. The thought brought a lump of guilt to his throat.

"Let's get underway. I'll cast off." He motioned to the wheel. "Are you comfortable steering while we motor away from the dock?"

"Yes." She made her way toward the wheel. He moved out of her path, but her backside brushed him.

Heat burst through Alejandro. What the hell?

He didn't understand why he kept reacting to Julianna. She was his ticket to an independent life. He needed to control himself. A mistake could cost him his freedom from his father and the monarchy.

Some distance from Julianna would be good. Alejandro walked forward to the bow.

Maybe he should hit the clubs later tonight and connect with a pretty young thing. That would be the fastest way to get rid of whatever tension had built up and was stirring inside of him.

He pulled up a bumper, removed the bowline from the cleat and tossed the line onto the dock.

She stared up at the wind indicator. "Won't it look weird to be sailing at this hour?"

"No." He stepped over the lifeline, jumped onto the dock and moved to the aft section of the boat. "I always take out my new boats at night so people can't see the designs."

Julianna touched the wheel. "Sounds like boatbuilding is a competitive field."

"Everyone is looking for an edge." Alejandro pulled up the other bumper and unfastened the line from the boat's stern cleat. The rope fell to the dock. He stepped onto the boat with his left foot, shoved the boat away from the dock and hopped aboard with his right foot. "I'd rather they not steal mine."

"Confident."

"If I wasn't, I would crew on someone else's boat for the Med Cup. A boat that was a top contender."

Julianna reached back, shifted the motor to forward and twisted the throttle. She steered clear of the dock and headed out to open water. "Do you race a lot?"

"Not as much as I would like due to my royal obligations, but I hope that will change in the near future."

And it would. After Julianna married Enrique and they had a baby, Alejandro would have as much time as he wanted for business and sailing.

"Looks like there's a nice easy breeze tonight." She shot him an expectant look. "Ready for the mainsail."

It wasn't a question.

Interesting. She knew what to do without him saying a word. He hadn't expected that from her. Saying you enjoyed sailing while sipping a glass of wine and knowing what to do when you were onboard were two completely different things. Alejandro hadn't known what kind of sailor the princess was. So far, he was impressed by her knowledge. "I'll raise the main."

As he moved forward to the starboard side of the mast, she turned the boat head to wind.

Pointing the bow into the wind wasn't something instinctual. That took experience or good instruction. Whichever the case for Julianna, his respect increased.

"You know what you're doing out here." Alejandro yelled to be heard over the motor. He raised the mainsail with the halyard. "How long have you been sailing?"

"Since I was seven." She tailed the halyard and secured the line at the cleat on the top of the cabin. "My grandparents taught me how to sail on the Black Sea. Best vacation ever. How long have you sailed?"

"As long as I can remember." Alejandro shifted to the port side of the mast to hoist the jib, a triangular sail set forward of the main. He saw no other boats on the water. "Both my parents sail."

Julianna turned the wheel right to ease the bow starboard and trimmed the mainsail so it filled with the wind. The boat steadied and glided forward through the water. "I can't imagine anyone not sailing if they lived here."

The awe in her voice made him smile. "Me, neither."

She throttled down the motor, shifted to neutral and killed it.

The sudden quiet gave way to the sound of the hull cutting through the water and the breeze against the sails. Better get to it and make the most of the time they had out here.

Her sailing skills impressed him, but he wasn't going to assume what she knew or didn't know. "Ready for the jib."

She held the starboard sheet in her hand. One step ahead of him again. "Ready."

He hoisted the jib while she tailed the jib halyard. She secured the sheet by wrapping the rope around a cleat.

Alejandro moved aft to the cockpit. "Nice work."

With a wide smile, she gripped the wheel. "Thanks."

He gave her a compass heading.

Her eyes widened. "You want me to take the helm?"

She sounded like a teenager who'd been given the keys to a brand-new car. He almost laughed. "You've got the wheel."

"I do, don't I?" Her grin was brighter than the full moon. She repeated the heading and turned toward the dock.

"Want to go back?" he asked.

As she shook her head, the cap didn't budge. "I want to make sure I have my bearings and know what the area looks like for our return."

Smart thinking. "You've sailed at night before."

"A few times, but I'd do the same thing if it were daytime."

His respect for her sailing abilities went up yet another notch. Alejandro trimmed the jib, adjusting the sheet to match her course and ensure the sail filled properly. Julianna adjusted the mainsail to match the heading.

He reached back and raised the motor out of the water. Now they would really move.

La Rueca accelerated through the water. Julianna kept her course, making minor corrections as she headed upwind. She seemed to have a feel for the boat as well as the wind.

"I love it out here." The look of pure joy on Julianna's face took Alejandro's breath away. "This is heaven. And you're an angel for doing this for me."

No angel. Not when he was getting turned on watching

her sail. The gleam in her eyes. Her smiling lips. Her flushed cheeks.

He focused on the sails. They had filled perfectly, no trimming necessary.

"We're going to need to tack," she said.

He held onto the jib sheet. "Whenever you're ready."

"Tacking."

Alejandro bent over to avoid the boom as it swung across to the other side. The sails luffed, flapping in the wind. He pulled in the sheet. She trimmed the main.

Julianna sailed at a forty-five-degree angle to the wind.

The boat heeled. She leaned over the side to stare at the bow.

As the boat headed upwind, she tacked back and forth to keep the boat moving. With each direction change, the two of them worked together managing the sails with the sheets. Words weren't necessary. They both knew what to do. Perfectly in sync, like they'd done this a hundred times together. Alejandro continued to be amazed by Julianna's knowledge and skill.

He'd never seen someone with such a natural talent. She handled the boat as if it were an extension of herself. She seemed to know when the wind was going to change, and the perfect course to set to maximize the boat's speed.

With the wind on her face, she stared up at the full moon.

His heart lurched. She was truly stunning.

"This is even better than I imagined." Julianna's gaze met his. "Being out here on the sea like this… It's intoxicating."

He felt the same way being around her. "You steer like you've been sailing on the sea your entire life."

"Thanks," she said. "I love the way your boat responds."

"I love the way the boat responds to you." He wondered how she would respond to him, to his touch, to his kisses.

She eyed him curiously. "I'm sure she responds this way with any helmsman."

"Guess again," he admitted. "You handle *La Rueca* better than anyone else."

"Including you?"

"Yes."

She laughed. As before, the sweet sound carried on the wind. Alejandro wanted to reach out and capture it, a song to remind him of this perfect sail.

He wished the evening wouldn't have to end. As much as he'd like to keep Julianna out here all night, he couldn't. They'd sailed longer than he intended.

"Come about," he said. "And head downwind."

"Can't we head up a little farther?"

"It's time to go back." The disappointment in her eyes knotted his stomach. "You don't want to sneak into the palace when it's daylight. If your maid finds a blond wig and pillows in your bed…"

"That would be a disaster." Julianna gripped the wheel until her knuckles turned white. "Coming about."

The boat turned around. They sailed with the wind at their backs, running with the wind.

But Julianna no longer smiled. The sparkle disappeared from her eyes. She looked so…resigned.

Alejandro didn't like the change in her. Being out here on the water had set her free. The sailor with him tonight was the real Julianna. He didn't want her to put on a princess mask and have to wear it for the rest of her life. "Perhaps another time we can—"

"There can't be another time." She sounded dejected, sad. "This is my last sail. At least until Enrique changes his mind."

Her words echoed through his brain. He firmly rejected them. "I know it's forbidden and you can't risk being caught, but you're so happy out here."

"It's my fate."

Screw fate. Happiness was important, too.

Her last sail?

Not if Alejandro had any say in the matter.

CHAPTER SIX

With the boat secured to the dock, Jules stood in the cockpit. She checked a sheet and wrapped it in a figure-eight pattern around a cleat. No way was the rope coming undone. Too bad her future couldn't be secured as easily.

The sail was over. With a sigh, she glanced at the bow. Soon she would be back in the palace. The thought squeezed her heart.

Below deck, Alejandro rummaged around, looking for a sail bag. Before long it would be time to go.

Emotion welled up inside her. She didn't want to return to reality yet. Nothing awaited her except a life of duty. Okay, she was being a total drama princess, but this once she would allow herself that luxury.

As the breeze picked up, the mast, standing so tall and strong, caught her attention. She closed her eyes and breathed in the salt air. The wind caressed her face. She could almost believe she was…free.

"Found it," Alejandro said from below.

Her eyelids flew open.

He climbed into the cockpit. "I need to organize the equipment."

"I'll do it for you now."

"It's too late."

Maybe for him. "I'll help you stow the sails."

"Good idea." Alejandro stood on the luff side of the mainsail. "We'll get out of here faster with two pairs of hands."

Her shoulders slumped. She should have offered to do the sails on her own. Getting out of here faster was the last thing she wanted.

She took the leech side. Together, they flaked the sail, layering the fabric across the boom. He secured the main with ties.

"What about the jib?" she asked.

He turned off the boat's running lights. "I'll take care of it when I get back."

Back? He was going out after this. To a club? The thought made her spirits sink lower. She should forget about it. Him. But she couldn't. "Where are you going?"

"I'm walking you back to the palace."

His chivalry pleased her, but she'd found her way to the dock on her own. She didn't need to be escorted back. A slow walk through the park on the way to the tunnels would keep her free a little while longer. Jules wanted as much extra time outside the palace as she could get. "I can find my own way."

"I know you can, but I'm going to escort you back."

"Okay." Jules caved like a house of cards. Truth was, she liked being with Alejandro and wanted to spend more time with him. Oh, she'd see him around the palace, at events and during meals. But given his relationship with Enrique, this might be their last chance to be alone.

She felt a pang in her heart.

The moonlight cast shadows on his face. With his strong jaw, nose and high cheekbones, he did look more pirate than prince. Too bad he wouldn't kidnap her, sail away with her on his boat and ravish her...

A smile tugged on the corners of her mouth. She couldn't help herself from daydreaming and fantasizing.

Alejandro was a hottie. He'd come to her rescue more than once. He might consider himself a black sheep, but black knight might be a better term after the sail tonight. He'd gone out of his way for her. Jules would be eternally grateful to him.

If only she could thank him, not with words, but a...kiss. A kiss would make tonight's sail more perfect. She stared at his full, soft-looking lips. A kiss under the full moon.

"Julianna?" Alejandro asked.

Desire flowed through her veins. "Yes?"

"You okay?"

"I'm just thinking." Of kissing him. All she had to do was rise up and touch her lips to his. Tempting, undeniably so. But the rebellious act of sailing was more than enough for the evening, for a lifetime really.

At least her lifetime. Jules took a deep breath.

"About our sail." She touched the boat's wheel, running her fingertips over the smooth edge. "I want to remember everything about tonight."

Everything except Alejandro.

Forget about kissing him. If she was to be Enrique's wife, she needed to bury all memories of Alejandro deep in her heart. Otherwise she would make herself and her marriage miserable, wanting what she couldn't have.

Not that Jules had real feelings for him or vice versa. They'd just met. She was getting carried away after a lovely evening with a fellow sailor. Alejandro hadn't flirted with her. He'd barely noticed her beyond her sailing abilities.

The setting with its full moon, starry sky and ocean breeze was perfect for two people to connect, to kiss. Yet he hadn't gotten caught up in the romantic atmosphere. That was a little…annoying. Maybe he didn't find her attractive.

What was she thinking? She shouldn't want him to hit on her.

"It's too bad we couldn't take pictures," he said.

"Yes." But having a photograph of tonight was too big a risk. If Enrique found it…

Enrique.

Maybe he was the reason Alejandro hadn't made a move on her. He might be the black sheep of the family, but he was an honorable man and not about to kiss his brother's fiancée.

She respected that. Respected him.

If only Enrique was more like his younger brother…Jules swallowed a sigh.

Alejandro double-checked the ties. "Ready to go?"

She took a final glance around. Everything had been stowed or secured, but she was in no hurry to leave.

Waves lapped against the hull. The boat rocked with the incoming tide. The sound and motion comforted her. She ran her hand along the deck, a final farewell to *La Rueca*.

Regret mixed with sadness. "I'm ready."

She exited the boat without taking Alejandro's hand. She didn't need his help. Not anymore.

Touching him again, feeling her small hand clasped with his larger, warm one, would make putting tonight behind her harder. Being with him made her feel so different. She didn't know if that was freedom calling or not. But real life beckoned, or rather would with the sunrise.

Tears stung her eyes. Blinking them away, she headed up the dock. Her nonskid shoes barely made a sound against the wood.

Would the memory of tonight fade into nothingness as she embraced her role as Enrique's fiancée and wife? Jules hoped not.

She glanced up at the sky. A shooting star arced across the darkness.

I wish this didn't have to end.

The thought was instantaneous, and her entire body, from the top of her head to the tips of her toes, felt that way. She kept her gaze focused on the sky. The star and its tail vanished.

What a waste of a wish. Jules should have wished for Enrique to change his mind instead. She blew out a puff of air.

Time to stop pretending. She wasn't living a fairy tale, but it wasn't a Gothic novel, either. She needed to face up to her responsibilities.

Climbing the steep hillside, she ignored the burn in her thighs.

Alejandro caught up without sounding winded or breaking a sweat. He walked alongside her, shortening his stride to match hers. "I hope you enjoyed your sail."

"I did." She forced the words from her tight throat. Making small talk wasn't going to be easy. The walk back made her realize how prisoners at the Tower of London must have felt on their way to the executioner. Though Jules faced a life sentence, not death. A sentence she'd chosen for herself, for the sake of her brother, her children and her country. "Thank you so much for tonight."

"I should be the one thanking you."

Alejandro's easy smile doubled her heart rate. She wanted

to scream and cry. If he'd been the firstborn... No, a man like him would never need an arranged marriage to secure a bride. No matter what the amount of that bride's dowry.

"Watching you sail tonight has been a true pleasure, Julianna," he continued. "You're very skilled. Amazingly so."

His words made her stand taller. She needed to focus on the positives, not wallow in what-could-have-beens or what-ifs. "Plying me with compliments, huh?" she quipped.

"I'm telling you the truth."

The sincerity of his words lifted her burdened shoulders and lightened her heavy heart. "That means more to me than you can imagine."

His gaze locked with hers. Seconds turned into a minute. The way he looked into her eyes made her think he was going to kiss her. Jules wanted him to kiss her. Anticipation surged.

She leaned toward him and parted her lips. An invitation and a plea.

"You should be at the helm of *La Rueca* in the Med Cup," he said.

Her breath caught in her throat. "What did you say?"

He repeated the words.

A strong yearning welled up inside of her, a longing that didn't want to be ignored. She started to speak then stopped herself.

What he said was impossible. In fact, he looked as surprised at his words as Jules did. He must have been joking.

She pushed aside her disappointment and laughed. "Oh, yes. That's exactly what I should do. Princess Julianna of Aliestle, helmsman."

Alejandro didn't joke back. His smile disappeared. His eyes darkened.

"You're not laughing," she said.

His jaw thrust forward. "I'm not kidding."

Of course, he was. Jules reached the top of the hill and continued along the paved path through the park. "It's been a lovely evening. Please don't spoil it by teasing me."

"I'm serious." The determined set of his chin made him look formidable. A lot like his father. But she remained unnerved by that. "If *La Rueca* places in the top five, the resulting publicity will boost my boatyard's reputation and raise the island's standing in the eyes of the yachting world. To do that I need you steering the boat."

"Wait." What he said confused her. "You said you were confident in the boat. In your crew."

"That was before I saw you sail. I need you, Julianna."

His words smacked into her like an unwieldy suitcase on wheels a porter couldn't handle and nearly knocked her on her backside. No one had ever needed her before.

"I'm floored. Flabbergasted. Flattered." Jules bit her lip to stop from rambling. She needed to be sensible about this, not emotional. "But we both know I can't race with you. The Med Cup is right before the wedding. Enrique and my father are unlikely to change their minds and allow me to compete, even with you."

"This will be our secret."

Jules considered what he was saying...for a nanosecond. "That's...that's..."

"Doable."

"Insane," she countered. "If I get caught—"

"We'll make sure you aren't."

A mix of conflicting emotion battled inside Jules. Part of her wanted to grab the moment and make the most of the opportunity. But common sense kept her feet planted firmly on the ground, er, path. She forced herself to keep walking toward the grotto.

"We're not talking about a midnight sail with the two of us. I'd have to practice with a crew in daylight. They'd figure out I'm not a boy the first time I said anything." Coming up with a list of reasons this was a bad idea was too easy. "Let's not forget the race officials. A crew roster will be necessary. We can't overlook the media coverage. The press will have a field day if my identity is discovered."

"For someone who's never sailed on the ocean you sure know a lot about what's involved with racing."

"I've raced in lakes, and I've followed various racing circuits for years. I know enough…" Her voice raised an octave. She took a calming breath. It didn't help. "Enough to know that with me at the helm, the odds are you'll lose. I'm not experienced enough."

"Are you trying to convince me?" he asked. "Or yourself."

"You."

"I say you're qualified enough. I want you to be my helmsman."

She felt as if she'd entered a different dimension, an alternative universe. Perhaps this was a dream and La Isla de la Aurora didn't exist. She would wake up in her room at the castle in Aliestle, not engaged. "Consider what you're saying, Alejandro. You're crazy if you want to risk the Med Cup on someone like me."

"Maybe I'm crazy. Certifiably insane. But I know what I saw tonight out on the water. No one else handles *La Rueca* as well as you."

"Have them practice more," she said. "It's late. I must get back to the palace before the sun rises."

She quickened her pace, leaving Alejandro behind. The

sooner she reached the grotto, the better. She couldn't listen to him anymore. It hurt too much to think racing on the ocean was even a possibility. That had never crossed her mind given her father's restrictions.

The footsteps behind her drew closer. "Don't run away."

"I'm heading in the wrong direction if I wanted to do that."

"Stop."

Jules did. She owed him that much for tonight's sail.

He placed his hand on her shoulder.

She gasped, not expecting him to touch her.

"Please," he said. "Consider what I'm saying."

Warmth ebbed from the point of contact. She struggled against the urge to lean into him, to soak up his strength and confidence. She wanted to, but couldn't. She shrugged away from his hand and counted to twenty in French. "I've considered it. No."

"Racing will make you happy." He wasn't giving up for some reason. "You love to sail."

"I love to sail, but it isn't my entire life." Jules didn't dare look at Alejandro. She couldn't allow herself to be swayed, even if she was tempted. "I have a duty to my family and country. That is more important than some…hobby."

The word used derisively by her father tasted bitter on her tongue. Sailing was a pastime, but it represented the freedom to live as she wanted and a tangible connection to the mother she didn't remember.

"I can't risk upsetting Enrique." The reality of her situation couldn't be ignored. "If he finds out—"

"Do you really think Enrique's going to send you back to Aliestle and walk away from a hundred-million-dollar dowry because you went sailing?"

Her jaw dropped. So did her heart. *Splat*.

Jules knew her father had set aside a large amount of money for her dowry, but not *that* much. She closed her mouth. She'd always known suitors were after the money, not her. Still the truth stung. "I...can't."

"Yes, you can," he urged. "It'll be worth the risk."

"For you, maybe. Not for me." If Enrique didn't marry her, she'd find herself trapped in a worse marriage, in an old-fashioned country with archaic, suffocating traditions. Her efforts to help Brandt and Aliestle would be futile. Plus, she had her children to consider. "I would love to race. But I can't do all the things I want to do. I must consider the consequences."

"Consider the consequences if you don't race."

The word *no* sat on the tip of Jules's tongue. That word would end further discussion. But her heart wasn't ready to do that yet. She wanted to know what racing might feel like. But reality kept poking at her, reminding her what was at stake. "There are no consequences if I don't race."

Alejandro held her hand. "Your happiness, Julianna."

"I'll find happiness."

"Life on the island will be good for you, but Enrique is self-involved. He'll most likely ignore you."

"Ignoring me will be better than trying to control me," she admitted. "And I'll be happy once I have children. I've always wanted to be a mother. Children will bring me great happiness and joy. I'll devote myself to being the best mother I can be. That will make me very happy."

"Will children be enough?"

They had to be.

"I'm sorry, Alejandro." Julianna pulled her hand out of his. "I must find contentment in the life I'm meant to live. If I believe I can or should have more, that will make the days unbearable."

"You're a wonderful, brave woman."

"If I was brave, I'd say yes even though it would be a really bad idea."

"It could be sheer brilliance."

"Or an utter disaster."

"You want to." Alejandro gazed into her eyes. "I can tell."

Her pulse skittered. She flushed. She did want to. More than anything. "I told you. It doesn't matter what I want. I can't."

"What's really stopping you?"

"Common sense." She raised her hand in the air to accentuate each point. "Duty. Obligation."

"Royal duty doesn't mean making yourself a slave."

"It's not slavery, but a responsibility to build something better."

"I'm trying to build something better here on the island. But you can't pretend to be something you're not," Alejandro said. "However much we love people or have loved them, we still have to be the person we are meant to be. Follow your heart," his voice dipped, low and hypnotic.

Emotion clogged her throat. She'd followed her heart once. Tonight. The thought of doing so again made her mouth water. "I…"

"Say yes," he encouraged. "You won't regret racing."

Oh, she would regret it. Jules had no doubt.

But tonight's glimpse of freedom had spoiled her and made her feel carefree and alive. She wasn't ready for that feeling to end.

"Yes." Her answer went against everything she'd been raised to do or be. She needed to reel herself in and set clear boundaries to temper this recklessness. She remembered her plan from this morning. "I'm saying yes for the same reason I sailed tonight. Once I marry Enrique, things will change. I must honor my husband and my marriage. I will step fully into my role of the crown princess who will one day be queen."

"The people of La Isla de la Aurora have no idea how fortunate they are to have you as their future queen."

"Let's make sure I'm not caught so one day I *can* be their queen."

"That's the number one priority," Alejandro said. "I'll take every precaution to keep your identity a secret. I have as much to lose with this as you do."

His words didn't make any sense. This had nothing to do with him. "What do you mean?"

Alejandro hesitated.

"I want to know what you have to lose," she said.

"My freedom," he admitted. "Once you and Enrique marry and have children, I'll be free from all royal obligations. I can concentrate on business and not have to worry about any more princely duties."

Enrique had said Alejandro didn't want to be royalty anymore. She'd thought Enrique had been exaggerating. Maybe that was what Alejandro had meant about being the person he needed to be. "You really want to turn your back on all your duties?"

"Yes."

She admired his being true to himself while dealing with some of the same burdens she had as a royal, but his wanting to break off completely from his obligations and birthright saddened her. Yet she had to admit, she was a tad envious. Alejandro would sail off into the sunset and do what he wanted, whereas she would carry the weight of two countries' expectations on her shoulders for the rest of her life.

At least she knew he would do everything in his power to keep them from getting caught. "I guess we both have something to lose."

"We're in this together, Julianna."

Yes, they were, but the knowledge left her feeling unsettled. Being out here alone with him did, too. His nearness disturbed her. His lips captured her attention. She still felt an overwhelming urge to kiss him. Even if he was the last man she should kiss.

Keep walking. Julianna saw the grotto up ahead. "We'd better get into the tunnel before someone sees us out here."

"No one will see us." Alejandro spoke with confidence. "I own this place."

"What place?"

He motioned to the land surrounding them. "The dock. The park. Everything you see."

She tried to reconcile this new piece of information with what she knew about him. Enrique had made Alejandro sound as if only sailing mattered to him. "You're a boatbuilder and a real estate investor?"

He nodded. "My goal is to turn the island into a travel hotspot. Most of the tourist traffic goes to other islands along the coast of Spain. La Isla de la Aurora doesn't have enough quality hotels, resorts and marinas to attract the big spenders. My father and brother have a more low-key vision of how to improve the economy. But the Med Cup has helped attract the yachting crowd. Now I have to get the travel industry onboard."

Impressive. And unexpected. He was so much more than she'd originally thought. Not that anything he owned or said or did should matter to her.

But it did. A lot.

She chewed on the inside of her cheek.

"As I mentioned, *La Rueca*'s result in the Med Cup could help that happen sooner," he said. "If we finish well."

We. The realization of what she'd agreed to hit her full force. Pressure to do well. Practice time. Being with Alejandro, a man she was attracted to. One who would be related to her when they finished racing. Oh, what a tangled web she was weaving. No way would she be able to escape unscathed.

"This isn't going to work." Doubts slammed into her like a rogue wave. "Someone at the palace will notice I'm not around if we have to practice a lot."

"Don't worry." He tucked a stray strand of blond hair up into the wig and adjusted the cap on her head. "I'll figure everything out. Trust me."

Jules shivered with desire and apprehension. She would have to trust him in a way she'd never trusted anyone before.

"Do you really think we have a shot at doing well?" she asked.

One side of his mouth tipped up at the corner. "With you at the helm, we have a good shot at not only placing, but winning."

CHAPTER SEVEN

THE SOUND OF voices woke Julianna. Lying in bed, she blinked open her eyes. Morning already. The bright sunlight made her shut her eyes again. But she'd glimpsed enough to know this wasn't her room back in Aliestle. She hadn't been dreaming.

Last night had been real. The sail. Alejandro.

A shiver ran down her spine.

She'd agreed to race, to be on his crew.

Somehow, she would have to be Enrique's conventional princess-fiancée and Alejandro's helmsman. And not let the two roles collide. Her temples throbbed thinking about trying to negotiate between the two different worlds without anyone figuring out what she was doing.

"The princess is sleeping, sir." Yvette's voice became more forceful. "I don't want to wake her unless it's necessary."

"This is important," a male voice Jules recognized as Brandt's said.

She opened her eyes and raised herself up on her elbows.

Yvette wore the traditional castle housekeeper uniform—a black dress with white collar and apron. Her brown hair was braided and rolled into a tight bun. She had the door cracked and held onto it with white knuckles, as if to keep an intruder out. Jules pictured Brandt standing on the other side, trying to sway the young maid with a flirtatious smile.

"I'm awake, Yvette," Jules said. "Send Brandt in."

"The princess is no longer sleeping, sir." Yvette opened the door all the way. "You may come in."

Brandt strode in, looking every inch the crown prince in his navy suit, striped dress shirt and colorful tie. He laughed. "I was out clubbing most of the night yet you're the one in bed. Must have been an exciting night watching TV?"

Jules shrugged. The night had been more exciting than she imagined. She hadn't been able to fall asleep when she'd returned to the palace. Too many thoughts about Alejandro had been running through her brain. Each time she closed her eyes, she'd seen his handsome face, as if the features had been etched in her memory.

She watched her maid head into the bathroom. "What is so important?"

"Prince Enrique wants you downstairs now."

Jules glanced at the clock. A quarter past ten. "Nothing is listed on my schedule."

If so, Yvette would have never allowed her to sleep in. The maid always made sure Jules was ready on time for her scheduled events.

Brandt raised a brow. "It's a surprise."

Her brother sounded amused. That set off warning bells in her head. "Care to enlighten me about this surprise?"

"No."

She tossed one of her pillows at him.

He batted it away. "Hey, don't shoot the messenger. I'm only doing as requested. I assumed you'd rather have me wake you than Enrique."

Alejandro would have been better. Especially if he woke her with long, slow kisses... She pushed the thought away as she fought a blush. Steering the boat was her responsibility, not kissing him. "I'll get dressed."

Brandt held up his hand as if to stop her. "That won't be necessary."

She drew back. "Excuse me?"

Mischief filled his eyes. "Enrique said a robe and slippers are fine."

She made a face. "I don't like the sound of this."

"No worries," Brandt said. "Bring Yvette. She and I will ensure your reputation isn't sullied."

If Jules had been caught last night, her reputation would have been more than sullied. "You've been spending too much time with Father. It's influencing your vocabulary."

"I happen to like sullying young maidens."

She rolled her eyes. "Give me five minutes. I'll meet you in the hallway."

"Don't take any longer," he cautioned. "Enrique said this is important."

Worry shivered down her spine. Had Enrique found out about last night? But if that were the case, why wouldn't he want her to dress before coming downstairs?

Brandt strode out of the room and closed the door behind him.

Jules slid out from under the covers and stood on the rug. Her simple white nightgown looked nothing like what a stylish princess would wear to bed. Her father forbade her to wear any sort of pajamas that were too pretty or feminine because she wasn't married. Forget sexy lingerie. She felt lucky wearing underwire bras decorated with lace. The castle's head housekeeper confiscated purchases she deemed inappropriate by King Alaric's standards.

Yvette returned, holding a lavender-colored, terry-cloth robe and matching slippers. "ma'am."

"I'd rather dress."

"I don't think there is time, ma'am."

Jules heard the sympathy in Yvette's voice. "Do you have any idea what's going on downstairs?"

"No, Ma'am." Yvette helped her into the thick robe. "But people have been arriving at the palace since early this morning. I'm surprised the noise didn't wake you."

Jules had been dead to the world once she'd quieted her thoughts of Alejandro and fallen asleep. She couldn't remember the last time she'd slept so soundly. She didn't remember any of her dreams. A rarity for her. "I didn't hear a thing."

"You must have been tired, ma'am."

She nodded.

Lines creased Yvette's forehead. "Are you feeling well, ma'am? Should I request a doctor be sent to the palace?"

"No worries, Yvette," Jules said. "I'm not sick. Let's go see what Enrique's surprise is all about."

Something good, she hoped. And something that had nothing to do with last night.

Alejandro stared at the attractive, stylish women carrying boxes into the palace's large music room. These weren't members of the normal staff. Not with those long legs and short skirts. His curiosity piqued, he decided to take a closer look and entered the Grand Hall.

Enrique paced with his hands clasped behind his back. Wrinkles creased his forehead. Sweat beaded at his brow.

The crown prince looked nothing like the oil paintings of the island's rulers hanging on the walls alongside him.

But Alejandro had seen his brother this way once before, when he prepared for what would turn out to be a disastrous date with a famous movie actress. The spoiled, pampered, egotistical couple had clashed from the moment they said hello. Each expected the other to cater to their whims.

"What are you up to, bro?" Alejandro asked.

"I wondered when the scent of perfume would lead you here." Enrique dabbed his forehead with a linen handkerchief. "Look, but don't touch. The women are being paid handsomely for their services."

Alejandro raised a brow. "I didn't realize you paid for female services."

"Not those kind of services, moron." Enrique sneered. "This is a surprise for Julianna."

"A surprise. Really?"

"Don't sound so shocked." He continued pacing. "She is going to be my wife."

Alejandro wasn't about to forget about that. He'd resisted tasting her lips last night for that very reason. But her agreeing to be his helmsman made up for the lack of kisses.

Asking her to join his crew wasn't his smartest move given consequences involved, but he believed *La Rueca* had a better chance of winning with her behind the wheel. She'd also looked so happy sailing. He wanted to show her how beautiful life could be here. All he had to do was douse his attraction for her, and things would be fine.

"I know." He tried to sound nonchalant, even if he was a little...envious. Enrique hadn't had much luck in the dating department, but he'd hit the jackpot finding a bride. Not that

Alejandro was in the market for one himself. "But you've never gone to so much trouble for a woman before."

Any trouble, really. Enrique expected women to fall at his feet. Those with dreams of being a princess and queen would until they tired of his self-centeredness. But Julianna was different...

"The royal wedding will generate a tremendous amount of publicity." He lowered his voice. "Julianna must be dressed appropriately for the ceremony and reception."

Too bad Enrique needed to feed his ego, not please Julianna the way she deserved to be pleased and cherished. Alejandro rolled his eyes in disgust.

"The princess is always at the top of the Best Dressed Lists." He hadn't been able to sleep last night. He'd searched the internet to learn more about Julianna. "She is a fashion icon for women, young and old."

"In everyday clothing, yes," Enrique said. "Being a princess bride is different. I have assembled the top experts here. A dress designer and her team, makeup artists, hairstylists and many others. This is all for her."

Alejandro rolled his eyes. "Don't pretend any of this is for Julianna. It's about how you want her to look when she's with you."

"This is important. The royal wedding will change the island's fortune and future. Everything must go perfectly." Enrique sounded more like a spoiled child than a crown prince. "Today's trial run of our wedding day preparations will work out any kinks and problems. The dress designer will also take care of alterations needed on the wedding gown."

Practical, perhaps, but so not romantic. Julianna was practical. Her words last night about her embracing her marriage told Alejandro that. But the woman who had sailed with stars in her eyes also seemed like the kind who liked the hearts, flowers and violin type of romance. Arranged marriage or not.

"Alterations?" he asked. "I didn't think Julianna had a wedding dress yet."

Enrique smirked. "She has one now."

The look on his brother's face worried Alejandro. "What have you—?"

"Good morning, gentlemen." Julianna walked toward them with Brandt at her side and her maid following.

Julianna looked regal wearing a bathrobe and slippers. Every strand of her hair, worn loose this morning, was perfectly placed. She'd applied makeup, too. Not as much as she usually wore, but enough for him to notice the difference from her clean face last night. No one would guess the perfectly groomed princess had another side, one that had taken her out onto the sea with him until early this morning.

She stopped in front of them. "I was told you wanted to see me, Enrique."

Her formal tone contradicted the casual way she'd spoken on the boat and during the walk back to the palace.

"I do." Enrique beamed. "I have a surprise for you, my lovely bride."

The corners of her mouth tipped up, but her eyes didn't sparkle the way they had last night. Of course, no one would notice that except Alejandro. He found it strange she showed no hint of the woman he'd spent hours sailing with. Her mask was firmly in place, a disguise like the sailing clothes she'd worn.

Julianna rubbed her hands together. Excited or cold, he couldn't tell. "I love surprises," she said.

Alejandro didn't think she would like this one. She wanted

freedom, not be told what to wear and how to act on her wedding day. He needed to warn her so she would be prepared. "Why don't you grab Father, Enrique? I'm sure he'll be interested in seeing this."

"Father is attending his weekly breakfast meeting with the head of the Courts. Something you would know if you had a clue about what went on around here." Enrique extended his arm, and Julianna laced her arm around his. "Ready for your surprise?"

She nodded with a hint of anticipation in her eyes.

The woman always hoped for the best. Alejandro respected that about her, but he knew she would only be hurt that much more.

The doors to the music room opened.

Alejandro stared at the floor. He didn't want to see her disappointed.

Julianna gasped.

His gaze jerked up. White satin, tulle and miniature white lights covered the walls of the music room. A thick, white rug lay on the hardwood floor. A white silk curtain separated a third of the room from the rest of it. No expense had been spared in transforming the space into a spa complete with a private beauty salon and a massage table.

Impressive. Enrique had managed to get it right this time. If only his motivation had been for his bride and not himself. Alejandro glanced over at Julianna.

She surveyed the entire room with wide-eyed wonder. "What is all this?"

"Everything you'll need to prepare for our wedding day," Enrique said proudly. "This will be your bride room."

"Oh, Enrique." Her smile widened. "I can't believe you would go to all this trouble."

Don't believe it, Alejandro wanted to shout. This was nothing but smoke and mirrors on the part of his brother. Ambition and pride run amuck à la Lady Macbeth. But Alejandro saw how moved Julianna was. He wanted her to be happy, even if that meant she was happy with his brother. Enrique might get Julianna the princess, but Alejandro took fierce delight in getting Julianna the sailor.

"This is amazing, Enrique," Brandt said. "Thank you so much."

Even Brandt had been fooled.

Enrique kissed the top of Julianna's hand, the gesture as meaningless as the over-the-top display in the music room.

"It was no trouble at all." Enrique's smooth tone made Alejandro want to gag. "Anything for my princess bride."

Julianna's eyes didn't sparkle, but they brightened. She looked relieved, pleased with what she saw in the music room and with her fiancé. "Thank you."

Warmth and appreciation rang out in her voice. Perhaps she would be content, even happy, in this marriage. But Alejandro couldn't shake his misgivings.

Enrique's chest puffed out. "There's more."

Alejandro had to admit he was curious, but in a train-wreck-waiting-to-happen kind of way.

With a grand gesture of his arms, Enrique motioned for the curtain to be opened. Two young women, both dressed in the same hot pink above the knee dresses and black sling-back stilettos, opened the white silk curtains to reveal a wedding gown on a busty mannequin wearing a diamond tiara and a long lace veil.

"Surprise," Enrique shouted with glee.

Julianna gasped again. Not in a good way this time. A

look of despair flashed across her face before her features settled into a tight smile.

Alejandro didn't blame her for the reaction.

A cupcake. That was his first impression of the gown. The frilly dress with big puffy sleeves, sparkling crystals and neatly tied bows would look perfect on a Disney princess, but not on Julianna. She would look like a caricature of a princess bride in that dress.

Julianna should wear a more sophisticated, elegant gown with sleek lines to show off her delicious curves. He imagined her walking down the cathedral aisle in such a dress and pictured himself waiting for her...

What the hell?

Alejandro shook the image from his head. He wasn't looking for a girlfriend, let alone a bride. Especially one who was already engaged and held the key to his freedom.

Julianna stared at the spectacle of a dress in front of her. Tears welled in her eyes.

"I told you she would like this." A smug smile settled on Enrique's lips. "She's crying tears of joy."

Alejandro balled his hands. He barely managed to keep his fists at his sides. He wanted to punch his brother in the nose and knock some sense into his inflated, ego-filled head.

The guy had to be a narcissist not to realize Julianna was horrified, not joyful. Either that, or Enrique was that dense about women.

"That is my sister's wedding dress?" Brandt asked with a tone of disbelief.

Enrique nodded, visibly pleased with himself. "I told the designer to create a royal wedding dress fit for a fairy-tale princess bride."

"When?" Julianna muttered. "When did you tell her that?"

"A while ago," Enrique admitted. "When my father decided I should wed."

Julianna pressed her lips together. Alejandro didn't have to be a mind reader to know what she was thinking. Enrique had requested the gown for a generic bride, not with Julianna in mind.

More proof this show today was for Enrique's benefit, no one else's. He knew exactly how *he* wanted things. Who cared about anyone else, including his bride who hadn't even been considered in the dress design?

Alejandro had come up against his brother's ego many times. He'd lost most battles and won a few, but he'd never been so angry with Enrique as he was now.

"Try on the dress," Enrique urged.

Alejandro waited for Julianna to speak up, to say she wanted to pick out her own wedding dress.

She squared her shoulders.

He smiled. This should be good.

"Let's go see how the dress looks on me, Yvette." Julianna set off toward the wedding dress with her maid in tow.

Alejandro stared in disbelief. Julianna had no problem yesterday speaking up to him, showing sass and spunk when it came to Boots's name and being helmsman. He couldn't understand why she remained silent now.

He glanced at Brandt. Surely the crown prince would stand up for his big sister? But he followed Julianna without saying a word.

What was going on? Alejandro watched from the other side of the music room as they approached the atrocious wedding gown.

"I knew this was a good idea," Enrique said in a low, but singsong manner.

Alejandro gritted this teeth. "A bride should choose her own gown."

"This was part of the wedding negotiations with King Alaric."

"The king approves of Julianna wearing a dress you picked out?" Alejandro asked.

Enrique nodded. "King Alaric paid for all of this, including the wedding gown I commissioned months ago. The old fool is so desperate to have grandchildren he agrees to anything I ask for. He's giving me an extra ten million if I keep Julianna from ever sailing again. Imagine that."

"I can't." Outrage tightened Alejandro's jaw until it ached. For that amount of money, Enrique would never change his mind about Julianna sailing again. "Especially since she seems to enjoy the sport."

"She'll get over it." Enrique's brush-off bothered Alejandro more than usual. "Remember, she has me. That will be enough for her."

His brother's uncaring attitude roused Alejandro's protective instincts. Someone had to take a stand for her. "Julianna might be happier if—"

Enrique cut him off. "Her happiness isn't my priority. I only care about her dowry, ability to produce heirs and obeying my orders."

Alejandro had never seen his brother act so callous. "This is wrong."

"I'm treating her the way she expects to be treated. Women in Aliestle are used to being ordered about. It's all they know."

"Enrique, don't—"

"Enough." Enrique sneered. "If you say a word to Julianna or Brandt about any of this, I'll shut down the Med Cup this year."

"You can't cancel the race."

"I can, and I will."

With the threat hanging in air, he strutted toward the others like a proud peacock.

Alejandro seethed. He needed his brother to marry if he wanted to be released from his princely duties and obligations. But what would the cost of that freedom be?

He stared at Julianna. She touched the skirt of the wedding dress with a hesitant hand. She claimed marrying Enrique was better than returning to Aliestle. Alejandro had his doubts.

The women in pink removed the frothy confection of a wedding gown from the mannequin. Julianna and her maid followed them behind a white, fabric-paneled screen.

Enrique's threat made it impossible for Alejandro to take action. Not that he could stop the royal wedding since Julianna wanted to marry his brother. But Alejandro could do something else.

He could make the Med Cup race memorable for Julianna. He could show her how skilled and talented she was. He could make her see she deserved the best from the crew, the staff and most especially, her husband.

That was the least Alejandro could do for the beautiful princess bride. And he would.

I look like a puff pastry.

Jules stared at her reflection in the three-part mirror with horror. She couldn't believe Enrique wanted her to wear this monstrosity at their wedding. She'd thought for a few short moments he'd wanted to make her happy and gone to all this trouble to make her feel…special. But he hadn't.

Do you really think Enrique's going to send you back to

Aliestle and walk away from a hundred-million-dollar dowry because you went sailing?

Alejandro's words reaffirmed what she knew in her heart and her mind. Enrique only cared about her dowry. He'd made it sound like all this had been for her, but it was really for him. She'd overheard the manicurist talking to the hairstylist about putting together a list of improvements for the crown prince. No one cared about Jules's opinion.

Thank goodness Enrique hadn't stuck around long. Otherwise she might have said something impolite. At least she didn't feel quite so guilty about agreeing to sail in the Med Cup and going behind his back.

One of the women in pink raised the hem of the dress. Tulle scratched Jules leg. "We'll need to add another ruffle."

No. Her stomach churned. Not another ruffle. The dress had too many as it was.

She inhaled to calm herself. The potent mixture of the different perfumes the women wore made her cough. Her eyes watered.

Delia, the dress designer, and her team jotted notes and marked the dress with pins.

Jules tried to ignore them. She needed a distraction. A quick survey of the room yielded nothing. Alejandro must have left before Enrique. She would have to rely on her own imagination.

She imagined being on *La Rueca* and holding the wheel in her hands. The metal felt smooth beneath her palms. The boat heeled and water splashed against her face and wet her clothes. Alejandro manned the jib sheet, his flexed muscles glistening from a combination of sweat and water. He glanced back at her. His handsome face filled with pleasure, his dark eyes gleaming with hunger for her. An answering desire sparked low in her belly as the wind whipped through her hair—

"With the dreamy look in your eyes, you must be picturing your wedding day," a woman's voice broke through Julianna's thoughts.

She turned off the romantic scene playing in her head and brought herself back to the present.

"You look gorgeous, ma'am." Delia motioned to the women in pink. "Let's button up the back to see how the gown fits."

Jules didn't—couldn't—say anything. She'd rather daydream about sailing with Alejandro than think about marrying a man who would have a wedding gown designed for a nameless, faceless bride. A dress more suited for a younger woman who wanted to be a fairy-tale princess, not a woman a couple of years away from turning thirty. The thought of walking down the aisle wearing the dress filled her with dread.

Don't think about that. She imagined herself with the wind on her face, the taste of salt in her mouth and Alejandro next to her.

Someone pulled on the left side of dress. "It's a little tight."

Jules pretended the lifeline tugged against her, keeping her attached to the boat. With iffy weather and big waves, falling overboard could be fatal.

As would be continuing to fantasize about Alejandro.

"It'll fit," another woman said.

The pressure around Jules's midsection increased. She felt as if she were caught in the middle of a tug-of-war game. The air rushed from her lungs, forced out by whatever was being tightened around her.

"Can't breathe," Jules croaked.

"Release the buttons and strings," Delia ordered.

The women did.

"Thank you," Jules said.

"Sorry, Ma'am." Delia's cheeks flushed. "The dress is too large in the bust and too small in the waist. I'll take measurements so I can alter the gown."

Enrique must have given the measurements for his idea of the perfect bride. Jules wasn't surprised he wanted an eighteen-year-old woman with the proportions of a real-life Barbie doll. She remembered the room he'd picked out for her with the garden view to make her happy. One of Enrique's problems was he assumed everyone's tastes were the same as his own or should be.

Using a measuring tape, the designer and her assistants took measurements and scribbled notes.

Jules wanted to laugh at the absurdity of it all, but despair crept along the edges of her mind, threatening to swamp her. The reality of what kind of marriage she would have had become clearer.

Running away, giving up duty and family for happiness, no longer seemed like such a drastic measure. She could shuck the awful dress and flee. No more grinning and bearing it. No more doing what everyone else wanted her to do.

But that behavior wasn't any more her than the wedding gown. Jules wanted a better future for her children and her country. She had a plan. She would have to be content with her sailing rebellion.

"That is all we need, Ma'am," Delia said. "I'll start to work on the alterations right away. I shall also remove some of the bows and layers. Prince Enrique talked about a fairy-tale princess dress. That led me to believe you were younger. My mistake."

"You've worked hard on the dress, Delia. The craftsmanship and quality are outstanding. I know you've delivered the wedding dress Prince Enrique asked for," Jules said. "But I'm twenty-eight. Not eighteen. Anything you can do to make the gown a little more...subdued would be appreciated."

Delia bowed her head. "I understand, ma'am."

The woman's empathetic tone told Jules the designer understood. Was that enough to make up for her having to wear the dress and marry an egotistical crown prince? She exhaled on a sigh.

Enrique was to be her husband. She had to make the best of the situation and the most of the opportunity. Jules straightened. "So where am I to go next?"

"The massage table, ma'am." Yvette read from a sheet of paper. "Then you're to have a pedicure and manicure before seeing the hairstylist and makeup artist."

"I'll be all made up with nowhere to go," she said, trying to sound lighthearted and cheerful.

"You do have someplace to go, ma'am." Yvette waved a piece paper. "I received an updated itinerary for today. You, Prince Brandt and the royal family are attending the ballet tonight."

Jules hoped that included Alejandro. Her heart bumped. The thought of seeing him again—make that racing with him—was the only thing keeping her going right now.

Thank goodness she'd said yes to being his helmsman or she didn't know what she would do. The memory of racing would keep her going until she had children to love.

Maybe she would get pregnant right away.

On her wedding night.

With Enrique.

The thought of being intimate with him seared her heart. Tears stung the corners of her eyes. She looked up at the elaborate crystal chandelier hanging from the ceiling and blinked. Twice.

Jules knew better than to let her emotions show. She'd been trained from a young age to hide her true feelings. She had to be more careful or someone might discover the truth about how she felt.

Shoulders back. Chin up. Smile.

She looked at Yvette. "So, which ballet will I be seeing?"

CHAPTER EIGHT

The sun had yet to peek over the horizon. As Jules made the early morning trek to Alejandro's boat dock, her headlamp illuminated the way through the darkness. The scent of cut grass hung in the air. The smell was new, different from the night before. Someone must have mowed yesterday. Or maybe she was paying closer attention this time.

Knowing where she was going made the walk easier. But the stillness was a little eerie. Even the insects seemed to have called it a night. If only she had gotten more sleep...

Jules yawned.

The four-hour ballet and the dessert afterward had dragged on into the wee hours of the night. She'd slept for three hours before having to wake and prepare for this practice. She felt half-asleep.

Too bad the Lilac Fairy from the ballet couldn't lead a handsome prince to Jules. A kiss might wake her up, especially if the kiss came from a certain prince.

Alejandro.

Warmth balled in her chest.

He'd been at the ballet for the first act, long enough to

slip a note about this morning's practice into Jules's beaded clutch. He'd left the royal family's private box before the start of the first intermission, well before the kissing happened in act two. She'd been sad to see him go. Not for any other reason than she enjoyed his company, she decided.

Jules knew she would never be anything more than Alejandro's sister-in-law. Anything more would be wrong. But she allowed herself the luxury of daydreaming about him until her wedding day. A guilty pleasure, yes. But a necessary one if she wanted to make it through her engagement without losing her mind.

Jules wanted to like her future husband. She wanted to fall in love with him. But he wasn't making it easy. He'd paraded her around like a puppet bride on a string during both intermissions. Enrique didn't want a wife; he wanted a fashion accessory.

She shivered with disgust at the way he'd showed her off and talked about her as if she weren't there. At least he hadn't tried to kiss her good-night.

Forget about it. Him. She needed to focus on sailing.

But Jules couldn't muster the same level of enthusiasm she'd felt venturing out here yesterday. Partly because of what had happened with Enrique, but also because she would be meeting the crew for the first. She wouldn't be Julianna, but J.V., a nineteen-year-old male university student from Germany who knew enough English sailing commands to be an effective helmsman.

Jules wore the same disguise as before, but she didn't know if she could pull off her new identity. The waist of her pants slipped down her hips. She pulled the pants up and rolled the band. Maybe that would make it fit better.

A wave of apprehension swept over her.

Alejandro thought she could do it, but the man exuded confidence. He thought he could do anything. He seemed to believe the same of her, too. Jules wished she was as certain, but all she felt were...misgivings.

At the top of the hill, she stopped.

The sun broke through the horizon casting beautiful golden rays of light through the sky. She inhaled, filling her lungs with the briny air.

Dawn brought a new day, a new beginning. This was hers. She needed to grab it with both hands.

Freedom.

Excitement shot all the way to the tips of her toes.

Alejandro needed her. Well, she needed him and *La Rueca*. Jules would do whatever she had to do until the Med Cup was over to create memories that would last a lifetime, ones she could share with her children, and she hoped, someday, with her husband.

Not even thinking about Enrique could burst the enthusiasm energizing her now. Jules wiggled her toes inside her boat shoes. She wanted to be down on the dock. She wanted to sail.

Jules removed the headlamp, switched off the power and shoved the device in her windbreaker's pocket. She hurried down the path, eager to climb aboard *La Rueca*.

Men stood on the dock and in the boat. Navy, black, red and white seemed to be the colors of choice for their clothing. Two wore baseball caps. Good, she wanted to fit in.

Still butterflies filled her stomach. She kept descending moving closer to the boat.

A few men glanced her way, gave her the once-over, but not in the way she was used to. That was okay. She didn't want them looking at her too closely.

She studied each and every one of the faces. The crew contained a mix of nationalities and ages. But she didn't see Alejandro with them.

Anxiety rocketed through her.

Where was he? Alejandro hadn't mentioned not being here on his note. She couldn't do this without him. Jules wanted to stop moving, but that would look odd. She didn't want to make the crew suspicious. She forced one foot in front of the other.

Please be here.

A familiar head with dark hair popped up from below deck. Alejandro.

Relief washed over her. She quickened her pace to reach him—the boat—faster.

With the dark stubble on his face, he looked very much like a pirate captain and king. His smile made her breath catch in her throat. "Good morning, J.V."

The rich, deep sound of his voice made her heart turn over.

Jules acknowledged him with a nod. The less she said, the better. She kept her hands at her sides, too. She didn't want to wave back like a girl, or worse, a princess.

"This is J.V.," Alejandro announced. "The one I told you about. Wait until you see him at the helm. *La Rueca* turns as if she's sailing on rails."

Jules straightened, pleased by his compliment. Living up to his words might be hard. What if she'd gotten lucky the other night with a perfect combination of wind and sea?

The others didn't say anything. They eyed her warily.

Jules wasn't offended. She understood their caution. Alejandro had given her the nod of approval, but she was an unknown quantity. She would have to earn their respect with her sailing. She only hoped she could.

"Hi," Jules said in the deepest voice she could manage.

She shoved her bare hands in her jacket pockets. Shaking hands with anyone would be a bad idea. She'd trimmed her nails and removed the polish, but her hands still looked feminine. Maybe she needed a pair of sailing gloves.

"I'm Phillipe." The bald man with clear, blue eyes spoke with a French accent. She recognized him from races she'd watched on television. "Tactician."

Before she could acknowledge him, Phillipe walked away, unimpressed by her. Uh-oh. This could be interesting since they would have to work closely together.

"I'm Mike. One of the grinders." The burly, brown-haired man, whose job was to crank the winch, sounded like an American. He yawned. "I hope all our practices aren't going to be at the crack of dawn."

Wanting to say as little as possible, Jules glanced at Alejandro.

"J.V. can't miss any of his classes at the university," he answered. "The wind is good in the morning."

"This morning," Mike agreed. "But these early wake-up calls are going to mess with my social life, skipper."

"Chatting on Facebook can wait until after the Med Cup, mate." A bleach blond with a tanned face stepped forward. Friendliness and warmth emanated from his wide smile. "I work the bow. Sam's the name. From New Zealand. Welcome aboard, J.V."

She smiled at him, feeling a little strange that no one could tell she wasn't a boy. Okay, she didn't want to be recognized, but it made her wonder. Were her features that masculine? Was that the reason her father had such a hard time marrying her off?

"Dude, I'm not talking about Facebook," Mike said to

Sam. "This girl I met at the club last night is so hot. She's interested, too."

Sam laughed. "In getting away from you."

"Yeah, right. That's why she gave me her number," Mike countered. "I'm texting her as soon as we finish practice. Talk about an amazing rack."

As a red-haired, Irish-sounding guy asked to see the woman's picture, heat rushed to Jules's cheeks. She turned her face away so no one would notice. Her brothers didn't talk like that in front of her. Not even Brandt, who probably considered admiring "racks" a pastime.

"No pics right now, Cody. We'll finish the rest of the introductions later," Alejandro said. "Let's take advantage of the wind and have J.V. show us what he can do."

Jules swallowed around the anchor-size lump lodged in her throat. If she messed up...

No, she shouldn't imagine making any mistakes.

The other crewmembers took their positions.

Alejandro had put his faith in her. She couldn't let him down.

With her insides shaking, Jules boarded *La Rueca*. She removed Brandt's sunglasses from her pocket and put them on. The dark lenses would protect her eyes from the rising sun, but also hide them.

She was a world away from the life she lived, but her training would help her today. A helmsman needed to be cool, calm, calculating. Just like a princess.

Shoulders back. Chin up. Smile.

Jules did all three. As her fingers tightened around the wheel, she widened her stance. The position felt familiar, comfortable.

"Ready?" Alejandro asked.

She would prove to the crew Alejandro hadn't made a mistake by giving her the helm. "Ready, skipper."

Her smile widened. She sounded like a German. Maybe she could pull this off.

Julianna had done it. Pride filled Alejandro. She'd proved her worth as a helmsman with some world-class sailing.

The three hours on the water went by faster than anyone expected. No one wanted to return to the dock. But Julianna needed to get back to the palace before anyone realized she wasn't asleep in her bed as they thought.

Standing on the dock, Alejandro picked up a line. He glanced at the cockpit where Julianna studied one of Phillipe's charts. With her sunglasses on top of her hat, she looked every bit a teenager. No one suspected differently. Maybe people only saw what they expected to see. The disguise made her appear younger, but nothing could hide her high cheekbones, lush lips or smooth complexion.

Alejandro could watch her all day long and never get bored.

"Skipper," Sam called from the bow. "Toss me the line."

Alejandro did.

"The kid's good." Sam hooked the end around a cleat. "Quiet, but he knows what he's doing. The way he maneuvered around that buoy. Sweet. It's like he's got a sixth sense when it comes to wind shifts."

"Told you."

Sam nodded. "But J.V. seems a bit...soft. We need to take him out. Harden him up. Make him drink until he pukes."

Alejandro's muscles tensed. Having Julianna out here without a bodyguard was bad enough. Granted, he could protect her. No doubt his security detail wasn't far away given his sneaking out of the palace hadn't been necessary this morning. But he wouldn't put her in harm's way, not even for a little hazing by the crew. "J.V. is young. He lives with his overprotective family. If we have some fun with him like that, he won't be allowed to sail with us."

"Okay, but he's wound pretty tight. Maybe a woman—"

"Leave the kid alone," Alejandro interrupted. "That's an order."

"If you change your mind—"

"The kid's a natural. We need to mentor J.V., not introduce him to a life of debauchery."

"You've never had a problem with debauchery before." Sam grinned knowingly. "Let me guess. The kid has a hot sister."

Julianna was hot. Alejandro smiled.

"You dog." Sam laughed. "I didn't know you liked young pups."

Alejandro didn't. "She's a bit older than J.V., but I'll take what I can get."

That was the case with Julianna until she married. Then he'd be free and she'd be with... He didn't want to think about that.

"Okay. I'll put my plans to corrupt the youngster on hold." Sam winked. "Until you've had your fill of his sister."

A good thing Julianna couldn't hear them. She was huddled with Phillipe going over race strategy in German. No one knew the Frenchman was fluent. Fortunately Julianna was, too. Otherwise her cover would have been blown.

Day one had been a success. Only time would tell what the rest of the days would bring.

But Alejandro was...hopeful.

Jules walked back to the palace through the dark tunnel. The four-footed creatures running alongside her beam of light didn't bother her. Meeting the crew and being accepted by them exhilarated her. The image of Alejandro with his eyes full of pride, a wide smile on his handsome face and the dawning sun gleaming in his hair gave her a boost of energy.

The darkness beyond her headlamp seemed to go on forever, but she didn't care. Jules felt as if she'd already been crowned queen. The only thing she needed was a hot shower. Okay, a nap wouldn't hurt.

She reached the staircase to her closet and climbed the steep, narrow steps to the landing.

Alejandro's plan had worked. Relief flowed through her veins. Sailing on his crew was going to work out fine. She could race and then marry Enrique. No one would know the truth.

Jules pressed on the latch. The secret door opened. She stepped out of the dark passageway and into the closet.

She'd told Yvette not to disturb her this morning and allow her to wake up on her own. But Jules stood at the closet door and listened. No sounds. Yes! Her escape and return had gone off without a hitch.

She closed the secret door.

All she had to do was undress, hide the sailing clothes and—

The closet door opened. Yvette dropped the towel in her hand and gasped.

Stunned, Jules jumped back.

No, no, no, no, no.

Heart pounding, she lurched forward and placed her hand over Yvette's mouth. "Shhhh. Don't scream."

Fear filled Yvette's brown eyes. "Waah wuh wah ma puhsa."

Jules struggled to comprehend the words. She hoped being

in the closet would mute their voices. "I'm going to lower my hand. Do not scream. Understand?"

Yvette nodded.

Jules lowered her hand from the maid's mouth. "What did you say?"

"Please don't hurt my princess."

Hurt. Princess. Yvette hadn't recognized her. Jules could still escape.

Her relief lasted no longer than a breath. Escaping into the tunnels wasn't an option. An investigation into the mysterious closet intruder might reveal the tunnels' existence. Worse, she couldn't allow Yvette to be traumatized by this.

Jules's best choice, her only choice, was to come clean and hope for the best. A miracle.

"It's me, Yvette," Jules whispered. "Julianna."

The young woman's brows knotted, but fear remained in her eyes. "Princess Julianna?"

"Yes." Jules pulled off the baseball hat, wig and the nylon cap holding all her hair.

Yvette gasped. "I just saw you asleep in your bed, ma'am."

"You saw pillows and a blond wig," Jules admitted. "Not me."

Yvette stared at her as if she was an extraterrestrial with three eyes, two mouths and purple skin. "What are you doing in your closet dressed like a boy, ma'am?"

The knowledge of the secret tunnels remained safe. For now. "I've been sailing."

Another gasp. "That is forbidden, ma'am."

"Which is the reason for my disguise." Jules needed Yvette to understand what was at stake. "Please, I beg you. Keep my secret in your heart. Never repeat a word of this to anyone."

Especially the tabloids or her father. Fear of discovery made Jules's stomach roll with nausea.

"I don't understand why you would disobey the king, ma'am." The maid sounded dumbfounded. "You've never..."

"I felt as if I had no other choice." In for a penny, in for a pound. Jules needed Yvette's help. That required honesty. Perhaps the truth would bring compassion. "Once I marry Enrique, my life will be the same as it is back home, with similar restrictions. Enrique has forbidden me from sailing again. I know I'm disobeying my father, but I need a taste of freedom. When Alejandro asked me to be on his racing crew—"

"You're sailing with Prince Alejandro?" Yvette's eyes widened, as if scandalized.

Jules nodded.

"But his reputation—"

"May be bad, but I assure you, Prince Alejandro has been a total gentleman."

Unfortunately.

"If King Alaric finds out or Prince Enrique—"

"Neither has to find out. Only Alejandro and you know what I'm doing. The crew thinks I'm a college kid from Germany."

Yvette said nothing. Her eyes looked contemplative. Maybe she was too stunned for words. Or maybe she was totaling how much she could make selling this story to the media.

Jules knew her freedom, at least what little she'd found sailing with Alejandro, would vanish with one wrong word. She took the maid's hands in hers. "I know what I'm asking is wrong, but please don't tell anyone."

The seconds ticked by.

"I'll keep your secret, ma'am," Yvette said. "I pledge my loyalty and promise to help you."

Her words nearly knocked Jules over. "Oh, thank you. I'll find some way to make it up to you. I promise."

"That isn't necessary, ma'am." Compassion shone in Yvette's eyes. "I understand."

"You do?"

"Yes, ma'am. I'd love to escape my job as a palace maid, move to Milan or Paris and work in the fashion industry." Wistfulness echoed in the maid's words.

A kindred spirit. "You have the talent."

"Thank you, ma'am."

"I'm sure we aren't the only ones who wish for something different."

Yvette nodded.

"I can't do much about Paris or Milan, but I can see about getting you a job here on the island."

"Thank you, ma'am, but my family needs me in Aliestle. I don't want to hurt my sisters' marriage prospects."

"I understand, but if you change your mind let me know." Jules had more in common with her maid than she realized. She smiled. "Having your help, Yvette, is going to make sailing in the Med Cup so much easier. Here's what we'll need to do…"

CHAPTER NINE

As the days flew by, Jules juggled between playing the role of J.V. and being Princess Julianna. Whenever anyone wanted to see her in the morning, Yvette said the princess was sleeping. No one was the wiser, at the palace or on the crew, in spite of a close call when a strong gust of wind nearly blew her cap and wig off her head.

Jules had found a way to do her duty, as was required by her father and country, and experience freedom, as her heart and soul longed for. But guilt niggled at her.

Being on Alejandro's crew was a crazy, fun adventure, but a temporary one. Her wedding day, however, was right after the Med Cup, yet she'd barely thought about it. Or her groom.

Prince Enrique wasn't the man of her dreams, but he was to be her husband and the father of her children. Their marriage would last for the rest of her life. She couldn't ignore her fiancé, even if he'd been ignoring her.

If love was to blossom, someone had to make the first move. That someone was going to have to be her.

With her resolve in place, Jules walked to Enrique's office. The sound of her heels against the marble floor echoed through the hall.

Enrique's assistant wasn't behind his desk, but the door to the inner office was ajar.

She tapped lightly. "Enrique?"

"Julianna." He rose from a large walnut desk. His gray suit, white dress shirt and red tie were a far cry from Alejandro's casual boating clothes and sexy, carefree style, but Enrique looked regal and handsome. "What brings you here?"

Jules entered the office. "I've hardly seen you this week."

She preferred sailing with Alejandro or her own company to being with Enrique. But she needed to make sure their marriage started out on a solid footing even if he saw her as nothing more than his royal broodmare and arm candy.

"True, but I've been thinking about you." Enrique smiled, but the gesture seemed to be more of an effort to placate her. "You must understand, my princess. There is much work to attend to."

"Yes, you have been busy." She wanted him to show her she hadn't misjudged him. She wanted him to do something to make her want to be with him the way she wanted to be with Alejandro. "Will you be joining us for dinner tonight?"

Enrique hadn't eaten with them the past four nights. Not even her father worked that much, and he was king. Aliestle was a small country, but wealthier and more influential than this island.

"I regret missing dinners." Enrique motioned to the papers on his desk. "But I am working more now so I can take a few days off after the wedding."

I, not we. Disappointment weighed her down. For their marriage to work, she needed Enrique to meet her halfway. "Just a few days for our honeymoon?"

He nodded. "I can't afford to be away any longer."

"I understand." Look at the bright side, Jules thought. They hadn't spent any time alone. Whenever they attended an official event, a security detail and the press accompanied them. And each time they were together, Enrique managed to irritate her more. A short honeymoon might be best. "Duty first."

He sat. "Your sense of duty appeals to me, Julianna."

Her obedience was second only to her dowry.

Stay positive. Enrique might want to lead her around like a champion show dog on a leash, but their daughters could be doctors and lawyers if they were raised on La Isla de la Aurora. Jules forced a smile. "Thank you."

"How is the wedding planning coming along?" he asked.

The question struck her as odd. Enrique made most of the decisions about the royal wedding. Either he was trying to be polite or he thought her that clueless. Neither boded well. But she kept her pride in check. "The wedding coordinators seem to have everything in hand. But I manage to keep myself...occupied."

Her day started at 3:00 a.m. in preparation for the morning sails. Jules returned to the palace for more sleep before heading to town to make appearances and attend functions.

"I love going into the capital," she admitted.

The coastal town looked like something from a postcard with its pastel buildings with tiled roofs, the coffee shops with umbrella covered tables and the open-air markets where people could buy everything from fresh fish to vegetables. Businesses closed in the afternoon for siesta. The relaxed pace reminded her of Alejandro.

Don't think about him now.

"The people are charming," she added.

The citizens of La Isla de la Aurora embraced their Spanish heritage. They spoke English and Spanish with ease often mixing the two languages. Wherever she went, smiles greeted her. The genuine warmth of the people touched her heart. Jules felt accepted here in a way she'd never felt back home. That gave her another reason for wanting this marriage to work. She liked living on the island.

"You've been tired lately," he said with what sounded like a hint of concern. She was surprised he'd noticed.

"A little." Jules made do with what sleep she could squeeze in. "I'm working hard to learn my new role."

Here at the palace and on the boat.

"You're doing well." He sounded pleased. "I saw your picture in the paper this morning. You were at the hospital."

She nodded. "I enjoy visiting the patients, especially the children. There's this little boy. His name is—"

"Stop visiting the hospital until after the wedding," he interrupted. "You could catch a nasty germ there."

"I'm sure you wouldn't want to get sick." The words slipped out.

"That's for certain."

She swallowed a sigh. Once again he was only concerned about himself. "I'm just tired, Enrique. Don't be concerned about catching germs, I'm healthy."

"I know."

Jules drew back. "You do?"

"Our palace doctor spoke with yours."

She didn't know what to say. Had all her fiancés been told about her medical record? Not that she had anything to hide, but still… She hated the lack of privacy. That would never happen to one of her brothers.

Enrique glanced at his computer monitor, distracted by whatever had popped up on his screen. "Is there anything else?"

No, you egotistical tyrant-wannabe, Jules would have said if she had a choice, but she didn't say a word. Like it or not, Enrique was going to be her husband. She couldn't spend the rest of her life fantasizing about his younger brother. She had to make this relationship with Enrique work. Somehow.

"Perhaps we could go out," she suggested. "Just the two of us. On a date," she clarified, so he got the point.

"A date. What a sweet thought. But that's not possible with our upcoming nuptials." He placed his fingers on his keyboard. "Don't fret, my princess. We'll have plenty of time for dates after we're married."

Their first kiss would be at the wedding ceremony. Their first date would be on their honeymoon. The thought of her wedding night made her nauseous.

She straightened. "I'll leave you to your work."

Enrique didn't look up. He didn't mutter a goodbye. The only sound was his fingers tapping on the keyboard.

So much for meeting her halfway. She walked to the doorway.

Time to face facts. If not for the PR opportunity at the wedding, he'd send a proxy to stand in for him as groom at the ceremony.

Enrique was going to have to have a complete change of heart about her and the marriage for things to work. Even then she wondered if love was possible.

But Jules knew one thing. No longer would she feel any guilt for sailing. She'd tried to make things better, but Enrique had shut her down.

Nothing was going to stop her from having the time of her life with Alejandro and the crew. Nothing at all.

Alejandro couldn't focus. All he wanted to do was look at the picture of Julianna on the cover of this morning's newspaper. He stared at the black and white photograph.

No one would call this vibrant, warm woman an ice princess. The smile on her face reached all the way to her eyes. Those same eyes looked brighter, more alive.

Alejandro wondered if he—make that the sailing—had brought about those changes. Or had it been Enrique?

He hadn't seen the royal couple together in a few days. Enrique had skipped several dinners. Alejandro hadn't minded one bit. He enjoyed spending time and talking with Julianna even with his father and Brandt there. The more Alejandro learned about her, the more he wanted to know. He couldn't wait to see her tonight.

He glanced at the clock. Only two.

The thought of waiting until dinnertime to see Julianna didn't sit well. If he returned to the palace early, he could see if she wanted to spend time with Boots. She enjoyed playing with the kitten.

Alejandro liked playing with her. Or would, if he could…

He'd settle for being alone with her.

She might be on his boat every morning, but so was the rest of the crew. They couldn't talk openly or in a language he was comfortable speaking. She had to play a role, and so did he.

Leaving with her from the dock might raise suspicions, so she always headed back to the palace alone while he went off to the boatyard.

He looked at the clock again.

Why not take the afternoon off? He rarely did so.

After a quick talk with the boatyard foreman about what needed to be completed today, Alejandro returned to the palace. He found Boots sound asleep in the apartment. The kitten didn't stir when Alejandro picked him up. He went to Julianna's room and knocked on her door.

No answer.

Alejandro knocked again. Nothing.

Damn. He felt becalmed, as if all the wind had left his sails.

"Are you looking for Princess Julianna, sir?"

He turned to face one of the palace housekeepers with a feather duster in her hand. "Yes, Elena, I brought Boots by for a visit."

"Every day the princess tells me how much the kitten is growing." Elena's smile deepened the lines on her face. She'd been working at the palace for as long as he could remember. She used to sneak him food when he'd been grounded for some infraction or other. "The princess is right, sir."

Alejandro hadn't noticed any changes in the kitten. He glanced down. Boots may have gained some weight. But they'd only been living at the palace a little over a week. That didn't seem long enough for the kitten to grow.

Then again Alejandro felt as if he'd known Julianna for years not days. He felt so comfortable around her. "The princess has been sneaking Boots treats. That's probably why."

Elena nodded. "I saw the princess head down to the beach about a half an hour ago."

"Thank you."

Alejandro returned the kitten to the apartment and then headed to the beach.

Clear blue waves rolled to shore. Off in the distance, Julianna sat on the sand. She didn't seem concerned about her white Capri pants getting dirty.

A seabird soared overhead. The white wings contrasted against the blue sky. Another bird swooped and dipped its feet into the water, but the talons came up empty.

Julianna wasn't alone. Her bodyguard, Klaus, stood back. Far enough to give the princess privacy but close enough to react if needed. Alejandro acknowledged Klaus with a nod before approaching Julianna.

As he made his way toward Julianna, the wind caught in her hair. Strands went every which way. She pushed the hair off her face.

He would have liked to do that for her. He remembered how her hair felt, soft as silk, when strands had slipped out of her wig. But with Klaus behind them, Alejandro would have to keep his hands to himself. "Hello, Princess."

Julianna glanced up at him. The combination of the sky and her short-sleeved shirt accentuated the blueness of her eyes. She smiled, looking pleased to see him. "Hi."

"Enjoying the peace and quiet?"

"Yes. I was raised to fear being on my own, but I like it." She raised a handful of sand into the air and let the granules sift from her fingers. A hill of sand formed. "Especially out here by the water."

"I don't want to disturb you."

"You're not." She patted the spot next to her. "Sit."

He did.

Julianna carved into the sand until a rustic castle took shape.

"You need a bucket and a shovel to build a proper castle," he said.

She stuck out her tongue. "Who said anything about this being proper?"

He laughed. "My mistake."

"This castle is different. Special."

Her wistful tone intrigued him. "Tell me about it."

"In this castle, you're allowed to do whatever you choose. The only rule is to follow your heart."

Alejandro shoved his hands into the warm sand to help her dig a moat. "A good rule for any castle, proper or not."

She nodded. "Marriage is encouraged, but only if you've found your one true love."

His hands worked right next to hers. If he moved his left hand, he could touch her. The bodyguard would be none the wiser. Klaus couldn't see past their backs or hear what they were saying. Alejandro inched his hand closer. "Weddings must be rare."

One side of the castle collapsed. She knocked the rest away and started over. "Divorces are rarer."

A little farther... Anticipation built.

Alejandro wanted to touch her, to feel her soft skin against his once more, but doing so would be wrong. He moved his hand away from hers.

"That would be a different kind of castle." While she occupied herself making another mound of sand, Alejandro pulled out his phone, typed in a text message for Ortiz and hit Send. "What about royal duty?"

"Royalty does not exist."

That surprised him. Sailing aside, she seemed so keen on being a perfect princess and having little princes and princesses to keep the royal bloodline going.

"All people are created equal in my castle," she continued. "Whether male or female, wealthy or poor."

"Sounds like a nice place to live."

"It would be nice." Jules stared at the sand. "If I could build it."

The longing in her voice touched his heart. "La Isla de la Aurora isn't perfect, but it's an enjoyable place to live. Though you won't have the kind of freedom here as you'd have in your castle."

She laughed. "It's a fantasy. No place like that exists."

"True." But the freedom he craved did. Her marriage to Enrique would give Alejandro what he wanted. No more pressure or orders to fulfill his royal duties and obligations. Yet was marriage to his brother what Julianna wanted?

"Your castle may be a fantasy, but if that's your dream I don't understand why you want to marry Enrique."

"It's my duty."

"You have a duty to yourself."

She stopped digging in the sand. "I was raised to do whatever is best for Aliestle. I've always known a marriage would be arranged for me. That is the custom. And marrying Enrique is what's best for my family and my country."

She sounded genuine. Patriotic. Alejandro's respect for her grew knowing the sacrifice she was making. "You hold duty in a much higher esteem than I do. You're ready to dive headfirst into an arranged marriage knowing you're sacrificing your dreams. I can't wait to escape the demands of palace life. We are very different."

Her gaze met his. "You want what's best for your country."

"Yes."

"So do I. We're just going about it differently."

Julianna might think so, but he knew better. She was far more worthy than him. "My brother doesn't deserve you."

She shrugged. "He would say I don't deserve him the way I've been sneaking around behind his back."

Alejandro sprung to her defense. "You're helping the island. Once we place—"

"Win."

Her confidence pleased him. "Yes, win, I'll be able to draw more attention to the sailing and tourism here. But my father and brother..."

"They have different ideas."

"They have taken a completely different path," Alejandro said. "Enrique thinks my efforts are too radical. He believes a royal wedding will accomplish the same thing as my plans." Alejandro drew lines in the sand. He wanted to make his own mark somehow. "But I'm not going to let them stop me. I'll turn this economy around and show them."

"I'm certain you will."

He appreciated her confidence. He also liked how her blond hair shone beneath the afternoon sun. So beautiful.

One of the garden staff sprinted across the beach with his arms loaded with colorful buckets, shovels and other sand tools. He placed them on the sand. "Compliments of Ortiz, Your Highnesses."

Julianna's grin lit up her face. "Please thank him for me."

The young man bowed before walking away.

She shot Alejandro a suspicious glance. "You sent a text to Ortiz asking for all this."

"Sometimes being a prince comes in handy."

The gratitude sparkling in her eyes made it difficult for Alejandro to breathe. "Thank you."

He ignored the quickening of his pulse and handed her one of the shovels. "Let's see if we can build you a castle that will last."

CHAPTER TEN

THAT EVENING, Jules floated down the staircase on her way to dinner. Her sling-back heels felt more like ballet slippers as she descended and the hem of her cocktail dress swooshed above her knees. An afternoon with Alejandro had been exactly what she needed. Building a sand castle had been fun, but being with him had made her heart sing. He'd told her about growing up on the island and listened when she spoke. Something men in Aliestle, including her brothers, rarely did.

Jules wondered if he was in the dining room. Anticipation danced through her. She couldn't talk to him as freely as she had on the beach, but being with him during the meal would be enough.

Realization dawned. She had a huge crush on him.

She giggled like a schoolgirl. That would explain her growing affection toward him. Though crushing on her future brother-in-law probably broke every rule in the princess handbook.

Well, she never claimed to be perfect. Besides, she'd never let the crush go anywhere.

She entered the dining room to find Alejandro and Enrique involved in a heated discussion. As soon as they saw her they stopped talking.

She saw three place settings on the table large enough to seat twenty-four. "Is no one else joining us?"

Enrique kissed the top of her hand. He seemed big on that gesture. But he'd made an effort. She shouldn't complain.

"My father is dining with old friends," he said.

"Brandt is dining with new friends," Alejandro explained. "He took Klaus with him."

No doubt with a push from Alejandro. She would have to thank him later. "Lucky me. I'm a fortunate woman to be dining with two handsome princes."

Enrique stared down his nose at his brother. "Though one of us is handsomer than the other."

Alejandro half-laughed. "In your dreams, bro."

Jules wondered what Enrique would do or say. She hoped nothing.

He ignored his brother and escorted her to the table. That pleased Jules. But his stiff formality overshadowed how suave and debonair he looked tonight in his dark suit. If only he would relax and not always be so…on.

A footman pulled out her chair, and she sat. A server placed a napkin across her lap.

Alejandro took his seat in one easy, fluid motion. He was definitely relaxed. Still he looked stylish in his own right wearing a button-down shirt and black pants. Not too fancy, but not casual. Just…right.

Her admiring gaze met his and lingered. The temperature in the room seemed to increase. Her heart rate kicked up a notch.

His mouth quirked.

Oh, no. He must realize she was staring.

Jules looked away. She took a sip of ice water, but the liquid did nothing to cool her down.

Enrique sat at the head of the table in King Dario's place. The ornate chair befit the king with his confidence and majestic splendor better than his son, who didn't quite emanate the right amount of regality and power. In time that would come, Jules told herself. With more…maturity.

The light from the chandeliers dimmed. Lit candles in foot-tall crystal holders provided a warm glow. Platinum-rimmed china set atop silver chargers stood out on the crisp, white linen tablecloth. A stunning bouquet of roses and lilies in an elaborate silver vase added a light floral fragrance to the air.

A table fit for a future king. And queen, she reminded herself.

"Romantic," Alejandro said.

Very. She forced her gaze off him and onto Enrique. This would be the perfect opportunity for her fiancé to show Jules he was willing to make an effort with their relationship. Oh, she wanted to dine with Alejandro, but if Enrique held out an olive branch, or a red rose in this case, she would gladly accept what he offered.

"You know." Alejandro pushed back from the table. "I'm sure you both would prefer an intimate dinner for two."

He glanced at Jules. She didn't know whether to thank him for the suggestion or not. Her heart debated with her mind over the outcome each wanted. She looked at Enrique, holding her breath while waiting for his answer.

"That's generous of you, but the table is set for three. You're already seated," Enrique said. "Please stay and dine with us. I'd like to finish our discussion."

Relief mingled with disappointment. Jules would get to spend more time with Alejandro, but Enrique should have taken his brother up on his offer. If he'd listened to her in his office, he would have jumped at the opportunity for them to share a romantic dinner alone.

But he hadn't, and he didn't.

Was he that dense or was he trying to make some kind of point? Did he want a chaperone present so rumors couldn't start? No matter what the reason, his decision stung.

She stared into her water glass, not wanting to participate in the brothers' conversation about Alejandro's most recent real estate purchase—a run-down hotel on the opposite side of the island.

The servers brought out the first course. Gazpacho.

Jules waited for Enrique to take the first sip, then did so herself. The cold tomato-based soup was one of her favorites. This version had a little more spices than she was used to, but she liked the tanginess.

Enrique wiped his mouth with a napkin. "I heard the two of you were out on the beach building sand castles today."

Jules stirred uneasily. She didn't want to risk saying too much so took a sip of white wine. The Albarino tasted crisp and fresh, a perfect complement to the acidity in the soup.

"Yes, I bumped into Julianna on the beach," Alejandro said much to her relief. "She was having trouble making a sand castle with her hands so I asked Ortiz to send out some proper tools to use."

"Tools." Enrique snickered. "You mean, toys."

Alejandro didn't look at his brother. He picked up his wineglass and sipped, the same way she had.

Jules recognized the impatience in his eyes. He was trying hard not to say anything. She respected him for not losing his temper. It couldn't be easy letting so much roll off his back. Maybe she could make it a little easier on him this time. He'd come to her assistance by speaking up before, now she could return the favor.

"Having the buckets and tools delivered was a sweet gesture." The afternoon had been a pure delight. The time had flown by with all the talking and laughter. She'd shared her dreams with Alejandro, something she'd never done with anyone else. Not even Brandt.

But Alejandro made her feel safe and, like the people on this island, accepted. He seemed to know her so well—better than her own family. It was easy to open up around him. He'd become a good...friend.

"And much appreciated," she added for Alejandro's benefit. "I would have never been able to build my castle without those items. Especially one that..."

"Lasts." Alejandro raised his glass to her. "Now everyone can live..."

"Happily ever after," she said with a smile.

"You shouldn't have been out there so long." Enrique scowled, seemingly oblivious to how close she'd gotten to his brother. "You're sunburned."

Jules touched her face. "Where?"

He studied her as if she were flawed and should be returned to the store for a refund. "Your nose."

"Fair skin," she said.

"I didn't notice it when you were in my office," Enrique said.

Thank goodness this hadn't been the result of sailing. That would have been a total disaster. "I must not have put on enough sunscreen this afternoon."

"The sun is strong here," Alejandro said. "I should have reminded you."

Enrique nodded, one of the few times she'd seen him agree

with his brother. "Makeup will hide the redness. But if you get sunburned any worse, the wedding pictures will be ruined."

Jules knew he expected her to make him look good. She'd have to layer zinc oxide on her nose during the race. Not only would that protect her skin from the sun's harsh rays, but the thick, white lotion would help disguise her face better. "I'll be more careful when we're out tomorrow."

Enrique eyed her suspiciously. "Planning to build more sand castles?

A lot more careful. She swallowed. Another sunburn would be a dead giveaway she wasn't spending much of the daylight hours asleep in her bed. "No, but I plan to be outside. I was hoping you could join me."

Alejandro nodded his approval.

Enrique didn't notice. "I have meetings."

"You've heard about our afternoon, Enrique," Alejandro said. "Tell us about yours."

"It was more interesting than playing in the sand." Enrique described his day in minute detail.

Jules mouthed the word "thanks." She appreciated Alejandro shifting the focus off her and onto Enrique's favorite subject—himself.

Courses paired with wines to complement the flavors of the dish came and went. Enrique droned on with Alejandro chiming in with comments spoken and muttered under this breath.

The differences between the two brothers became more distinct. Enrique was so focused on himself and his role as crown prince and future king, nothing else mattered. She wasn't sure if he cared who sat at the table with him as long as someone was present to hear him speak.

But Alejandro wasn't perfect, either. His blatant disdain

for the responsibilities thrust upon him by his royal birth and his lack of respect for the monarchy made her question his priorities. She wished he wasn't so intent on turning his back on his duty.

Still she enjoyed his company. No one had ever made her feel so...good, capable, alive. Underneath his casual, sailor exterior, Jules saw a man—a prince—who loved his country with his whole heart, the same as her. But he'd been pushed aside due to the birth order and forced to live in Enrique's shadow. And for that, he blamed the monarchy and the rules that accompanied it.

Neither brother was Prince Charming, and that was okay. Such a prince was the thing of legends and fairy tales, like the expectation of her being the perfect princess. Being perfect wasn't possible.

Too bad no one else seemed to realize that.

Jules slumped in her chair, overcome by weariness and emotion. She straightened only to want to relax again. She focused on the food and tried to tune everything else out. It wasn't hard to do.

As soon as the servers cleared the dessert dishes, Jules wiped her mouth and folded her napkin. "Thank you for the pleasant company, gentlemen. I'm going to retire for the evening."

Both men rose as she stood.

"Good night, Julianna," Alejandro said.

"Sleep well," Enrique said. "I want to see my bride's pretty blue eyes sparkling tomorrow."

She moved away from her chair and waited for Enrique to offer to escort her, but his feet remained rooted in place.

Alejandro's gaze met hers in silent understanding. "Sweet dreams."

Jules acknowledged him with a smile. She didn't dare trust her voice. She wanted to have sweet dreams, but she feared the wrong brother would be starring in them. Not only tonight.

But every night for the rest of her life.

Alejandro's temper flared, but he maintained control.

For Julianna's sake.

She walked out of the dining room with her head high, but the disappointment in her eyes was unmistakable.

Alejandro remained standing until she disappeared from sight. He turned to Enrique. "Why didn't you escort Julianna to her room?"

Enrique had already sat. He motioned to the wine steward to refill his empty glass. "She said she was tired."

Anger burned in Alejandro's throat. "That's why you should have walked with her."

His brother's gaze sharpened. "Why do you care what I do with Julianna?"

Good question. Alejandro sat. He downed what remained in his wineglass. He wanted to say he felt indifferent about her, but he would be lying. He enjoyed being with her whether on the boat or here at the palace. But, rudeness aside, that didn't explain why his brother's treatment of her bothered him so much. "I wouldn't want her to leave the island."

That much was true.

"Never fear, little brother." Enrique snickered. "She can't leave."

"Can't?"

"If Julianna doesn't marry me, she'll be forced to marry a nobleman from Aliestle." His lip curled in disgust. "Any woman with half a brain would want out of that backward country."

Alejandro hated that she had only those two options. She deserved so much more. "Julianna has more than half a brain. She's very intelligent."

"That is why she doesn't mind how I treat her. She knows she must marry me," Enrique explained. "She'll put up with anything I do or say to keep from having to spend the rest of her life stuck in archaic Aliestle where men treat her worse."

Julianna had admitted as much to Alejandro, but that didn't excuse Enrique's behavior. "Her misfortunate situation gives you carte blanche to be ill-mannered and rude to her. How... noble."

Enrique snorted. "This is rich. Relationship advice from the man who goes through women as if they were selections on a menu."

"I may have never been involved in a serious relationship for an extended period of time, but I know women. Better, it seems, than you, bro," Alejandro said. "Julianna isn't an obedient automaton. She has feelings. Dreams. She deserves—"

"She deserves what I see fit to give her."

"Enrique..."

"As long as she obeys and provides me with heirs, be assured she'll have all she needs."

"She needs to be loved and accepted for who she is," Alejandro countered. "If you continue treating her poorly and taking advantage of her situation, you'll alienate her until she can't take it anymore. Is that what you want?"

Enrique leaned back in their father's chair. "You've come up with all this about her after spending an afternoon playing in the sand?"

"You've missed dinners this week," Alejandro replied. "You can learn a lot about a person over seven course meals."

Especially Julianna once she let her guard down and opened up.

"Come on, Alejandro," Enrique cajoled. "You don't care about Julianna. You want to make sure I marry."

"With your marriage comes my freedom from royal obligations."

That was the one thing Alejandro wanted more than anything. Somehow with his growing concerns over Julianna's future he'd lost sight of that. How had that happened?

Letting physical attraction and friendship get in the way of what he wanted made no sense. Julianna was hot, but she was also a princess. She might enjoy sailing, but she would never walk away from her title or her duty. Not for anything in the world. She wanted to help her brother, her country and her future children. The fact that she was willing to marry Enrique after his treatment of her spoke volumes about her priorities and was a not-so-subtle reminder…

As soon as the Med Cup finished and she married, Alejandro needed to say goodbye. She belonged with his brother, not him.

The truth stung. A sharp pain sliced into his heart. He reached for his wineglass, but it was empty.

"Treat her better." If Enrique did that, he would give Julianna what she wanted—more freedom, a throne and children.

Especially children.

I've always wanted to be a mother. Children will bring me great happiness and joy. I'll devote myself to being the best mother I can be. That will make me very happy.

Julianna's words echoed inside Alejandro's head. He wanted her to be happy. That wasn't like him. He'd never considered a woman's happiness beyond the moment at hand. He hadn't worried about how she felt after. That didn't make him much better than Enrique who wasn't considering Julianna's happiness at all.

The truth hit Alejandro like a sucker punch.

He didn't want to have anything in common with his brother.

"Do it for yourself, but for me and the island, too." And Julianna. "Heirs must be your first priority."

Enrique's forehead creased. "You want out of the line of succession that badly?"

"Yes." Alejandro did. But this wasn't about him anymore. Julianna needed babies to love. He was finally figuring out why this had become important to him.

Maybe if she were happy, he might be happy, too.

Alejandro tossed and turned all night. Images of Julianna flashed in his mind like photographs in a digital picture frame. Her long legs exposed by her short dress. Her playful smile on the beach. Her parted lips as she steered *La Rueca*. Her passion-filled eyes as she looked at him.

The last one was pure fantasy.

With a grimace, Alejandro tried to fall asleep for the fourth time. But he couldn't stop the slide show playing in his brain. He kept thinking about her, about wanting to be with her, about wanting to touch her.

Not only touch her.

Alejandro punched his pillow. Maybe if he was more comfortable...

Nothing helped. The harder he tried not to think about her, the more he did. Some of the thoughts were going to require a cold shower if he wasn't careful.

He didn't want to take that chance. He jumped out of bed, dressed for sailing and headed to the boat.

That would keep him...distracted.

La Rueca bobbed in the water. This past week, he'd gotten used to the activity of the crew preparing for a sail or cleaning up afterward. Today, she looked lonely tied to the dock with her running lights off and no crew around.

Better remedy that. Alejandro hopped aboard. The boat rocked with the incoming tides. The wind increased, jostling the lines that secured the boat to the dock. Metal clanked against metal. The waves picked up momentum, hitting the hull with more force.

He glanced at the horizon. Orange and red fingers of sunlight poked their way into the dark sky.

Red sky at night, sailor's delight. Red sky at morning, sailor's warning.

The nursery rhyme used to predict weather played in his head. A red sky might mean a more challenging sail this morning. That would be a good test for the crew with the race coming up.

Especially Julianna.

He had no doubt she'd rise to the challenge. The more situations she was exposed to, the more experience she could rely upon come race day. He'd have to make sure they came up with a good excuse to explain her absence during the three days of races. Sleeping in late wouldn't cut it.

An image of Julianna's twinkling blue eyes, her smiling mouth and her sunburned nose formed in his mind. At least that picture was more innocent than others he'd imagined.

He laughed.

"Care to let me in on the joke?"

Alejandro's heart lurched. He could recognize Julianna's melodic voice anywhere.

He whipped around to face the dock. The beam of light from her headlamp blinded him. He shielded his eyes. "You're here early."

She removed her headlamp, turned it off and shoved it in her pocket. "Couldn't sleep."

Her, too. Alejandro doubted for the same reasons as him.

Lust probably wasn't in the innocent princess's vocabulary. Not that anyone would mistake Julianna for anything but a too thin, gawky teen in those baggy clothes.

Anyone, except him.

He saw a beautiful woman who was willing to disguise herself to experience a taste of freedom. She'd grabbed the golden ring with both hands and wasn't going to let go until she had to. Julianna was…special. He'd never met a woman like her. If only…

Don't go there. He'd decided what he needed to do once she married. But she was here now.

Alejandro shifted his weight. He needed some distance. "I'm going to get the sails."

He stepped below deck without waiting for her to respond. He didn't want to care what she said.

A musty scent filled his nostrils. He'd always found familiarity in the smell, but he would have rather breathed in Julianna's sweet fragrance. Her usual scent when she wasn't pretending to be a teenage boy.

He shook his head. She'd gotten under his skin. He needed to get her out of there.

Alejandro felt a presence behind him. He didn't need to turn around to know who it was. "Julianna."

"I'll help you."

"Thanks." He faced her. The sails, equipment and slope of the hull didn't leave a lot of room. With her down here, the space felt more cramped. Or maybe he was more aware of her. "But I've got them."

"We'll have things ready for the crew faster with two pairs of hands."

He'd said something similar to her after their first sail together. That seemed like a lifetime ago.

The boat tilted to one side, as if hit by a mischievous wind or a powerful surge.

Julianna widened her stance.

The boat jolted and leaned the opposite way. Jules flew into Alejandro. He caught her, as he had in the foyer that first morning when she'd arrived at the palace.

He stared down at her face. Her body pressed against his. "The princess is in my arms yet again."

She was nothing like the woman he'd held then. Or maybe she'd taken off the mask and allowed her true self to show. Whichever, he didn't want to let her go. His arms tightened around her.

Attraction sizzled. A need burned deep within him. He fought against the ache with every ounce of self-control he had.

The race began tomorrow. The royal wedding would occur next week. She would be out of his life…

The same longing he felt filled Julianna's eyes. Her lips parted.

A sense of urgency drove him. He lowered his mouth to hers, capturing her lips with a kiss.

She gasped, but didn't back away.

His lips ran over hers, tasting and soaking up her sweetness. He knew he was crossing the line.

What he was doing was wrong on so many levels. But he didn't care. Maybe he'd care later, but at this moment the kiss consumed him. She consumed him.

Julianna arched toward him, her breasts pressing against

his chest, her arms entwining around his chest. She opened her mouth further, deepening the kiss. Her eagerness thrilled him. Blood roared through his veins. He pulled her closer, until he felt the rapid beat of her heart.

His tongue explored her mouth with abandon, burning with her sweet heat. Sensation pulsated wildly through him. Passion grew. Self-control slipped.

A soft moan escaped her throat. So sexy.

Alejandro wanted more. He wanted all of her. But he'd take whatever she was willing to give him.

He leaned back against the sail bags, pulling her with him. His hands cupped her round bottom. Fabric bunched. Too much clothing was in the way.

Alejandro slid his hand under her jacket and...

Voices sounded above them.

Julianna jerked away so fast she almost fell on her butt. She regained her balance and touched her hand to her mouth. "I-I'm sorry. I shouldn't have..."

Her red cheeks and ragged breathing made her look so turned-on and sexy, but Alejandro couldn't pretend he didn't hear the regret in her voice. He tried to regain control. Not easy with his body on fire and aching for more kisses. More Julianna.

But she was right. They shouldn't have done this.

"I'm the one who kissed you." He knew better, but when he was around her he couldn't think straight. "I apologize."

She stared down her nose at him. "I kissed you back."

Always the princess even when passion filled her eyes, a flush stained her neck and cheeks and her lips were swollen. Alejandro bit back a smile. She would be upset if he thought this was funny.

"Alejandro?" Phillipe yelled.

"Ju—J.V. is helping me with the sails." Alejandro needed to calm down and cool off. Or they would blow her cover. But he couldn't stop thinking how perfect her lips felt against his. He'd kissed many women, but no kiss had ever felt like this. "Be up in a minute," he added, not wanting anyone to come down here.

"What now?" she asked.

More kisses. That was what he wanted. But Julianna wasn't some woman he'd met at a club or on the beach or at a sailing regatta. She was Enrique's future wife and Alejandro's ticket out of the royal life he abhorred. Even if his brother was out of the picture, she wasn't a fling. He wasn't looking to get serious with anyone.

Alejandro had too much going on with his boat business, properties and plans for the island to get involved in a serious relationship with any woman. Let alone with a princess.

He wanted to be freed from his princely duties, not be caught up trying to live up to her expectations. She would want him to remain a prince. She would challenge him to be more and embrace his birthright. He'd seen her act that way with Brandt. That behavior and pressure didn't appeal to Alejandro in the slightest. He'd spent too much of his life justifying himself and his actions. Continuing on that path would be hell on earth.

Julianna was the last woman Alejandro should want to be with. She was a perfect princess, with a royal heart and soul. Duty and country motivated her. She would use her role on La Isla de la Aurora to make a difference in Aliestle. He would never be able to make a princess like her happy. He wouldn't want to try. Even if he liked kissing her.

And wanted to kiss her again.

So what now?

"We sail," he answered.

CHAPTER ELEVEN

THREE HOURS OF sailing with high winds and waves kept Jules's mind off Alejandro's kisses. Thank goodness she'd needed to focus on steering the boat, or she would have been sighing, staring and swooning.

Pathetic.

But she couldn't help herself. The way Alejandro made her feel overwhelmed Jules. Which was why she'd hurried up the dock back toward safety without a word as soon as the crew was ready to leave.

She may have apologized, but it wasn't because kissing Alejandro had felt wrong. Kissing him had felt oh-so-right. As if that was what she should be doing today, tomorrow and every day for the rest of her life. That was why she'd been sorry. Feeling that way while engaged to Enrique wasn't fair to either man.

She jogged through the park, eager to return to the palace and the sanctuary of her room. The suite provided all she needed—a means to escape and a lovely view from the windows. Enrique had been right about that. The pretty, colorful blossoms soothed her. She could use some soothing now.

Enrique.

She wove her way through the rocks in the grotto, passed through the wrought-iron gate and locked it behind her.

She didn't want to think about her fiancé now.

Not with the effects of Alejandro's kisses lingering.

The tunnel seemed darker and longer, and the smell of moisture and mold more pronounced. Each of her nerve endings seemed heightened in sensitivity. Her lips still tingled. The ache deep inside her that had started the moment his lips captured hers had grown exponentially since then.

Alejandro stirred something inside her. She was torn by her desire of wanting more and her guilt of knowing better.

Was this what passion felt like?

If so, the feeling frightened her even as it thrilled her. Allowing herself to be carried away by the strong current of emotion would be stupid. She had to be rational about this.

He hadn't proclaimed his undying love and affection. He'd simply kissed her until she couldn't think straight. He'd made her feel so special, like the only woman in the world.

Would that be the only time she ever felt like that? Her heart hoped not.

"Julianna."

The sound of Alejandro's voice sent a shiver of pleasure down her spine, but brought a twinge of uncertainty, too. She stopped walking. "I thought you were going to the boatyard."

He caught up to her. The beam from his flashlight pointed at the dirt floor. "I wanted…"

You. She held her breath.

"…to talk with you," he finished.

Disappointment squeezed her heart even though she knew his wanting her was as likely as her living happily ever after.

Alejandro reached forward and tilted her headlamp so the light shone up. "We never got a chance to talk on the boat."

Her uncertainty increased three-fold. "A hard day of sailing. We needed to focus."

"You didn't smile much."

"I had a lot on my mind." Like now. She started walking. "I should get back to the palace."

Being so close to him sent her out-of-whack emotions spiraling into the danger zone. His scent made her want to lean in closer for another sniff. His warmth made her want to seek shelter in his arms. And his lips made her want to forget what her future held.

He fell into step next to her, his flashlight swinging at his side. "Tell me what's on your mind."

"You mean on the boat?"

"And now."

Jules didn't know where to start. She took a deep breath. It didn't help.

"Julianna," he prompted.

"You. You were…are…on my mind." There, she'd said it. Even though she figured Alejandro had guessed as much.

"You've been on my mind, too. We're equal."

Not even close. Jules had never felt this way about any man, not even Christian, whom she believed at the time she loved. Of course, she'd been sixteen then.

Not that she was in love with Alejandro. Except…

She wanted to be with him on the boat, off the boat, all the time. She wanted to sneak out of the palace for good and sail off into the sunset with him. And Boots. They wouldn't have to sail—they could walk, run, drive or fly. She wasn't particular on the mode of transportation as long as they were together. The thought of being without Alejandro…

What was she thinking?

Being with him was impossible. What she felt now was a crush. The new sensations he had awakened with his kiss were causing her to feel this way.

Not...love.

"About this morning below deck," Alejandro said.

"It's okay." Jules didn't dare look at him. No one could ever know how much his kisses had affected her. "Each time I exit this tunnel, I enter a whole new world full of wonderful, but forbidden things. Freedom. Sailing. Kissing."

"You've never—"

"I've been kissed." The surprise in his voice made her cheeks grow hot. Jules was embarrassed enough by letting a crush get so out of control. She wasn't about to tell him she could count on one hand the number of times she'd been kissed. "But I'm not...as experienced as you."

"I couldn't tell."

Well, she *could* tell *he* was an expert kisser. That kind of expertise took...practice.

Alejandro has a horrible reputation. Worse, his taste in women is far from discriminating. Royalty, commoner, palace staff, it doesn't matter.

Yvette's words were the cold dose of reality Jules needed. She was probably one in a long line of women who'd come before. A part of her—okay, her heart—didn't want to believe that, but she'd allowed this to go way further than it should. Romanticizing his kisses made no sense. "Kissing you was a nice addition to my adventure."

"Adventure?"

She nodded. "Escaping the palace, wearing a disguise and sailing on *La Rueca*'s crew. It's all been a grand adventure, a fantasy I've been able to experience for a brief time, but I know it's not...real."

"The sailing has been real. Kissing you was—"

"Not real." If the kisses weren't real, neither were her feelings. "I mean, we kissed. But we were caught up in the moment. Two consenting adults in each other's arms. The opportunity presented itself. A kiss was bound to happen."

"Perhaps we should find out if the kisses are real or not."

Jules's gaze flew up to meet his.

His intense gaze seemed to penetrate all the way to her soul. Her breath caught in her throat. She'd never felt so exposed, so naked before.

A chill rushed through her. Goose bumps prickled her skin. "We...can't."

"Why not?"

Her heart slammed against her chest. Logically she knew what she should say, but those words would contradict what her heart and her lips wanted her to do. "This can't go anywhere."

Alejandro traced her jawline with his fingertip. "I know."

His light-as-a-feather touch tantalized. Teased. Tempted. "I'm marrying Enrique."

"I know that, too." Alejandro's rich voice seeped into her, filling all the empty places with warmth. "The race begins tomorrow. This may be our last opportunity to be alone."

Jules's chest tightened. "This has to be the last time."

He nodded and lowered his hand from her face. "That would be for the best."

At least he agreed. Still, nerves gripped her. "But I..."

Silence hung between them, but instead of pushing them apart Alejandro drew closer. "Your move, Princess."

Her move. Jules had never been in this position before,

but she knew what she had to do. She raised her chin and pressed her lips against his. Hard.

A mistake? Probably.

But she wanted—needed—to kiss him one more time. She wanted to remember what his kiss felt like and how he made her feel.

Jules wrapped her arms around him and leaned in close. She tasted a mix of salt and heat. So delicious. She wanted to remember every detail, each texture.

As she deepened the kiss, sparks shot through her.

Okay, this kiss was real. She'd give him that.

The kiss made her quiver with pleasure and burn with desire.

But Jules didn't know if the way she felt was real or not. She didn't care. She just wanted to keep kissing him.

Because once she finished, Jules knew she would never kiss Alejandro again.

Tensions ran high the next morning. The first day of the Med Cup had arrived. Alejandro couldn't believe how calm and cool Julianna was. She impressed the entire crew with her composure. She steered like a pro. The entire team worked together. The sweat and hard work enabled *La Rueca* to win their first race. Alejandro's goal was one step closer.

And so was saying goodbye to Julianna.

He ignored the knot in his gut.

His father excused him from eating dinner at the palace that night. But Alejandro didn't feel like celebrating as he sat at a tapas bar with the crew so he headed back to the palace.

Julianna.

She should have been with the crew tonight. With him.

Alejandro wanted to take her in his arms and kiss her until she begged him to stop or give her more. But he couldn't.

This has to be the last time.

He'd agreed. Logically that made the most sense, but the way he felt about her didn't make sense at all.

The kitten was waiting when Alejandro entered the apartment. "Hey, Boots."

The kitten meowed.

Alejandro got an idea. "Want to go see Julianna?"

Another meow.

That was good enough for him. He swooped up the cat and went to Julianna's room.

In the hallway, Yvette sat on a chair outside the door and read. She lowered her book. "Are you here to see Princess Julianna, sir?"

"Yes." He showed her the kitten. "Boots wants to see her."

As if on cue, the cat meowed.

"I'm sorry, sir. The princess is sleeping."

Alejandro looked around. No one else was in the hallway. He smiled. "Please tell her I'm here."

"I'm sorry, sir," Yvette repeated with a hint of disapproval this time. "Princess Julianna has an upset stomach and asked not to be disturbed until morning. Would you like me to tell her you and Boots paid a visit?"

"No, thanks. I'll see her tomorrow." Disappointment settled over the center of his chest. Alejandro wanted to see her now. "Good night."

He returned to his apartment feeling out of sorts. He played with Boots using the laser pointer, but the kitten had more fun.

The entire time, Alejandro couldn't stop thinking about

Julianna. The passion in her eyes when they kissed. The exhilaration on her face during the race.

He had to see her for a minute. Yvette wasn't about to let him pass, but he knew another way.

With a flashlight in hand, Alejandro used the secret door in his apartment to enter the tunnels. He wove his way around until he reached the staircase leading to Julianna's room. Each step brought him closer to her. He stood on the landing and pulled the latch. The secret door opened.

Alejandro had been here before to leave her disguise and other gear she needed. He'd never thought twice about entering her closet.

But this time, he hesitated.

This can't go anywhere.

I know.

I'm marrying Enrique.

I know that, too.

His conversation with Julianna echoed through his head. Yes, he wanted to see her. Hell, he wanted to kiss her.

But Julianna didn't want that.

I'm marrying Enrique.

Alejandro might want to see her, but he couldn't. She was determined to marry his brother. He wasn't going to do something that both he and Julianna might regret. He knew better than that.

Alejandro closed the secret door.

This was for the...best.

The morning of the race, Julianna had instructed Yvette to tell anyone who came to the door she was suffering from a stomach virus. No one, especially Enrique, would want any part of that.

Hours later, she stood with her hands on the wheel, nervous and excited. Adrenaline coursed through her veins.

They were halfway through the course, running ahead of their closest competitor.

The tension and noise level had increased from yesterday's match. The winds and waves had, too. Both had turned stronger over the last twenty-four hours. That made her job harder.

Water splashed into the cockpit. A foul weather suit kept her dry. Each member of the crew had a responsibility and knew what to do. Hers was to steer the boat. She focused her attention on the direction the boat sailed. She couldn't think about anything else.

Or anyone else.

But Jules knew where Alejandro had been since the boat had left the dock. Her gaze was automatically drawn to him at midbow. Water dripped from his hair and his foul weather gear. He looked sexy and in his element. The sheer joy on his face tugged on her heart and her dreams.

One more day of racing. A week until her wedding. And it would be all over.

A sense of loss assailed her. She ignored it. Now wasn't the time.

Each of the crew worked to keep the *La Rueca* sailing as fast as she could with adjustments to the sails. Others sat aft, trying to keep the weight on the stern.

The boat sailed downwind, surfing the waves that got bigger by the minute. The up and down motion of the boat reminded her of a thrilling roller coaster ride. More than once her stomach ended up in her throat, but she didn't mind one bit.

Jules tightened her grip on the wheel. She needed to hold

a steady course, but didn't want to plow into a wave and risk the possibility of broaching.

Water hit her face and dripped down her cheeks. She tasted salt on her lips and in her mouth.

This was what she dreamed about. Freedom in its purest form.

She had no regrets. Well, one. Alejandro. But that wasn't as much a regret as a what-might-have-been. Kissing him again had left a wound on her heart. One she hoped would heal in time.

"*Dragon Rider*'s broached," Sam yelled from the midsection of the bow.

Jules could barely hear him, but she'd heard enough. Their competitor had heeled too far to one side and was lying broadside. Her stomach clenched. She hoped the crew were tied in. It would be easy to capsize or break the mast in these waves.

Everyone searched for the boat. The sails and waves got in the way. The mast must be in the water or someone would see it.

"Does it look like they are going to recover?" Alejandro's voice sounded strained.

"I see them," Sam shouted.

"Me, too," Mike yelled. "They are knocked down."

Jules inhaled sharply, but held the course.

"Has the boat righted itself?" Phillipe, who was nearest to her, asked.

"No," Mike said.

The answer sent a chill down Jules's spine.

"Man overboard," a voice called over the radio.

"Trimming up for beam reaching," she said without a moment of hesitation.

Alejandro jumped off the deck and grabbed the radio. "*La Rueca* is responding."

The energy level tripled. A sailor was in the water. A life was at stake. The race no longer mattered. Every able-bodied vessel was required to offer assistance.

He looked at Jules. Confidence and affection shone in his eyes. "You can do this."

She nodded once.

As she turned the boat from the starboard side, the mainsail and jib trimmers went to work. No one wanted to waste any time, but they had to be careful. They didn't want to broach as well.

"Get a fix on the person in the water," she ordered Phillipe. With the race on hold, he needed another job. Jules needed to make sure she didn't run the sailor over.

"I've got the beacon," Alejandro said, moving toward the stern.

She knew he was clipped in, but she bit her lip, worried about his safety out there. And the other boat. They'd been fighting the waves all day. *If he went overboard...*

Don't think. Just steer.

"I see him," Mike yelled.

Jules heard the collective sigh of relief, but the sailor wasn't safe yet.

Alejandro threw the overboard buoy toward the sailor in the water. The buoy was state of the art with a lighted pole, life ring, flotation jacket and location beacon.

"Sailor has the beacon," Phillipe said. "You've sailed past him on the aft side."

"Coming about," she ordered. "Trim up."

Jules gave the second order even though it wasn't necessary. They knew what to do. She sailed over the waves. Tacking back, she guided the boat toward the buoy.

Alejandro stood on the bow, clipped into the jackline. Sam was nearby, too. They looked out at the water. Alejandro was too far away for her to hear him so he directed her with hand signals.

She slowed down, luffing leeward of the sailor in the water. The wind against the loose sails sounded like thunder. The crew shouted. The noise level kept rising. She must be getting closer.

Jules focused, pushing the boat to its limits to reach the sailor as quickly as possible.

A helicopter flew overhead.

Mike used a recovery hook to grab the buoy's line, pulling the buoy and the person toward them. Cody grabbed the buoy pole and dragged it back toward the stern.

"The other boat's righted," he said.

Thank goodness, but she couldn't celebrate yet. She kept the sails luffing so the boat wouldn't drift into the person bobbing in the water. Mike and Phillipe hauled the man onboard. His face was pale, but he looked relieved to be aboard. Water poured from his foul weather gear.

"We've got your sailor," Alejandro radioed. "But due to the weather conditions an exchange isn't possible."

"We're dropping out to recover," the voice replied.

Bummer, Jules thought. But two other boats were still racing. Her questioning gaze sought Alejandro's. He smiled at her, sending her heart into a pirouette.

"We'll keep going," he said over the radio.

"Thanks and good luck," the voice replied. "Tell your newest crew member to enjoy the ride."

"Will do," Alejandro said. "The extra weight will come in handy with these waves."

The guy on the radio laughed.

"Time to finish the race," Alejandro announced to the crew.

Everyone took his position with a cheer.

"We can win this." The confidence in Alejandro's voice kept her focused. "J.V."

"Coming about," she said.

It was as if the rescue had never happened. If not for their extra passenger it might have all been a dream.

But as they sailed toward the finish line, Jules knew it was real. Like Alejandro's kisses.

The bow crossed the finish line.

The crew cheered. Jules laughed.

They'd won.

Won!

La Rueca would be in the finals tomorrow.

Excitement rocketed through her. She stared at Alejandro. A grin lit up his face. So handsome. So dear to her heart.

He gave her a high-five. She would have preferred a hug, but being able to touch him was enough. For now.

"I've never seen anyone sail like you did today," he said. "Awe-inspiring."

"You're the best, J.V.," Sam said.

"Thanks for the ride." The sailor they'd rescued, Robert, shook her hand. "We underestimated you, kid. You're one helluva a helmsman."

Jules smiled, but didn't say anything. Her voice would give her away. She couldn't fake a deep tone now. Not with delighted joy exploding like fireworks in her chest.

The boat docked. People were waiting for them. A medical crew stood in front of the crowd.

"Looks like you'll need a checkup," Alejandro said to their guest.

Robert had changed into spare dry clothes down below. "I'd rather hit the bar and wait for my boat to arrive."

"Maybe there's a pretty doc or nurse to keep you company, mate," Sam said.

"One can hope." Robert saluted Jules and the rest of the crew. "Thanks again. Good race, but watch out for us next year."

Alejandro laughed. "We'll have our eyes open looking back at you the entire way."

Robert grinned wryly. "With this kid driving, you might be."

As he left with the medical crew, people pushed forward.

"Look at all these fans, mates," Sam said. "Smile. The media is here, too."

Jules's heart slammed against her chest. A horrible sense of dread replaced the wonderfulness of the moment. The press took pictures, asked questions, followed up.

So not good.

She ducked her head and pulled her cap lower.

"You may find yourself a pretty girl out of this, J.V.," Sam teased with a slap on Jules's back.

Jules forced a smile. Anything would be better than the truth coming out.

"Don't worry," Alejandro whispered so only she could hear.

She appreciated his words, but she was worried. Terrified. Her future, her country's future and her children's future were all at stake. The press circled like a school of hungry piranhas. She swallowed around the spinnaker-size lump in her throat.

The sea of people standing on the dock grew larger. Some held cameras. A few shouted questions in a variety of languages: Spanish, German, French, Italian and English. She understood most of the questions, but she pretended not to hear them.

Her insides trembled, but she maintained her composure. A teenage boy would relish the attention after winning a race, not run away. Still her feet were itching to take off.

Who was she kidding?

If she could jump into the water and swim away without drawing attention to herself, she would.

"We need to get you out of here," Alejandro whispered.

"I can swim."

"So can the sharks." He tried to lead her away from the mob, but the crowd pushed closer. "It'll be okay."

She clung to his words even though her doubts multiplied by the seconds. Camera flashes blinded her. Reporters shoved microphones and digital recorders in her face. Arms reached for her.

Jules cringed. Bodyguards never let crowds get so close. She wasn't used to being touched like this. Her anxiety level spiraled.

Someone touched her cap.

"Please don't." She held it on her head with both hands. "Alejandro."

He tried to help her. "Leave the kid alone."

Another person grabbed the cap off her head. The wig went with it, leaving her wearing a nylon cap.

People gasped. A horrible silence fell over the crowd.

"It's a girl," a man shouted.

"A woman," another yelled.

"Hey," a woman said. "Isn't that the princess who's going to marry Crown Prince Enrique?"

The air rushed from her lungs. Her worst nightmare was coming true. Everyone would know her true identity now. Including Enrique and her father.

Her heart and her head felt as if they might explode.

Hundreds of people surrounded her, but she'd never felt so alone. And she had only herself to blame.

Life as she knew it was over.

Had it been worth it?

She glanced at Alejandro. He'd removed his sunglasses. The warmth in his eyes drove her goose bumps away.

"Do not worry," he said softly. "I'm here. You won't have to face this alone."

His words gave her the strength she needed. She knew sailing with Alejandro had been worth it. No matter what the consequences.

Shoulders back. Chin up. Smile.

Jules fell back into the training that had been ingrained in her since she was a little girl. She removed the plastic cap hiding her blond hair.

Goodbye J.V., hello Princess Julianna.

She answered the questions being shouted at her. Alejandro stood next to her the entire time. He downplayed the situation by answering questions as well. She appreciated his efforts. The rest of the crew stayed by her, too, though they looked confused. Phillipe's brows furrowed. Mike's mouth gaped. Cody scratched his head. Sam stared at her as if she were a ghost.

But Alejandro's presence gave her strength. Courage.

A good thing, too. When her father and her fiancé discovered what Jules had done, she was going to need all that and more.

CHAPTER TWELVE

BACK AT THE PALACE, Jules couldn't stop shaking. Not even a hot shower helped. She put on a conservative pink dress, befitting a princess and future queen. With trembling hands, she applied makeup and styled her hair in an updo.

What was her father going to say? Do about her disobedience?

Yvette fastened a strand of pearls around Jules's neck. "You look like a proper princess, ma'am."

She hadn't been acting like one. "Thank you."

A knock sounded on her door. Jules's heart pounded in her ears. She wasn't ready.

Yvette answered the door. "It's Prince Brandt, ma'am. He's here to escort you to the sitting room."

As soon as Jules stepped into the hallway, her brother hugged her. "Father requests your presence."

She stepped out of Brandt's embrace. "Yvette said he arrived like a bull from Pamplona. Snorts and all."

"I've never seen him so angry." The concern in Brandt's voice matched her own. "I'm worried what he'll do."

She wanted to ease Brandt's concern even though she was apprehensive, too. "Don't worry. Father will be...fair."

At least she hoped so.

"I screwed up." Brandt hung his head. "Klaus is beside himself for leaving you alone so much."

Jules touched her brother's shoulder. Love for him filled her heart. "Neither of you are to blame for this."

Only her.

She descended the stairs, mindful of each step so she didn't stumble.

"But if I hadn't been partying so much—"

"Please, Brandt." Straightening, Jules composed herself. She couldn't duck for cover now. "Don't get in the middle of this."

It would be bad enough without dragging him or Alejandro into this.

Alejandro.

His name brought a welcome rush of warmth through her cold body. She'd survived the onslaught of questions on the dock with him at her side. If she had the same help tonight…

No, that was too much to ask of him. Her father was too rich, too powerful. He could destroy everything Alejandro worked so hard to build.

The sitting room loomed in front of her like a black hole. She entered with Brandt at her side.

A tense silence filled the air. Alejandro, Enrique, King Dario and her father rose from their seats.

Compassion filled Alejandro's eyes. He'd shaved, removed his earring and pulled his hair away from his face and secured it at his nape. He looked regal and princely in his suit, dress shirt, tie and leather shoes. Respectable. Her heart squeezed tight. She missed the pirate.

Enrique had dressed similarly. The two men had never

looked as much like brothers as tonight. Enrique glared at Alejandro with accusation and a frown on his lips.

She hated knowing she would push the two men farther apart.

Concern clouded King Dario's face. He pressed his lips together and clasped his hands behind his back. Sweat beaded on his brow.

Her father's gaze burned with fury. His lips thinned with anger. "How dare you disobey me, Julianna Louise Marie!"

Shoulders back. Chin up.

No way could she smile. Jules looked him in the eyes. She wanted to be strong for Brandt's and Alejandro's sake, as much as her own. "I apologize for my actions, sir. I didn't mean to cause any trouble."

"Trouble?" Alaric's features hardened. "You have brought disrepute onto our family and country. Pictures of you looking windswept and wild, hardly the way a princess should appear in public, are everywhere. Papers, television, the Internet."

Jules felt everyone's eyes on her, especially Alejandro's. She tried not to cower, but she'd never seen her father so full of rage.

Enrique sneered. "You looked like a boy."

"It was a disguise," she explained, cutting him with a quick glance.

"The fact you needed a disguise should have been the first sign this was a mistake." King Dario patted his forehead with his handkerchief. "You're the future queen of La Isla de la Aurora, Julianna. This kind of behavior is unacceptable."

"I'll say." Enrique glowered at her. "Your father and I told you not to sail. You're supposed to be a conservative princess. Not a…wild child."

Her temper rose. "I wasn't—"

"You were." Her father's voice boomed like a thunderstorm in November. "I watched a tape of the race on the flight. You not only disobeyed me but put yourself in danger. You could have been killed sailing the way you did today."

Heat stole into her face. Her breath burned in her throat.

"Jules is fine, Father. She saved a sailor's life," Brandt said bravely. He'd never stood up to their father before and she was proud he'd found the courage to do that. "It's my fault Klaus wasn't with Jules. I partied too much, and he was with me."

Her muscles tensed, nervous what her father would say.

"This has nothing to do with you, Brandt," Alaric replied sharply. "Your sister knew what I expected of her. She must accept the consequences."

Dread shuddered through her. Jules knew what her punishment would be—to spend the rest of her life in Aliestle.

She glanced at Alejandro. Her heart cried. She would never see him again.

"King Alaric." Alejandro stepped forward. "I am Prince Alejandro Cierzo de Amanecer. King Dario's second son."

"You mean, the spare." King Alaric's curt voice lashed out. "You're the idiot who put my daughter's life in danger."

Jules drew in a sharp breath at the insult. She couldn't stand the thought of her father taking out his anger on Alejandro.

"Yes, but Julianna's safety is of the utmost concern to me, Your Majesty." The regal air emanating from him made him seem more like a future king than second in line for the throne. "I take full responsibility for what's happened. Julianna disobeying you was one hundred percent my fault. I took her sailing. I asked her to be part of my crew and race in the Med Cup. I'm the one who should be punished, not her."

Jules stared at Alejandro, full of pride and…love.
I love him.

Love was the only explanation for her feelings, ones that went far deeper than friendship and future familial bonds. She couldn't stop thinking about the way he looked at her, kissed her, stood by her side and wanted to take the blame for all of this.

Alejandro had to have feelings for her. Otherwise why would he be standing up for her now? Her heart wanted her to go to him, but too many things needed to be resolved first.

Jules couldn't allow Alejandro to take the blame. She hadn't been a dutiful princess. She'd disobeyed. She needed to stand up and be accountable for her actions, not let a wonderful, giving man suffer consequences meant for her.

Joy provided strength. Love gave her courage.

Alejandro embraced his role as a prince tonight to protect her. She needed to embrace her role as a black sheep to accept her punishment and protect him.

"Thank you, Alejandro." An unfamiliar sense of peace rested in her heart. "But I can't allow you take the blame for my actions."

His eyes implored her. "It's my blame to take."

Her heart melted. She allowed her gaze to linger, longer than what was considered proper. She loved the gold flecks and the concern she saw in his brown eyes. "No."

"Yes," Enrique countered. "All this is Alejandro's fault, King Alaric."

"It's not. I knew what I was getting myself into, Father." Jules stared up at her father, who towered over her with a face full of contempt. "I was so desperate for a taste of freedom, I allowed my desire to override everything else. Alejandro's not to blame. It's my fault. But I have no regrets over what I have done."

The affection and pride in Alejandro's eyes made her heart want to dance and sing. Whatever consequence she faced would be worth it. If she hadn't disobeyed, she would never have gotten to know him, kiss him and fall in love with him.

"Your stepmother worked so hard to turn you into a proper Aliestlian princess." Her father spoke with disdain. "But you have always been too much like your mother."

Jules smiled. "Thank you, Father."

His nostrils flared. "It isn't a compliment."

Her smile didn't waver. She would cherish the words no matter what fate had in store for her. "It is to me, sir."

The wrinkles on her father's forehead deepened. He stared at her with a look of bewilderment then turned his attention to King Dario. "I trusted you with my most prized possession. You promised she would be safe, yet you allowed this to happen."

"We had no idea she was sailing." King Dario sounded contrite.

"Her well-being is our number one priority," Enrique added.

Jules hated how they spoke as if she wasn't present. "I'm right here, gentlemen."

Alaric ignored her. "If that's the case, how come no one noticed she was missing from the palace? Not even her fiancé?"

"I've been busy with work and wedding plans," Enrique answered hastily.

Alaric's lips snarled. "Wedding plans are women's work."

Enrique flinched.

"My brother had no idea because he works nonstop as

crown prince. He would have no reason to suspect anything was amiss because Julianna didn't allow the sailing to affect her obligations as his fiancée," Alejandro explained. "There was no harm done."

"No harm?" Her father's ruddy complexion reddened more. "Her blatant disobedience has thrown Aliestle into chaos. A small feminist movement has taken her participation in the race and run with it. They are holding rallies across the land and protesting for equal rights. It's disgusting."

No, it was progress. The kind of change Jules wanted to influence in her country. Satisfaction flowed through her.

Approval gleamed in Alejandro's eyes. He knew what this meant to her.

She smiled at him.

He smiled back.

"This situation is completely out of hand and unacceptable," Alaric announced. "I'm canceling the marriage contract."

Panic clawed into her heart. Jules didn't want to return to Aliestle. She wanted to stay on the island with Alejandro.

What now? Did she dare defy her father again?

As the king's words echoed through the room, Alejandro stared at Julianna. The distress on her face twisted his insides.

Emotions clamored in his heart, demanding to be acknowledged. Not respect or attraction or friendship. Deep feelings. Intense feelings. Ones that scared him.

Not love. He knew better than to fall in love. This had to be…something else.

Still his hand itched to reach out to take hold of Julianna.

He wanted to protect her from the fallout and make everything better.

Brandt cleared his throat. "Father, please—"

"This does not concern you," Alaric said through clenched teeth.

But it concerned Alejandro. He wanted to punch King Alaric in the nose and free her from this tyranny. But that wasn't what Julianna wanted him to do. And it certainly wouldn't help her with her father. In fact, acting out the fury balling in his gut would cause more trouble for his own family.

Alejandro's frustration rose.

If she returned to Aliestle, her sense of duty would lead her to marry whatever nobleman her father picked out.

Alejandro couldn't allow that to happen. She had to stay on the island. No matter what. "Your Majesty, if I may…"

King Alaric glared at him. "Haven't you done enough already?"

"Sire." The old-fashioned word felt weird coming off Alejandro's tongue, but perhaps it would resonate with the misguided and medieval King Alaric. "Julianna needs to remain on La Isla de la Aurora."

"Why?" Scorn laced King Alaric's word.

"Because I want to stay here, Father," Julianna said.

She smiled softly at Alejandro.

His heart turned over. And that hurt like hell because to do the right thing, he had to let her go.

"The people are wild about her, sire." Alejandro had been in his brother's shadow his entire life, but this time he belonged there. Only Enrique could give Julianna the kind of life she was raised for, the kind of life she wanted. She wanted to use her position as the crown prince's wife to influence change and give her people a better future. She could accomplish all she desired and more as the future queen. "Julianna has touched their hearts with her compassion and friendliness. They've embraced her as their princess, and one day they'll love her as their queen."

"My daughter was raised to be a queen," Alaric admitted.

"Everyone can tell she has received the finest training." Alejandro fought the desire to claim her for himself. But too much was at stake. He could never give Julianna what she wanted and make her happy, even if she wished to be with him. He swallowed around the lump of emotion in his throat. He had to push aside his own desire and do what was best for her. "You say her actions have caused chaos, sire. But her countrywomen see someone they can relate to and rally around. A respected and beloved leader. As the future queen of La Isla de la Aurora, Julianna will be able to do that for women not only in Aliestle and here on the island, but all over the world."

"Please consider my youngest son's words." Appreciation gleamed in Dario's eyes. "Alejandro may not be a conventional prince, but he is wise for his age and speaks the truth."

That was the first compliment his father had ever given him. And the words couldn't have come at a better time.

"Julianna has enchanted the entire island," Enrique added. "And all of us."

Especially Alejandro. But his feelings didn't matter. Julianna would get what she wanted and by default, so would he. He wanted freedom from the monarchy, not a princess bride who dreamed of happily ever afters.

His thoughts tasted like ashes in his mouth. But he had to be realistic. He didn't want to be a prince. He avoided romantic entanglements like the plague. It would...never work.

King Alaric looked at each one of them, but his assessing gaze lingered on Alejandro. "So it seems."

"I stand by the marriage contract," Enrique announced. "I want to marry Julianna."

Her face showed no change of emotion, but his brother's words crushed into Alejandro like a left hook. He resisted the urge not to carry her off to his boat and sail away. But he was the second son, the spare. He wasn't what Julianna needed.

"I don't know." King Alaric's gaze bounced between Alejandro and Julianna. "There seems to be a strong...connection between these two."

"Friendship, sire." Enrique sidled closer to Julianna, as if to reclaim his prize. "They both enjoy sailing."

Alaric looked doubtful.

Perceptive man, Alejandro had to admit. Other than passion, there wasn't anything binding him to Julianna. There couldn't be. "We are friends, sire."

"There will be complications if Julianna has done more than sail with her friend Alejandro," Alaric said. "If there is any reason to doubt the paternity of an heir, the embarrassment to our family name..."

Julianna flushed.

Anger surged. Alejandro couldn't believe her father was questioning her virginity. He balled his hands into fists. "I assure you, sir—"

King Alaric cut him off. He stared at his daughter as if she were a peasant, not a princess. "Is there any reason you shouldn't marry Enrique?"

The question mortified Julianna. Her heart pounded in her chest, so loudly she was certain everyone could hear it. But no one said anything. They stared, waiting for her to answer.

Her father with his dark, accusing eyes.

King Dario with compassion.

Enrique with panic.

And Alejandro with hope.

Is there any reason you shouldn't marry Enrique?

Yes, a big reason. A six-foot-two-inch-tall reason with dark hair and dark eyes.

Alejandro.

Jules loved him, but couldn't understand why he kept talking about her being a future queen. She wanted to stay on the island, but with Alejandro, not his brother.

She made a silent wish from her heart.

Claim me.

Jules wanted Alejandro to forget about everything. His family, her family and their two countries. She wanted him to declare his love and claim her for himself.

Alejandro gave her an encouraging smile filled with warmth.

Relief washed over her. Her tense muscles relaxed. He would come to her rescue once again and claim her. Everything would turn out fine.

"You can still do your duty and help your country," Alejandro insisted. "All you have to do is tell your father that marrying Enrique is what you want."

Emotion tightened her throat. Her body stiffened with shock.

No. She didn't want that. She loved Alejandro. His actions told her he had feelings for her, too.

There was something between them. Something special.

Yet he wanted her to marry his brother. Jules struggled to breathe. She stared at him.

His smile disappeared. His expression turned neutral.

Why was he doing this?

And then something clicked in her mind and she remembered...

Once you and Enrique marry and have children, I'll be free from all royal obligations. I can concentrate on business and not have to worry about any more princely duties.

The truth hit her with stark clarity. She didn't want to believe it, but nothing else made sense.

Alejandro might have feelings for her, but the feelings didn't run deep enough. He chose not to act upon them. He wasn't willing to sacrifice what he wanted. His freedom was more important than duty. Love. Her.

Julianna's heart froze, leaving her feeling cold and empty.

Despair threatened to overwhelm her, but she didn't give in to it. She needed to answer her father's question.

A million thoughts jumbled her mind. But one kept coming back to her. Her actions on the island had created the very sort of change she desired in Aliestle.

Was that enough reason to marry Enrique?

She looked at Brandt. If she didn't go through with the wedding now, the repercussions would reflect badly on her brother. He was the one who was supposed to be escorting her safely to marriage. The Council of Elders would blame him, so would the press. Their plans to help their country would never come to fruition if she returned home.

Before Alejandro and getting caught up in a fantasy, she'd had a plan—a life outside of Aliestle, helping Brandt and her country, falling in love with her husband and becoming a mother. She might not achieve all of those things now, but she could have some of them.

That would have to be enough.

Shoulders back. Chin up. Smile.

"There isn't any reason I shouldn't marry Enrique, Father." Jules sneaked a peek at Alejandro. The gold flecks in his eyes burned like flames. Somehow she would have to learn to live with Enrique as her husband and Alejandro as her brother-in-law. And be satisfied with that. She swallowed a sigh. "No reason at all."

"I am satisfied." Alaric proclaimed after a long minute. "The marriage contract will be honored, provided Julianna not sail in the Med Cup tomorrow. I'll be here to see to it that she remains in the palace all day long."

Every one of her nerve endings cried out in protest. Jules had earned the spot in the final, but she remained silent as any proper princess would.

"As will I," King Dario said.

"Me, too," Enrique agreed.

Alejandro nodded. "Julianna is a skilled helmsman, but I agree it's best she doesn't sail."

Even he was taking their side. Her heart shattered into a million pieces, each one jabbing into her at the same time. If love and passion brought this kind of pain, she would rather go back to how she lived before arriving on the island.

With what strength she had left, Jules forced all her emotions to a deep, dark place. She'd survived before by sleepwalking through life. That was how she would survive again.

The dullness in Julianna's eyes struck at Alejandro's heart. He knew she was upset at being banned from the race. Competing in the Med Cup had been important to her. At least she was getting what she wanted. She could help her brother and her country now.

But the lack of emotion on her face and her lifeless eyes bothered him. Concerned, he turned toward her. "Jul—"

"There's no reason for you to remain at the palace, Alejandro." King Dario interrupted him with a pointed glare. "Return to your villa and prepare for tomorrow's race."

Alejandro didn't want to leave. He wanted to stay near Julianna. "I don't mind staying here."

"Go." His father touched his shoulder. "Keep your distance until the wedding."

Julianna didn't glance Alejandro's way. He knew why.

She'd put her princess mask back on.

He wanted to reach out to her, to shake some sense into her, but he couldn't. He'd pushed aside his own feelings to help her be a proper princess again. A mistake, probably.

But that was what she needed. More than she needed him.

Alejandro had to let Julianna go so she could fulfill the royal duty that was so important to her. She wouldn't disappear from his life. She would disappear into being his distant sister-in-law. Thinking about it now, having her leave the island might have been easier to deal with.

"Perhaps you should stay away after the wedding, too," King Alaric said. "I'll see to it you're well compensated, Alejandro."

His temper flared. He wasn't about to allow Julianna's father to pay him off to stay away. "That isn't necessary, sir. I know my place."

"You're now free from your royal obligations, my son," Dario announced. "I know this is what you've always wanted."

Alejandro nodded. But he didn't feel any relief. No happiness. "Thank you, Father."

He'd gotten what he set out to get—his freedom. He'd never have to step back inside the palace or appear at openings, dinners or charity events. He was free to live his life as he wanted—building boats, racing and turning around the island's economy. No more royal orders. No more royal interference.

But it felt...anticlimactic. Wrong.

Julianna moved closer to Enrique.

Sharp pain sliced Alejandro. A black void seemed to engulf his heart. Seeing her so willingly embrace her future with Enrique shouldn't hurt so badly.

Alejandro shook off the feeling. He was jealous and feeling guilty for what he'd done. That was all.

Enrique had won again. No doubt his brother would punish him for going behind his back.

"Under the circumstances," Enrique said. "I do not think it wise for you to be my best man."

"I agree." Alejandro looked at Julianna. "You're the best helmsman I've had the privilege of sailing with. You'll be missed."

"Thank you for allowing me to sail on your boat." She spoke politely as if he were some hired help.

The ice princess had returned. But he knew she wasn't cold and heartless, but warm and genuine. He wanted to rip the mask off her face so he could see the real Julianna.

"Good luck with the race tomorrow," she added.

She'd earned *La Rueca* the spot in the finals tomorrow. But she had known her father would never allow her sailing to continue once the truth was out.

"I know you want to sail, Julianna," Alejandro said. "But it's best if you resume your life and do what is best for your country and mine. I don't see any other—"

"No explanations are needed, sir." She emphasized the last word with a haughtiness that put him in his place. "I know my duty. I always have. I was using you as a means to an end, one last hurrah before settling into the life I've chosen. No hard feelings, right?"

Each of her words pierced his heart like a dagger. He had hard feelings, ones that were becoming difficult to ignore and fight.

Using him? Okay, he'd used her to do well in the race.

Alejandro hated to think what she said was true. They'd shared good times, their hopes and their dreams, and hot kisses. Maybe she didn't have feelings for him or maybe she was back to pretending. It didn't matter.

The next time he saw her, they would be required to wear polite faces and share a meaningless conversation. Everything in the past would seem like nothing more than a dream.

No hard feelings, right?

"Right." Alejandro bowed. "I wish you much happiness. All of you."

With that, he packed his bag, picked up Boots and left the palace feeling worse than he'd ever felt in his entire life.

CHAPTER THIRTEEN

THE TWO KINGS, satisfied to have the marriage between their children moving forward, retired to the library to have a brandy. Jules sat in the sitting room with Enrique. He'd wanted to talk with her alone. She didn't blame him. She figured he wanted to talk about his brother.

Alejandro.

Her heart ached.

Who was she kidding?

She felt as if her heart died when Alejandro left. The raw hurt in his eyes made it hard for her to breathe. She'd hurt him with her words. Worse, she'd done it on purpose. She'd lashed out in her own hurt because he'd been unwilling to make a commitment to her.

She wanted to scream and cry, but instead she sat showing no emotion on her face. The way she'd done her entire life, except for the time she'd spent with Alejandro. Sailing, talking, building castles in the sand.

The best time of her life.

Don't think about him. As he'd said, she had to resume her life...

"I understand how easy it must have been to get carried away with the sailing, but I must know..." Enrique rose from the damask-covered settee. He stood in front of her, towering over her while she remained seated. His mouth narrowed into a thin line. "Did you have sex with my brother?"

It wasn't as much a question as a demand. An easy one to answer, but she hesitated.

Jules knew her life on the island would be better than life in Aliestle, but not by much. Enrique would see to that. He only cared about himself. She would always be an extension of his persona to be controlled so she wouldn't embarrass him.

She stood and raised her chin. "I didn't have sex with Alejandro."

The tension on Enrique's face disappeared.

"But I'm in love with him," she admitted.

"I'm not surprised." Enrique sounded more amused than angry. "Alejandro has seduced many beautiful women and left a trail of broken hearts on this island. Someone as innocent as you never stood a chance. Do not worry. Once we're married, you'll forget him."

Surprise echoed through her. "You still want to marry me knowing I love another man?"

"Of course," Enrique said. "I thought he might have wanted sex from you. I realize he wanted to win the race so he could promote his business. But now that he received so much publicity today, winning the race, and therefore you, are no longer necessary."

His words took the wind out of her sails. "I'm a necessary part of his crew."

Enrique shrugged. "If that's true, why didn't he argue to have you race with him tomorrow?"

Feeling like she'd hit a reef and was taking on water fast, she struggled to breathe. To think. "Because of my father. And you."

"Believe that if it makes you feel better, but one day you'll realize the truth."

Jules knew the truth. Alejandro had told her it himself.

If La Rueca *places in the top five, the resulting publicity will boost my boatyard's reputation and raise the island's standing in the eyes of the yachting world. To do that I need you steering the boat.*

She narrowed her gaze. "Your brother wanted me so he could win the race. And you want me for my dowry."

Enrique grinned wryly. "Your royal bloodline doesn't hurt."

The two brothers were similar. Both men were selfish.

The realization hit her full force, the pain soul-deep.

But she couldn't entirely blame Alejandro for pursuing the freedom she was too scared to reach for herself.

She had let him go, but she couldn't let herself go. Surrendering and being obedient wasn't going to bring real change and happiness. She had to find her own path like Alejandro had done.

Effecting change meant not passively waiting and hoping, but required real, risk-taking leadership. The women's rights rallies weren't occuring because she'd been a dutiful princess, but because she'd been a defiant one who sailed in a race like her mother.

If she married Enrique, she would perpetuate the same repression her father had returned to in the wake of her mother's death. Jules wouldn't be an example for change, but of the status quo.

She'd been sleepwalking through life out of duty, but there was a higher duty: to be true to one's self.

However much we love people or have loved them, we still have to be the person we are meant to be.

Alejandro had been talking about his family when he'd spoken those words to her. Jules hadn't realized how much the words spoke to her soul until now.

Being true to one's self had more power to improve lives than she realized. Alejandro had taught her that. And she wanted to teach that to any children she had, both sons and daughters.

It was time for her to wake up for good. She needed to stand up for herself and go after what she wanted. She wanted to be the person her mother wanted her to be, the kind of person the women of Aliestle could be proud of.

She squared her shoulders. "La Isla de la Aurora might be more progressive, but you and Alejandro are as selfish as the men in Aliestle. Neither of you value women for who they are, but for what they can provide you."

"Why are you so surprised?" Enrique asked. "You agreed to an arranged marriage. Did you think this would turn into a love match?"

"Yes. I hoped it would." Ridiculous fantasy that it was. "Like my parents' arranged marriage."

Enrique laughed. "Love is a childish notion that royalty cannot indulge in."

His words strengthened her. "I appreciate you wanting to marry me, but I can't marry you. I ask to be released from our arrangement."

His eyes flared with surprise. "Because of Alejandro."

"No. He doesn't want me." The knowledge bit into her, but she refused to give it any measure. She'd awoken to possibilities thanks to Alejandro for which she would always be grateful. "But that doesn't mean I can't find love, a real love I can count on."

"What have you done?" King Alaric looked as if one of the blood vessels in his forehead might burst. "You march back in there and tell Enrique you were mistaken."

"I'm not mistaken about this, Father." All she'd learned while on this island paradise empowered her. "Enrique only wants my dowry."

"So?"

She boldly met her father's gaze. "So I want more from a marriage than that."

"You'll see what you end up with when we return home and you marry an Aliestlian."

His words unleashed something deep inside of her, something lying dormant for too long. "I'm not returning to Aliestle," she said with a new sense of conviction. "I'm not going to be forced into a marriage I don't want."

"This is your duty."

"Perhaps once, but no longer. I believe my mother would've understood."

"I will not stand for this impertinence." He stood, his nostrils flaring. "You will obey me or I will disown you. You will lose your title, your home, your allowance. I will strip you of your passport. You will have nothing left. No money. No home. No country."

The thought of losing everything hurt, but she had to follow her own path. Her own heart. Jules didn't need to be claimed by a man or rescued. She could take care of herself. "If that is what you must do, Father, go ahead."

"You are dead to me," he screamed.

Tears stung her eyes. She felt an odd mix of sadness and joy. But she held firm. For the first time in her life, she was completely free of duty. Until now, everything in her life had been planned out, dictated by others. "Father..."

He turned his back on her.

She would have to make her own way, create a new life for herself. She was in charge now. She got to decide who she would be.

But Jules already knew.

She was like her mother, Queen Brigitta. Jules was a sailor, and a sailor sailed. She needed to get back into the Med Cup race even if Alejandro didn't want her. She needed to do it for herself, her mother and for all the women in Aliestle.

"I'll always love you, Father."

And she walked out of the room to an uncertain future.

Alejandro barely slept. Early the next morning, he wandered through his villa, unable to shake his uneasiness and loneliness. Strange, given he was back home, free to race and do as he pleased.

Boots meowed, sounding sad as if he knew Julianna and her treats were gone.

Gone.

He'd let Julianna go so she could be happy. Now he was miserable.

Alejandro dragged his hand through his hair. He missed her already. He'd done everything on his own for so long and been self-reliant, but this past week and a half, he'd been in a partnership. One, he realized now, he didn't want to end.

Everything in his life—Boots, *La Rueca* and his plans for the island—had become built around Julianna. He cared what she thought about things. He valued her opinion. He was happier than he'd ever been when he was with her. She was happy, too.

That had to count for something.

Would it be enough?

He hoped so because he realized that he was willing to fight for it. For her.

Letting Julianna go had been the wrong decision. One he regretted with his whole heart. Somehow he had to show her happiness and love were as important as her sense of duty.

I love her.

His heart pounded a ferocious beat. Feelings he'd tried to ignore burst to the surface. He staggered back until he hit the wall.

Alejandro wasn't sure when it had happened, sailing or on the beach, but he loved Julianna. Body, heart and soul. He loved the way she could be so prim and proper, but yearn for adventure at the same time. He loved the way she sailed as if her life depended on it. He loved her smile, her laughter and her tears. He loved the way she made him want to be a better man.

He struggled to breathe.

Love might not always last, but they weren't his parents. Julianna was too important not to at least try. The life Alejandro wanted wasn't going to work unless she was a part of it.

"I've got to go after her," he said to Boots. "I have to convince her we have a future together."

Boots meowed.

Alejandro ran out the villa's front door.

The sun rose as he drove up the windy road to the palace. No red sky this morning, just golden-yellow and orange rays. The beginning of a beautiful day, he hoped.

The only other car on the road was his security detail following him. No matter what time of day, they were always right there behind him. His father must have forgotten to tell them their services were no longer required.

Inside the palace, he ran through the hallway to her room. Yvette wasn't sitting outside.

He knocked.

No one answered.

He knocked again.

"She's not here." Enrique slurred the words. He wore the same clothes as last night sans jacket and held a bottle of wine. "Julianna broke off the match. Alaric disowned her. She's gone."

Alejandro's heart soared. If Julianna called off the wedding and gave up on doing her duty, that might mean she loved him. If she didn't, he'd show her the feelings between them were real. "Where is she?"

"What is all the noise?" His father walked down the hallway in his robe and slippers. "Do you know what time it is?"

Enrique burped. "His fault."

"Where is Julianna, Father?" Alejandro asked.

"I don't know," Dario admitted. "I offered to let her stay in the palace until she sorted things out, but she said it was time for her to start doing things on her own."

"Is Klaus with her?"

"King Alaric forbid the bodyguard from going with her," Dario said. "I thought Klaus was going to cry. Brandt is with him now."

"Yvette?"

"She broke down." Dario shook his head. "Elena is with her."

"I must find Julianna, Father. I need to know she's safe." Alejandro had spent much of his life rebelling and retreating from his duty, wanting to be alone and doing everything himself. But not today. "I love her. I need to tell her that even if she doesn't feel the same way."

"She's an ice princess." Enrique swaggered down the hallway. "All that money gone. Gone. Gone."

"Alaric took away Julianna's passport so she's on the island," Dario said in earnest to Alejandro.

"It's a start." But where on the island would she go? She didn't know anyone that well.

His father placed a hand on Alejandro's shoulder. "I was wrong trying to control everyone. That is what drove your mother away. I didn't want to lose you, too, so I wouldn't allow her to take you. But I fear I have lost you anyway, Alejandro. We don't always see eye to eye, but I hope you know I love you and am proud of the man you've become."

Alejandro choked up. That was all he'd ever wanted from his father. "I love you, too."

"We'll have to start listening to each other as a family. Perhaps you can show me your plans for the properties you've purchased."

Alejandro nodded.

His father smiled. "Good luck with Julianna, son."

"Thanks." Alejandro ran to his car. The island wasn't that big, but searching for her alone would take too much time. The crew was preparing for the race.

The race.

No, Julianna was more important.

He saw a familiar car and sprinted over to his security detail. "We must find Princess Julianna. I don't care if you have to search every single hotel on the island. Find her."

For the next two hours, Alejandro searched to no avail. He checked the tunnels, the beach, the dock and the yacht club that was sponsoring the race. The narrow streets grew crowded as the town came alive. Excitement about the Med Cup finals filled the air.

Text messages from the crew asking where he was and why he wasn't at the boat preparing for the race, grew more frantic. They also wanted to know if J.V. was coming.

Alejandro didn't want them to know Julianna was missing. He finally sent a reply he never expected to send: Go without me.

He'd regret not looking for Julianna more than he'd regret missing the race.

The race.

He'd checked the yacht club earlier, but she might go to the boat to race.

Hope glimmered, the first time all morning.

Traffic clogged the roads. Impatient, Alejandro parked on the side of the road, exited the car and jogged to the marina.

Up ahead, a woman with long, blond hair wearing the colors of his crew headed toward the yacht club.

"Julianna," he yelled.

She didn't stop. Alejandro ran after her, but was going against the crowd of people. He found himself being pushed back.

He had to reach her somehow.

Alejandro saw a narrow opening between buildings. He worked his way over, but a large hedge blocked his way.

Nothing was going to stop him from reaching her.

Looking around, he saw a crate. He dragged it over and climbed over the hedge. His team jacket caught on a thorn and tore. He didn't care. He dropped down on the other side, jumped over some small plants until he made it to a paved walkway that led to the marina.

Alejandro ran, his legs pumping as fast as they could, but he'd lost sight of her. Julianna was…gone.

A bolt of grief ripped through him. His fault. He had no one else to blame.

He stared at the marina in the distance. A familiar mast caught his attention. *La Rueca* was heading out to the course to race.

Alejandro didn't know whether to laugh or cry. He pulled out his phone instead.

Good luck, he texted.

Sam replied: We've got J.V., no luck needed.

Alejandro read the message three times before the words sunk in. Julianna *had* been on her way to *La Rueca*. She'd made it onboard in time.

But he hadn't.

He laughed.

Now he would have to wait to see how things turned out both with *La Rueca* and Julianna. But at least he knew she was safe. That was enough. For now.

He texted Sam, asking him to hand his mobile phone to Julianna.

What? she asked.

He typed, You OK?

OK. You?

Alejandro typed a message and hit Send.

That was all he could do now.

He called his security detail and his father then made his way to the yacht club. There, he could watch the race unfold. His boat was out there with the woman he loved at the helm. He didn't want to miss a single minute of it.

The race was in its final leg. Not having Alejandro aboard was strange, especially during such a tight race. *La Rueca* had made up distance since heading upwind, but couldn't catch the lead boat.

Jules clutched the wheel, the wind whipping through her ponytail. The same frustration etched on the crew's face must be on hers. "We're going to run out of course."

"We'll never catch them this way," Phillipe agreed.

"Alejandro will be satisfied with second place." She thought about the text he'd sent as they headed out.

If we lose the race, we lose. But just being here, we've already won.

She'd already won her freedom. She'd lost her family and...

No. Jules needed to focus. "But he deserves a win."

"We can still win," Phillipe said confidently. "But it's going to take the best tack of your life. You up for it?"

She grinned. "Just tell me what to do."

"Not what, when," Phillipe explained. "The rules make it hard to overtake a boat. But if we can tack below and come ahead."

"We'd have luffing rights," she said.

Phillipe winked. "Our helmsman has read the rule book."

Jules nodded. Her hands trembled with excitement and nerves. She wanted to give Alejandro and *La Rueca* the victory.

"The lead boat is tacking on starboard," Phillipe yelled. "Wait for my call."

The crew readied themselves for the final maneuver. They were on port, left of the lead boat. Instead of passing behind their competitor, they were going to tack below them and try to gain the advantage and the lead.

"Now," the tactician ordered.

"Tacking." Julianna turned the wheel. She focused on her

job. She knew the other crewmembers were doing theirs, everyone in sync. The wind seemed to be on their side as well.

"Faster," Phillipe yelled.

Jules turned the wheel. Her hands and arms ached from three days of racing. She ignored the pain, thinking about Alejandro instead. This boat and race meant so much to him. Placing would give him more publicity so he could start turning the island into a sailing-centered tourist spot, but a win would be a huge boost to his boatyard.

He'd helped her. Jules wanted to do the same for him even if he didn't want her the way she wanted him.

She pressed the boat closer to the wind.

Phillipe whistled. "That's it. They're getting our dirty air now."

They edged out in front, taking both the lead and the wind.

"They're falling away," Mike called. "Looks like we can pull this off."

A few minutes later, the prow of *La Rueca* sailed between the buoys marking the finish line. They had done it. They had won the race!

Laughter overflowed along with deafening cheers. Jules wanted to celebrate along with the crew, but the victory was bittersweet.

Yes, she had proven herself. But now that the race was over, she had no idea what would happen. What would she do next?

Exhilaration shot through her. At least she was the one who got to answer that question, not anyone else.

The boat arrived at the marina. Alejandro stood on the dock with champagne bottles. A jubilant smile graced his face. Approval filled his dark eyes.

"Good race." He shook her hand, the pressure warm,

secure, making her ache to have him pull her into his embrace. "World class sailing out there, Julianna. You won the race for us."

For you, she wanted to tell him. But seeing him brought a rush of emotion. Tears welled in her eyes. She didn't want to start crying because she was afraid she wouldn't be able to stop.

"Thanks." She forced a smile even though his greeting broke her heart. Not that she expected anything else, but they had won the race. A hug would be...appropriate. "And it's Jules, not Julianna."

"Thank you, Jules," he said.

A member of the yacht club led the crew to a platform surrounded by fans and press. Trophies were handed out. Through it all, Jules kept stealing glances at Alejandro. She forced her attention off him. When a bottle of champagne ended up in her hands, she took a swig.

The crew cheered.

Sam grinned. "Now that's the proper way a princess should drink, mates."

She laughed.

Alejandro pulled her aside. "We need to talk."

Her heart beat as fast as a hummingbird's wings. She followed him to *La Rueca* and climbed aboard. "I'm not going to marry Enrique."

"I know." His mouth twisted with regret. "I'm sorry, Jules. I thought you and Enrique marrying was for the best, but I was fooling myself. I'm miserable without you. I thought I had to rely only on myself. But I needed you to sail the boat. And then I realized I need you in my life. I love you."

The air rushed from her lungs. "You do?"

"Yes. I do." His tender gaze caressed her face. "I love everything about you. From the way you drive a sailboat to the way you kiss me until I can't think straight. You can go from haughty royal to sweet young thing in about three seconds flat. That made it hard to know the real Julianna or Jules, but I realize she's all of you. And that's okay."

Jules stared up at him. "I'm sorry for what I said to you. I was hurt. Angry. Wrong."

"It's okay now." He squeezed her hand. "I'm here for you. I'll take care of you. I can be a prince if that's what you want. Though you'll never be a queen."

Joy flowed through her, filling up every space inside her. She touched his cheek. "I don't care about being a queen. I don't need you to be a prince. I love you, Alejandro. That's all that matters. But we'll have to take care of each other. Equally. I wouldn't have it any other way."

"Fine by me, Princess." He brushed his lips across hers. "You've already rescued me from being alone, from believing I was the black sheep who had to prove himself, from avoiding my problems with my family and running away from being a prince."

"We rescued each other."

"And we'll continue to do so." Alejandro dropped down on one knee. "I love you, Jules. There's no other woman I'd rather spend the rest of my life with. Will you do me the honor of being my wife?"

"Yes." She pulled him up and kissed him hard on the lips. "A hundred times, yes."

"I want you to pick out a ring you like." He pulled something out of his pocket. A thin piece of line knotted into a ring. "I hope this will do in the meantime."

Tears of love crested her lashes. "It'll do fine."

She'd been wrong. So very wrong.

Alejandro hadn't been selfish. He'd been afraid. But he was still the same dashing hero from her midnight sailing adventure. And she knew from the bottom of her heart, totally devoted to her. Love overflowed as he placed the handmade ring on her finger. A perfect fit.

Her heart sighed. "I'm ready to sail off into the sunset."

"Not yet," he said.

She looked up at him. "I thought..."

"I'm going to marry you, but first I want you to take some time to live your own life. To be on your own before we settle down. Maybe six months to a year. I want you to experience the freedom you've longed for. Travel, sail, whatever you want."

"I want to be with you."

"I want to be with you, but this is too important." He kissed each of her fingers. "Don't worry. I'm not about to let you have all that fun without me. Some things we'll do together. Others you'll do on your own. But know I'll be here to support, love and marry you when it's time."

"I'm counting the days."

"I'll have a real ring for you by then."

She stared at the rope on her finger and smiled up at him. "This ring is real. Like your kisses. Speaking of which..."

He lowered his mouth toward her. "I thought you'd never ask."

EPILOGUE

One year later...

STANDING ON THE deck of the eighty-five-foot sailboat, Jules listened to the wind against the sails. The sun shone high in the blue sky. The oiled teak gleamed. The old-fashioned schooner was something out of a dream or a pirate movie.

Contentment flowed through her. She'd spent the last year chasing her dreams. She'd sailed in numerous races, including winning a prestigious offshore race as part of an all-women's crew. She'd traveled and worked on women's rights issues. All the while Alejandro was there supporting, encouraging and waiting.

But this was the one dream she wanted to make come true.

She couldn't imagine a better place to get married. No heads of state, no strangers, no media in attendance. Only friends and family. Her father, stepmother and four brothers were here as well as Alejandro's father, mother and brother. Not quite a happy family, but Jules hoped in time differences could be...forgotten.

Alejandro squeezed her hand. He stared at her as though

she were the sun and his world revolved around her. She felt the same way about him.

"I pronounce you husband and wife." The ship's captain smiled. "You may kiss the bride."

Alejandro's lips pressed against hers, making her feel cherished and loved. Jules kissed him back with her heart and her soul. She wanted him to know how much he meant to her.

Those in attendance clapped and cheered.

"I feel like I'm dreaming," she whispered.

"Wake up, Princess." He brushed his lips across hers. "Your dreams are coming true."

"A happily ever after, too?"

"Nothing less will do." Alejandro ran his finger along her jawline. The caress sent tingles shooting through her. "But we have to do one thing first."

Anticipation buzzed through her. "What?"

"Sail off into the sunset."

Jules's heart overflowed with love. "Sounds perfect."

"Just like you."

"I'm not perfect."

His smile crinkled the corners of his eyes. "Then you're the perfect not-so-perfect princess for me."

* * * * *

MILLS & BOON®

Find out more about our
latest releases, authors
and competitions.

Like us on facebook.com/millsandboonaustralia

Follow us on twitter.com/millsandboonaus

Find us at millsandboon.com.au

Did you know
MILLS & BOON®
books are also available in

eBook?

Download yours from
your favourite online bookstore